POLAR STAR

MARTIN CRUZ SMITH

POLAR STAR

RANDOM HOUSE · NEW YORK

Grateful acknowledgment is made to the following for permission to
reprint previously published material:

Indiana University Press: Excerpts from "Brigantine" and "Wolf
Hunt" from *Songs to Seven Strings*, translated by Gerald Stanton
Smith.

Little, Brown & Company, Inc.: Excerpts from the poem "The
Guest" from *Poems of Akhmatova*, selected, translated and
introduced by Stanley Kunitz with Max Hayward. Translation
copyright © 1973 by Stanley Kunitz and Max Hayward. First
appeared in *The New York Review of Books.* Reprinted by permission
of Little, Brown & Company, Inc.

Library of Congress Cataloging-in-Publication Data
Smith, Martin Cruz.
Polar Star / by Martin Cruz Smith.
    p.   cm.
ISBN 0-394-57819-8
I. Title
PS3569.M5377P65   1989
813'.54–dc19

Manufactured in the United States of America
98765432
First Trade Edition

Book design by Debbie Glasserman

A Signed Limited First Edition of this book has been privately
printed by The Franklin Library.

For Em

I thank Captain Boris Nadein and the crew of the *Sulak;* Captain Mike Hastings and the crew of the *Oceanic;* Sharon Gordon, Dennis McLaughlin and William Turner for their hospitality in the Bering Sea. Valuable assistance was also provided by Martin Arnold, Kathy Blumberg, Captain D. J. (Jack) Branning, Knox Burger, Dr. Gerald Freedman, Beatrice Golden, Professor Robert Hughes, Captain James Robinson and Kitty Sprague.

Most of all I owe Alex Levin and Captain Vladil Lysenko for their patience.

There is a Soviet factory ship named the *Polar Star.* Neither it nor the *Sulak* is the *Polar Star* of this book, which is fiction.

CONTENTS

POLAR STAR

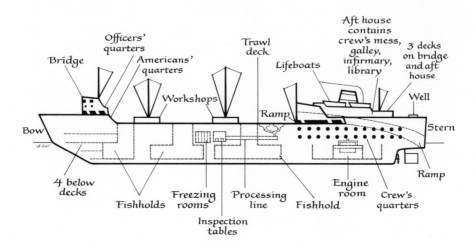

Bridge

Officers' quarters

Americans' quarters

Workshops

Trawl deck

Lifeboats

Aft house contains crew's mess, galley, infirmary, library

3 decks on bridge and aft house

Well

Bow

Ramp

Stern

Ramp

4 below decks

Fishholds

Freezing rooms

Inspection tables

Processing line

Fishhold

Engine room

Crew's quarters

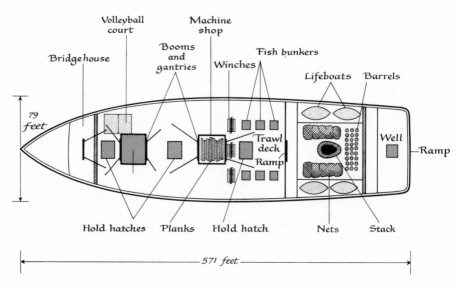

Bridgehouse

Volleyball court

Booms and gantries

Machine shop

Winches

Fish bunkers

Lifeboats

Barrels

79 feet

Trawl deck

Ramp

Well

Ramp

Hold hatches

Planks

Hold hatch

Nets

Stack

← 571 feet →

POLAR STAR

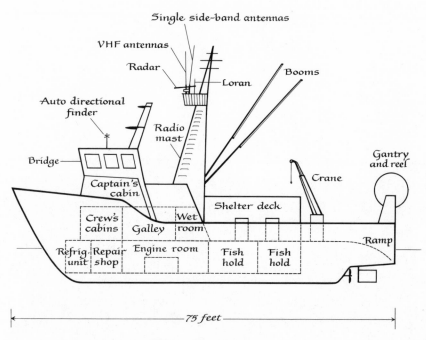

Single side-band antennas

VHF antennas

Radar

Loran

Auto directional finder

Booms

Radio mast

Bridge

Gantry and reel

Crane

Captain's cabin

Shelter deck

Crew's cabins

Galley

Wet room

Refrig unit

Repair shop

Engine room

Fish hold

Fish hold

Ramp

75 feet

THE EAGLE

I.

WATER

1 Like a beast, the net came steaming up the ramp and into the sodium lamps of the trawl deck. Like a gleaming pelt, mats of red, blue, orange strips covered the mesh: plastic "chafing hair" designed to ease the net's way over the rocks of the sea bottom. Like rank breath, the exhalation of the sea's cold enveloped the hair in a halo of its own colors, brilliant in the weepy night.

Water hissed from the net's plastic hair onto the wooden boards that provided footing on the deck. Smaller fish, smelts and herring, fell free. Starfish dropped like stones. Uprooted crabs, even dead, landed on tiptoe. Overhead, gulls and shearwaters hovered at the outer glow of the lamps. As the wind shifted the birds broke into a swirl of white wings.

Usually the net was tipped and disgorged headfirst into the forward chutes to begin with, then ass-end into the rear. Either end could be opened by releasing the knot of a "zipper," a nylon cord braided through the mesh. Though the men stood by with shovels ready for work, the trawlmaster waved them off and stepped into the water raining from the net's plastic hair and stared straight up, removing his helmet the better to see. The colored strips dripped like running paint. He reached and spread the hair from the mesh, then looked into the dark to find the other, smaller light riding the ocean swells, but already fog hid the catcher boat the net had come from. From his belt the trawlmaster took a double-edged knife, reached through the dripping plastic hair and sawed the belly of the net down and across. Fish began dropping by ones and twos. He gave the knife a last furious tug and stepped back quickly.

Out of the net and into the light spilled a flood of silver pollack, a whole school that had been caught en masse and dredged up like bright coins. There were thick, bruised-looking bullheads; overlapping waves of flatfish, blood-red on the eyed side, pale on the blind side; sculpin with heads like dragons; cod, some bloated like balloons by their air bladders, some exploded into soft tissue and pink slime; coral crabs as hairy as tarantulas. The bounty of the night sea.

And a girl. She slid loose-limbed like a swimmer as the fish poured from the net. On the deck she rolled lazily, arms awry, against a mound of sole, a bare foot tangled in crabs. A young woman, not a girl. Her hair was short and her blouse and jeans were sodden and twisted, heavy with water and sand, unprepared for any return to the world of air. The trawlmaster lifted a strand of hair that had wrapped itself across her eyes, revealing the open surprise in them, as if the ship's lamplit fog were golden clouds, as if she had risen in a boat sailing toward heaven itself.

2 Originally when it came down the rails in Gdansk, the *Polar Star*'s four superstructures had been a dazzling white and the gantries and booms a candy-yellow. The decks were clear; silver chains wound round the winches; the facing on the deckhouses was stylishly raked. In fact, the *Polar Star* had looked like a ship.

Twenty years of salt water had repainted it with rust. The top decks had accumulated wooden planks, full barrels of lubricating oil and empty barrels for fish oil, the refuse of piled nets and floats. From the black stack with its red Soviet band drifted the dark smoke of a diesel in poor condition. Now, seen from a distance with a good view of the hull battered by unloading side trawlers in bad weather, the *Polar Star* resembled not so much a factory ship as a combination factory and junkyard cast into the sea and making improbable headway through the waves.

Yet day and night the *Polar Star* efficiently caught fish. Not caught, that was wrong; smaller trawlers caught the fish and transferred their nets to the factory ship to be processed: headed, gutted, frozen.

For four months now the *Polar Star* had followed American catcher boats in American waters from Siberia to Alaska, from the Bering Strait to the Aleutian Islands. It was a joint venture. Simply put, the Soviets provided processing ships and took the fish, while the Americans provided trawlers and translators and took the money, all of this managed by a Seattle-based company that was half Soviet, half American. The crew of the *Polar Star* had seen the sun perhaps two days in that time, but then the Bering Sea was known as the Gray Zone.

THIRD MATE SLAVA BUKOVSKY walked the processing line while workers sorted the catch: pollack on a conveyor belt to the saws, mackerel and rays into the fish-meal hatch. Some of the fish had literally exploded as their air bladders expanded on the way from the bottom of the sea, and soft bits of them clung like mucus to caps, oilskin aprons, lashes, lips.

He passed the rotary saws to the "slime line," where workers stood in slots on either side of the belt. Like automatons, the first pair slit fish bellies open to the anus; the second pair sucked out livers and guts with vacuum hoses; the third pair washed slime from the skin, gills and cavities with saltwater jets; the last pair vacuumed the fish a final time and laid the trimmed and dressed result on a belt moving toward the freezers. In the course of an eight-hour watch the gutting and spraying spread a mist of blood and wet pulp over the belt, workers and walkway. They were not the usual Hero Workers, least of all the lean, pale man with dark hair loading the dressed fish at the end of the line.

"Renko!"

Arkady vacuumed pinkish water from one eviscerated belly, slapped the fish on the freezer belt and picked up the next. Pollack was not firm-fleshed. If it wasn't cleaned and frozen quickly, it would be unfit for human consumption and be fed to minks; if unfit for them, it would go to Africa as foreign aid. His hands were numb from handling fish little warmer than ice, but at least he wasn't working the saw like Kolya. In bad weather when the ship began to roll it took concentration to handle a frozen, slippery pollack around a blade. Arkady had learned to dig the toes of his boots under the table so that he wouldn't slide on the duckboards. At the beginning of the voyage and at the end, the entire factory was hosed down and scrubbed with ammonia, but meanwhile the fish room had a dank organic slickness and smell. Even the clicking of the belt, the whining of the saw, the deep rhythmic moan of the hull were the sounds of a leviathan that was resolutely swallowing the sea.

The belt stopped.

"You're Seaman Renko, aren't you?"

It took Arkady a moment to recognize the third mate, who was not a frequent visitor belowdecks. Izrail, the factory manager, stood at the power switch. He wore layers of sweaters and a black stubble almost to his eyes, which rolled with impatience. Natasha Chaikovskaya, a huge young woman in oilskin armor but with a feminine touch of lipstick, listed discreetly, better to see the third mate's Reeboks and unstained jeans.

"Aren't you?" Slava repeated.

"It's not a secret," Arkady said.

"This is not a dance class of Young Pioneers," Izrail told Slava. "If you want him, take him."

The belt started moving again as Arkady followed Slava aft, stepping over sluices where liquid slime and fish-liver oil ran through bilge holes directly out the side of the ship.

Slava stopped to scrutinize Arkady, as if trying to penetrate a disguise. "You are Renko the investigator?"

"Not anymore."

"But you were," Slava said. "That's good enough."

They climbed the stairs to the main deck. Arkady assumed the third mate was leading him to the political officer or to a search of his cabin, although that could have been done without him. They walked by the galley and the steamy smell of macaroni, turned left at a sign that exhorted "Increase production in the agro-industrial complex! Strive for a decisive upswing in the supply of fish protein!" and halted at the infirmary door.

The door was guarded by a pair of mechanics wearing the red armbands of Public Order Volunteers. Skiba and Slezko were two informers—"slugs" to the rest of the crew. Even as Arkady and Slava went through the door Skiba pulled out a notebook.

The *Polar Star* had a clinic bigger than most small towns could boast: a doctor's office, an examining room, an infirmary with three beds, a quarantine room and an operating room, to which Slava led Arkady. Along the walls were white cupboards with glass canisters of instruments in alcohol, a locked red cupboard with cigarettes and drugs, a cart with a green tank of oxygen and a red tank of nitrous oxide, a standing ashtray and a brass spittoon. There were anatomical charts on the wall, an astringent tang to the air. A dentist's chair sat in one corner. In the middle of the room was a steel operating table covered by a sheet. Soaked through, the cloth clung to the form of a woman underneath. Below the edge of the sheet dangled restraining straps.

The room's portholes were bright mirrors because it was black outside—0600, another hour's work to go before dawn. And as usual at this point in his shift Arkady was stupefied by the number of fish in the sea. His eyes felt like those portholes. "What do you want?" he asked.

"Someone has died," Slava announced.

"I can see that."

"One of the girls from the galley. She fell overboard."

Arkady glanced at the door, picturing Skiba and Slezko on the other side. "What has this got to do with me?"

"It's obvious. Our trade union committee must make a report on all deaths, and I am the union representative. You're the only one on board with experience in violent death."

"And resurrection," Arkady said. Slava blinked. "It's like rehabilitation, but it's supposed to last longer. Never mind." Arkady eyed the cigarettes inside the cabinet; they were *papirosi,* cardboard tubes with tobacco wads. But the cabinet was locked. "Where's the doctor?"

"Look at the body."

"Cigarette?"

Caught off stride, Slava fumbled in his shirt before coming up with a pack of Marlboros. Arkady was impressed. "In that case, I'll wash my hands."

The water from the sink tap was brown, but it rinsed the slime and scales off Arkady's fingers. A mark of veteran seamen was discolored teeth from drinking water from rusting tanks. Over the sink was the first clean mirror he'd looked into for a year. "Resurrection" was a good word. "Dug up," he decided, described him better. The night shift on a factory ship had drained what color his skin had ever had. A permanent shadow seemed to lie across his eyes. Even the towels were clean. He considered getting sick sometime.

"Where were you an investigator?" Slava asked as he lit the cigarette for Arkady, who filled his lungs.

"They have cigarettes in Dutch Harbor?"

"For what sort of crimes?"

"I understand that in the store in Dutch Harbor the cigarettes are stacked to the ceiling. And fresh fruit. And stereos."

Slava lost patience. "What sort of investigator?"

"Moscow." Arkady exhaled. For the first time he delivered his whole attention to the table. "And not for accidents. If she fell overboard, how did you get her back? I never heard the engines stop to pick her up. How did the body get here?"

"It is not necessary for you to know."

Arkady said, "When I was an investigator I had to look at dead people. Now that I am a simple Soviet worker I only have to look at dead fish. Good luck."

He took a step toward the door. It was like pressing a button. "She came up in the net," Slava said quickly.

"Really?" Arkady was interested in spite of himself. "That is unusual."

"Please."

Arkady returned and pulled the sheet off.

Even with her arms stretched back over her head, the woman was small. Very white, as if bleached. Still cold. Her shirt and pants were wrenched around her like a wet shroud. One foot wore a red plastic shoe. Slack brown eyes looked up from a triangular face. Her hair was short and blond, but black at the roots. A mole, a beauty mark by the mouth. He lifted her head, let it drop limply onto the table. Felt her neck, arms. The elbows were broken, but not particularly bruised. Her legs were stiff. More than from any fish, the reek of the sea came from her. There was sand in her shoe; she'd touched bottom. Skin was scraped from her forearms and palms, probably by the net on the way back up.

"Zina Patiashvili," Arkady said. She'd worked in the cafeteria ladling out potatoes, cabbage, compote.

"She looks different," Slava said analytically. "I mean, from when she was alive."

A double difference, Arkady thought. A death change and a sea change. "When did she go over?"

"A couple of hours ago," Slava said. He took an executive stance at the head of the table. "She must have been at the rail and fell over when the net was pulled in."

"Someone saw her?"

"No. It was dark. Heavy fog. She probably drowned as soon as she hit the water. Or died from shock. Or couldn't swim."

Arkady squeezed the flaccid neck again and said, "More like twenty-four hours. Rigor mortis starts from head to foot and it leaves the same way."

Slava rocked slightly on his heels, not from the motion of the ship.

Arkady glanced at the door and lowered his voice. "How many Americans are on board?"

"Four. Three are representatives of the company, one is an American Fisheries observer."

"Do they know?"

"No," Slava said. "Two were still in their bunks. The other representative was at the stern rail. That's a long walk to the deck. The observer was inside having tea. Fortunately, the trawlmaster was intelligent and covered the body before any Americans could see."

"The net came from an American boat. Didn't *they* see?"

"They never know what's in the net until we tell them." Slava pondered. "We should prepare a proper explanation, in case."

"Ah, an explanation. She worked in the galley."

"Yes."

"Food poisoning?"

"That's not what I meant." Slava's face turned red. "Anyway, the doctor examined her when we brought her in and he said she is only two hours dead. If you were such a good investigator you would still be in Moscow."

"True."

ARKADY'S SHIFT WAS over, so he went to the cabin he shared with Obidin, Kolya Mer and an electrician named Gury Gladky. No model seamen here. Gury was on the bottom bunk thumbing through a Sears catalog. Obidin had hung his overcoat in the closet and was washing slime that clung to his beard like webs on a feather duster. An oversized Orthodox cross swayed on his chest. His voice emanated as a rumble; if a man could speak comfortably from the grave, he would sound like Obidin. "That is the anti-Bible," he told Kolya as he looked at Gury. "That is the work of an anti-Christ."

"And he hasn't even seen the Sharper Image," Gury said as Arkady climbed to the upper bunk. In his leisure time, Gury always wore dark glasses and a black leather jacket, like a lounging aviator. "You know what he wants to do in Dutch Harbor? Go to church."

"The people have maintained one," Obidin said. "It is the last vestige of Holy Russia."

"Holy Russia? People? You're talking about Aleuts, fucking savages!"

Kolya counted pots. He had fifty cardboard pots, each five centimeters wide. He had trained as a botanist, and to hear him talk about the port of Dutch Harbor and the island of Unalaska was to imagine that the ship was going to put in at Paradise and he would have his choice of the Garden.

"Fish meal in the soil will help," he said.

"You really think they're going to make it all the way back to Vladivostok?" A thought occurred to Gury: "What kind of flowers?"

"Orchids. They're more hardy than you think."

"American orchids? They'd go over big, you'd need some help selling them."

"They're the same as Siberian bog orchids," Kolya said. "That's the point."

"This was all Holy Russia," Obidin said, as if nature agreed.

Gury pleaded, "Arkady, help me. 'That's the point'? We have one day in an American port. Mer here will spend it looking for fucking Siberian flowers, and Obidin wants to pray with cannibals? Explain to them; they listen to you. We spend five months on this oceangoing shitcan for that one day in port. I have room under my bunk for five stereos and maybe a hundred tapes. Or computer discs. All the schools in Vladivostok are supposed to get Yamahas—supposed to, at least. Someday. So anything compatible is worth a fortune. When we get home I'm not going down the gangplank and say 'Look what I got in America' and hold up pots of Siberian flowers."

Kolya cleared his throat. He was the smallest man in the cabin and had the unease of the smallest fish in an aquarium. "What did Bukovsky want?" he asked Arkady.

"That Bukovsky gives me such a pain in the ass." Gury studied the picture of a color television. "Look at this: 'nineteen inches.' How big is that? I had a Foton color set in my flat. It blew up like a bomb."

"There's something wrong with the tubes," Kolya said meekly. "Everyone knows that."

"That's why I had a bucket of sand by the set, thank God." Gury leaned out to look up at Arkady. "So what did the third mate want from you?"

There was just enough room between the overhead and the bunk for Arkady to wedge himself into a semi-sitting position. The porthole was open to a faint line of gray. Sunrise in the Bering Sea.

"You know Zina in the galley?"

"The blonde," Gury said.

"From Vladivostok." Kolya stacked his pots.

Gury grinned. His incisors were porcelain and gold, decoration as much as dental work. "Bukovsky likes Zina? She'd tie his cock in a knot and ask if he liked pretzels. He might."

Arkady turned to Obidin, who could be counted on for a judgment from the Old Testament.

"A slut," Obidin said, and examined the jars that lined the bottom of the wardrobe, the lid of each one plugged with a cork and a rubber pipe. He unscrewed one, releasing the sweet exhaust of fermenting raisins. He peered at a jar of potatoes.

"Is this dangerous?" Gury asked Kolya. "You're the scientist. These fumes, can they explode? Is there any vegetable or fruit he can't make alcohol from? Remember the bananas?"

Arkady remembered. The closet had smelled like a rotting tropical jungle.

"With yeast and sugar, almost anything can ferment," Kolya said.

"Women should not be on a ship," said Obidin. On a nail in the back of the closet was a small icon of Saint Vladimir. His thumb to two fingers, he touched his forehead, chest, right shoulder, left shoulder, heart, then hung a shirt on the nail. "I pray for our delivery."

Curious, Arkady asked, "From whom?"

"Baptists, Jews, Freemasons."

"Although it's hard to see Bukovsky and Zina together," Gury said.

"I liked her bathing suit," Kolya said. "That day off Sakhalin?" A warm-core ring of water had wandered north from the equator, making a false few hours of summer. "That string bathing suit?"

"A just man covers his face with a beard," Obidin told Arkady. "A modest woman keeps herself from public view."

"She's modest now," Arkady said. "She's dead."

"Zina?" Gury sat up, then removed his dark glasses and stood to be at eye level with Arkady.

"Dead?" Kolya looked aside.

Obidin crossed himself again.

Arkady thought that probably all three of them knew more about Zina Patiashvili than he did. Mostly he recalled that freak day off Sakhalin when she had paraded on the volleyball deck in her bathing suit. Russians loved the sun. Everyone wore the skimpiest possible bathing suit in order to apply the greatest amount of sunshine to pale skin. Zina, though, had more than a meager bathing suit. She had a Western body, a bony voluptuosity. On the infirmary table she looked more like a damp rag, nothing like the Zina walking up and down the deck, posing against the gunwale, her sunglasses black as a mask.

"She fell overboard. The net brought her back up."

The other three stared at him. It was Gury who broke the silence. "So why did Bukovsky want you?"

Arkady didn't know how to explain. Each man had his past. Gury had always been a *bizness* man, dealing inside and outside the law. Kolya had gone from academe to labor camp, and Obidin zigzagged from drunk tank to church. Arkady had lived with men like them ever since Moscow; nothing broadened acquaintanceship like internal exile. Moscow was a drab hive of apparatchiks compared with the diverse society of Siberia. All the same, he was relieved to hear a brusque knock on the cabin door and to see Slava Bukovsky's face again, even if the third mate did step in with a mock bow and address him with scorn.

"Comrade Investigator, the captain wants to see you."

3 Viktor Sergeievich Marchuk needed no uniform or gold braid to announce he was a captain. Outside the Seamen's Hall in Vladivostok Arkady had seen his face among the giant portraits of the leading captains of the Far East fishing fleet. But the picture had softened Marchuk's face and propped it on a jacket and tie, so that he looked as if he sailed a desk. The live Marchuk had a face with angles of rough-hewn wood sharpened by the trim black beard of an individualist, and he commanded his ship wearing the wool sweater and jeans of an outdoorsman. Somewhere in his past was an Asian, somewhere a Cossack. The whole country was being led by a fresh breed of men from Siberia—economists from Novosibirsk, writers from Irkutsk and modern mariners from Vladivostok.

The captain seemed at a loss, though, as he pondered the confusion on his desk: a seaman's dossier, a code book and cipher table, scrap paper covered with rows of numbers, some circled in red, and a second page of letters. He looked up from them as if trying to get

Arkady into focus. Slava Bukovsky took a tactful step away from the object of the captain's attention.

"It is always interesting to meet members of the crew." Marchuk nodded at the dossier. " 'Former investigator.' I radioed home for details. Seaman Renko, these are some details." A heavy finger thudded on the deciphered letters. "A senior investigator for the Moscow prosecutor's office dismissed for lack of political reliability. Next seen in the lesser metropolis of Norilsk on the run. No great shame, many of our finest citizens came east in chains. As long as they reform. In Norilsk you were a night watchman. As a former Muscovite, you found the nights brisk?"

"I'd burn three oil cans of tar and sit in the middle of them. I looked like a human sacrifice."

While Marchuk lit a cigarette, Arkady glanced around. There was a Persian carpet on the floor, a sofa built into the corner, a nautical library on railed shelves, television, radio and an antique desk the size of a lifeboat. Over the sofa was a photo of Lenin addressing sailors and cadets. Three clocks told local, Vladivostok and Greenwich mean time. The ship ran on Vladivostok time; the log was kept on GMT. Altogether, the captain's dayroom had the look of a private study that merely happened to have lime-green bulkheads for walls.

"Dismissed for destruction of state property, it says here. The tar, I assume. Then you managed to sign on at a slaughterhouse."

"I dragged reindeer on a kill floor."

"But again it says you were dismissed for political instigation."

"I worked with two Buryats. Neither of them understood Russian. Maybe the reindeer talked."

"Next you show up on a coastal trawler in Sakhalin. Now, this, Seaman Renko, really amazes me. To work one of those old trawlers is to be on the moon. The worst work for the worst pay. The crews are men on the run from their wives, from child support, from petty crimes, maybe even manslaughter. No one cares, because we need crews on the Pacific coast. Yet here it is again: 'Dismissed for lack of political reliability.' Please tell us, what did you do in Moscow?"

"My job."

Marchuk brusquely waved blue smoke aside. "Renko, you've been on the *Polar Star* almost ten months. You didn't even leave the ship when we returned to Vladivostok."

When a seaman disembarked he had to pass the Border Guard, frontier troops of the KGB.

"I like the sea," Arkady said.

"I am the leading captain of the Far East fleet," said Marchuk. "I am a decorated Hero of Socialist Labor, and not even *I* like the sea that much. Anyway, I wanted to congratulate you. The doctor has revised his estimate. The girl Zina Patiashvili died the night before, not last night. In his capacity of trade union representative, Comrade Bukovsky will naturally be responsible for preparing the report on the matter."

"Comrade Bukovsky is no doubt equal to the task."

"He's very willing. However, a third mate is not an investigator. Besides yourself, no one on board is."

"He seems a young man of initiative. He already found the factory. I wish him luck."

"Let's be grown men. The *Polar Star* has a crew of two hundred and seventy deckhands, mechanics and factory workers like you. Fifty of the crew are women. We are like a Soviet village in American waters. News of an unusual death on the *Polar Star* will always find an interested ear. It is vital that there be no suggestion of either a cover-up or a lack of concern."

"So the Americans already know," Arkady guessed.

Marchuk conceded the point. "Their head representative has visited me. The situation is even more complicated by the fact that this unfortunate girl died two nights ago. You speak English?"

"Not for a long time. Anyway, the Americans on board speak Russian."

"But you don't dance."

"Not recently."

"Two nights ago we had a dance," Slava reminded Arkady. "In honor of fishermen of all nations."

"I was still cleaning fish. I just glanced in on the way to my shift." The dance had been held in the cafeteria. All Arkady had seen from the door were figures bouncing in the lights reflected from a ball of mirrors. "You played the saxophone," he said to Slava.

"We had guests," Marchuk said. "We had two American catcher boats tied up to the *Polar Star* and American fishermen at the dance. It's possible you might want to speak to them. They do not speak Russian. Of course this is not an investigation; that will, as you say, be carried out by the appropriate authorities when we return to Vladivostok. Information should be gathered now, however, while memories are fresh. Bukovsky needs the assistance of someone with experience in such matters and with a command of English. Just for today."

"With all respect," Slava said, "I can ask questions with complete correctness and no help from Renko at all. We must keep in mind that this report will be studied by the fleet, by departments of the Ministry, by—"

"Remember," Marchuk said, "Lenin's thought: 'Bureaucracy is shit!' " To Arkady he said, "Seaman Patiashvili was at the dance, which was held about the time you say she died. We count ourselves fortunate in having someone with your skills on the *Polar Star,* and we assume that you count yourself fortunate to have an opportunity to serve your ship."

Arkady looked at the litter of papers on the desk. "What about my political reliability?"

Marchuk's smile was all the more startling in contrast to his beard.

"We do have an expert on your reliability. Slava, some interest in Seaman Renko has been expressed by our friend Comrade Volovoi. We would not want to start any enterprise without Volovoi."

FILMS WERE PRESENTED twice a day in the cafeteria. All Arkady could see from the hall were murky images on a screen set up on the stage where Slava and his band had performed two nights before. A plane was landing at an airport with modern architecture: a foreign locale. Cars swung to the terminal curb: limousines, maybe a few years old and a little dented but definitely American. In American accents voices addressed each other as "Mr. This" or "Mr. That." The camera focused on foreign wingtip shoes.

"Vigilance Abroad," said someone wandering out. "All about the CIA."

It was Karp Korobetz. Barrel-chested, with a hairline that started within a millimeter of his brows, the trawlmaster resembled those massive statues erected after the war, the soldier hoisting his rifle, the sailor firing his cannon, as if victory had been gained by primitive man. He was the model worker of the *Polar Star.*

In fact, on display in the hall was a board that kept count of the competition between the three watches, the winner each week being awarded a gold pennant. So many points were awarded for the quantity of fish caught, for the quality of fish processed, for the percentage of the all-important quota. Karp's team won the pennant month after month. Because Arkady's factory team had the same shift, they won too. YOU ARE BUILDING COMMUNISM BY FEEDING THE SOVIET PEOPLE! said the banner over the board. That was him and Karp!

The trawlmaster idly shook out a cigarette. Deckhands didn't take much notice of crew that worked below. He hardly glanced at Slava. On the screen, white packets were being passed from one secret agent to another.

"Heroin," Karp said.

"Or sugar," said Arkady. That was hard to get too.

"Trawlmaster Korobetz was the one who found Zina." Slava changed the subject.

"What time was that?" Arkady asked.

"About 0300," Karp said.

"Was there anything else in the net?"

"No. Why are *you* asking questions?" Karp demanded in turn. The quality of his gaze had changed, as if a statue had opened its eyes.

"Supposedly Seaman Renko has experience in matters like this," Slava said.

"In falling overboard?" Karp asked.

"Did you know her?"

"I only saw her around here. She served food." Karp's interest was growing all the time. He tried Arkady's name like a bell. "Renko, Renko. Where are you from?"

"Moscow," Slava answered for Arkady.

"Moscow?" Karp whistled appreciatively. "You must have really fucked up to end up here."

"But here we are, all of us proud workers of the Far East fleet," Volovoi said as he joined them, and with an eye to another new-comer, an American boy with freckles and a bush of springy hair who was coming warily down the hall. "Bernie, go in, please," Volovoi urged him. "It's a spy story. Very exciting."

"You mean we're the villains, right?" Bernie had a sheepish grin and only a slight accent.

"How could it be a spy story otherwise?" Volovoi laughed.

"Think of it as a comedy," Arkady suggested.

"Yeah." Bernie liked that.

"Please, enjoy yourself," Volovoi said, although he had stopped laughing. "Comrade Bukovsky will find you a good seat."

The first mate took Arkady down the hall to the ship's library, a room where a reader had to slip sideways between the stacks. In such a limited collection it was interesting to see who was represented. Jack London was popular, as were war stories, science fiction and a field of literature called tractor romances. Volovoi dismissed the librarian and sat himself at her desk, pushing to one side her tea cozy, pots of glue and books with broken spines to make room for a dossier he pulled out of his briefcase. Arkady had tried to stay out of the political officer's way, hanging back at meetings and avoiding entertainments. It was the first time the two of them had ever been alone.

Although Volovoi was the ship's first mate and habitually wore a canvas fishing jacket and boots, he never touched the helm, a net or a navigational chart. The reason was that a first mate was the political officer. There was a chief mate for more mundane matters having to do with fishing and seamanship. Very confusing. First Mate Volovoi was responsible for discipline and morale; for hand-painted signs in the corridor that proclaimed "Third shift wins gold pennant for socialist competition!"; for announcing the news every noon on the ship's radio, mixing telegrams to proud crew members about babies born in Vladivostok with items from revolutionary Mozambique; for running movies and volleyball tournaments; and most important, for writing a work and political evaluation of every member of the crew from the captain on down, and delivering that judgment to the Maritime Section of the KGB.

Not that Volovoi was a weakling. He was the ship's champion weight lifter, the kind of redhead whose eyes were always pink, whose eyelids and lips had a crust of eczema, whose meaty, well-kept hands had golden hair. Crewmen called political officers "invalids" for their lack of real work, but Fedor Volovoi was the healthiest invalid Arkady had ever seen.

"Renko," Volovoi read, as if familiarizing himself with a problem. "Chief investigator. Dismissed. Expelled from the Party. Psychiatric rehabilitation. You see, I have the same file the captain has. Assigned to labor in the eastern section of the Russian Republic."

"Siberia."

"I know where the eastern section is. I notice also that you have a sense of humor."

"That's basically what I've been working on for the last few years."

"Good, because I also have a more complete report." Volovoi placed a thicker dossier on the desk. "There was a murder case in Moscow. Somehow it ended with you killing the city prosecutor, an unexpected twist. Who is Colonel Pribluda?"

"An officer of the KGB. He spoke for me at the inquiry, which decided not to charge me."

"You were also expelled from the Party and kept for psychiatric observation. Is that the fate of an innocent man?"

"Innocence had nothing to do with it."

"And who is Irina Asanova?" Volovoi read the name.

"A former Soviet citizen."

"You mean a woman whom you helped to defect and who has since been a source of slanderous rumors about your fate."

"What are the rumors?" Arkady asked. "How far off?"

"Have you been in contact with her?"

"From here?"

"You've been questioned before."

"Many times."

Volovoi flipped the pages of the dossier. " 'Political unreliability.' . . . 'Political unreliability.' Let me tell you what is humorous to
me as first mate. In a few days we will be in Dutch Harbor. Everyone
on this ship will go into port for shopping, with one exception: you.
Because everyone on this ship has a Number One seaman's visa, with
one exception: you. I must assume you have only a Number Two visa
because those people who should know believe you cannot be trusted
with foreigners or in a foreign port. Yet you are the man the captain
wants to assist Bukovsky, even to help him speak to the Americans
on board or to those on the trawlers. That's either humorous or very
odd."

Arkady shrugged. "Humor is such a personal thing."

"But to be expelled from the Party . . ." The invalid liked hitting
that nail, Arkady thought. Never mind dismissal and exile; the real
punishment, the fear of every apparatchik, was losing his Party card.
Molotov, for example, was denounced for writing up the murder lists
of thousands of Stalin's victims. He wasn't in real trouble, though,
until they took away his card.

"Membership in the Party was too great an honor. I could not
bear it."

"So it seems." Volovoi pondered the file again. Perhaps the words
were too painful. He lifted his eyes to the bookshelves, as if no story
there could be so tawdry. "The captain, of course, is a Party member.
Like many sea captains, however, he has a decisive nature, a personality that enjoys risk. He's astute about fishing, about avoiding ice-
bergs, simply going to starboard or port. But politics and human
personality are more complicated, more dangerous. Of course he

wants to know what happened to the dead girl. We all do. Nothing is more important. That's why the proper control of any inquiry is vital."

"I've heard that before," Arkady admitted.

"And didn't listen. Then you were a Party member, a high official, a man with a title. I see by your file that you haven't been on shore for almost a year. Renko, you're a prisoner on this ship. When we return to Vladivostok, while your cabin mates return to their girl-friends or families, you will be met by the Border Guard, an arm of State Security. You know that or you would have left the ship the last time we were home. You have no home, no place to go. Your only hope is a strongly positive evaluation from the *Polar Star.* I am the officer who writes that evaluation."

"What do you want?"

"I expect," Volovoi said, "to be closely and quietly informed before any report is made to the captain."

"Ah." Arkady bowed his head. "Well, it's not an investigation; it's only asking questions for a day. I'm not in charge."

"Since Slava Bukovsky speaks little English, it's obvious you will do some of the questioning. Questions have to be asked, the truth ascertained, before any proper conclusion can be reached. It's impor-tant that no information be given to the Americans."

"I can only do my best. Would you like accidental death? We've considered food poisoning. Homicide?"

"It's also important to protect the name of the ship."

"Suicide comes in many forms."

"And the reputation of the unfortunate worker."

"We could declare her still alive and name her the Queen of Fisherman's Day. Whatever you want. Write it out and I'll sign it right now."

Volovoi slowly closed the dossier, dropped it into his briefcase, pushed back his chair, and stood. His pinkish eyes became a little redder and more fixed, the instinctive reaction of a man sighting a natural enemy.

Arkady gazed back. *I know you too.* "Do I have permission to leave, Comrade?"

"Yes." Volovoi's voice had gone dry. "Renko," he added as Arkady turned to go.

"Yes?"

"Suicide, I think, is what you're best at."

4 Zina Patiashvili lay on the table, her head resting on a wooden block. She had been pretty, with the nearly Grecian profile that Georgian girls sometimes possessed. Full lips, a graceful neck and limbs, a black pubic stripe and a head of blond hair. What had she wanted to be, a Scandinavian? She had gone into the sea, touched bottom and returned with no apparent signs of corruption aside from the stillness of death. After the tension of rigor mortis all flesh became slack on the bone: breasts sagged on the ribs, mouth and jaw were loose, eyes flattened under half-open lids, the skin bore a luminous pallor mottled with bruises. And the smell. The operating room was no morgue, with a morgue's investment of formaldehyde, and the body was enough to fill the room with an odor like the stench of soured milk.

Arkady lit a second Belomor straight from the first and filled his lungs again. Russian tobacco, the stronger the better. On a medical chart he drew four silhouettes: front, back, right side, left.

Zina seemed to levitate in the flash of Slava's camera, then settle back on the table as her shadow faded. At first the third mate had resisted attending the autopsy, but Arkady had insisted so that Slava, already hostile, couldn't later claim any findings were prejudiced or incomplete. If this was a last twinge of professional pride on Arkady's part, he didn't know whether to be amused at himself or disgusted. The adventures of a fish gutter! At this point, Slava was snapping pictures like a combat-hardened photojournalist from *Tass*, while Arkady felt ill.

"Altogether," Dr. Vainu was saying, "this trip has been a great disappointment. Back on land I had a good trade in sedatives. Vale-ryanka, Pentalginum, even foreign pills. But the women on this boat are a group of Amazons. Not even many abortions."

Vainu was a young consumptive who generally received patients in his leisure suit and slippers, but for the autopsy he wore a lab coat with an ink-stained pocket. As always, he chain-smoked cigarettes laced with anti-stormine for seasickness. He held the cigarette be-tween his fourth and little fingers, so that every time he took a puff his hand covered his face like a mask. On a side table were his surgical tools: scalpels, protractors, clamps, a small rotary saw for amputations. On the table's lower shelf was a steel pan holding Zina's clothes.

"Sorry about the time of death," Vainu added airily, "but who in his right mind would believe a trawl would pick her up more than a day after she went over?"

Arkady tried to smoke and draw at the same time. In Moscow a pathologist did the actual work and the investigator only walked in and out. There were laboratories, teams of forensic specialists, a professional apparatus and the steadying hand of routine. One com-fort of the past few years had been the idea that he would never have to deal with victims again. Certainly not a girl out of the sea. A salty rankness underlay the smell of death. It was the smell of all the fish that had come down the factory line, and now of this girl from the same net, her hair matted, her arms, legs and breasts purpled with pooled blood.

"Besides, estimating a time of death from rigor mortis is very chancy, especially in cold conditions," Vainu went on. "It's only a contraction caused by chemical reactions after death. Did you know that if you cut a fish fillet before rigor mortis the flesh will still shrink and get tough?"

The pen slipped from Arkady's hand and his boot kicked it when he stooped for it.

"You'd think this was your first autopsy." Slava picked up the pen and surveyed the table clinically. He turned to the doctor. "She seems pretty bruised. Think she hit the propeller?"

"But her clothes weren't torn. Fists, not a propeller, from my experience," Vainu said.

Vainu's experience? He was trained in broken bones and appendectomies. Everything else was handled with green liniment or aspirin because, as he said, the infirmary dealt primarily in alcohol and drugs. That was why the table had restraining straps. The *Polar Star* had run out of morphine a month ago.

Arkady read the top of the chart: "Patiashvili, Zinaida Petrovna. Born 28/8/61, Tbilisi, G.S.S.R. Height: 1.6m. Weight: 48k. Hair: black (dyed blond). Eyes: brown." He handed the clipboard to Vainu and started walking around the table. Just as a man who is terrified of heights will concentrate on one rung at a time, Arkady spoke slowly and moved from detail to detail.

"Doctor, will you indicate the elbows are broken. The small amount of bruising suggests they were broken after death and at low body temperature." He took a deep breath and flexed her legs. "Indicate the same for her knees."

Slava stepped forward, focused and took another shot, picking angles like a movie director on his first film.

"Are you using color or black-and-white?" Vainu asked.

"Color," Slava said.

"On the forearms and calves," Arkady continued, "indicate a pooling of blood, not bruising, probably from the position she was in after death. Indicate the same on the breasts." On the breasts the blood under the skin looked like a second, liverish pair of areolas. He wasn't up to this, Arkady thought; he should have refused. "On the left shoulder, left side of the rib cage and hip some faint bruises evenly spaced." He used a ruler from the lab table. "Ten apparent bruises in all, about five centimeters apart."

"Could you hold the ruler a little steadier?" Slava complained and took another shot.

"I think our former investigator needs a drink," Vainu said.

Silently Arkady agreed. The girl's hands had the feel of cool, soft clay. "No signs of broken nails or any tissue under them. The doctor will take scrapings and examine them under a microscope."

"A drink or a crutch," Slava said.

Arkady took a deep pull on the Belomor before he opened Zina's mouth wide.

"Lips and tongue do not appear bruised or cut." He closed her mouth and tilted her head to look down her nostrils. He squeezed the bridge of her nose, then pulled the eyelids up from elliptical irises. "Indicate discoloration in the white of the left eye."

"Meaning what?" Slava asked.

"There are no signs of a direct blow," Arkady went on. "Possibly shock from a blow on the back of the skull." He rolled Zina onto her shoulder and pulled brine-stiffened hair from the nape of her neck. The skin there was bruised black. He took the clipboard from Vainu and said, "Cut her."

The doctor selected a scalpel and, still smoking a cigarette with a long ash, made a slice the length of the cervical vertebrae. Arkady cradled the head as Vainu probed.

"This is your lucky day," the doctor said dryly. "Indicate a crushed first vertebra and base of the skull. This must be a little triumph for you." He glanced at Arkady and then at the saw. "We could bring the brain out to make sure. Or crack the chest and examine the air passages for seawater."

Slava snapped a picture of the neck and straightened up, swaying a little as he stood.

"No." Arkady let her head settle on the block and closed her eyes. He rubbed his hands on his jacket and lit a second Belomor from the first, sucking fiercely, then sorted through the clothes in the pan. If she had drowned there would have been ruptures in her nose and mouth; there would have been water in her stomach as well as in her lungs, and when she was moved she'd still be seeping like a sponge. Besides, Vladivostok had enough investigators and technicians who'd be happy to carve her up and analyze her down to her atomic elements. The pan held a red plastic shoe of Soviet manufacture, loose blue exercise pants, panties, white cotton blouse with a Hong Kong label and a pin that said, "I ♥ L.A." An international girl. In a pocket of the pants was some sodden blue pasteboard that had been a pack of Gauloises. Also a playing card, the queen of hearts. A romantic girl, Zina Patiashvili. Also a sturdy Soviet condom. But a practical one too. He looked at her waxy face again, at the scalp already withdrawing from the black roots of her blond hair. The girl was dead, leaving her fantasy life behind. He always became angry at autopsies—at the victims as well as the murderers. Why didn't some people just shoot themselves in the head the day they were born?

The *Polar Star* was in a turn, trailing after its catcher boats.

Arkady steadied himself unconsciously. Slava braced himself at the table while trying not to touch it.

"Losing your sea legs?" Vainu asked.

The third mate stared back. "I'm fine."

Vainu smirked. "At least we should remove the viscera," he told Arkady.

Arkady took the clothes from the pan. They were daubed with fish blood, torn here and there by fish spines, no more than you'd expect from a ride in a net. There might have been an oil smudge on a pants knee. Spreading the blouse, Arkady noticed a different sort of rustiness on the front flap, not a rip but a cut.

He returned to the body. There was maroon discoloration on the limbs, breasts and around the navel. Maybe it wasn't all blood pooling; maybe he'd been too quick to say that just to get away from her. Sure enough, as he spread the belly from the navel he saw a puncture, a narrow stab wound about two centimeters long. Just what a fisherman's knife would leave. Everyone on the *Polar Star* had a knife with a white plastic handle and a 20-cm. double-edged blade for gutting fish or cutting net. Signs throughout the ship advised: "Be ready for emergencies. Carry your knife at all times." Arkady's was in his locker.

"Let me do that." Vainu elbowed Arkady aside.

"You found a bump and a scratch," Slava said. "So what?"

Arkady said, "It's more than the usual wear and tear, even for a high dive."

Vainu staggered from the table. Arkady thought he must have opened the wound more because a short length of intestine, purplish-gray and slick, stood out of it. More of it rose with a life of its own, and continued to emerge from the girl's belly through a bubbling collar of salt water and pearly ooze.

"Slime eel!"

Slime eel or hagfish. By either name, a primitive but efficient form of life. Sometimes the net brought in a halibut two meters long, a beast that should have weighed a quarter ton and was nothing but a sack of skin and bones and a nest of slime eels. The outside of the fish could be untouched; the eels entered through the mouth or anus and forced their way into the belly. When an eel appeared in the factory the women scattered until the men had hammered it to death with shovels.

The eel's head, an eyeless stump with fleshy horns and a puckered mouth, whipped from side to side against Zina Patiashvili's stomach; then the entire eel, as long as an arm, slid seemingly forever out of her, twisted in midair and landed at Vainu's feet. The doctor stabbed, snapping the scalpel in two against the deck. He kicked, then grabbed another knife from the table. The eel thrashed wildly, rolling across the room. Its main defense was a glutinous, pearly ooze that made it impossible to hold. One eel could fill a bucket with slime; a feeding eel could cover bait in a cocoon of slime that not even a shark would touch. The tip of the knife broke off and flew up, cutting Vainu's cheek. He tripped, landed on his back and watched the eel squirm toward him.

Arkady stepped into the passage and returned with a fire ax, which he swung, blunt-end down, on the eel. With each blow the eel thrashed, smearing the deck. Arkady lost his balance on the slime, caught himself, turned the hatchet edge down and cut the eel in half. The two halves went on twisting separately until he had chopped each of them in two. The four divided parts twitched in pools of slime and blood.

Vainu staggered to the cabinet, pulled the instruments from the sterilizing jar and poured the alcohol into two glasses for Arkady and himself. Slava Bukovsky was gone. Arkady had a fleeting memory of the third mate bolting for the door a moment after the eel appeared.

"This is my last trip," Vainu muttered.

"Why didn't anyone notice she was missing from work?" Arkady asked. "Was she chronically ill?"

"Zina?" Vainu steadied his glass with both hands. "Not her."

Arkady drained his own glass in a swallow. A little antiseptic, but not bad.

What sort of doctor, he considered, did factory ships generally have? Certainly not one with curiosity about the whole range of physical dysfunction, of deliveries, childhood diseases, geriatrics. On the *Polar Star* there wasn't even the usual maritime hazard of tropical diseases. Medical duty on the waters of the North Pacific was pretty boring, which was why it drew drunks and medical school graduates assigned against their will. Vainu was neither. He was Estonian, from a Baltic republic where Russians were treated like occupying troops. Not a man with a great deal of sympathy for the crew of the *Polar Star*.

"No problems of dizziness, headaches, fainting? No problems with drugs? You didn't treat her for anything?"

"You saw her records. Absolutely clean."

"Then how is it that no one was surprised by the absence of this able-bodied worker?"

"Renko, I have the impression you are the only man on board who didn't know Zina."

Arkady nodded. He was getting that impression, too.

"Don't forget your ax," Vainu said as Arkady started for the door.

"I'd like you to examine the body for signs of sexual activity. Get her fingerprints and enough blood for typing. I'm afraid you'll have to clean out the abdomen."

"What if . . . ?" The doctor stared at the eel.

"Right," Arkady said. "Keep the ax."

. . .

SLAVA BUKOVSKY WAS bent over the rail outside. Arkady stood beside him as if they were taking the air. On the trawl deck mounds of yellow sole waited to be shoveled down the chute to the factory. An American nylon net was strung between two booms, and a net needle—a shuttle with a split tip—hung from an ongoing repair. Arkady wondered if it was the net Zina had come up in. Slava studied the sea.

Sometimes fog acted like oil on water. The surface was dead calm, black, a few gulls hovering over a trawler he could make out only because American boats were so bright, like fishing lures. This one was red and white, with a crew in yellow slickers. It swung in and out behind the *Polar Star*'s stern, the factory ship's rusty hull looming forty feet above the trawler. Of course, the Americans went out only for weeks at a time, whereas the *Polar Star* was out for half a year. The American boat was a toy in the water; the *Polar Star* was a world unto itself.

"That doesn't usually happen at autopsies," Arkady said softly.

Slava wiped his mouth with a handkerchief. "Why would anyone stab her if she was already dead?"

"The stomach has bacteria. The puncture was to let the gases out, to keep her from floating. I can carry on alone for a while; why don't you catch up when you feel better?"

Slava stiffened up from the rail and folded his handkerchief. "I'm still in charge. We will do everything like a normal investigation."

Arkady shrugged. "In a normal homicide investigation, when you find the body you go over the ground with a magnifying glass and metal detectors. Look around you. Is there any particular wave you want to examine?"

"Stop saying 'homicide.' That's rumor-mongering."

"Not with those wounds."

"It could have been the propeller," Slava said.

"If someone hit her over the head with it."

"There were no signs of a struggle—you said so yourself. It's your attitude that is the greatest problem. I'm not going to let your antisocial posturing compromise me."

"Comrade Bukovsky, I'm just a worker off the factory line. You are an emblem of the radiant Soviet future. How can I compromise you?"

"Don't play the worker with me. Volovoi told me about you. You made a big mess back in Moscow. Captain Marchuk was crazy to let you off the line."

"Why did he?" Arkady was genuinely curious.

"I don't know." Slava seemed as confused as Arkady.

ZINA PATIASHVILI'S CABIN was the same as Arkady's in space and layout, four people living in what could pass for a fairly comfortable decompression chamber: four bunks, table and bench, closet and sink. The atmosphere itself was different. Instead of male sweat, the air contained a powerful mix of competing perfumes. Rather than Gury's pinups and Obidin's icon, the closet door was decorated with Cuban postcards, sappy International Women's Day greeting cards, snapshots of children in Pioneer scarves, magazine pictures of movie stars and musicians. There was a smiling picture of the roly-poly Soviet rock star Stas Namin, a scowling photo of Mick Jagger.

"That was Zina's." Natasha Chaikovskaya pointed to Jagger.

The other cabin mates were "Madame" Malzeva, the oldest worker from Arkady's factory line, and a little Uzbek girl named Dynama in honor of the electrification of Uzbekistan. Her family had done the innocent girl no favor, because in more sophisticated parts of the Soviet Union a "dynama" is a flirt who wines and dines on a man's money, then goes to the rest room and disappears. Mercifully, her friends called her Dynka. Her black eyes balanced anxiously on enormous cheekbones. Her hair was done up in two ponytails that looked like black wings.

For such a somber occasion Natasha had eschewed lipstick, compromising with a tall haircomb. Behind her back she was called Chaika, for the broad-shouldered limousine of that name. She could have smothered Stas Namin with one squeeze; Jagger wouldn't have had a chance. She was a shot-putter with the soul of Carmen.

"Zina was a good girl, a popular girl, the life of the ship," Madame Malzeva said. As if holding court in her parlor, she wore a tasseled shawl and darned a sateen pillow with stitched waves and the invitation VISIT ODESSA. "Wherever there was laughter, there was our Zina."

"Zina was nice to me," Dynka said. "She'd come down to the laundry and bring me a sandwich." Like most Uzbeks, she couldn't pronounce "zch"; she just dropped it.

"She was an honest Soviet worker who will be badly missed." Natasha was a Party member with the Party member's ability to sound like a tape recording.

"Those are valuable testimonials," Slava said.

A top bunk was stripped. In a cardboard box designed for holding thirty kilos of frozen fish were clothes, shoes, stereo and cassettes, hair rollers and brushes, gray notebook, a snapshot of Zina in her bathing suit, another of her and Dynka, and an East Indian jewelry box covered with colored cloth and bits of mirror. Over the bunk a framed panel screwed into the bulkhead gave the occupant's assignment in case of emergency. Zina's post was the fire brigade in the galley.

Arkady could tell immediately who occupied the other bunks. An older woman always had a lower, in this case one lined with pillows from other ports—Sochi, Tripoli, Tangiers—so that Madame Malzeva could repose on a soft atlas. Natasha's bunk held a selection of pamphlets like *Understanding the Consequences of Social Democratic Deviationism* and *Toward a Cleaner Complexion.* Perhaps one led to the other; that would be a propaganda breakthrough. On Dynka's upper bunk was a toy camel. More than men did, they had made a real home out of their cabin, enough for him to feel like an intruder.

"What interests us," Arkady said, "is how Zina's disappearance went unnoticed. You shared this cabin with her. How could you not notice that she was gone for a day and a night?"

"She was such an active girl," Malzeva said, "and we have different shifts. You know, Arkasha, we work at night. She worked during the day. Sometimes days would pass without our seeing Zina. It's hard to believe we will never see her again."

"You must be upset." Arkady had seen Madame Malzeva cry at war movies when the Germans got shot. Everyone else would be screaming "Take that, you fucking Fritz!" but Malzeva would be sobbing into her babushka.

"She borrowed my shower cap and never returned it." The old woman raised dry eyes.

"It would be good to gather testimonials from her other mates," Slava suggested.

"What about her enemies?" Arkady asked. "Would anyone want to hurt her?"

"No!" the three women said as a chorus.

"There's no call for such a question," Slava warned.

"Forget I asked. And what else was Zina's?" Arkady scanned the photomontage on the closet door.

"Her nephew." Dynka's finger went tentatively to a snapshot of a dark-haired boy holding a bunch of grapes as big as figs.

"Her actress." Natasha pointed to a picture of Melina Mercouri looking pouty and wreathed in cigarette smoke. Had Zina seen herself as a sultry Greek?

"Any boyfriend?" Arkady asked.

The three women looked at one another as if they were consulting; then Natasha answered, "Not any one man especially that we were aware of."

"No one man," said Malzeva.

Dynka giggled. "No."

"Fraternization with all your mates is the best course," Slava said.

"Did you see her at the dance? Were you at the dance?" Arkady asked them.

"No, Arkasha, not at my age," Malzeva said, dusting off some coyness. "And you forget that the factory line still processed fish during the dance. Natasha, weren't you sick?"

"Yes." When Slava, erstwhile musician, gave a start, Natasha added, "I may have looked in at the dance." In a dress, Arkady guessed.

"Were you at the dance?" Arkady asked Dynka.

"Yes. The Americans dance like monkeys," she said. "Zina was the only one who could dance like them."

"With them?" Arkady asked her.

"It seems to me there is a certain unhealthy sexuality when Americans dance," Madame Malzeva said.

"The dance was meant to encourage friendship between workers of both nations," Slava answered. "What does it matter who she danced with if she had an accident later that night?"

Arkady poured the box of effects onto Zina's bunk. The clothes were foreign and worn to the last thread. Nothing in the pockets. The tapes were of the Rolling Stones and Dire Straits variety; the player was a Sanyo. There was no ID, nor had he expected any; her paybook and visa would be in the ship's safe. Lipsticks and perfumes lay in the hollow of the bunk; how long would the scent of Zina Patiashvili linger in the cabin? Her jewelry box had a string of fake pearls and half a deck of playing cards, all the queen of hearts. Also a roll of "pinkies," ten-ruble notes, held together by a rubber band. It would take more time to go through the effects than he had at this moment. He put everything back into the box.

"Everything's here?" he asked. "All her tapes?"

Natasha sniffed. "Her precious tapes. She always used her headphones. She never shared them."

"What are you trying to find?" Slava demanded. "I'm tired of being ignored."

"I'm not ignoring you," Arkady said, "but you already know what happened. I'm more slow-witted; I have to go step by step. Thank you," he told the three women.

"That's all, comrades," Slava said decisively. He picked up the box. "I'll take care of this."

At the door Arkady paused to ask, "Did she have fun at the dance?"

"It's possible," Natasha said. "Comrade Renko, maybe you should go to a dance sometime. The intelligentsia should mix with workers."

How Natasha had settled on this label for him Arkady didn't know; the slime line was not an avenue of philosophers. There was something ominous in Natasha's expression he wanted to avoid, so he asked Dynka, "Did she seem dizzy? Sick?"

Dynka shook her head, so that her ponytails rode back and forth. "She was happy when she left the dance."

"At what time? Where was she going?"

"To the stern. I can't say what time it was; people were still dancing."

"Who was she with?"

"She was alone, but she was happy, like a princess in a fairy tale."

It was a fantasy far better than what men usually put together. These women believed they were sailing the seas with all the ordinary intrigues of a women's apartment, as if you couldn't step outside into the wide sea and simply disappear. During the ten months that Arkady had spent on board, he felt more and more that the ocean was a void, a vacuum into which people could be drawn at any moment. They should hang on to their bunks, and hold on for their lives if they stepped on deck.

When Slava and Arkady reached the deck, they found Vainu jackknifed over the rail, his lab coat smeared with blood and slime. The ax lay at his feet. He held up two fingers.

". . . more," he blurted and turned his face back into the wind.

A void or a well of too much life. Take your pick.

5 Arkady happily followed Slava toward the stern. He could almost breathe in the view: a lone figure at the rail, a catcher boat in the middle distance, black sea folding into gray fog. It was a change from claustrophobia.

"Look around," Slava said. "You're supposed to be an expert."

"Right." Arkady stopped on command and turned, not that there was much to see: winches and cleats lit by three lamps that even at midday glowed like poisonous moons. In the middle of the deck was an open stairwell that led to a landing directly over the stern ramp. Stern ramps were a feature of modern trawling: the *Polar Star*'s ramp began at the waterline and tunneled up to the trawl deck on the other side of the aft house. All he could see of the ramp was the part below the well, and all he could see of the trawl deck were the tops of the booms and gantries beyond the smokestack. Around the stack were oil barrels, spare cables and hawsers. On the boat deck, lifeboats hung on davits. On one side was emergency gear: fire axes, a pike, gaff and spade, as if fire could be fought like foreign troops.

"Well?" Slava demanded. "According to the girl this is where Zina was headed. Like someone in a fairy tale." He stopped in mid-stride and whispered to Arkady, "Susan."

"Soo-san?" Arkady asked. Now, there was a name that lent itself to Russian pronunciation.

"Shh!" Slava blushed.

The figure at the rail wore a hooded canvas jacket, shapeless pants and gum boots. Arkady had always avoided the Americans. They rarely came down to the factory, and above deck he felt he was watched, that he was expected to try to make contact with them, that he would compromise them, if not himself.

"She's taking a net." Slava stopped Arkady at a respectful distance.

Susan Hightower's back was to them as she talked into a hand-held radio. It sounded as if she were alternately answering the *Eagle* in English and giving instructions to the bridge of the *Polar Star* in Russian. The catcher boat approached, putting its shoulder to the waves. A rattling came from below. Arkady looked down the well to see a cable of scarred red-and-white buoys spill down the grooved, rust-brown slope of the ramp. "If she's working," he said, "we can talk to the other Americans."

"She's the head representative. As a courtesy, we must speak to her first," Slava insisted.

Courtesy? Here they were shivering and ignored, but Slava was in the throes of social embarrassment.

On the water, the cable straightened as it played out twenty-five, fifty, a hundred meters, each buoy riding its own crest. As the line spread to its full length, the American boat approached on the port side and kept pace.

"This is very interesting," Slava announced heartily.

"Yes." Arkady turned his back to the wind. At this longitude there was no land between the North and South Poles and breezes built quickly.

"You know how in our Soviet fleet we come so close to transfer fish," Slava went on. "There are battered hulls—"

"Battered hulls are a signature of the Soviet fleet," Arkady agreed.

"This system the Americans taught us, the 'no contact' system, is cleaner, but it is more intricate and demands more skill."

"Like sex between spiders," Susan said without turning her head.

Arkady admired the technique demanded. From the American trawler a fisherman with a strong arm threw a gaff over the trailing line. Another fisherman ran the line along the gunwale to the stern, where a full net of fish covered the trawler's narrow deck. "They're connecting," Susan told the radio in Russian.

Like spiders having sex? An interesting comparison, Arkady thought. A buoy line was a relatively fine thread. Not only were the boats at a distance, but they were moving up and down in relation to each other. If the ships separated too much, the line would snap from the pressure; too little and the net wouldn't leave the trawler or would drop toward the bottom, where vertical drag could break the line and lose gear and fish worth one hundred thousand dollars in American money.

"Coming in," Susan said as the net slipped off the trawler's deck. At once the weight of the bag made the *Polar Star* slow half a knot. The catcher boat veered off, while winches far back on the factory ship's trawl deck started hauling the line in.

Susan gave Arkady no more than a glance as he stepped to the rail beside her. He thought she must be wearing layers of sweaters and pants to appear so shapeless because her face was thin. She had brown eyes and the kind of concentration you see in a girl on a balance beam who doesn't give a damn about the rest of the world.

"Fifty meters," she was saying in Russian.

Gulls started to gather. It was always a mystery how there could be not a bird in sight, then suddenly by the tens they would appear, as if the fog were a magician's cape.

Behind its vanguard of buoys, the incoming net, its orange-and-black plastic hair glimmering wet, surged toward the *Polar Star*. Behind them a trawlmaster crossed the deck and ran down the stairs of the stairwell, taking his position on the landing over the ramp. The slim cable rose taut and dripping. Buoys bounced up the ramp. Dragged by its steel bridle, the bag surged out of the water and onto the ramp's lower lip.

"Ease off!" Susan ordered in Russian.

The *Polar Star* slowed almost to the point of wallowing. There was a necessary caution to hauling in thirty tons of fish that lost buoyancy and doubled in weight as they left the water. Any more tension on the winch or forward motion to the ship and the line could part. On the other hand, a dead stop could force the bag into the propeller screws. Patiently the cable eased the bag half onto the ramp as the ship coasted at dead slow. There the bag paused as if exhausted, water pouring out, crabs and starfish dripping out.

Susan asked Arkady, "You're from the factory?"

"Yes."

"The mystery man from the Lower Depths."

Slava pulled Arkady to the stairwell rail. "Don't bother her now."

At the well they looked down at the trawlmaster as the ramp's steel-mesh safety gate swung up and two men in hard hats, life jackets and lifelines around their waists dragged heavy messenger cables down the ramp to the bag. The closer they came to the net, the more steeply the chute curved down to the water. A floodlight in the well showed where, at the belly of the waiting bag, the ramp dropped dead away.

The lead man shouted, slipped and clung to his lifeline. It was a deckhand named Pavel; his eyes had gone white with fright.

From the landing the trawlmaster encouraged him. "You look like a drunk on a dance floor. Maybe you'd like a pair of skates."

"Karp," Slava said with admiration.

Karp's shoulders stretched his sweater. He turned his broad head up to them and grinned, displaying golden dental work. He and his team were taking an extra shift, another reason they were the favorites of the first mate. "Wait until we reach the ice sheet," he yelled up. "Pavel will do some real skating on the ramp then."

Arkady remembered the half-mended net he had seen earlier on the trawl deck.

"Did you cut Zina out?" he called down to Karp.

"Yeah." The gold left the smile. "So?"

"Nothing." It was simply interesting to Arkady that Karp Korobetz, that exemplar among the trawlmasters, had taken the chance of ruining expensive American mesh rather than pouring the fish out and waiting for her body to emerge.

Below them, Pavel was struggling to untangle the bridle of the net so that his teammate could attach the G-hooks of the messenger cables and relieve the weight on the buoy line. It was one thing for a cable to snap and fly wildly on an open deck; in the close tunnel of the ramp, a broken cable would be a whip in a barrel.

"Were you at the dance?" Arkady called down to Karp.

"No," Karp yelled. "Hey, Renko, you never answered my question. What did they nail you for?"

Arkady detected the faint imprint of a Moscow accent.

Susan turned around. "Is there a problem?"

Pavel fell again, this time to midway down the net before his lifeline saved him. A wave flowed up the ramp and lifted the net so that it rolled indolently over the fisherman. Arkady had seen men die like this before. The weight of the bag wouldn't let the lungs breathe, and half the time the bag was in the water. Pavel's teammate shouted and pulled on the rope, but with Pavel beneath twenty tons of fish and net the line didn't budge. Yells didn't help. As another wave broke over the bag it rolled some more, like a walrus crushing a pup. Receding, the wave tried to suck the bag back to the sea, and the lifeline broke.

Karp jumped down from the landing onto the net—what was another hundred kilos compared to tons? With the next wave, he was up to his waist in freezing water, holding on to the net with one hand and with the other dragging Pavel from a kelplike mass of plastic chafing hair. Karp was laughing. As Pavel sputtered and climbed onto the back of the bag, the trawlmaster pulled himself up to the bridle and helped connect the G-hooks. It was all over in a second. What struck Arkady was that Karp had never hesitated; he had moved with such speed that saving another man's life seemed less an act of courage than a gymnast's spin around a bar.

The catcher boat swung back into the *Polar Star*'s wake, waiting for the call on the net's catch—so many tons, so much sole, crabs, mud. Gulls hovered at the mouth of the ramp, watching for any fish slipping through the net.

"Someone from the slime line is the last thing we need here now," Susan told Slava. "Take him to my cabin."

As soon as the G-hooks snapped shut, Karp and his deckhands moved quickly up the ramp, hauling themselves in step by step on one lifeline. The net began stirring behind them. The *Polar Star* had a Trip Plan, a quota of fifty thousand tons of fish. So many frozen fillets, so much fish meal, so much liver oil for a nation starved for protein to build the muscles that were building Communism. Say 10 percent was lost on board to freezer burn, 10 percent spoiled on shore, 10 percent was split between the port manager and the fleet director, 10 percent was spilled on unpaved roads to villages where there might or might not be a working refrigerator to save the last well-traveled fillets. No wonder the net rushed eagerly to the trawl deck.

SLAVA LED ARKADY forward past the trawl deck and midships by the white hangar of the machinists' shop. "Can you believe her accent? It's so good," he said. "Susan is a fantastic woman. That she can speak so much better than that Uzbek girl—what's her name?"

"Dynka."

"Dynka, right. No one speaks Russian anymore."

True. Upwardly mobile Russians in particular spoke the increasingly popular "Politburo Ukrainian." Ever since Khrushchev, the Ukrainian-born leaders of the country had spoken in crude, halting Russian, substituting *w*'s for *v*'s, until sooner or later everyone in the Kremlin, whether from Samarkand or Siberia, started sounding like a son of Kiev.

"Say your name," Arkady asked.

"Slawa." Slava eyed Arkady suspiciously. "I don't know what it is, but you always seem to be getting at something."

On the dark seam where fog met the horizon was the glow of another catcher boat working a trawl.

Arkady asked, "How many boats do we have with us?"

"We usually have a fleet of four: the *Alaska Miss,* the *Merry Jane,* the *Aurora* and the *Eagle.*"

"They were all at the dance?"

"No. The *Alaska Miss* had a crew change coming and the *Aurora* had a steering-gear problem. Since we'd stopped fishing for the night and since we're about to go to Dutch Harbor, they decided to leave

for port early. We only had two boats at the dance, the same two
we have now."

"You have a good band?"

Carefully Slava said, "Not the worst."

The forward deck was divided between a volleyball court on one
side and a loading deck, which they walked across. Netting covered
the court. Despite this, sometimes a ball escaped into the water;
then the captain would turn the *Polar Star* around right to the
bobbing dot, a task equivalent to steering a giant sow through heavy
mud. Volleyballs were scarce in the Bering Sea.

The Americans on board lived in the forward house, on the deck
below the officers' cabins and the bridge. Susan had yet to arrive, but
the three others had assembled in her cabin. Bernie was the freckled
boy Arkady had met outside the cafeteria with Volovoi. His friend
Day wore steel-rimmed glasses that emphasized a scholar's doll-like
earnestness. Both reps wore jeans and sweaters that were at once
shabby and superior to any Russian clothing. Lantz was a National
Fisheries observer charged with making sure the *Polar Star* didn't
take fish of an illegal type, sex or size. As he was about to go on duty,
he wore oiled coveralls, a plaid shirt with rubber sleeves, a rubber
glove on one hand and a surgical one hanging like a handkerchief
from his shirt pocket. Acting half asleep, he lounged on the built-in
bench, curling up because he was so tall, a cigarette stuck in his
mouth. While they waited for Susan, Slava talked with the three of
them in Russian with the enthusiastic ease of friends, contemporar-
ies, soulmates.

Susan's cabin was no great step up from crew quarters. Two bunks
instead of four, which she had to herself as the lone American
woman. There was a waist-high ZIL refrigerator and the metallic
aroma of instant coffee. A typewriter and manuscript boxes on the

upper bunk and, stacked in cartons, books—Pasternak, Nabokov, Blok. Arkady saw Russian-language editions that would have sold in seconds at any Soviet bookstore or for hundreds of rubles on a Moscow back street. It was like coming upon cartons of gold. Susan could read these?

"Explain again, please," Day asked Slava. "Who is he?"

"Our workers have many talents. Seaman Renko is a worker from the factory, but he has experience with the investigation of accidents."

"It's terrible about Zina," Bernie said. "She was great."

Lantz blew a ring of smoke and asked lazily in English, "How would you know?"

"What happened to her?" Day asked.

Arkady groaned inwardly as Slava answered, "It seems Zina became ill, went out on deck and perhaps lost her balance."

"And perhaps came up in the net?" Lantz asked.

"Exactly."

"Did anyone see her fall over?" Bernie asked.

"No," Slava said. This was the primal error of first-time investigators, the tendency to answer questions rather than ask them. "It was dark, you know, and foggy after the dance and she was alone. These things happen at sea. This is the information we have so far, but if you know anything . . ."

Assisting Slava was like following a lemming. The three Americans shrugged and said in unison, "No."

"We were supposed to wait for Susan, but I don't think we have any more questions," Slava told Arkady.

"I don't have any," Arkady said, and then switched to English. "I am impressed with your Russian."

"We're all graduate students," Day said. "We signed on to improve our Russian."

"And I'm struck by how well you knew our crew."

"Everyone knew Zina," Bernie said.

Day said, "She was a popular girl."

Arkady could see Slava mentally translating, trying to keep up.

"She worked in the crew's galley," Arkady said to Day. "She served you food?"

"No, we eat in the officers' mess. She worked there at the start of the trip, but then she transferred."

"We did see Zina on deck—at the stern rail, in fact," Bernie said.

"Where your station is?"

"Right. There's always a company rep at the stern when the fish are transferred. Zina would come out and watch with us."

"Often?"

"Sure."

"Your station is . . . ?" Arkady turned apologetically to Lantz.

"The trawl deck."

"You were on watch when the net bearing Zina came on deck?"

Lantz brushed cigarette ash from his sweater and sat up. For such a tall boy he had a small skull and the raked hair of a narcissist. "It was cold. I was inside having some tea. The deckhands know they're supposed to tell me when a bag is coming up the ramp."

Even belowdecks in the din of the factory line, Arkady knew when a net was coming aboard by the high whine of the hydraulic winch and the shift in the ship's engines from half speed to dead slow as the net cleared the water, followed by the return to half speed as it came up the ramp. In his sleep he knew when fish were coming on board. Nobody had needed to call Lantz from a glass of tea.

"You enjoyed the dance?" Arkady asked.

"Terrific dance," Bernie said.

"Especially Slava's band," said Day.

"You danced with Zina?" Arkady asked.

"Zina had more interest in the motorcycle gang," Lantz said.

"Gang?" Arkady asked.

"Fishermen," Bernie explained. "American fishermen, not yours."

"Boy, your English is really good," said Day. "You're from the factory?"

"The slime line," Susan said as she entered and threw her jacket on a bunk. She pulled off a wool cap, releasing thick blond hair cut short. "You started without me," she told Slava. "I'm the head rep. You know you don't talk to my boys without me."

"I'm sorry, Susan." Slava was contrite.

"As long as it's clear."

"Yes."

Susan had taken command, that was obvious, with the imperious manner small people sometimes have of inserting themselves into the center of a situation. Her eyes darted around the cabin, taking roll call.

"It's about Zina and the dance," Bernie said. "This Seaman Renko with Slava said he didn't have any questions, but I think he does."

"In English," she said. "I heard." She turned to Arkady. "You want to know who danced with Zina? Who knows. It was dark and everyone was bobbing up and down. One second you're dancing with one person and the next you're dancing with three. You dance with men or women or both. It's like water polo without the water. Now, let's talk about you. Slava told me you have experience with accidents."

"Comrade Renko served as an investigator for the Moscow prosecutor's office," Slava said.

"And what did you investigate?" she asked Arkady.

"Very bad accidents."

She studied him as if he were auditioning for a part and not doing well. "How convenient that you happened to be cleaning fish on the factory line of this ship. An investigator all the way from Moscow? Fluent in English? Cleaning fish?"

"Employment is guaranteed in the Soviet Union," Arkady said.

"Fine," Susan said. "I would suggest that you save all your other questions for Soviet citizens. Zina is a Soviet problem. If I hear you've approached any American stationed on this ship again, I'm going straight to Captain Marchuk."

"No more questions," Slava said and pushed Arkady to the door.

"I have a last question," Arkady said. He asked the men, "You're looking forward to Dutch Harbor?"

This broke the tension a little.

"Two more days," Bernie said. "I'm going to the hotel, get the best room, sit in a hot shower and drink an ice-cold six-pack of beer."

"Soo-san?" Arkady liked saying it that way, making her name Russian.

"Two more days and I'm gone," she said. "You'll get a new head rep in Dutch and I'll be flying out of the fog to California, so you can say good-bye to me now."

"The rest of us are coming back," Day assured Slava. "We have two more months of fishing."

"Just fishing," Slava promised. "No more questions. We should always keep in mind that we are shipmates and friends."

Arkady remembered that on the voyage out from Vladivostok the *Polar Star* had staged exercises in camouflage and radiation cleansing. Every Soviet seaman knew that in his captain's safe was a sealed packet to be opened on receipt of a coded signal of war; inside were instructions on how to avoid enemy submarines, where to make friendly contact, what to do with prisoners.

6 Usually Arkady didn't enjoy amusement rides, but he liked this one. Nothing fancy. The transport cage had a chain for a gate and a tire on the base to cushion its landings, but it lifted off the deck of the *Polar Star* with a satisfyingly taut jerk of the crane cable, swaying as it rose, and for a moment, in midflight, felt like an oversized birdcage that had taken wing. Then they cleared the side and began dropping toward the *Merry Jane.* Next to the looming hull of the factory ship any catcher boat looked diminutive, even though the *Merry Jane* was forty meters long. It sported the characteristic high bow of a Bering Sea trawler, a forward wheelhouse and stack, a mast hung with antennae and lamps, a wooden deck with a side crane of its own, and a stern ramp and gantry with three neatly reeled nets. The hull was blue trimmed white, the wheelhouse white trimmed blue, and the boat looked bright as a toy as it rubbed against the black sea fender of the *Polar Star.* Three fishermen in slickers steadied the cage as it descended to the deck. Slava unhooked the chain and stepped out first. Arkady followed; for the first time in almost a year he was off the factory ship. Off the *Polar Star* and onto an American boat. The fishermen vied with one another to pump his hand and ask enthusiastically, "Fala Português?"

There were two Diegos and one Marco, all short, dark men with the soulful eyes of castaways. None of them spoke any Russian or much English. Slava hurried Arkady up the wheelhouse stairs to meet Captain Thorwald, a pink-faced, bear-sized Norwegian.

"Crazy, isn't it," Thorwald said. "It's American-owned, that's all. The Portuguese, they spend ten months of the year fishing here, but they have families in Portugal. They make a fortune here compared with what they could at home. Same with me. Well, I go home to shovel snow off the walk, they go home to fry sardines. But two months on land is enough for us."

The captain of the *Merry Jane* wore pajamas open to gold chains nesting on a chest of red hair. Russians supposedly traced their ancestry back to Viking raiders; "Russ" meant red, for the hair of the invaders. Thorwald looked as if nothing less than Viking pillage would wake him up.

"They don't seem to speak English," Arkady said.

"That way they don't get into trouble. They know their jobs, so there's not much need for conversation. They may be little fuckers, but next to Norwegians they're the best."

"High praise," Arkady said. "Beautiful boat."

The luxurious bridge alone was a revelation. The chart desk was teak lacquered to an agate gleam; the deck bore a carpet thick enough for a member of the Central Committee; and at each end of the wide, padded console was a wheel with its own high upholstered swivel chair. The chair on the starboard side was surrounded by the color monitors of fish-finders, radar screens and the digital readouts of radios.

Thorwald reached inside his pajama pants to scratch. "Yah, this is built solid for the Bering. Wait till you see us in the ice sheet. To bring a boat like the *Eagle* up here, to me that's really crazy. Or to bring women."

"You knew Zina Patiashvili?" Slava asked.

"When I fish, I fish. When I fuck, I fuck. I don't mix them up."

"Wise," Arkady said.

Impervious, Thorwald went on, "I didn't know Zina and I didn't go to the dance because I was in the wardroom with Marchuk and Morgan trying to show them where to trawl. Sometimes I don't think the Russians and Americans are after fish at all."

Slava and Arkady descended to the galley, where the crew had assembled for a meal of salt cod and wine, hardly the midday fare on a Soviet ship. Fishing was arduous work, but again Arkady was struck by the amenities on the *Merry Jane:* the big range with sliding bars to keep food from flying in heavy seas, the table covered by antiskid pads, the cushioned banquette, the coffee machine with its pot strapped in place. There were homey touches: hanging from a lamp cord, a wooden model of a sailing boat with eyes painted on the bow; a poster of a whitewashed village on a beach. Very different from the galley of the inland trawler Arkady had served on off the coast of Sakhalin. There the crew ate with no room to take off their coats, and everything—groats, potatoes, cabbage, tea—tasted of mildew and fish.

As they ate, the Portuguese watched a videotape. Aside from a polite nod, all interest in their guests was gone. Arkady understood. If someone was coming to ask them questions, he should speak their language. After all, when Russians were mucking around in rowboats the Portuguese had an empire that circled the world. On the screen was the hysterical narration and languid action of a soccer match.

"Zina Patiashvili?" Slava asked. "Does anyone here know Zina?

Does . . . do you . . . have you?" He turned to Arkady. "This is a waste of time."

"Football," Arkady said as he sat down.

The Diego next to Arkady poured him a tumbler of red wine. *"Campeonato do Mundo.* You?"

"Goalie." Twenty years ago, Arkady realized.

"Forward." The fisherman pointed to himself, then to the other Diego and Marco. "Forward. Back." He aimed his finger at the television. "Portugal white, *inglês* stripe. Bad."

As all three fishermen winced, a figure in a striped jersey broke away and scored. How many times had they already seen the tape of this game, Arkady wondered—ten times, a hundred? Over a long voyage, men tend to tell the same tale over and over. This was the more refined torture of high technology.

While Diego averted his eyes from the television Arkady showed him the snapshot of Zina and Dynka.

"You stole that," Slava said. "Zina." Arkady watched the fisherman's eyes slide from woman to woman equally. He shrugged. Arkady showed the picture to the other two crewmen and got the same reaction, but then the first Diego asked to see the photo again.

"No baile," he told Arkady. *"A loura da Rússia. A mulher com os americanos."* He became passionate. *"Entende? Com americanos."*

"She danced with the Americans. That's what I thought," Arkady said.

"Beba, beba." Diego refilled his glass.

"Thank you."

"Muito obrigado," Diego instructed him.

"Muito obrigado."

"Meo pracer."

• • •

ARKADY HELD ON to the center bar as the transport cage swung down to the second trawler. Slava was looking more and more miserable, like a bird caged with a cat.

"This is upsetting the work schedule."

"Look on it as a holiday," Arkady said.

"Ha!" Slava soberly regarded a gull hovering outside a bilge hole of the *Polar Star* waiting for slops to drop. "I know what you're thinking."

"What?" Arkady was mystified.

"That since I was onstage I could see who Zina was with. Well, you're wrong. When you're onstage playing, the lights are right in your eyes. Ask the other members of the band; they'll tell you the same thing. We couldn't see anyone."

"You ask," Arkady said. "You're in charge."

The *Eagle* was smaller than the *Merry Jane,* red and white, lower to the water, sporting a side crane and a gantry with a single reel. Another difference was that not a single fisherman was on deck to greet them. They stepped out onto wooden planks empty except for the dregs of the boat's last tow: limp flatfish, skeletal crabs.

"I don't understand," Slava said. "Usually they're so friendly."

"You feel something, too?" Arkady asked. "A certain coolness. What language will we be speaking, by the way? Swedish? Spanish? What kind of Americans will these be?"

"You're going to embarrass me, aren't you?"

Arkady looked Slava over. "You're wearing your jogging shoes, your jeans. You're the picture of a Young Communist. I think we're ready to face the captain."

"Some assistant I have, a regular fugitive."

"Worse, someone with nothing to lose. After you."

The *Eagle*'s bridge was smaller than the *Merry Jane*'s and had no carpeting or teak, but otherwise was more what Arkady had supposed an American bridge would be like: a veritable space capsule's array of color monitors banked around and behind the captain's chair; a circle of radar screens and the cathode-green of fish-finders that targeted schools of fish as shifting orange clouds. Radios hung from the overhead, their ruby numbers floating in the static of open channels. The chrome hoods of the compass and repeater were polished to shine like crystal. In all, glitter without clutter.

The man in the captain's chair fit in. Fishermen were usually scarred by exposure to knives, spines and frayed ropes, and coarsened by cold air and brine, but Morgan seemed to have been abraded by something sharper. He was lean to the point of gaunt, with prematurely gray hair. Although he wore a cap and sweatshirt, there was about him and his ship's bridge a sense of monkish order, of a man who was happiest alone and in control. As he unwound from his chair Slava gave him a nod of obeisance, and it occurred to Arkady that the third mate would have made a good dog.

"George, this is Seaman Renko. Or you can call him Arkady." To Arkady, Slava said, "Captain Morgan."

The captain gave Arkady's hand a brief squeeze. "We're sorry about Zina Pishvili."

"Patiashvili." Slava shrugged as if either the name was ridiculous or it didn't really matter.

"Pashvili? Sorry." Morgan said to Arkady, "I don't speak Russian. Ship-to-ship communications go through the company reps on the *Polar Star*. Perhaps you should ask a rep to join us, because right now we're losing trawling time and that means we're losing money. Can I offer you a drink?" On the chart chest was a tray with three tumblers and a bottle of Soviet vodka. Better than what the Soviets drank at home: export-quality vodka. He lifted the bottle a millimeter off the tray, as if measuring the minimum of hospitality. "Or are you in a rush?"

"No, thank you." Slava could take a hint.

"Why not?" Arkady asked.

Slava hissed, "First wine, now vodka?"

"It's like New Year's Eve, isn't it?" Arkady said.

Morgan poured Arkady half a glass and, bemused, one for himself. Slava abstained.

"Nazdrovya," Morgan said. "Isn't that it?"

"Cheers," said Arkady.

Arkady drank his in three swallows, Morgan in one that he followed with an even smile of excellent teeth. "You don't want a company rep," he said.

"We'll try to do without." The last thing Arkady wanted was Susan joining them.

"Well, Arkady, ask away."

Morgan was so assured that Arkady wondered what would faze him.

"Is this boat safe?"

Slava started. "Renko, that's—"

"It's okay," Morgan said. "This is a seventy-five-foot Gulf boat with a North Sea rig. That means it was originally built to tend oil platforms in the Gulf of Mexico and then was refitted to come up here for the crabbing boom. When crabs went bust, they put on the gantry for trawling and some extra plating for hitting the ice. The real money went where it counts, into electronics. We don't have all the amenities of our round-headed friend and his three dwarfs over on the *Merry Jane,* but we do catch more fish."

"Did you know Zina?"

"Just to see. She was always friendly, waving."

"And dancing?"

"I didn't have the pleasure of dancing with her myself. I was in the wardroom going over charts with my good friends Captains Marchuk and Thorwald."

"Do you like the joint fishery?"

"It's exciting."

"Exciting?" Arkady had never thought of it that way. "How so?"

"After Dutch we're going up to the ice sheet. Soviet captains are intrepid. Last year you people had a whole fishing fleet, fifty boats, iced in off Siberia and almost lost them all. You did lose a factory ship, and the only reason the whole crew didn't go down with it was because they were able to cross the ice."

"Those were Soviet boats," Arkady said.

"Right, and I don't want to end up like a Soviet boat. Don't get the wrong idea; I like Russians. It's the best joint fishery. Koreans will steal half of every bag. The Japanese are too proud to cheat but they're colder than the fish." Morgan was the sort of man who smiled while he reassessed a situation. "Arkady, how is it I don't recall ever meeting you on the *Polar Star*? You're a fleet officer or from the Ministry or what?"

"I work in the factory."

"The slime line," Slava said.

"And you speak fluent English and investigate accidents? I'd say you're overqualified for cleaning fish." There was a candid, glass-blue quality to Morgan's eyes that told Slava and Arkady what liars he thought they were. "It was an accident?"

"There's no doubt of it," Slava said.

Morgan had kept his eyes steadily on Arkady. His gaze moved to the net now idle on the gantry, then to two crewmen in oilskin coveralls coming up the outside stairs from the deck, and then back to Arkady. "Okay. It's been a delightful social call. Just remember, these are American waters."

The narrow bridge became crowded as the fishermen entered. These were the Americans he had been curious about since he'd heard Lantz describe them as the "motorcycle gang." In the Soviet Union, where two wheels chained to an internal combustion engine were the symbol of personal freedom, bikers were called Rockers. The authorities were always trying to channel Rockers into approved motordromes, but the gangs slipped away like Mongols on the loose, took over whole villages, then vanished before a state motor patrol could arrive.

The larger fisherman had a sallow face, hooded eyes and the strong, hanging arms of someone who has spent time shoving crab pots and nets. Not a smooth man. He looked Arkady up and down. "What is this shit?"

"This, Coletti," Morgan explained, "is the joint venture. The man with our old friend Slava speaks English well enough to teach you. We'll make it fast and clean."

"Renko, this is Mike." Slava introduced the younger fisherman, an Aleut with fine Asian features on a broad face. "Mike is short for Mikhail."

"A Russian name?" Arkady asked.

"Up here there are a lot of Russian names." Mike had a soft, hesitant voice. "There were a lot of crazy Cossacks around here way back."

"At one time the Aleutians and Alaska all belonged to the czars," Morgan told Arkady. "You ought to know that."

"Do you speak Russian?" Here was someone who could have talked to Zina.

"No. I mean, we use expressions," Mike said, "without, you know, really knowing what they mean. Like if you hit your thumb with a hammer, right? Or when we go to church, some of that's in Russian."

"There's still a Russian church in Dutch Harbor," Slava said.

The Aleut dared a glance at Coletti before saying, "We're really sorry about Zina. It's hard to believe. Every time we brought in a bag of fish there she'd be at the stern rail giving us a big wave. Rain or shine, night or day, she was there."

"You danced with her?" Arkady asked.

Coletti cut in. "We all did."

"And after the dance?"

"When we left, the dance was still going on." Coletti held his head at an angle, getting a fix on Arkady.

"Zina was still dancing?"

"She left before us."

"Did she seem ill in any way? Drunk, dizzy, light-headed? Nervous, preoccupied, afraid?"

"No." Coletti answered questions like a Moscow militiaman, the type that volunteered nothing.

"Who did she leave with?" Arkady asked.

"Who knows?" answered a late arrival as he came up the galley stairs onto the bridge. This third crewman raised peaked brows in mock concern, as if the party had started without him. A gold ring decorated his left ear; a leather thong tied his long hair into a ponytail. His beard was wispy, almost feminine, like that of a young actor. He didn't offer to shake hands because he was wiping his own on a greasy rag. He said, "I'm Ridley, the engineer. I wanted to add my own condolences. Zina was a great kid."

"Then you talked to her at the dance?" Arkady asked.

"Well . . ." Ridley paused apologetically. "Your captain laid out a generous spread for us as soon as we got on board. Sausages, beer, brandy. Then we visited with the Americans, Susan and her boys. Old friends, so there was more beer and vodka. As I understand it, it's against your regulations to have liquor on board, but it runs like a gusher every time I've been on the *Star*. Plus there's the time factor. The *Star* runs on Vladivostok time, which is three hours earlier than ours. You start a dance at nine P.M., that's midnight to us. At that hour we relax real fast."

"It was a good dance?"

"Best rock 'n' roll band in the Bering Sea."

Slava shook his head under the force of flattery.

"The truth is," Ridley added in a confessional tone, "I think we're an embarrassment when we get on the *Polar Star*. We get drunk and try to live up to the reputation of being wild Americans."

"No, no," said Slava.

"Yes, yes," said Ridley. "The Russians are so hospitable. We get stoned and you go on smiling, picking us up off the floor. I got so drunk I had to come back early."

Every crew had a natural leader. Even in the tight quarters of the *Eagle*'s bridge, Coletti and Mike had taken a perceptible step toward the engineer.

"Do I recognize you?" Arkady asked.

"Ridley spent two weeks on the *Polar Star*," Slava said.

Ridley nodded. "The voyage before this. The company wants us to be familiar with Soviet techniques. I can tell you that after working with Soviet gear my opinion of Soviet fishermen is higher than ever."

Arkady remembered Ridley being pointed out. "You speak Russian?"

"No, there was a whole lot of sign language. Language is not one of my talents. Look, I had an uncle who lived with us. He studied

Esperanto, the international language. Finally he finds a woman who also studies Esperanto. In Washington State there had to be about five people. Anyway, she comes over and we're all in the parlor waiting for this big moment, two people speaking Esperanto, like a glimpse of the future. It takes about ten seconds to see that they don't understand each other at all. She's asking for the wine, he's telling her the time. That was the Russians and me. Sorry. Just out of curiosity, did you serve in Afghanistan?"

"I was too old to do my 'internationalist duty,' " Arkady said. "Did you serve in Vietnam?"

"Too young. Anyway, I don't even remember saying good night to Zina. What happened? Did she disappear?"

"No, she came back."

Ridley enjoyed the answer, as if he'd found someone worth talking to. "Came back from where?"

"As I understand it," Morgan said, trying to put the conversation back on conventional rails, "her body was picked up by our net and was found when the bag was opened on the *Polar Star.*"

"Jesus," Ridley said, "that must have been a moment. She fell over?"

"Yes," Slava said.

Coletti pointed at Arkady. "I want to hear him say it."

"It's too soon for that," Arkady answered.

"Fuck that!" Coletti exploded. "We don't know what happened to Zina. We don't know if she took a swan dive or what, but we were off that fucking boat before anything happened."

"Coletti." Morgan stepped in front of him. "Someday I'm going to open up your head just to see how small your brain is."

Ridley eased Coletti back with a touch. "Hey, we're all friends. Take it easy like Arkady. See how he watches."

"Yes." Morgan noticed; he told Arkady, "We apologize. Whatever happened to Zina was a tragedy, but we hope it doesn't affect the joint venture. We all believe in it."

"We'd be shit out of work if we didn't have it," Ridley said. "And we like making new friends, having Slava play his sax or explain all about perestroika and how the Soviet Union from top to bottom is thinking in new ways."

"Thinking in new ways" was a catchphrase of the new men in the Kremlin, as if Soviet brains could be rewired like circuit boards.

"Are you thinking in new ways?" Ridley asked Arkady.

"I try."

"A senior man like you has to keep up," Ridley said.

Slava said, "He just works in the factory."

"No." Coletti disagreed as if he had special information. "I used to be a cop and I can smell another cop. He's a cop."

BEING LIFTED BY cage up the *Polar Star*'s hull was like floating across a great curtain of suppurating steel.

Slava was furious. "We made fools of ourselves. This is a Soviet affair; it has nothing to do with them."

"It doesn't seem to," Arkady agreed.

"Then what is there to be cheerful about?"

"Oh, I think of all the fish I didn't see today."

"That's all?"

Arkady looked down through the open bars of the cage at the catcher boat below. "The *Eagle* has a low hull. I wouldn't take it into the ice."

"What do you know about trawlers?" Slava demanded.

There had been the Sakhalin trawler. Captured from the Japanese during the war, it was a little drift trawler, a porous wooden hull around an ancient diesel. Wherever paint peeled, ghostly Japanese markings emerged. There was no trouble getting a berth on a vessel overdue to sink, especially when the captain had a simple quota: cram the hold with salmon until the boat shipped water. As the new man, Arkady was stuffed into the warp hole; when the net was pulled in he had to run in a crouch around and around, coiling a hawser spiked with frayed metal threads. As the hawser filled the hole he circled on all fours like a rat in a coffin, then climbed out to help shake the net. By the second day he could barely raise his hands, though once he got the knack he developed the first shoulders he'd had since the army.

The lesson of that foul little boat was that fishermen had to be able to get along in a confined space for long periods of time. All the rest—knowing how to wind or mend—meant nothing if a man set his shipmates on edge. Arkady had never seen as much antagonism on that trawler as he had witnessed on the glittering bridge of the *Eagle*.

The cage swayed with Slava's agitation. "You had a day off, that's all you wanted."

"It was interesting," Arkady granted. "Americans are a change."

"Well, I can promise you that you're not getting off the *Polar Star* again. What are you going to do now?"

Arkady shrugged. "There were people on special duty during the dance. I'll ask whether any of them saw Zina on deck or below. Try to find out when the Americans actually left the ship. Talk to people who were at the dance. Talk to women she worked with in the galley. I want to talk to Karp again."

"After we talk to the women we'll split up," Slava said. "I'll take Karp. You take the crew belowdecks—that's more your style."

The cage cleared the side and began its descent toward the familiar scrofulous deck and the barrels heaped like a high-tide line of sea trash around the stack.

"You put people off," Slava said. "The crew on the *Eagle* are usually great guys. Susan is generally an angel. Why is everyone nervous? We're in American waters."

"A Soviet boat is Soviet territory," Arkady said. "They should be nervous."

7 To a fanfare of trumpets white lines emanated from a red star. Natasha pushed the fast-forward button to the image of a white clockface on a blue background. Fast forward again to the slanted logo of *Novosti News,* then the silent picture of a man reading accounts of stale events into two microphones, then fast forward again until finally a slim girl in a skintight Lycra warm-up outfit appeared on the television screen. She had a dappling of freckles across her nose, hoop earrings and braided hair the color of brass. She began stretching like a willow bending in a strong wind.

In the ship's cafeteria, facing the glow of the connected television and VCR, outfitted in sweat suits and aerobic gear, twenty women of the *Polar Star* tilted grudgingly like sturdy oaks. When the girl bent forward and touched her nose to her knees, they took only slight bows, and when she ran lightly in place, the women sounded like an enthusiastic, thundering herd. Though Factory Worker Natasha Chaikovskaya was in the lead, not far behind her was

Olimpiada Bovina, the massive chief cook of the crew's galley. Like a little ribbon on an oversized box, a powder-blue sweatband decorated Olimpiada's brow. Sweat leaked from the band, welled around her small eyes and flowed poignantly like tears down her cheeks as she pursued the graceful, tireless acrobat on the screen.

When Slava called her name, Olimpiada abandoned her trotting and puffing with the wistful reluctance of a masochist. They talked to her at the back of the cafeteria. She had the fruity voice of a mezzo-soprano.

"Poor Zina. A smile is gone from the galley."

"She was a hard worker?" Slava asked.

"And cheerful. So full of life. A tease. She hated to stir the macaroni. We have macaroni often, you know."

"I know," Arkady said.

"So she would say, 'Here, Olimpiada, is some more good exercise for you.' We will miss her."

Slava said, "Thank you, Comrade Bovina, you can—"

"An active girl?" Arkady asked.

"Certainly," Olimpiada said.

"Young and attractive. A little restless?"

"It was impossible to keep her in one place."

Arkady said, "The day after the dance she didn't come to work. Did you send someone for her?"

"I needed everyone in the galley. I can't have all my girls wandering around the ship. I run a responsible kitchen. Poor Zina, I was afraid she was sick or overtired from the night before. Women are different, you know."

"Speaking of men . . ." Arkady said.

"She kept them in line."

"Who was at the head of the line?"

Olimpiada blushed and giggled into her hand. "You will think this is disrespectful. I shouldn't say."

"Please," Arkady said.

"It's what she said, not what I said."

"Please."

"She said that in the spirit of the Party Congress she was going to democratize her relationship with men. She called it 'Restructuring the Males.' "

"There weren't one or two men in particular?" Arkady asked.

"On the *Polar Star*?"

"Where else?"

"I don't know." Olimpiada suddenly became discreet.

Slava said, "You've been very helpful, Comrade Bovina."

The chief cook chugged back to her position in the class. The girl on the screen spread her arms and rotated them; she seemed light enough to fly. Through the power of television, all across the Soviet Union this young dancer had become the new ideal of Soviet women, a shining, bobbing icon. Sleek Latvian women, Asiatics in felt tents and settlers in the Virgin Lands all watched the show and copied her every move. Thanks to the VCR, the ladies of the *Polar Star* could follow suit, though looking at their broad backs and outstretched powerful arms, Arkady was put less in mind of birds than of a squadron of bombers lifting off.

The VCR was a Panasonic, a prize of the ship's last visit to Dutch Harbor, and had been adapted to Soviet frequencies. There was a flourishing black market for Japanese VCR's in Vladivostok. Not that Soviet VCR's like a top-of-the-line Voronezh weren't good— they were fine for Soviet videotapes—it was just that Soviet machines lacked the ability to tape shows. Also, just as Soviet railroad tracks were a wider gauge than foreign ones in order to prevent an invasion by train, Soviet VCR's took a larger tape to prevent an influx of foreign pornography.

"Women!" Slava was disgusted. "To reduce a subject of such importance as restructuring to so trivial a level. And I'm sick of you asking questions and going off in different directions. I have my own ideas and I don't need assistance from you."

Olimpiada looked over her shoulder to see Slava storm out of the cafeteria. Natasha half turned from the television and fixed her black gaze on Arkady.

WHEN HE WAS a boy Arkady had little lead soldiers, the heroic General Davydov's saber-wielding cavalrymen, the sly General Kutuzov's artillerymen and the scowling grenadiers of Napoleon's Grand Army, all kept in a box beneath his bed, where they rolled together in a melee as he took the box out, played with the pieces and then slid them back home. Like casualties, they soon lost their original coats and faces of paint and he daubed them afresh, less carefully each time.

Skiba and Slezko looked like a pair of those grenadiers toward the end of their careers: fierce, with mottled pink-and-gray chins, spots of gold in their teeth, identical except that Skiba had black hair and Slezko gray. They were on the midship deck, the same place they had been during the dance when their duty had been to watch the transport cage that carried the American fishermen from and to their boats.

"The *Merry Jane* was tied up to the *Eagle*, which was tied up to our starboard side?" Arkady asked.

"We prefer answering the third mate," Skiba said.

"I can tell the captain that you refused to answer questions."

Skiba and Slezko looked around the deck and then at each other until a telepathic decision was made.

"More private," Slezko said. He led the way inside, downstairs, around a machine shop and through a door into a dank, badly lit room with sinks and stalls. The sinks were brown from the ship's water; the stalls had concrete benches with holes. In Moscow, informers always wanted to meet in public toilets; in a desert, an informer would unearth a toilet to talk in.

Skiba folded his arms and leaned against the door as if he were temporarily in the hands of the enemy. "We will answer a question or two."

"The arrangement of boats was as I described?" Arkady asked.

"Yes." Slezko closed the porthole.

"Chronologically, by our time, when did the Americans leave?" Arkady opened the porthole.

Skiba consulted a notebook. "The captain and crew of the *Alaska Miss* returned to their boat at 2300 and immediately cast off. One crewman of the *Eagle* returned to his boat at 2329; then two others and the captain returned at 2354. The *Eagle* cast off at 0010."

"When the trawlers cast off, how far did they go?" Arkady asked. "A hundred meters? Out of sight?"

"It was too foggy to tell," Slezko said after much consideration.

"When the Americans left, did any Soviets see them off?" Arkady asked.

While Skiba referred to his notebook Arkady's eye fell on the newspapers stuffed in baskets by the stalls; crumpled headlines on top announced, BOLD REFOR— and NEW AGE O—. Skiba cleared his throat. "The head rep Susan came out on deck with them. Captain Marchuk shook hands with Captain Morgan and wished him good fishing."

"No undue fraternization," Arkady said. "There was no one else?"

"Correct," Skiba said.

"From 2230 on, who else did you see on deck?"

"Oh." Skiba thumbed through his notebook, flustered but also angry, as if he'd known there would be a surprise question. "The captain I said already. At 2240, the Americans Lantz and Day headed aft." He pivoted to be sure. "At 2315, Comrade Taratuta." She was in charge of the captain's quarters and galley.

"Which direction?"

As Slezko held up his left hand and then his right, Skiba faced the door and then away.

"From aft—" Slezko began.

"To forward," Skiba finished.

"THINKING IN NEW WAYS. What does this mean?" Gury asked. "The old ways meant Brezhnev—"

"No," Arkady corrected him. "They may mean Brezhnev, but you don't say his name. Brezhnev no longer exists, only the problems of old ways, obstructionism and foot-dragging."

"It's confusing."

"All the better. A good leader mystifies people at least half the time."

Gury had spent a month reading two American books, *In Pursuit of Excellence* and *The One-Minute Manager*, a feat of concentration that was religious considering how little English he understood. Arkady had translated much of these chronicles of business greed, and the collaboration had, at least in Gury's mind, made them fast friends.

Now Arkady watched Gury test condoms in a tub. Users called them "galoshes," and they came rolled in talc, two to a paper envelope. Powder exploded as he inflated each condom, tied it and plunged it under water. A film of talc covered his leather jacket.

The site Gury had chosen for this consumer review was an empty fuel bunker. Although the bunker had supposedly been flushed, there was an acrid edge to the air and the promise of a petroleum-based headache. In the absence of vodka, a lot of sailors sniffed fumes; they would be found laughing or crying uncontrollably or dancing off the walls. Or Thinking in New Ways, Arkady guessed.

As champagne-sized bubbles worked their way to the surface of the tub and broke through a scum of talc, Gury fumed. "Lack of quality control. Basic lack of management commitment and product integrity."

He tossed the condom onto a growing pile of tested and rejected ones, unwrapped another one, blew it up and held it under water. His plan was not only to buy radios and cassette players in Dutch Harbor, but also to smuggle aboard as many batteries as possible in elastic, watertight containers that could be secreted in an oil drum.

Getting condoms was no problem; Gury ran the ship's store. The problem was that the KGB had informers that not even Volovoi knew about. Someone always seemed to know about the book in the sand bucket or the nylon stockings in the anchor well. Unless, of course, Gury was himself one of those extra ears of the Committee for State Security. Everywhere Arkady had gone a different informer had appeared—in Irkutsk, at the slaughterhouse, even in Sakhalin. Setting out from Vladivostok on the *Polar Star*, he had simply assumed that one of his cabin mates was an informer, but whether it was Gury, Kolya or Obidin, paranoia could fight friendship just so long. Now they all seemed comrades.

"How will you get the batteries on board?" Arkady asked. "They're going to search everyone coming back to the ship. Some they'll strip-search."

"I'll come up with an idea."

Gury was always coming up with ideas. The latest was a book that would teach anyone to Think in New Ways in a minute. "The crazy thing," he went on, "is that I was convicted of Restructuring. I was doing away with state planning, offering initiatives—"

"You were convicted of illegally buying a state-owned coffee roaster, selling coffee privately, and doctoring the beans with fifty percent grain."

"I was just a premature entrepreneur."

Bubbles trailed to the surface and popped. "You sold condoms to Zina," Arkady said.

"Zina was not a girl to take chances." Gury threw the latest failure on the pile, picked up another and sneezed. "At least not that kind."

"She bought them regularly?"

"She was an active girl."

"Who with?"

"Who not? She wasn't a slut necessarily; she didn't take money; she didn't like to be obligated. *She* did the choosing. A modern woman. Aha!" He tossed a condom on the good pile. "Quality is on the upswing."

"Is this really where the country is headed?" Arkady asked. "A nation of entrepreneurs happily sorting out condoms, cars, designer furniture?"

"What's wrong with that?"

"Gogol's great vision of Russia was of a troika madly dashing through the snow, sparks flying, the other nations of the earth watching in awe. Yours is of a car trunk stuffed with stereo equipment."

Gury sniffed. "I'm thinking in new ways. Clearly you're not."

"Who were Zina's friends?" Arkady asked.

"Men. She slept with you; then she wouldn't sleep with you again, but she didn't hurt your feelings."

"Women?"

"She got along with Susan. You've talked to her?"

"Yes."

"Fantastic, isn't she?"

"Okay."

"She's beautiful. You know how sometimes after a ship passes the wake will glow with a bioluminescence? Sometimes when I've just missed seeing her on the ship there will be that glow."

" 'Bioluminescence'? Maybe you could bottle it and sell it."

"You know," Gury said, "there's a hardness in you I worry about. Finding out you were an investigator has made me see you with new eyes. Like there's someone else inside you. Look, I just want to make money. The Soviet Union is about to leave the nineteenth century, and there are going to be—" He found he was waving a condom as he spoke, laid it down and sighed. "Everything's going to be different. You were such a help to me with those books. If we could combine them with the inspirational words of the Party . . ."

In spite of himself, Arkady knew the clichés. They had poured from the Party like a rain of stones, rising to the ankles, to the knees. "Like, working class, vanguard of restructuring, both broadening and deepening ideological and moral victory?"

"Exactly. But not the *way* you say it. I believe in restructuring." Gury found he was waving a condom again. "Anyway, don't you think we should leave stagnation and corruption behind?" He caught Arkady's glance at the tub. "Well, I wouldn't call this corruption—not real corruption. Brezhnev's daughter was smuggling diamonds, having orgies, fucking a gypsy. *That's* corruption."

"Zina had no special man?"

"You're starting to sound like an investigator, that's the scary part." Gury tested another condom. "I told you, she was very democratic. She was different from other women. Let me give you some advice. Find out what they want to hear and then give it to them. If you get serious, Arkady, they'll nail you like Obidin's Christ on a cross. Lighten up."

Gury seemed sincerely concerned. They were cabin mates and comrades, both with troubled pasts. Now that Arkady thought about it, who was he to sneer at another man's aspirations, given the lack of any of his own except to lie low and survive? Where did this righteousness come from? He thought he'd killed it long ago. "Okay, you're right," he said. "I'll think in new ways."

"Good." Relieved, Gury dunked another condom. "New and profitable ways, if possible."

As an experiment, Arkady gave it a try. "Say you don't just mask the smell from the Border Guard. Take another approach. When we get back to Vladivostok, misdirect the dogs by getting them to sniff something else. Collect some dog or cat urine and smear it on some crates."

"I like that," Gury said. "The new Arkady. There's still hope for you."

8 It was evening when Arkady returned to the captain's cabin. The sea-green walls gave the room a proper underwater aspect. Around the desk's glittering collection of glasses and bottles of mineral water sat Marchuk, First Mate Volovoi and a third man, who was not much larger than a child. He had eyelids dark from lack of sleep, hair wild as straw and an unlit navigator's pipe drooping from his mouth. What made him remarkable was that Arkady had never seen him before.

Slava had already begun. At his feet was a canvas sack. "After my visit to the *Eagle,* I conferred with First Mate Volovoi. We agreed that with the aid of the ship's Party activists and volunteers, we would be able to canvass the crew of the *Polar Star* and determine the location of every crew member on the night of Zina Patiashvili's disappearance. This enormous task was completed in two hours. We learned that no one saw Seaman Patiashvili after the dance, and that no one was with her when she fell overboard. We made special inquiries among the co-workers of Comrade Patiashvili, as much to lay rumor to rest as to find answers. There are those whose first instinct is to turn accident into scandal."

"Also," said Volovoi, "we had to take into account our unusual situation, working with foreign nationals in foreign waters. Was undue fraternization with these nationals a factor in the tragic death of this citizen? Facts had to be faced. Hard questions had to be asked."

This was good, Arkady thought. Here he'd been running around the ship while Slava and the Invalid were polishing a speech.

"Again and again," Slava said, "these suspicions were put to rest. Comrades, there is no testimony with more weight in any socialist court than the thoughts of those workers who toiled side by side with the deceased. In the galley I heard it time after time. 'Patiashvili was an unstinting cook's assistant,' 'Patiashvili never missed a day,' and"—Slava lowered his voice out of respect—" 'Zina was a good girl.' Similar sentiments were echoed by her cabin mates; I quote, 'She was an honest Soviet worker who will be badly missed.' That from Natasha Chaikovskaya, a Party member and herself a decorated worker."

"They will all be commended for their forthright statements," Volovoi said.

No one had greeted Arkady yet. He wondered whether he should disappear or become part of the furniture. Another chair would be useful.

"I again enlisted the aid of Comrade Volovoi," Slava told the captain. "I asked Fedor Fedorovich, 'What kind of girl was Zina Patiashvili?' He said, 'Young, full of life, but politically mature.' "

"Typical of Soviet youth," Volovoi said. For the occasion he wore a shiny running suit typical of political officers. It hadn't occurred to Arkady before that the first mate's cropped red hair looked like the stubble on a pig's snout.

Slava said, "The trawlmaster, who first found her body, was badly shaken."

"Korobetz," Volovoi reminded the others. "His deck team leads the ship's socialist competition."

"I questioned him and his team. Although he had only ever seen her in the cafeteria, he too remembered a worker who gave unstintingly."

Of mashed potatoes? Arkady wondered.

As if he could read minds, the Invalid slipped Arkady a brief malevolent glance before holding up his end of the duet. "Still, we must face the mystery of what happened to her on the night of her death. Not only for her sake, but for that of all her comrades, that they may move past this unhappy event and again put their full effort into productive ends."

"Just so." Slava couldn't agree more. "And that is what we have accomplished today. We established that Zina Patiashvili was at the dance held at the cafeteria that night. I myself was in the band, and I can attest to the heat generated within a closed space by active dancers. This led me to inquire among the female crew members who attended whether at any time they felt uncomfortable because of the heat. Yes, a number of them answered; they had to leave the cafeteria and go out on deck for fresh air. I then returned to the infirmary and asked the ship's doctor whether Zina Patiashvili had ever complained of dizziness or headaches. His answer was affirmative. Earlier Dr. Vainu had performed an autopsy on the deceased. I asked him whether there were any signs of violence that could not possibly be accidental. 'No,' he said. Were there any signs he found difficult to explain? I asked. 'Yes, there was discoloration on the torso and limbs, and there were evenly spaced bruises along the ribs and hips that he could not explain. Also, there was a small puncture of the abdomen.

"Comrades, there is no mystery. I myself retraced the steps of Zina Patiashvili the night of her disappearance. She was not seen in the passageways leading to her cabin, nor on the trawl deck. The only place she could have gone was to the stern. If she had fallen over the side directly into the water, yes, the marks on her body would be difficult to explain. However, alone and in the dark, Zina Patiashvili did not fall over the side rail but over the rail that surrounds the open stairwell above the stern ramp, hitting the back of her head as she fell on the stairs. Sliding down the steps, she also bruised her front and limbs."

A rather handy "also," Arkady thought. Marchuk earnestly studied the autopsy report on his desk. Arkady felt for him. Viktor Marchuk wouldn't be a captain without a Party card, and he wouldn't be trusted to fish with Americans unless he was a Party activist. An ambitious man, but still a "sailor's captain." The anonymous guest in the third chair rested his head on his hand. He wore the enlightened expression of a person who actually enjoyed the wrong notes in an amateur piano recital.

"There's a landing on those stairs," Marchuk said.

"Exactly," Slava agreed, "and there the body of Zina Patiashvili rested while the dance went on. She lay with her body pressed against the outer rail of the landing, which explains the bruising of the ribs and hips. Then, when the dance was over and the *Polar Star*'s work began again, her body rolled as the ship moved. As you know, our designers bend their efforts to build the safest ships in the world for our Soviet seamen. Unfortunately, not every freak event can be foreseen. There is no protective rail on the inner side of the landing. Zina Patiashvili rolled free and fell onto the ramp. There is a safety gate further up the ramp to protect anyone falling down from the trawl deck, but not anyone falling from the well. Unconscious and unable to cry out, Zina Patiashvili slid down the ramp and into the water."

Slava related his conclusion as if it were a radio play. In spite of himself, Arkady saw it: the girl from Georgia in her jeans and bleached hair leaving the smoke and heat of the dance; feeling light-headed, staring into the soft oblivion of the fog, stepping carelessly back toward the rail of the well . . . No, frankly, he couldn't see it. Not Zina, not the girl with the queen of hearts in her pocket, not alone, not that way.

Unexpectedly Captain Marchuk asked, "What do you think of this theory, Comrade Renko?"

"Very exciting."

Slava went on. "I do not have to explain to veteran seamen how briefly Zina Patiashvili could have survived in such near-freezing waters. Five minutes? Ten at the most. The only question left is the puncture wound in the abdomen, a wound brought to our attention by Seaman Renko. Renko, however, is not a fisherman and is not trained or familiar with trawling gear. Has he ever handled a cable frayed from dragging forty tons of fish over the rocks of the sea floor?"

Well, yes, Arkady thought, but he didn't want to interrupt when the third mate was building to a climax, or at least to an end. Slava opened the sack on the floor, brought out a loop of 1-cm. steel cable and held it up triumphantly. In a few places steel threads fanned out like spikes.

"Cable like this, frayed like this," Slava said. "It's a fact that the body of Zina Patiashvili came up in the net. We seamen know that the net is drawn by worn cables. We know that as the net is drawn through the water the cables vibrate, making any frayed threads into virtual saws. That's what cut Zina Patiashvili. End of mystery. A girl went to a dance, became overheated, went out on deck alone for air, fell overboard and, I am sorry to say, died. But that is *all* that happened."

Slava displayed the section of cable to Volovoi, who affected great interest in it, and to the stranger, who waved it aside, and to Marchuk, who was busy reading a new document. The captain had a feline manner of stroking his trim black beard as he concentrated on the page.

"According to your report, you recommend no further inquiry on board, and that any outstanding questions be left to the proper authorities in Vladivostok."

"Yes," Slava said. "Of course the decision is yours."

"There were some other recommendations, as I remember," Volovoi suggested. "I saw the report only for a moment."

"That is correct," Slava answered dutifully. It was really wonderful, Arkady thought, almost as good as table tennis. "If there is one lesson to be learned from this tragic incident it is that safety can never be taken for granted. I propose two firm recommendations. First, that during evening social events volunteers be placed on watch at either side of the stern deck. Second, that social events be held as much as possible during the daytime."

"Those are useful recommendations that I'm sure will be discussed with great interest at the next all-ship meeting," Volovoi said. "The entire ship owes you their thanks for your labor, for the completeness and speed of your inquiry, and for the factual, clearsighted nature of your conclusion."

Tolstoy's aristocrats spoke effervescent French. The grandsons of the Revolution spoke plodding, measured Russian, as if each word were so many centimeters that when carefully laid end to end would inevitably lead to consensus, and spoken politely and soberly because it was the genius of Soviet democracy that all meetings should reach

comradely unanimity. Say a worker came before a factory committee
and pointed out that they were turning out cars with three wheels,
or told a farm committee they were turning out calves with two
heads. Such news never stopped a calm, experienced committee
from marching in single formation.

Marchuk sipped from a glass, lit another cigarette, a Player's with
rich, foreign smoke, and studied the report, his head down. The
angle accentuated the Asiatic cast to his cheeks. The captain looked
like a man made for subduing the taiga, not for nosing through
bureaucratic jargon. The stranger in the oatmeal sweater smiled
patiently, as if he'd wandered by chance into this meeting, but was
in no great hurry to leave.

Marchuk looked up. "You conducted this inquiry with Seaman
Renko?"

"Yes," Slava said.

"I see only your signature at the bottom."

"Because we did not have an opportunity to speak before this
meeting."

Marchuk motioned Arkady closer. "Renko, do you have anything
to add?"

Arkady thought for a moment and said, "No."

"Then do you want to sign it?" Marchuk offered a thick fountain
pen, a Monte Cristo, right for a captain.

"No."

Marchuk screwed the cap back on the pen. This was going to be
more complicated.

The Invalid poured himself more water and said, "As Seaman
Renko did not do the bulk of the work, and as the recommendations
are purely those of the third mate, there's no need for Renko's
signature."

"Let's see." Marchuk turned back to Arkady. "You disagree with the conclusion that we leave the loose ends for the boys in Vladivos-tok?"

"No."

"Then with what?"

"Only . . ."—Arkady searched for precision—"the facts."

"Ah." For the first time the man in the oatmeal sweater sat up, as if he had finally heard a word in a language he understood.

"Excuse me," said Marchuk. "Seaman Renko, this is Fleet Elec-trical Engineer Hess. I have asked Comrade Hess to contribute his able mind to our meeting tonight. Explain to him and to me how you can disagree about the facts and agree with the conclusion."

The *Polar Star* hadn't seen the fleet in six weeks and wouldn't see it again for another four. Arkady wondered where Hess been hiding, but he concentrated on the question at hand.

"Zina Patiashvili died the night of the dance," Arkady said. "Since she was not seen belowdecks on her way to her cabin, she probably went either to some other compartment in the aft house or, as the third mate says, onto the stern deck. However, when people faint they drop, they do not take a running start so that they can flip over a rail that would have come up to Zina's ribs. There are marks characteristic of drowning, none of them present with Zina, and when they open her lungs in Vladivostok they'll find no salt water. The characteristic marks present on the body—the livid-ity on the forearms, calves, breasts and belly—result only *after* death, from being on all fours for a period of time, and the bruises on the ribs and hips come not from resting against a rail but from being packed viciously against hard protuberances. She was killed on the *Polar Star* and stowed on board. As for the puncture of the belly, it was done with the single stab of a sharp knife. There were no scratches or sawing, and there was little bleeding. The facts are that before being thrown over she was stabbed to prevent her from floating to the surface. Another proof that the cut was not made by a net bringing her up was that she was thirty fathoms down on the sea bottom, long enough for slime eels to penetrate the puncture wound, enter her and nest in her."

"There's nothing in your report about eels," Marchuk said to Slava. Fishermen hated slime eels.

"More?" Arkady asked.

"Please."

"Her co-workers state that Zina Patiashvili was a ceaseless toiler, yet the Americans say she appeared at the stern rail every time, day or night, that the catcher boat *Eagle* delivered a net. Often that coincided with Zina's watch, which meant that she dropped her work whenever she cared to and was gone for half an hour at a time."

"You say Soviets lie and Americans tell the truth?" Volovoi asked as if uncertain about a distinction.

"No. Zina spent the dance in the company of the Americans from the *Eagle*, dancing with them and talking to them. I do not think a woman runs to a stern rail in the middle of the night or in the rain to wave to a boatful of men; she runs to wave to one man. The Americans are certainly lying about who that might be."

"You mean one of our boys was jealous?" Marchuk asked.

"That would be slander," Volovoi stated, as if this disposed of the question. "Of course, if there were derelictions in the galley, if any worker gave less than her full time, there will be a stern rebuke."

"Water?" Marchuk lifted a bottle to Volovoi.

"Please."

Bubbles danced in the Invalid's glass. There was an ominous curve to Marchuk's smile, but the words would stay Soviet, level and businesslike.

"The problem," Marchuk defined it, "is the Americans. They will watch to see whether we conduct an open and forthright investigation."

"We will," Volovoi said. "In Vladivostok."

"Naturally," Marchuk said. "However, this is a unique situation and may require a more immediate effort." He offered the Invalid a cigarette. All this was still within the bounds of Soviet discussion. Sometimes there were immediate crises, such as at the end of each month when the quota could be fulfilled only by turning out cars with three wheels. The equivalent on a fishing boat was to meet the tonnage quota by turning the entire catch, foul or fresh, into fish meal.

"The doctor agreed with Comrade Bukovsky," Volovoi pointed out.

"The doctor," Marchuk said, trying to take the suggestion seriously. "The doctor was even wrong about the time of death, as I remember. A good doctor for the healthy, not so good with the ailing or dead."

"The report may have some flaws," Volovoi conceded.

Full of regret, Marchuk addressed himself to Slava. "Excuse me, the report is shit." To Volovoi he added, "I'm sure he did his best."

The last Russian ship the *Polar Star* had seen was an off-loader that had taken three thousand tons of sole, five thousand tons of pollack, eight thousand tons of fish meal and fifty tons of liver oil in exchange for flour, hams, cabbage, cans of film, personal mail and magazines. Arkady had been part of the crowd on deck that day. He hadn't noticed any tiny fleet electrical engineer riding the block and tackle.

Under his muff of hair Anton Hess's face was half forehead, the other features squeezed into a southern hemisphere of rounded brows, sharp nose, broad upper lip and dimpled chin, all lit by two amiable blue eyes. He looked like a German choirmaster, someone who had collaborated with Brahms.

Still using the measured tones of Soviet authority, of facts reluctantly stated, the first mate decided to take the offensive.

"Seaman Renko, for our information, is it true you were dismissed from the Moscow prosecutor's office?"

"Yes."

"Is it also true that you were expelled from the Party?"

"Yes."

There was a somber pause suitable for a man who had confessed to two incurable diseases.

"May I be blunt?" Volovoi begged Marchuk.

"Please."

"From the start I was against the involvement of this worker in any inquiry, especially one involving our American colleagues. I already had a dossier of negative information on Seaman Renko. Today I radioed the KGB in Vladivostok for more information, not wanting to judge this seaman unfairly. Comrades, we have a man with a shady past. Exactly what happened in Moscow no one will say, except that he was involved in the death of the prosecutor and in the defection of a former citizen. Murder and treason, that is the history of the man before you. That's why he runs from job to job across Siberia. Take a look: he has not thrived."

True, Arkady admitted. His boots, crusted with scales and laced with dried slime, were not the footwear of a thriving man.

"In fact," Volovoi went on, as if only the greatest pressure could bring the words to his lips, "they were looking for him in Sakhalin when he signed on the *Polar Star*. For what, they don't say. With his kind, it could be any of a million things. May I be candid?"

"Absolutely," said Marchuk.

"Comrades, Vladivostok will examine not what happened to a

silly girl named Zina Patiashvili but whether we as a ship have maintained political discipline. Vladivostok will not understand why we involve in such a sensitive inquiry anyone like Renko, a man politically so unreliable that we don't let him ashore in an American port."

"An excellent point," Marchuk agreed.

"In fact," Volovoi said, "it might be wise not to let any of the crew ashore. We reach Dutch Harbor in two days. It might be best not to give them port call."

At this suggestion, Marchuk's face darkened. He poured more water for himself, studying the silvery string of liquid. "After four months' sailing?" he asked. "That's what they've been sailing for, that one day in port. Besides, our crew is not the problem; we can't stop the Americans from going ashore."

Volovoi shrugged. "The representatives will report to the company, yes, but the company is half Soviet-owned. The company will do nothing."

Marchuk screwed out his cigarette and produced a smile that had more irony than humor. Etiquette seemed to be wearing thin. "The observers will report to the government, which is American, and the fishermen will spread tales to everyone. The tale will be that I hid a murder on my ship."

"A death is a tragedy," Volovoi said, "but an investigation is a political decision. Any further investigation on board would be a mistake. On this I must speak for the Party."

In a thousand communes, factories, universities and courtrooms, the same words could have been spoken at that same instant because no serious meeting of manager or prosecutors was ever complete without someone finally speaking for the Party, at which point the niceties of debate would come to an end and the cigarette smoke would be cleared by that decisive, ineluctable phrase.

But this time Marchuk turned to the man on his right. "Comrade Hess, do you have anything to say?"

"Well," the fleet electrical engineer said, as if he had just thought of something. His voice had a timbre like a woodwind with a cracked reed, and he talked directly to Volovoi. "In the past, comrade, everything you say would have been correct. It seems to me, however, that the situation has changed. We have a new leadership that has called for more initiative and a more candid examination of our mistakes. Captain Marchuk is symbolic of this young, forthright leadership. I think he should be supported. As for Seaman Renko, I also radioed for information. He was not charged with either murder or treason. In fact, there is a record of his being vouched for by a Colonel Pribluda of the KGB. Renko may be politically reckless, but there has never been a question of his professional abilities. Also, there is an overriding consideration. This is a unique joint program we have undertaken with the Americans. Not everyone is happy that Soviets and Americans are working together. What will happen to our mission? What will happen to international cooperation if a story spreads that any Soviets who fraternize with Americans will have their bellies slit and be thrown overboard? We should show a sincere and genuine effort now, not only in Vladivostok. Third Mate Bukovsky has great energy, but he has no expertise in this area. None of us does except for Seaman Renko. Let us proceed with more confidence; let's find out what happened."

For Arkady this was curious, like watching the dead rise. For once the Invalid hadn't ended the debate.

Volovoi said, "Sometimes the ugly rumor of the moment has to be overlooked. This is a situation to be contained, not stirred up or publicized. Consider: if the Patiashvili girl was murdered, as Seaman Renko insists, then we have a murderer on board our ship. If we do encourage an investigation on board, whether run intelligently or ineptly, what will be this person's natural reaction? Anxiety and fear—in fact, a desire to escape. Once in Vladivostok that will do him no good at all; a proper investigation in our own port will find him already in our hands. Here, however, the situation is different. The open sea, American boats and, most dangerous of all, an American port. Premature zeal here will prompt desperate acts. Wouldn't it be possible, even logical, that a criminal fearing exposure would abandon his group during its turn in Dutch Harbor and try to escape Soviet justice with the claim that he was seeking political asylum? Isn't this what prompts many so-called defectors? Americans are unpredictable. As soon as a situation becomes political it gets out of hand, a circus, the truth vying with lies. Of course in time we would get the man back, but is this the right light for a Soviet ship? Murder? Scandal? Comrades, no one would argue that this crew does not, under normal circumstances, deserve a port call after four months' hard work at sea. However, I would not want to be the captain who risked the prestige and mission of an entire fleet so that his crew could buy foreign running shoes and watches."

After such immaculate spadework by the Invalid, Arkady thought the issue was buried again. Hess, however, answered immediately.

"Let's separate your concerns. An investigation on board creates an abnormal situation, and an abnormal situation prevents a port call. It seems to me that one concern can resolve the other. We're a day and a half from Dutch Harbor, which is time enough for us to reach more definite conclusions about this poor girl's death. If it still seems suspicious in thirty-six hours, we can then decide not to allow the crew a port call. If not, let them have their well-earned day on shore. Either way, no one escapes and there will still be a full investigation waiting when we return to Vladivostok."

"What about suicide?" Slava asked. "What if she threw herself overboard, down the well, or wherever?"

"What about that?" Hess asked Arkady.

"Suicide is always a borderline issue," Arkady said. "There's the suicide who names fellow criminals before locking the garage door and starting the car. Or the suicide who paints 'Fuck the Soviet Writers Union' on the kitchen wall before putting his head in the oven. Or the soldier who says 'Consider me a good Communist' before he charges a machine gun."

"You are saying that the political element is always different," Hess said.

"*I* will determine the political element," Volovoi said. "I am still the political officer."

"Yes," Marchuk said coolly. "But not the captain."

"On such a delicate mission—"

Hess cut Volovoi off. "There's more than one mission."

There was a pause, as if the entire ship had veered in a new direction.

When Marchuk offered Volovoi a cigarette, the lighter's flame lit a fan of capillaries spreading in the first mate's eyes. Exhaling, Volovoi said, "Bukovsky can do another report."

"Bukovsky and Renko strike a good balance, don't you think?" Hess asked. To Arkady he said, "I've taken over the second mate's cabin. My door will be open to you."

Volovoi hunched forward as consensus, the goal of Soviet decision-making, rolled over him.

Marchuk changed the subject. "I keep thinking about that girl being on the bottom, about the eels. Renko, what were the odds a net would find her? A million to one?"

Arkady's participation in the meeting had been an order, but also an honor, as if a toe had been invited to the deliberations of the brain. Marchuk's question was a gesture of that inclusion.

"A million to one is about the odds that Comrade Bukovsky and

I will find anything," Arkady said. "Vladivostok has real investigators and real laboratories, and they know what to find."

"The inquiry here and now is what matters," Marchuk said. "Report the facts as you find them."

"No," Arkady said. "I agree with Comrade Volovoi; leave this for Vladivostok."

"You're reluctant, I understand," Marchuk sympathized. "The important thing is you can redeem yourself—"

"I don't need to redeem myself. I agreed to spend a day asking questions. The day is over." Arkady started for the door. "Comrades, good night."

Marchuk got to his feet, stunned. Stupefaction turned into the rage of a powerful man whose good intentions had been betrayed. Meanwhile Volovoi sat back, scarcely believing this turn of fortune.

"Renko, you say someone killed this girl and you won't find out who?" Hess asked.

"I don't think I could—and I'm not interested."

Marchuk said, "I'm ordering you."

"I'm refusing."

"You forget you're speaking to your captain."

"You forget you're speaking to a man who has spent a year on your slime line." Arkady opened the door. "What can you do to me? What could be worse?"

Wind had rolled the fog back into one dense bank. Arkady was crossing the deck intent on bed when he saw his cabin mate Kolya at the rail. A clear night always brought Kolya on deck, as if the moon were lit only for him. His hair curled up around a wool cap while his long nose pointed toward phenomena.

"Arkasha, I saw a whale. Just its tail, but it went straight down, so it was a humpback."

What Arkady admired about Kolya was that even though the botanist had been chased off land he went on collecting scientific data. He had the courage of a monk willing, in spite of his meekness, to be tortured for his beliefs. Shining in his hands like a little French horn was his prize, a highly polished old-fashioned brass sextant.

"Are you done with the captain?" Kolya asked.

"Yes."

Kolya had the delicacy not to ask any more questions, such as, Why didn't you tell your friends you were an investigator? Why aren't you an investigator now? What did you find out about the dead girl? Cheerfully he said, "Good. Then you can help me." He gave Arkady a watch. It was plastic, digital, Japanese. "The top button lights the readout."

"Why are you doing this?" Arkady asked.

"It keeps the mind alive. Ready?"

"Okay."

Kolya put his eye to the sextant telescope and sighted on the moon, swinging the index arm along the arc. As he had once explained to Arkady, sextants had the charm of being archaic, simple and complicated all at the same time. In essence, a pair of mirrors mounted on the arc brought an image of the moon down to the horizon, and the arc marked how many degrees off a right angle with the horizon the moon was at a precise instant.

"Mark."

"10:15.31."

"22:15.31." Kolya corrected to nautical hours.

As a Young Pioneer, Arkady had once performed celestial navigation. He remembered being surrounded by nautical almanacs, sight-reduction tables, scratch paper, charts and parallel rules. Kolya did it all in his head.

"How many almanacs have you memorized?" Arkady asked.

"Sun, moon and Ursa Major."

Arkady looked up. The stars seemed immensely bright and faraway, with colors and depth, like a blazing night.

"There's the Little Bear." Arkady looked straight up.

"You'll always see the Little Bear here," Kolya said. "At this latitude we're always under the Little Bear."

When Kolya did calculations his eyes took on a fixed, inward look, a kind of bliss. Arkady could tell he was subtracting the moon's refraction, adding the parallax, moving on to the moon's declination.

"You've been under the Little Bear too long. You're round the bend," Arkady said.

"It's no harder than blindfold chess." Kolya even smiled to prove he could talk while he thought.

"Does it ever bother you that the sextant is based on the idea that the sun goes around the earth?"

Kolya faltered for a second. "Unlike some systems, it works."

Once declination was fixed, Kolya's brain would review its memorized tables. It was the sort of endeavor only a quietly manic personality would pursue, like looking for whales in the dark. Not so dark, in fact. As the swells lifted the moon's reflection, the sea seemed to be breathing slowly and steadily.

During his first months at sea, Arkady had spent a lot of time on deck watching for dolphins, sea lions and whales, just to see them moving. The sea gave the illusion of escape. But after a time he realized that what all these creatures of the sea had, as they swam this way and that, was a sense of purpose. It was what he didn't have.

He peered back at the Little Bear and its long tail ending in Polaris, the North Star. A Russian folktale said Polaris was actually a maddened dog tied by an iron chain to the Little Bear, and that if the chain ever broke it would be the end of the world.

"Don't you ever get angry, Kolya? Here you are, a botanist, hundreds of kilometers from land."

"Only a hundred fathoms from the sea floor. And there's more land all the time. The Aleutian Islands are still building."

"I think I would call that the long view," Arkady said. He could feel his friend's anxiety; Kolya always became anxious when Arkady was depressed.

"Have you ever considered how much the Volovois of the world cost us?" Kolya was changing the subject, as if a good riddle was always balm. "What are we paid?"

"I thought you were shooting the moon."

"I can do both. What are we paid?"

That was complicated. The *Polar Star*'s pay was shared on a coefficient from 2.55 shares for the captain to .8 share for a second-class seaman. Then there was a polar coefficient of 1.5 for fishing in Arctic seas, a 10 percent bonus for one year's service, a 10 percent bonus for meeting the ship's quota, and a bonus as high as 40 percent for overfulfilling the plan. The quota was everything. It could be raised or lowered after the ship left dock, but was usually raised because the fleet manager drew his bonus from saving on seamen's wages. Transit time to the fishing grounds was set at so many days, and the whole crew lost money when the captain ran into a storm, which was why Soviet ships sometimes went full steam ahead through fog and heavy seas. Altogether, the wage scale of a Soviet fisherman was only a little less intricate than astronomy.

Arkady guessed, "Around three hundred rubles a month for me."

"Not bad. But did you factor in the Americans?" Kolya reminded him.

Because there were Americans on board, the work rules were different: a lower quota and a slower pace to impress the visitors with the humaneness of the Soviet fishing industry.

"Say three hundred twenty-five rubles?"

"For a first-class seaman three hundred forty rubles. For you two hundred seventy-five. For an invalid like Volovoi, four hundred seventy-five."

"This is cheery," Arkady said. But he was amused by his cabin mate's virtuosity, and Kolya grinned fiercely, like a juggler demanding the test of one more ball added to the ones already in the air.

"Fish! We're here for fish, not mathematics, Comrade Mer!"

Volovoi stepped out of the shadow of a companionway, his running suit iridescent in the moonlight. There was something particu-

larly gloating about his saunter, and Arkady realized that the first
mate had followed him in triumph from the captain's cabin. As
usual, Kolya automatically looked away.

Volovoi's hand reached out and took the sextant. "What's this?"

Kolya said, "It's mine. I was taking a reading from the moon."

Volovoi glanced at the moon suspiciously. "What for?"

"Finding our position."

"You clean fish. What do you need to know our position for?"

"Just curiosity. It's an old sextant, an antique."

"Where are your charts?"

"I don't have any charts."

"You want to know how far we are from America?"

"No. I just wanted to know where we are."

Volovoi unzipped the jacket of his running suit and slipped the
sextant inside. "The captain knows where we are. That should be
enough."

Walking away, the Invalid didn't say a word to Arkady; he didn't
need to.

And so to bed.

The cabin was black as a grave, a proper abode. Kolya curled up
with his flower pots while Arkady pulled off his boots and climbed
into his bunk, pulling a sheet tight around his shoulders. A vinegary
scent from Obidin's home brew tinged the air. Before he drew his
second breath, he was asleep. It was sleep like a lightless void, one
he knew well.

ON MOSCOW'S GARDEN RING, near the Children's Library and the
Ministry of Education, stood a three-story building with a gray

fence, the Serbsky Institute of Forensic Psychiatry. The fence was topped by thin wires invisible from the street. Between the fence and the building guards patrolled with dogs trained not to bark. On the second floor of the institute was Section Four. Along the parquet hall were three general wards that Arkady saw only on the day he arrived and the day he left, because he was held at the end of the hall in an "isolator," with a bed, toilet and one dim bulb. On arrival, he was bathed by orderlies, two old women in white, and shaved by a fellow patient, head, armpits and pubis so that he would be as clean and hairless as a babe for the doctors, then dressed in striped pajamas and a beltless robe. There was no window, no day or night. The diagnosis was "pre-schizophrenic syndrome," as if the doctors could confidently predict.

They injected caffeine under the skin to make him talkative, followed by a needle of sodium barbital into the vein of his arm to depress his will. Sitting on white stools, full of concern, the doctors asked, "Where is Irina? You loved her, you must miss her. You made plans to meet? What do you think she's doing now? Where do you think she is?" They moved from arm to arm to the veins of his legs, but the questions were always the same, as was the humor of the situation. Since he had no idea where Irina was or what she was doing, he answered everything in full, and since the doctors were convinced he knew more, they thought he was holding out. "You're suffering under a delusion," he told them. It didn't help his case.

Frustration naturally led to punishment. The favorite was the lumbar puncture. They strapped him to the bed, swabbed his spine with iodine, and with one vigorous push inserted the needle. The puncture was a twofold experience, the agony of the probing needle and, for hours afterwards, spasms exactly like the comical reaction of a frog's leg to an electric current.

It was hard work for everyone. After a while they dressed him only in a robe, the easier to get at veins. The doctors removed their lab coats and labored in their uniforms, dark blue with the red shoulder boards of the militia.

Between sessions they kept him quiet with aminazin. It was so quiet that he could hear through two sets of closed soundproofed doors the scuffing of slippers in the hall during the day, the squeak of the guard's shoes at night. The light was never off. The door's peephole would blink: doctor's rounds.

"Better to talk to us and let go of this paranoia. Otherwise there will always be more questions, another interrogator when you least expect it. You really will go crazy."

True, Arkady felt himself losing control. From the street he could hear the occasional siren of a police car or fire engine, klaxons muffled in concrete, and he pouted like a dead man whose grave has been transgressed. *Leave me alone.*

Arkady squirmed in his straps. "Just what is 'pre-schizophrenic syndrome'?"

The doctor beamed, encouraged. "It is also called 'sluggish schizophrenia.' "

"It sounds terrible," Arkady had to admit. "What are the signs?"

"A wide variety. Suspicion and uncommunicativeness—you recognize those? Listlessness? Rudeness?"

"After injections, yes," Arkady confessed.

"Argumentativeness and arrogance. An abnormal interest in philosophy, religion or art."

"What about hope?"

"In some cases," the doctor said, "absolutely."

The truth was that the interrogators gave him hope simply because they wouldn't have brought him here if Irina wasn't well. The KGB liked nothing more than to write off a defector as "another émigré waiting on tables"; or "The West wasn't such a soft bed after all, even for whores"; or "They squeezed her dry and then threw her out, and now she wants to come back, but of course it's too late." When they demanded whether he was trying to reach her, his hope soared. Was she trying to reach him?

To protect Irina he changed his tack. He wanted to babble nothing, not even in his most feeble condition, so he thought about her as little as he could in order to purge her from his mind. In a sense, the doctors did achieve the schizophrenia they had predicted. Even as he took heart that she had survived, he tried to wipe her face from his memory, to make her a blank.

Besides the robe, Arkady had a green enamel jug, the perfect gift, something you couldn't swallow, cut or hang yourself with. Sometimes he would put the jug in front of the door so that the doctors would knock it over when they came in. Then not for a week, just enough to create the smallest uncertainty in the staff. One day they marched in as a group and took the jug away.

This time they used insulin. Insulin was the most primitive tranquilizer; in fact, it induced coma.

"Then let us tell you. She's married. Yes, this woman you're shielding is not only living in the luxury afforded traitors, but she's living with another man. She's forgotten you."

"He's not even listening."

"He hears us."

"Try digitalis."

"He could go into shock. Then we'd have nothing."

"Look at his color. Another minute you'll be pounding on his chest."

"He's faking. Renko, you're faking."

"He's white as snow. That's not faking."

"Shit."

"Better give it to him right away."

"Okay, okay. Fuck."

"Look at the eyes."

"I'm giving it to him."

"Ones like him can slip away on you, you know."

"Bloody bastard."

"Still no pulse."

"He'll be fine by tomorrow. We'll start again, that's all."

"Still no pulse."

"He'll be babbling like a parakeet tomorrow, you'll see."

"No pulse."

"I still think he's faking."

"I think he's dead."

NO, JUST HIDING in the deep faraway.

"Only half dead," judged a visitor. His squat nose wrinkled as he sniffed the astringent air of the isolator. "I'm taking you to more rigorous accommodations, away from this health spa."

Because Arkady recognized the voice he made an effort to focus on a heavy Slavic head with piggish eyes and jowls that seemed to ooze out of a brown-and-red uniform with the star-and-dagger patch of the KGB.

"Major Pribluda?"

"Colonel Pribluda." The visitor pointed to new epaulets, then tossed a paper bag at the orderly who rushed in. "Get him dressed."

It was always bracing to see the effect that a brute in the right uniform could have, even on the medical community. Arkady had thought he was lost forever, like a larva in the center of a hive, yet in ten minutes Pribluda had him out on the street. Wrapped in pants and a coat admittedly two sizes too large, but out and shivering in the snow until Pribluda contemptuously shoved him into a car.

The car was a badly dented Moskvitch missing its wipers and rearview mirror, not a Volga with official plates. Pribluda pulled away from the curb quickly, looking forward and back through his open window, then pulled his head back and erupted with a laugh. "Not a bad actor, eh? By the way, you look terrible."

Arkady felt ridiculous. Giddy with freedom and exhausted by the short walk, he slumped against the door. "Didn't you have papers for my release?"

"Not with my name on it; I'm not dumb enough for that, Renko. By the time they find out you'll be out of Moscow."

Arkady took another look at Pribluda's shoulder boards. "Did they promote you? Congratulations."

"Thanks to you." Pribluda had to pull his head in and out both to drive and to hold a conversation. "You made me look very smart when you came back. Let the girl run off and sell herself on the streets in New York; what state secrets did she have? You were a good Russian; you did what you had to and then came back."

Flakes caught on Pribluda's hair and brows, making him the picture of a coachman. "The problem is the prosecutor. He had many friends."

"He was KGB, too."

For a block, Pribluda acted offended. "So you see my point," he said finally. "People think you know more than you do. For their own safety, they have to wring you like a rag until they get every last drop, and I don't mean of water."

"Where is Irina?" Arkady asked.

Pribluda reached around and pushed snow off the windshield as he drove. Ahead, an East German Wartburg sedan, built like an inverted bathtub, made a complete 360 degrees on the trolley tracks.

"Fascist!" The colonel stuck a cigarette in his mouth and lit it. "Forget her. For you she's as good as dead—worse than dead."

"That means she's either very sick or very healthy."

"For you it doesn't matter."

The car swung through a gate and bounced over what at first seemed unlikely ruts in the center of Moscow, but Arkady dimly saw a railroad switching yard with ramps built over rails so that trucks could cross. A field of trains like so many armored hosts were standing in the snow, with flatcars of cable reels, tractors and prefab walls half erased by white. In the distance, appearing to rise in the falling snow, were the Gothic spires of Yaroslavl Station, the gateway to the East. Pribluda stopped the car between two passenger trains, one with the short, helmeted locomotive of a commuter line, the other with the long red coaches of the *Rossiya,* the Trans-Siberian Express. Through the windows Arkady could see travelers taking their seats.

"You're joking."

"In Moscow you're surrounded by enemies," Pribluda said. "You're in no condition to protect yourself, and I won't be able to rescue you twice—not here. The same would be true in Leningrad, Kiev, Vladimir—anywhere near. You need to go where no one wants to follow you."

"They'll follow me."

"But they'll be one or two instead of twenty, and you'll be able to keep moving. You don't understand; you're dead here already."

"Out there I'll be as good as dead."

"That's what will save you. Believe me, I know how their minds work."

Arkady couldn't deny the truth of that; the line between "them" and Pribluda was fine enough.

"Just two or three years," the colonel said. "With the new regime, everything is changing—though not all for the best as far as I'm concerned. Anyway, give them a chance to forget you and then come back."

"Well, it was a good act," Arkady said, "but you got me out too easily. You made a deal."

Pribluda killed the engine, and for a moment there was no sound except the settling of snow, all those tons of flakes gently blanketing the city.

"To keep you alive." The colonel was exasperated. "What's wrong with that?"

"What did you promise?"

"No contact, not even the possibility of contact between you and her."

"There's only one way you could promise 'not even the possibility of contact.' "

"Stop playing the interrogator with me. You always make everything so difficult." Under his cap Pribluda had little eyes driven deep as nails. It was a strange place to find embarrassment. "Am I your friend or not? Come on."

Each red railroad car bore a golden hammer and sickle and a plaque that read MOSCOW–VLADIVOSTOK. Pribluda had to carry Arkady up the high steps of the platform to a "hard class" section. Exotic families in skullcaps and brilliant scarves camped on bedrolls, their berths occupied by new appliances still in packing cases— goods they could buy only in Moscow. Brown children peeked through curtains rolled up like bunting. Women opened bundles, releasing a buffet's smell of cold lamb, kefir, cheese. Students heading for the Ural Mountains stacked skis and guitars. Pribluda talked to the conductress, a top-heavy woman wearing what looked like an airline captain's cap and a short skirt. Returning, he stuffed into Arkady's overcoat a through ticket, an envelope of rubles and a blue work pass.

"I've made arrangements," Pribluda said. "Friends will take you off in Krasnoyarsk and put you on a plane for Norilsk. You'll have a job as a watchman, but you'd better not stay too long. The main thing is, once you're above the Arctic Circle you'll be too much trouble to bring back. It's just for a few years, not a lifetime."

Arkady had never hated anyone as much as he once had Pribluda, and he knew Pribluda had loathed him in return. Yet here they were, as close to friends as each other had alive. It was as if everyone traveled the world in the dark, never knowing where he was going, blindly following a road that twisted, rose and fell. The hand that pushed you down one day helped you up the next. The only straight road was . . . what? The train!

"I meant it about the promotion," Arkady said. "That's good."

On the platform a row of conductresses were raising batons, signaling that the express was ready to leave. Ahead, the locomotive released its air brakes and a tremor ran the length of the cars. Still the colonel lingered.

"You know what they say?" He smiled.

"What do they say?" Arkady wondered. Pribluda was not known for humor.

"They say some waters are too cold even for sharks."

IF THE HOSPITAL had left Arkady dazed, the motor yard in Norilsk made him numb. To keep from freezing, trucks were left running all night on Siberian diesel fuel, the cheapest on earth. Or else fires had to be carefully set under the engine block but away from the fuel line. The problem was that the surface was actually a thin cover of moss and dirt over permafrost, and as the frost around the fires melted and refroze, the ground became an icy swamp.

One night in his second month on the job, Arkady was building a fire in the black space under a Belarus earthmover, a ten-wheeler the size of an iron house, when he saw figures approaching from opposite sides of the yard. Truck drivers wore boots, quilted jackets, caps. These two were in overcoats and hats and stepped daintily across the rutted ice. The one skirting a coal pile picked up a pickax and carried it with him. Theft of construction equipment, the sacred property of the state, was not unusual; that's why there were watchmen like Arkady. If you want it, take it, he thought. The two men stood in the shadows and waited. The temperature was 10 degrees below zero and Arkady began to freeze. It felt like burning on a spit. He stuffed a glove in his mouth to keep his teeth from chattering. In the dark he saw the two men shivering, arms folded, hopping in place, their breath crystallizing and drifting to the ground. Finally, on wooden legs, they gave up and gathered at the fire in the oilcan. The one with the pickax held it up and carefully peeled his fingers back; when the ax dropped and bounced smartly off his knee he didn't seem to feel a thing. The other was so cold he cried tears that froze in waxy stripes down his face. He tried to smoke, but his hands were shaking too hard to get out one cigarette, and half the pack spilled into the can and onto the ice. Finally, slowly, as bent and unsteady as if they were walking into violent wind, they moved away. Arkady heard one fall: a muffled impact and an agonized curse. A minute later he heard car doors shut and an engine start.

Arkady dragged himself on his elbows to the burning can. He emptied kerosene into the fire and vodka into himself, and in the morning he didn't return to his hostel. He went to the airport and boarded a plane east, farther into Siberia, like a fox heading for deeper woods.

He was pretty safe. With the Siberian labor shortage, any strong back got double pay with no questions asked for laying railroad ties, sawing ice or slaughtering reindeer, because Siberian managers had their quotas too. A man carving ice with a chain saw, his face encased with frost, might be an alcoholic, a criminal, a bum or a saint. What were the odds? Once the quota was fulfilled, then a local apparatchik would check names against a list of persons in whom the militia or the KGB had an interest. But each of these work camps was a minuscule dot in a landmass twice the size of China. That was why workers were so prized: Siberia's mere fifteen million inhabitants facing an envious one billion Chinese! By the time any agent of State Security arrived Arkady was gone.

The interesting thing was that although Irina was Siberian he never saw a woman like her, not in all the villages and work camps that he passed through. Certainly not among the Uzbeks or Buryats, nor among the women who tended cement mixers like so many milkmaids around a cow. Nor among the Young Komsomol princesses who came to pose on tractors for six months and then flew home, having fulfilled their lifetime quota of volunteer labor.

Yet when he cared to, he could stand on the duckboards of a work camp and be sure that the next woman to jump from a truck to the mud, jacket open, scarf around her hair, lunch pail in hand, would be Irina. Somehow she had returned, and through a trail of incredible coincidences had arrived at the very same place he was. His heart would stop until she landed and looked up. Then he would be sure that Irina was the next one. It was like a children's game.

So he didn't think of her.

At the end of his second year, escaping the Border Guard on Sakhalin, he crossed to the mainland and boarded a southbound train, reconnecting with the red Trans-Siberian Express after all this while. But this time he rode the platform because he smelled like a fishnet. At dusk he arrived at Vladivostok, the "Lord of the Ocean," the major Pacific port of the Soviet Union. Under tall, fluted streetlamps well-fed, well-dressed people filled the sidewalks. Motorcycles raced buses. Across from the terminal a statue of Lenin pointed to the Golden Horn, Vladivostok's bay, and on the rooftop above Lenin's steel brow glowed a welcome in neon script: FORWARD TO THE VICTORY OF COMMUNISM!

Forward? After two years of exile, Arkady had ten rubles in his pocket; the rest of his money was back on the island. A seaman's hostel was only ten kopeks a night, but he had to eat. He followed the buses to the Shipping Administration, where a board displayed the status of every civil vessel that claimed Vladivostok as its home port. According to the board, the factory ship *Polar Star* had put to sea that day, but when Arkady wandered to the docks he saw it still taking on cargo and fuel. Floodlit gantries lifted barrels that had passed inspection by the Border Guard, army veterans outfitted by the KGB in navy-blue uniforms. Their dogs sniffed each barrel, although how the animals could smell anything over the dockside odors of diesel fuel and the ammoniated steam of refrigeration plants was hard to understand.

In the morning Arkady was the first man into the Seamen's Hall, where a clerk admitted that the *Polar Star* was still in port and still needed a worker on the factory line. He took his work pass behind a steel door to be stamped by the Maritime Section of the KGB. On the desk were two black phones for local offices and a direct red phone to Moscow. Arkady was surprised because for coastal fishing there were no such precautions. The black phones were no danger, he felt, unless they called Sakhalin. If anyone bothered to check his name on the red phone, this would be as far as he got.

"There are Americans," warned the KGB captain in charge.

"What?" Arkady had been watching the phones.

"There are Americans on the boat. Just be natural, friendly but not overfriendly. Better to say nothing at all, in fact." He stamped the work pass without even reading the name on it. "I'm not necessarily saying hide."

But isn't this what Arkady did, hide? First in the deep faraway of the psycho ward. Then, after Pribluda revived him, in Siberia and on the ship, carrying on inert and semidead?

NOW, ASLEEP IN his narrow bunk, he asked himself, *Wouldn't it be good to be alive again?*

Zina Patiashvili had swum back. Maybe he could, too.

10 In the morning, showered and shaved, Arkady took the long walk to the *Polar Star*'s white wheelhouse and the cabin of the fleet electrical engineer for advice.

"You're lucky," Anton Hess said. "You caught me between going off duty and coming on. I was just making tea."

His accommodations were no larger than a crew cabin, except that they were for one man rather than four, leaving room for a desk and a wall map that appeared to show every Soviet fishing fleet in the North Pacific. On a rubber pad on the desk was, instead of a samovar, a coffee maker, the sort that might grace a Moscow apartment.

Hess had the sort of look Arkady had once seen on submariners returning from a polar voyage. Eyes red and sprung, step shuffling and uncertain. The little man's hair was stiff and wild, as if attacked by a cat, and his sweater reeked of pipe tobacco. The coffee dripped in greasy black drops. He poured out two mugs, added a generous amount from a cognac bottle, and gave a mug to Arkady. "Confusion to the French," he said.

"Why not?" Arkady agreed.

The coffee delivered a kick to his heart, which started beating anxiously. Hess sighed and allowed himself to sink in slow motion into a chair, from where his eyes fixed wearily across the room on a waist-high vertical glass tube with a stand and cord for the radiation of ultraviolet rays. Sunlight. Vitamin D. During winter in Siberia they would ring children around tubes like this.

Hess's pale face smiled. "My wife insisted I bring it. I think she wants to believe I'm in the South Pacific. Good tea?"

Tea for coffee, French for Americans. Hess had an ease for misleading that struck Arkady as appropriate.

There was no such thing as a fleet electrical engineer; it was a title of convenience that allowed an officer of the KGB or of naval intelligence to move from ship to ship. The question was which of these agencies the amiable Anton Hess belonged to. The best indicator was Volovoi, who was the political officer and who regarded Hess with both respect and animosity. Also, these days the KGB tended to be a strictly Russian club, where a name like Hess was a liability. The navy tended to promote competence, with the exception of Jews.

On the map Alaska yearned toward Siberia. Or was it the other way around? Either way, Soviet trawlers dotted the sea from Kamchatka, across the island arc of the Aleutians and down to Oregon. Arkady hadn't appreciated before how well the American coast was covered. Of course, in Soviet-American joint ventures Soviet trawlers functioned as processors; each fleet shared its company of American catcher boats. Only a great factory ship like the *Polar Star* could operate independently with its own family of American boats. The red dot for the *Polar Star* was about two days north of Dutch Harbor and nowhere near other fleets.

"Comrade Hess, I apologize for bothering you."

Hess shook his head, exhausted but indulgent. "Not at all. Whatever I can do."

"Very well," Arkady said. "Let's say that Zina Patiashvili did not accidentally stab, beat and throw herself overboard."

"You've changed your mind." Hess was delighted.

"And let's say we investigate. Not a real investigation with detectives and laboratories, but with the meager resources we have on hand."

"You."

"Then we must consider the slim possibility of actually finding something out. Or of discovering a great many things, some of which we did not set out to find. This is where I need your counsel."

"Really?" Hess sat forward, his whole attitude suggesting rapport.

"See, my vision—which is that of a man who cuts fish in the hold of a ship—is very limited. You, however, think in terms of the entire ship, even of the entire fleet. The work of a fleet electrical engineer must be difficult." Especially so far from the fleet, Arkady thought. "You would be aware of factors and considerations I know nothing of. Perhaps of factors I *should* know nothing of."

Hess frowned as if he couldn't imagine what these could be. "You mean there might be some reason not to ask questions? And if there were such a reason, that it would be better to ask no questions at all rather than to stop questions once you've begun asking them?"

"You've expressed it better than I could," Arkady said.

Hess rubbed his eyes, fumbled with a tobacco pouch, filled and tamped his pipe. It was a navigator's pipe designed to hang out of the way while its smoker studied charts. He lit it with short sucks of air, sounding like a radiator.

"I can't think of any such reason. The girl seems to have been ordinary, young, a little loose. But I have a solution for your concern. If you come across anything especially unusual, anything that bothers you, then please feel free to come to me first."

"Sometimes you might be hard to find." After all, I didn't even know you existed until last night, Arkady thought.

"The *Polar Star* is a large ship, but it's still only a ship. Captain Marchuk or his chief mate always knows where I am."

"His chief mate, not his first mate?"

"Not Comrade Volovoi, no." Hess smiled at the idea.

Arkady wished he knew more about the man. German communities had been invited to settle, cultivate and tone up the Volga for hundreds of years, until the Great Patriotic War, when Stalin ripped them out in advance of the fascist invasion and shipped them overnight to Asia.

Hess scrutinized Arkady in the same way. "Your father was General Renko, is that right?"

"Yes."

"Where did you do your service?"

"Berlin."

"Really? Doing what?"

"Sitting in a radio shed, listening to Americans."

"Intelligence work!"

"Hardly so grand."

"But you monitored enemy movements. You didn't make any mistakes."

"I didn't set off a war accidentally."

"That's the best test of intelligence." Hess pushed his hair back, but it rose again like a stiff beard. "Just tell me what you need."

"I'll need to be released from my usual duties."

"Of course."

Arkady kept his voice level, but the truth was that every word brought blood rushing through his veins in a sensation that was shameful and intoxicating. "I can work with Slava Bukovsky, but I'll need an assistant of my own choice. I'll have to question crew members, including officers."

"All reasonable, if done quietly."

"And question Americans, if necessary."

"Why not? There's no reason for them not to cooperate. After all, this is just a fact-finding preliminary to the official investigation in Vladivostok."

"I don't seem to get along with them."

"I believe the head representative's cabin is directly below mine. You could talk to her now."

"Anything I say seems to annoy her."

"We're all out here together peacefully fishing. Talk about the sea."

"The Bering Sea?"

"Why not?"

Hess sat with his hands on his belly like a little German Buddha. He looked too comfortable. Was he KGB? Sometimes it took a sharp stick to find out.

Arkady said, "The first time I heard of the Bering Sea I was eight years old. We had the encyclopedia. One day we received in the mail a new page. All the subscribers to the encyclopedia were mailed the same insert, along with instructions on how to cut out Beria so that we could tape in vital new information about the Bering Sea. Of course Beria had been shot by then and was no longer a Hero of the Soviet Union. It was one of the rare times I ever saw my father truly happy, because it gave him so much pleasure to cut off the head of the secret police."

If Hess were KGB the inquiry would be over now. Even so, his smile wore the strain of a man whose new dog has proven to be a biter. "You killed the Moscow prosecutor, your boss. Volovoi was right about that."

"In self-defense."

"A number of others died too."

"Not by my hand."

"A German and an American."

"Them, yes."

"A messy business. You also helped a woman defect."

"Not really." Arkady shrugged. "I had the chance to wave good-bye."

"But you didn't go yourself. When all was said and done, you were still a Russian. That's what we count on. You know seals?"

"Seals?"

"In the winter. How they hide under the ice sheet near a hole, just coming up to breathe? Is that a little bit like you right now?"

When Arkady didn't answer, Hess said, "You shouldn't confuse the KGB and us. I confess that sometimes we seem hard. When I was a cadet, far back in the days of Khrushchev, we set off a hydrogen device in the Arctic Sea. It was a hundred-megaton bomb, the largest ever detonated then or since. Actually, it was a fifty-megaton warhead wrapped in a uranium case to double the yield. A very dirty bomb. We didn't warn the Swedes or the Finns, and we certainly didn't tell our own people who were drinking milk under this rain of fallout a thousand times worse than Chernobyl. We didn't tell our fishermen who sailed in the Arctic Sea. I signed on as a third mate, and my mission was to use a Geiger counter without telling anyone else on board. We caught one shark that measured four hundred roentgens. What could I say to the captain—to throw his quota overboard? His crew would ask questions, and then the cry would spread. But we let the Americans know, and the result was that Kennedy was frightened enough to come to the table and sign a test-ban treaty."

Hess let his smile fade and held Arkady's eyes, the way an executioner might briefly show his professional face to a son. Then he brightened. "Anyway, for most of the crew, sailing on the *Polar Star* is no different from working in a factory anywhere, with the positive aspect of visiting a foreign port and the negative one of seasickness. For some, however, there is the attraction of freedom. It's the aura of the wide sea. We are far from port. The Border Guard is on the other side of the earth and we are in the world of the Pacific Fleet."

"Does this mean I have your support or not?"

"Oh, definitely," said Hess. "Support and growing interest."

As he left the cabin Arkady saw the informers Skiba and Slezko slip around the end of the passageway. Walk, don't run, don't trip, Arkady thought. Don't bust your lips before you tell the Invalid what seaman visited the fleet electrical engineer's accommodations. Carry the news as if it were a mug of tea from Hess himself. Don't spill a drop.

SUSAN WAS AT her cabin table, resting her head on one hand and letting cigarette smoke curl in the mop of her hair. It was actually a very Russian pose, poetic, tragic. Slava was with her and they were dining on soup and bread, which Arkady suspected the third mate had brought straight from the galley.

"I'm not interrupting?" Arkady asked. "I wouldn't have stopped, but your door was open."

"It's my rule to keep my door open when Soviet men come to call," Susan said. "Even when they come bearing strange breakfasts."

Out of her jacket and boots she was practically a girl. Brown eyes and blond hair made an interesting contrast but were hardly unique. She had neither the complete ovalness nor the Slavic cheekbones of Russian women. The cigarette marked a fuller mouth, and etched around her eyes were those first lines that made a woman more real. But she was too thin, as if Soviet food wouldn't take. Admittedly the soup was a pasty liquid dappled with grease. She idly dredged bones, which she dropped back in the stew.

"It's sweet butter," Slava pointed out to her. "I told Olimpiada, 'No garlic cloves.' Anyway, you must visit Lake Baikal. Sixteen percent of the world's fresh water is contained in that lake."

"How much is contained in this bowl?" Susan asked.

Arkady began, "I was just wondering—"

Slava took a deep breath. If Arkady was going to ruin the intimacy of a civilized repast, the third mate would make him pay. "Renko, if you have questions you should have asked them yesterday. I think I hear them calling you on the slime line."

"I've noticed," Susan said. "You're always 'just wondering.' Wondering what?"

"How do you like fishing?" Arkady asked.

"How do I like fishing? Christ, I must love it or I wouldn't be here, right?"

"Then do it like this." Arkady took the spoon from her hand. "Fish. If you want the bones, then do as you're doing and trawl the bottom. But everything is at a different level. Cabbage and potatoes are a little higher off the bottom."

"Baikal has indigenous seals. . . . blind fish. . . ." Slava tried to hold the thread of his monologue. "Many species of . . ."

"To catch an onion is more difficult," Arkady explained. "You must use a mid-water pelagic trawl to hunt them down. Ah!" He scooped one up in triumph. A burnt pearl.

"What about meat?" Susan asked. "This is a meat stew."

"Theoretically." Arkady gave her back her spoon.

Susan ate the onion.

Slava lost patience. "Renko, your shift is on duty."

"This may seem a silly question," Arkady said to Susan, "but I was wondering what you wore to the dance."

She laughed in spite of herself. "Not my prom dress, that's for sure."

"Prom?"

"Crinoline and corsage. Never mind, let's say I wore my basic shirt and jeans."

"A white shirt and blue jeans?"

"Yes. Why do you ask?"

"Did you leave the dance for fresh air? Perhaps went out on deck?"

Susan was silent. She sat back against the bulkhead and studied him with a flare of confirmed distrust. "You're still asking about Zina."

Slava was outraged, too. "That's over; you said so last night."

"Well," Arkady said, "I changed my mind this morning."

Susan said, "Why are you so fixated on Americans? On this factory ship with hundreds of Soviets, you keep coming back to us. You're like my radio; you work in reverse." She pointed her cigarette to a speaker built into a corner of the cabin. "In the beginning I wondered why it didn't work. Then I climbed up and found a microphone. See, it did work, just not the way I expected." She tilted her head and blew smoke that drifted toward Arkady like an arrow. "When I get off at Dutch Harbor, no more imitation radio or imitation detectives. Never again. Any more questions?"

"I didn't know anything about this," Slava assured Susan.

"Are you taking your books with you?" Arkady asked.

On the upper bunk were the typewriter and cartons of books that Arkady had admired before. What Soviet poetry and toilet paper had in common was scarcity due to the inadequacies, despite the largest forests in the world, of the Soviet paper industry.

Susan asked, "You want one? Besides being a slime-line worker and an investigator, you're also a book lover?"

"Some books."

"Who do you like?" she asked.

"Susan is a writer," Slava said. "I like Hemingway myself."

"Russian writers," Susan told Arkady. "You're Russian and you have a Russian soul. Name one."

"You have so many." More good books than the library on board, he thought.

"Akhmatova?"

"Naturally." Arkady shrugged.

Susan recited: " ' "What do you want," I asked. "To be with you in Hell," he said.' "

Arkady picked up the next verse: " 'He lifted his thin hand/and lightly stroked the flowers:/"Tell me how men kiss you,/Tell me how you kiss." ' "

Slava looked back and forth from Susan to Arkady.

"Everybody knows that one by heart," Arkady said. "People do when books can't be bought."

Susan dropped her cigarette into her soup, rose, grabbed the first book she could reach on the upper bunk and threw it at Arkady. "That's a good-bye gift," she said. "No more questions, no more 'wondering.' I'm lucky you only surfaced at the end of the trip."

"Well," Arkady suggested, "actually you may have been luckier than that."

"Tell me."

"You were dressed like Zina. If someone did throw her overboard, it's good they didn't throw you by mistake."

11

The cabin of the late Zina Patiashvili had the privacy of a dream; merely by turning on the lamp Arkady felt like a trespasser.

Dynka, for example, came from a race of Uzbeks and there was her own toy camel, a Bactrian from a miniature Samarkand, standing on the pillow of her upper bunk. There were Madame Malzeva's embroidered cushions, each a sachet redolent of talcs and pomades. Her scrapbook of foreign postcards displayed minarets and crumbling temples. An embossed portrait of Lenin guarded Natasha Chaikovskaya's berth, but there was also a snapshot of a mother smiling timidly amid giant sunflowers, as well as a glossy photo of Julio Iglesias.

The bulkheads of the cabin were dyed a romantic maroon by a glass wind chime that hung before the porthole. The room was a little dizzying, a nautilus shell of colors, of inner folds and cushions, of warring perfumes as powerful as incense, of life crammed into a steel compartment. There were more pictures in evidence than before, as if the removal of Zina had released the last constraint on the three cabin mates remaining. The wardrobe door was decorated with more Uzbeks and Siberian construction workers shimmering in the watery reflection of the chimes.

Arkady was looking under Zina's stripped mattress when Natasha arrived. She was in a damp blue running suit, the universal outfit of Soviet sports. Sweat lay like dew on her cheeks, but her lipstick was fresh.

"You remind me of a crow," she told Arkady. "A scavenger."

"You're observant." He didn't tell her what she reminded him of, which was her nickname Chaika for the big limousine. An out-of-breath Chaika in a blue tarp.

"I was doing calisthenics on deck. They said you wanted to see me here."

Because Arkady was wearing rubber gloves from the infirmary his sense of touch took all his concentration. When he pulled open a slit in the mattress, a tape cassette slid out. "Van Halen," said the case. Rooting around inside the mattress, he came out with three more tapes and a small English-Russian dictionary. Flipping through it, he noticed some words underlined in pencil. The lines had the heavy assertiveness of a schoolgirl's, as did the words, which all had to do with sex.

"A major breakthrough?" Natasha asked.

"Not quite."

"Aren't there supposed to be two witnesses in a police search?"

"This is not a search by any official body; this is just me. Your cabin mate may have had an accident, maybe not. The captain has ordered me to find out."

"Hah!"

"That's what I'm thinking too. I was once an investigator."

"In Moscow. I heard all about it. You became involved in anti-Soviet intrigue."

"Well, that's one story. The point is, for the last year I've been in the hold of this ship. It's been an honor, of course, to take part in the process of preparing fish for the great Soviet market."

"We feed the Soviet Union."

"And a wonderful slogan it is. However, not expecting this particular crisis, I have not maintained my skills as an investigator."

Natasha frowned as if examining an object she didn't know quite how to handle. "If the captain has ordered you to carry out a task, you should do so happily."

"Yes. But there is another limitation. Natasha, we work together on the factory line. You've expressed the opinion that some men on the line are soft-bellied intellectuals."

"They couldn't find their pricks if they weren't tied on."

"Thank you. You come from different lineage yourself?"

"Two generations of hydroelectric construction workers. My mother was at the upper Bratsk Dam. I was brigade leader at Bochugany Hydroelectric Station."

"And a decorated worker."

"The Order of Labor, yes." Natasha accepted compliments stiffly.

"And a Party member."

"I hold that lofty honor."

"And a person of underestimated intelligence and initiative."

Arkady remembered that when Kolya lost a finger in the saw and blood was spraying from his hand over his face, the fish and everyone around him, it was Natasha who immediately tied her scarf tightly around his wrist, then made him lie down with his feet up and guarded him fiercely until a stretcher was brought. When he was taken to the infirmary, she searched on her hands and knees for the missing finger so it could be sewn back on.

"The estimation of the Party is sufficient. Why did you ask me down here?"

"Why did you leave construction work for the cleaning of fish? You got double pay at the dams, plus an Arctic bonus for some of them. You worked outside in the healthy air instead of in the hold of a ship."

Natasha crossed her arms. Her cheeks colored.

A husband. Naturally. There were more men than women at a construction site, but not as on a ship, where more than two hundred healthy men were trapped for months with perhaps fifty women, half of them grandmothers, leaving a ratio of ten to one. Natasha was always touring the deck in her running suit or fox-trimmed coat or, on a day with the merest hint of balminess, in a flower-print sundress that made her resemble a large, threatening camellia. Arkady was embarrassed for being so obtuse.

"Travel," she said.

"The same as me."

"But you don't go into the foreign ports; you stay on the ship."

"I'm a purist."

"You have a second-class visa, that's why."

"That too. What's worse, I have had a second-class curiosity. I have been so content on the factory line that I have not participated in the full social and cultural life of the ship."

"The dances."

"Exactly. It's almost as if I haven't been here at all. I know nothing about the women or the Americans—or, to be more particular, about Zina Patiashvili."

"She was an honest Soviet worker who will be badly missed."

Arkady opened the wardrobe. The clothes were on hangers in order of owner: Dynka's girl-sized apparel, Madame Malzeva's frowsy dresses, Natasha's giant red evening gown, sundresses, pastel running suits. He was disappointed in Dynka's clothes because he'd expected some colorful Uzbek embroidery or golden pants, but all he saw was a Chinese jacket.

"You took away Zina's clothes already," Natasha said.

"Yes, they were laid out for us very nicely."

Three wardrobe drawers held lingerie, stockings, scarves, pills, even a swimsuit in Natasha's drawer. The fourth was empty. He checked the backs and bottoms for anything taped to the drawers.

"What are you looking for?" Natasha demanded.

"I don't know."

"Some kind of investigator you are."

Arkady took a hand mirror from his pocket and looked under the sink and bench for anything taped to the underside.

"Aren't you going to dust for fingerprints?" Natasha asked.

"We'll get to that later." He checked under the berths, leaving the mirror propped against the books on Zina's mattress. "What I need is someone who knows the crew. Not another officer and not someone like me."

"I'm a Party member but I'm not a slug. Go talk to Skiba or Slezko."

"I need an assistant, not an informant." Arkady opened the wardrobe again. "There are only so many places to hide anything in a cabin like this."

"Hide what?"

He felt Natasha tensing beside him. He thought he'd sensed her doing it before. She seemed to tilt as he opened her drawer a second time. It was the swimsuit, of course, a green-and-blue bikini that wouldn't get past her knee. It was the suit Zina had worn with the sunglasses on deck that warm day.

The moral code on a ship was like the code of prison. The worst crime—more heinous than murder—was theft. On the other hand, it was only natural to divide up the possessions of someone dead. Either way, though, having the swimsuit and concealing it could cost Natasha her sacred Party card.

"I bet your cabin's the same as mine," Arkady said. "Everybody's always lending and borrowing from everyone else? Sometimes it's difficult to know whose is whose? I'm glad we found this."

"It was for my niece."

"I understand."

Arkady laid the bikini on the bed. In the mirror he watched Natasha's eyes remain on the wardrobe. He did feel shameless about the mirror, but he didn't have the time or means for an ethical, scientific investigation. Returning to Natasha's side, he again perused the clothes rack. As a kind of generalization it could be said that adult Russian women went through a metamorphosis that provided them with a Rubenesque bulk against northern winters. Zina had been Georgian, a Southerner. The only one of her three cabin mates who could have worn any of her clothes was little Dynka, and the only piece of apparel with the sort of dash that seemed like Zina was Dynka's red quilted Chinese jacket. In most foreign ports there were shabby stores that specialized in the cheap goods that Soviet mariners and fishermen could afford. Often the shops were in poor neighborhoods far from the dock, and groups of Soviets could be seen walking miles to save the cab fare. A prime souvenir was such a red jacket with golden Oriental dragons and snap pockets. The trouble was that this was Dynka's first voyage and they hadn't made any port calls yet. With a little thought he wouldn't have had to use the mirror at all. Now he felt even more ashamed.

As Arkady removed the jacket from its hanger Natasha's eyes grew like those of a girl watching her first magician. "And this," he said. "Zina lent this to Dynka before the dance?"

"Yes." More firmly she added, "Dynka would never steal anything. Zina was always borrowing money and never paying it back, but Dynka would never steal."

"That's what I said."

"Zina never wore it. She was always fussing with it, but she never wore it on board. She said she was saving it for Vladivostok." The words poured out of her with relief. There were no more glances at the wardrobe.

"Fussing?"

"Sewing it. Mending it."

The jacket seemed new to Arkady. He kneaded the quilting and the padded edge of the front. The label said "Hong Kong. Rayon."

"A knife?"

"One second." Natasha found one in an apron hanging by the door.

"You should carry your knife at all times," Arkady reminded her. "Be ready for emergencies."

He felt the quilting at the back and sleeves, then squeezed the edge at the neck and bottom hem. When he slit the hem at the center, a stone the size of a candy lozenge dropped into the palm of his hand. As he pinched the hem, more stones dropped until the hollow of his palm was filled with the red, light purple and dark blue of polished but uncut rubies, amethysts and sapphires. They didn't look like high-quality gems.

He poured the stones into a pocket of the Chinese jacket and snapped it shut, then pulled the rubber gloves off his hands.

"They could have come from Korea, the Philippines or India. No place we've been, so Zina got them from another ship. Let's just be happy that Dynka didn't try to wear this jacket past the Border Guard."

"Poor Dynka," Natasha muttered as she considered the prospect of her friend being arrested for smuggling. "How would Zina get the stones through?"

"She'd swallow them, sew the jacket and wear it down the gang-plank just as she said. Then she'd collect the stones later."

Natasha was disgusted. "I knew Zina was brazen. I knew she was a Georgian. But this . . ."

Arkady struck while the Chaika was still awed by his elementary reasoning and good luck. "See, I didn't know she was 'brazen.' I don't know anything about the crew. That's why I need you, Natasha."

"You and me?"

"We've worked on the same factory line for six months. You're methodical and you have nerve. I trust you, just as you can trust me."

She glanced at the jacket and swimsuit. "Or else?"

"No. I'll report I found them under her mattress. The third mate and I should have found them before."

Natasha pushed a damp curl away from her eyes. "I'm not the sort who squeals."

She had nice eyes, as black as Stalin's but nice. Striking, in fact, with the blue running suit.

"You wouldn't be informing; you'd be asking questions. You'd be telling me what other people say."

"I'm not sure."

"The captain wants to know what happened to Zina before we reach Dutch Harbor. The first mate says we shouldn't have a port call at all."

"That bastard! All Volovoi does is run the movie projector. We've cleaned fish for four months."

"You only have one more shift in the factory. Skip it. You'll be working with me."

Natasha studied Arkady as if really seeing him for the first time. "No anti-Soviet agitation?"

"Everything according to Leninist norms," he assured her.

There was one final hesitation. "You really want me?"

12 Arkady enjoyed the view from the crane operator's cabin: the top decks covered with nets and planks, the yellow gantries framing the fog, the gulls seesawing in the wind. Looking forward, around the gantries of the forward house was a spider's nest of wire antennas strung to catch low radio frequencies. An array of whip dipoles cast in the breeze for shorter frequencies. Two interlocked circles were a radio directional finder, and star-shaped antennas picked up passing satellites. Despite all appearances, the *Polar Star* was not alone.

"Bukovsky is happy about my selection?" Natasha asked.

"He will be." Arkady was pleased because the book from Susan was by Mandelstam, a wonderful poet, urban, dark and probably not Natasha's cup of socialist tea. Even if it was only a collection of letters, Arkady had already stashed it as tenderly as gold leaf under his mattress.

"Here he comes," Natasha said.

Indeed, the third mate was fairly flying across the forward deck and around a group of mechanics lazily batting a volleyball back and forth over the net.

She added, "He doesn't look happy."

Slava disappeared below and Arkady thought he could hear the reverberations of his Reeboks as they ran up three flights. In Olympic time the third mate emerged on the top deck and pushed into the crane cabin. "What is this about another assistant?" Slava gasped. "And why are you calling me to meet you? Who's in charge?"

"You are," Arkady said. "I thought we might have some fresh air and privacy here. A rare combination."

The crane cabin was the ultimate in privacy because the windows, broken and repaired with washers and pins like crockery, sloped in and forced intimacy whenever more than one person was inside. Still, the view could not be beat.

Natasha said, "Comrade Renko thinks I can be helpful."

"I've cleared Comrade Chaikovskaya with the fleet electrical engineer and the captain," Arkady said. "But since you are in charge, I thought that you should know. Also, I have to make a list of Zina's effects."

"We did that," Slava said. "We saw her old clothes, we examined the body. Why aren't you looking for a suicide note?"

"Victims rarely leave them. It will be very suspicious if that's the first thing we find."

Natasha laughed, then cleared her throat. Since she took up half the cabin, it was hard for her to be subtle.

"And what are you going to be doing?" Slava glared at her.

"Gathering information."

Slava laughed bitterly. "Great. Stirring up more trouble. I can't believe this. My first voyage as an officer and they make me trade union representative. What do I know about workers? What do I know about murder?"

"Everyone has to learn sometime," Arkady said.

"I think Marchuk hates me."

"He's entrusted a vital mission to you."

The third mate slumped against the bulkhead, his face sunk in misery, his curly hair limp with self-pity. "And you two, a pair of deuces from the slime line. Renko, what is this pathological need of yours to lift every rock? I know Volovoi will write the final report on this; it's always a Volovoi who writes the final— Look out!"

The wall below the crane cabin resounded as the volleyball bounced off. It fell back down to the deck and rolled by the mechanics, who glared up at the threesome in the cabin.

"See?" Slava said. "The crew has already heard all about their port call depending on this so-called investigation of ours. We'll be lucky if we don't end up with knives in our backs."

Gantries had another name, Arkady recalled: gallows. A succession of bright yellow gallows sailing through the mist.

"But you know what really gets me?" Slava asked. "The worse our situation becomes, the happier you are. What difference does it make whether there are two of us or three of us? Do you really think we're going to find out anything about Zina?"

"No," Arkady conceded. He couldn't help noticing that Natasha was starting to be affected by Slava's pessimism, so he added, "But we should take heart from Lenin."

"Lenin?" Natasha perked up. "What did Lenin say about murder?"

"Nothing. But about hesitation he said, 'First action, then see what happens.' "

. . .

WEARING RUBBER GLOVES, Arkady laid out on the operating table jeans and blouses with foreign labels. Paybook. Dictionary. Snapshot of a boy amid grapes. Postcard of a Greek actress with raccoon eyes. The intimate hardware of rollers and brushes still coiled with bleached hair. Sanyo cassette player with headphones and six assorted Western tapes. Bikini for a single sunny day. Spiral notebook. Jewelry box containing fake pearls, playing cards and pink ten-ruble notes. An embroidered Chinese jacket with a pocketful of gems.

The paybook: Patiashvili, Z. P. Born Tbilisi, Georgian Soviet Socialist Republic. Vocational school training in food industries. Three years working galleys of the Black Sea Fleet out of Odessa. One month in Irkutsk. Two months working in a dining car on the Baikal–Amur main line. Eighteen months at the Golden Horn Restaurant in Vladivostok. The *Polar Star* was her first Pacific voyage.

Arkady lit a Belomor and drew in the raw fumes. This was his first time alone with Zina—not the cold corpse but the inanimate odds and ends that held whatever soul was left. Somehow smoking made it more social.

Odessa always had been too rich and worldly. They didn't settle for smuggling semiprecious stones there; they brought in bars of Indian gold for the locals and bags of Afghan hash for trucking north to Moscow. Odessa should have been a natural habitat for a girl like Zina.

Irkutsk? Rabid Young Communists volunteered to lay railroad ties and fry sausages in Siberia, not a girl like Zina. So something had happened in Odessa.

He broke the wad of pink ten-ruble notes. A thousand rubles, a lot to take to sea.

Vladivostok. Waiting on table at the Golden Horn was a clever move. Fishermen drank by the bottle to make up for their relatively dry months at sea, and they regarded their hard-won Arctic bonuses as onerous burdens to be shared with the first warm woman they met. She must have done well.

Slut. Smuggler. Depending on politics or prejudice, it was easy to write off Zina as either a corrupted materialist or a typical Georgian. Except that usually it was Georgian men, not Georgian women, who were adept privateers. Somehow from the start Zina was different.

He fanned the playing cards. They were a collection, not a deck. A variety of cut-down Soviet cards, corners cracked, with bright-colored peasant girls on one side, the design of a star and sheaves of wheat on the other. Swedish cards with nudes. A British Queen Elizabeth on her Silver Jubilee. All of them the queen of hearts.

Arkady hadn't heard the Rolling Stones for a long time. He slipped the cassette into the tape deck and pushed "Play." From the speaker came a commotion like the sound of Jagger being dropped from a height onto a set of drums and then being pummeled by guitars; some things never changed. Fast forward. Stones in the middle of the tape. Fast forward. Stones at the end. He turned the tape over and listened to the other side.

He tore a strip of electrocardiograph paper from a roll and sketched an outline of the ship, marking the cafeteria where the dance was held, Zina's cabin and every possible route between the two. He added the position of each crew member on watch and the transport cage on the trawl deck.

Out with the Stones, in with The Police. "Her precious tapes," Natasha had said. "She always used her headphones. She never shared them."

Fast forward. With a following sea the ship seemed to be gathering speed, as if plunging downhill and blind through the snow. He couldn't see it, but he could feel it.

Why did Zina ship on the *Polar Star*? The money? She could have made more off sailors in the Golden Horn. Foreign goods? Fishermen could bring her whatever she wanted. Travel? To the Aleutians?

Out with The Police, in with Dire Straits.

He sketched the stern deck and the well to the ramp. There was room to kill her, but no place to hide her.

What had been in her pockets? Gauloises, a playing card, a condom. The three great pleasures in life? The card was a queen of hearts of a style unfamiliar to him. Fast forward. Below the *Polar Star* he drew the *Eagle*.

"Politically mature" was the label the Party applied to any young person who was not a convict, dissident or outspoken defender of Western music, which by itself was a whole arena of subversion. There were overage "hippies" who still listened to the Beatles and migrated to the Altai Mountains to meditate and drop acid. Kids tended to be "breakers," who danced to rap, or "metallisty," who saturated themselves in heavy-metal music and leather gear. In spite of her taste in music, in spite of her absences from the galley, in spite of her casual sleeping around, Zina was still, according to as conservative an arbiter as Volovoi, an "honest toiler and politically mature."

Which only made sense given the first mate's task of watching foreign provocateurs. Fast forward.

Slut, smuggler, informer. A neat and simple total. A sliding of beads on an abacus; answer as addition. A girl from Georgia. Education limited to ladling soup. Expanded to smuggling in Odessa. Sleeping around in Vladivostok. Informing at sea. An abysmal life begun and ended in ignorance, without morals, soul or a single reflective thought. At least it seemed that way.

Arkady noticed that on the Van Halen cassette the recording-proof tab had been punched. He put the tape into the player and heard a woman with a Georgian accent say, "Sing to me, just sing." It was Zina's voice; Arkady recognized it from the cafeteria. There was a microphone built into the corner of her player.

A man accompanied by a guitar answered:

"You can cut my throat,
You can cut my wrists,
But don't cut my guitar strings.
Let them tramp me in the mud,
Let them push me under water,
Only leave my silver strings alone."

As Arkady listened he found spoons in a desk drawer and looked for iodine crystals. Not finding crystals, he searched for iodine pills. There was a padlocked metal cabinet for radiation medicine—in other words, for war. He broke the lock by twisting a screwdriver through the shank, but there was nothing inside except two bottles of scotch and a booklet on the effective distribution of iodine and Vitamin E in case of nuclear explosions. He found the iodine in an open cabinet.

"Sing another," Zina said. "A thieves' song."

The man on the tape laughed and whispered, "That's the only kind I know."

Arkady couldn't put a name to the man's voice, but he did know the song. It wasn't Western at all, not rock or rap; it was by a Moscow actor named Vysotsky who had become famous underground throughout the Soviet Union by writing, in the most traditional Russian style, the plaintive and bitter songs of criminals and convicts, and by singing them accompanied by a seven-stringed Russian guitar, the most easily strummed instrument on earth. Magnatizdat, a tape version of samizdat, spread every song, and then

Vysotsky had sealed his fame by drinking himself, while still young, into a fatal heart attack. The Soviet radio offered such mindless pap—"I love life, I love it over and over again"—that you'd think people would caulk their ears; yet the truth was that no other country was so dependent on or vulnerable to music. After seventy years of socialism, thieves' songs had become the counter-anthem of the Soviet Union.

The singer on the tape wasn't Vysotsky, but he wasn't bad:

> *"The wolf hunt is on, the hunt is on!*
> *For gray prowlers, old ones and cubs;*
> *The beaters shout, the dogs run themselves until they drop,*
> *There's blood on the snow and the red limits of flags.*
> *But our jaws are strong and our legs are swift,*
> *So why, pack leader, answer us,*
> *Do we always run towards the shooters,*
> *And never try to run beyond the flags?"*

At the end of the tape Zina said, "I know that's the only kind you know. That's the kind I like." Arkady liked the fact that it was the kind she liked. But the next tape was completely different. Suddenly Zina was speaking in a low, weary voice. "Modigliani painted Akhmatova sixteen times. That's the way to know a man, to have him paint you. By the tenth time you must start to know how he really sees you.

"But I attract the wrong men. Not painters. They hold me as if I were a tube of paint they have to empty in one squeeze. But they're not painters."

Zina's voice could sound honeyed or as tired as death, sometimes all in one sentence as if she were casually playing an instrument. "There is a man on the slime line who looks interesting. Paler than a fish. Deep eyes, as if he were sleepwalking. He hasn't noticed me at all. It would be interesting to wake him up.

"But I don't need another man. One thinks he tells me what to do. A second thinks he tells me what to do. A third thinks he tells me what to do. A fourth thinks he tells me what to do. Only I know what I'm going to do." There was a pause; then, "They only see me, they can't hear me think. They have never heard me think."

What would they do if they could hear you? Arkady wondered.

"He'd kill me if he could hear me think," Zina said. "He says wolves mate for life. I think he'd kill me and then he'd kill himself."

On the fifth tape the tab had been removed and then taped over. The cassette began with a sibilant rustling of cloth and an occasional muffled thud. Then a man said, "Zina." It was a younger voice, not the singer.

"What kind of place is this?"

"Zinushka."

"What if they catch us?"

"The chief's asleep. I say who comes and goes here. Stay still."

"Take your time. You're like a boy. How did you get all this down here?"

"That's not for you to know."

"That's a television?"

"Pull them down."

"Gently."

"Please."

"I'm not going to get completely undressed."

"It's warm. Twenty-one degrees Celsius, forty percent humidity. It's the most comfortable place on the ship."

"How do you have a place like this? My bed is so cold."

"I'd climb into it anytime, Zinushka, but this is more private."

"Why is there a cot here? You sleep here?"

"We put in long hours."

"Looking at television. That's work?"

"Mental work. Forget about that. Come on, Zinushka, help me."

"You're sure you shouldn't be doing important mental work right now?"

"Not while we're taking a net."

"A net! When I met you at the Golden Horn you were a handsome lieutenant. Now look at you, at the bottom of a fishhold. How do you know we're taking a net?"

"You talk too much and kiss too little."

"How do you like that?"

"That's better."

"And that?"

"That's much better."

"And this?"

"Zinushka."

Evidently the microphone was voice-activated and she'd had no chance to turn it off. The recorder was probably in the pocket of her fisherman's jacket and either under her or hanging beside the cot. Arkady had two cigarettes left. On his match a flame bobbed toward his fingers.

HE WAS FIVE years old. It was summer south of Moscow, and in the warm nights everyone slept on the porch with doors and windows open. There was no electricity in the cottage. Luna moths flew in and danced above the lamps, and he always expected the insects to flare up like burning paper. Some of his father's friends, other officers, had come by for a buffet. The social pattern set by Stalin was of dinners starting at midnight and ending in a drunken stupor, and Arkady's father, one of the Leader of Humanity's favorite generals, followed this style, though while others got drunk he only got more angry. Then he would wind up the gramophone and always play the same record. The band was the Moldavian State Jazz Orchestra, an ensemble that had followed General Renko's troops on the Second Ukrainian Front, performing in their greatcoats in each town square the day after it had been liberated from the Germans. The tune was "Chattanooga Choo-Choo."

The other officers hadn't brought their wives, so the general had them dance with his. They were pleased; none of their wives was as slim and tall and beautiful. "Katerina, get in the spirit!" the general would order. From the porch, the young Arkady felt the floor shake under the shuffling of heavy boots. He didn't hear his mother's feet at all; it was as if they were spinning her through the air.

When the guests had left was always the worst. Then his father and mother would go to their bed behind a screen at the far end of the porch. First the two sets of whispers, one soft and pleading, one through the teeth of a rage that made the heart shrink. The whole house swayed like a seesaw.

One morning Arkady had a breakfast of raisin cakes and tea outside under the birches. His mother came out still in her night-shift, a gown of silk and lace his father had found in Berlin. She had a shawl over her shoulders against the morning cool. Her hair was black, loose, long.

Did he hear anything during the night? she asked. No, he promised, nothing.

As she turned back toward the house a branch reached out and plucked off the shawl. On her arms were the blue bruise marks of individual fingers. She lightly picked the shawl off the ground, replaced it on her shoulders and tied it tight by its end tassels. Anyway, she added, it was over. Her eyes were so serene that he almost believed her.

He could hear it now. "Chattanooga Choo-Choo."

"SERIOUSLY, ZINA, THE CHIEF would have my head and yours if he found out about this. You can't tell anyone."

"About what? *This*?"

"Stop it, Zina, I'm trying to be serious."

"About your little room here?"

"Yes."

"Who would care? It's like a little boys' club in the bottom of the ship."

"Be serious."

Each tape was thirty minutes long. As the last narrow band of black unreeled there was no way for Zina to turn the recorder off. Her companion would hear the *click* as the tape stopped.

"One moment it's all 'Zinka, I love you'; the next it's 'Zina, be serious.' You're a confused man."

"This is secret."

"On the *Polar Star*? You want to spy on fish? On our Americans? They're dumber than the fish."

"That's what you think!"

"Is that your hand?"

"Keep your eye on Susan."

"Why?"

"That's all I'm saying. I'm not trying to impress you; I'm trying to help you. We should help each other. It's a long voyage. I'd go crazy without someone like you, Zinka."

"Ah, we've stopped being serious."

"Where are you going? We still have time."

"You do. I don't. My shift is on and that bitch Lidia is looking for any reason to get me in trouble."

"A little minute?"

There was a rasp of canvas over the microphone, the sigh of a cot as a body stood up.

"You go back to your mental work. I have some soup to stir."

"Shit! At least wait until I look through the hole before you go."

"Do you have any idea how silly you look right now?"

"Okay, the way is clear. Go."

"Thank you."

"Zinka, tell no one."

"No one."

"Zinka, tomorrow?"

A door shut reluctantly. *Click.*

The other side of the tape started as a blank. Fast forward. It was all blank.

Arkady studied the spiral notebook. On the first page was pasted a map of the Pacific. Zina had added eyes and lips so that Alaska leaned like a bearded man toward a shy and feminine Siberia. The Aleutians reached out to Russia like an arm.

The last cassette started as Duran Duran. Fast forward.

On the second page was a photo of the *Eagle* anchored in a bay surrounded by snowy mountains. On the third page the *Eagle* wallowed in choppy water.

"Making a baidarka," the tape said in English. "It's like a kayak. You know what a kayak is? Well, this is longer, leaner, with a square stern. The old ones were made with skin and ivory, even with ivory joints so it just flowed through the waves. When Bering came with the first Russian boats, he couldn't believe how fast the baidarkas were. The best baidarkas have always come from Unalaska. You understand a word of this?"

"I know what a kayak is," Zina answered in slow and careful English.

"Well, I'll show you a baidarka and you'll see for yourself. I'll paddle it around the *Polar Star.*"

"I should have a camera when you do."

"I wish we could do more than that. What I'd like to do is show you the world. Go all over—California, Mexico, Hawaii. There are so many great places. That would be a dream."

"When I listen to him," Zina said on the second side, "I hear a first boyfriend. Men are like malicious children, but he is like a first boyfriend, the sweet one. Maybe he is a merman, a child of the sea. In a rough sea, on a big boat, I hold on to the rail. Down below, on his small deck, he stands with perfect balance, riding the waves. I listen to his innocent voice over and over again. It would be a dream, he says."

The next dozen pages were photos of the same man with straight dark hair. Dark eyes with heavy lids. Broad cheekbones around a fine nose and mouth. The American. The Aleut with a Russian name. Mike. Mikhail. The pictures, all taken from above and at a distance, showed him on the deck of the *Eagle* working the crane, posing on the bow, mending a net, waving to the photographer.

Arkady smoked the last intoxicating cigarette. He remembered Zina on the autopsy table in this same room, her sodden flesh and bleached hair. The body was as far removed from life as a shell on a beach. This voice, though—this was Zina, someone no one on the ship had known. It was as if she had walked in the door, sat across the desk in the shadow just outside the lamp's veil of light, lit her own phantom cigarette and, having finally found an understanding ear, confided all.

Naturally Arkady would have preferred to have the technical lab back in Moscow throwing an exciting array of solvents and reagents or mortar-sized German microscopes and gas chromatographs into the fight. He used what he could. In front of the spiral notebook he laid out spoons, pills and the card of fingerprints Vainu had taken from the body. He crushed the pills between the spoons, wrapped his sleeve around the handle of the spoon that held the pulverized iodine, struck a match and held it to the spoon's bowl. He moved both close to the notebook so that the fumes from the heated iodine would flow up the page opposite the map. The hot-iodine method was supposed to employ iodine crystals over an alcohol burner in a glass box. He reminded himself that in the spirit of the New Way of Thinking announced by the last Party Congress all good Soviets were willing to bend theory to practical application.

Iodine fumes reacted quickly to the oils of perspiration in a latent print. First a ghostly outline appeared of a whole left hand, sepia brown, like an antique photograph. Palm, heel, thumb and four fingers spread out, as they would have been while she held the book flat to paste in a picture. Then the details: whorls, deltas, ridges, radial loops. He concentrated on the first finger and compared it with the card. A double loop, like yin and yang. An island at the loop's right delta. A cut at the left delta. Card and page were the same; this was Zina's book and the imprint of her hand as if she were reaching out to him. There were two other prints, male by the size of them, rough, hurried marks.

As the match burned down, the hand began to fade, and in a minute it had disappeared. He repacked all the effects neatly. He'd found Zina. Now to find the lieutenant who called her Zinushka.

13 Belowdecks everything was built around fishholds. Noah's Ark must have had a fishhold. When he called Peter "a fisher of men," Christ must have appreciated the virtues of a tight fishhold. If cosmonauts ever sail on solar winds and collect specimens of galactic life, they will need a fishhold of sorts.

Yet for ten months the *Polar Star* had sailed with a forward fishhold that was inoperative. Various conjectures were offered to explain why the hold was out of commission: pipes kept cracking; there was an electrical short in the heat pump; the plastic insulation seeped some kind of poison. Whatever, the result was that off-loading ships had to make more frequent rendezvous to take the fish crammed into the *Polar Star*'s other two holds. Another result was that the area around the unused hold had been abandoned to stacks of barrel staves and steel plates. As the walkway became more crowded the crew tended to take a longer but faster route on deck.

A line of bulbs lit the way between the bulkhead and the hold. Access to it was a watertight door with a ramp to carry carts of frozen fish over the coaming. The wheel on the door was chained with an impressively large padlock. On one side of the door was a heat pump, its hood open to display a convincing tangle of unattached wires. On the other was an oilcan of tall capstan shafts. The bottom of the can stirred with rats. The ship hadn't been fumigated since Arkady came on board. It was interesting that rats ate bread, cheese, paint, plastic pipes, wiring, mattresses and clothes—everything, in fact, but frozen fish.

There seemed to be two Zinas. There was Zina as the public slut; then there was this private woman who dwelt within a world of hidden photographs and secret tapes. One tape could only be called dangerous. The amorous lieutenant had boasted of the fishhold's bedroom temperature and 40 percent humidity. Arkady had heard someone bother to mention a humidity ratio only once before: in the computer room back in militia headquarters on Petrovka Street in Moscow.

All well and good. Arkady had no argument with naval intelligence. Every Soviet fisherman on the Pacific coast knew that American submarines constantly violated his country's waters. On dark nights periscopes would pop out of the Tatar Strait. The enemy even followed Soviet warships right into Vladivostok harbor. What he couldn't understand was how a listening station in a fishhold would be able to hear anything. An echo sounder only told you what was directly below, and no submarine would venture under a trawler. As Arkady understood it, passive sonar like hydrophones could detect sound waves at a distance, but an old factory ship like the *Polar Star* had plating that was substandard—so thin that, pounding like a drum, it bowed in and out with each wave. It had been welded with the wrong beading, riveted with burned and undersized rivets, seamed with cement that wept, shored with timbers that creaked like bones. All of which made the ship more human, in a way, and even more trustworthy in the sense that a patched-up veteran, for all his complaints, was more to be trusted than a handsome recruit. Still, the *Polar Star* marched through the water like a brass band; its own noise would smother the whisper of any submarine.

Arkady had no interest in espionage. In the army, sitting for hours in a radio shack on the roof of the Adler Hotel in Berlin, he used to hum—Presley, Prokofiev, anything. The others asked why he didn't want to take a turn on the binoculars, to study the American shack on the roof of the Sheraton in West Berlin. Perhaps he lacked imagination. He needed to see another human to get interested. The fact was that in spite of Zina's tape, from the outside the fishhold looked like a fishhold.

The lieutenant had mentioned looking through a hole to Zina. There was no peephole that Arkady could see. The door had an ambient, clammy touch, nothing cozy about it. He pondered the shafts in the oilcan, and after a moment's indecision selected one. It was like lifting a hundred-pound crowbar; once he had it to his shoulders he wouldn't be able to casually brush off any rat that came with it. Sweat came just at the thought. But no rodent appeared, and when he inserted the shaft into the hasp of the padlock and gave it a twist, the lock popped open like a spring: another black mark for State Quality Control. The wheel lock itself wouldn't give until he got a foot against the pump. With grudging, metallic cries, it turned and he pushed the door open.

The interior of the hold rose through three decks of the *Polar Star*, a shaft of dark air lit by a dim bulb at Arkady's level. Ordinarily each level of a hold had its own deck, open in the middle to raise fish from below. This single precipitous drop was odd, as if there was no intention of using the hold at all. A watertight hatch covered the main deck overhead, sealing in a stale smell of fish and brine. The sides were covered with spaced wooden planks over the grid of pipes that usually circulated coolant. A ladder ran from the hatch down to the bottom deck two levels below. He swung onto the rungs and closed the door behind him.

As Arkady descended his eyes adjusted. Once in a while he caught sight of rats climbing the pipes away from him. Rats never tried to enter an operating cold store, a sign of intelligence. It occurred to him that a flashlight would have been a sign of intelligence on his part. There were so many rats that the sound of their movement was like a wind in the trees.

There should have been decks, block and tackle, crates covered in hoarfrost. The packing of a cold store was a maritime art. Cases of frozen fish not only had to be stacked but separated by planks to allow torpid air colder than merely freezing to circulate. Here there was nothing. At each level he descended was a door, a light socket and a thermostat. Each level was darker, and when he stepped off the last rung onto the wider bottom deck of the hold he was almost blind, though he felt the pupils of his eyes expand to their rims. This is a pit, he thought, the center of the earth.

He lit a match. The deck was more planking over a grid of pipes above a cement base. He saw orange peels, a piece of planking, empty paint cans and a blanket; someone had been using the hold to sniff fumes. There were comblike bones that explained what had happened to the ship's cat. What he did not see was a lieutenant of naval intelligence, a cot, a television or a computer terminal. Beneath the base was a double hull with tanks for fuel and water, enough space to smuggle contraband, maybe, but hardly to hide an entire furnished room. He inserted the broken board between wall planks. No secret door swung open. When subtlety didn't succeed he swung the board against the planks. Through the booming echoes came high-pitched protests from the gallery of rats overhead, but no officers of naval intelligence emerged.

Climbing back up the ladder, Arkady felt like a man returning to the surface of the water, as if he were holding his breath and swimming up to the bulb. Zina's tape made no sense anymore. Perhaps he'd misunderstood the conversation. Perhaps he could find some vodka in Vainu's office. A little vodka in a bright room would be nice. Back at the bulb, he pulled the door open and swung himself through to the deck. By now the barrel staves and heat pump had a homey, welcoming appearance. He slipped the broken padlock onto the wheel; Gury, the *biznessman,* would help him find another.

As Arkady started toward the factory the light over the coffer-dam went out, then the one over the heat pump. A figure stepped out of the dark and hit him in the stomach. While he bent and gagged a ball of wet rags was stuffed in his mouth. Another rag was tied tightly over his mouth. A sack was pulled over his head and shoulders, all the way down to his feet. Something like a belt was pulled tight over the sack and around his arms and chest. He re-acted the right way, breathing deeply and flexing his arms, and at once choked because the rags in his mouth had been soaked in gasoline. The cloths had pressed his tongue back into the soft pal-ate, and he was close to swallowing his tongue. So he blew out, trying to clear his tongue, and as he did so the belt was pulled tighter like a cinch.

He was carried—by three men, he thought. There would also be one man up ahead to clear the way or stall anyone coming, and possibly another man following to do the same. They were strong; they toted him as easily as a broomstick. He tried not to choke on the gasoline fumes. On long voyages, seamen got together to share fumes and get a little dizzy. A coil of acrid vapor teased its way down his throat.

They could have just thrown him down the fishhold; his body wouldn't have been found for days. So perhaps being hit, gagged and sacked was a good sign. He'd never been kidnapped before, not in all his years with the prosecutor's office, and he wasn't sure of the nuances of being beaten and seized, but it was clear they didn't want to kill him right away. Probably they were crew members irate about the possibility of losing their port call. Even if they kept him in the sack, he might recognize a voice if they whispered.

It was a short promenade. They stopped and a door wheel turned. Arkady was unaware of the men making any rights or lefts; had they returned to the fishhold? The only watertight entrances at this level were to the holds. The door opened with the clap of splitting ice. A furnace emits a fiery blast; a cold store, with a temperature of minus 40 degrees centigrade, emits a more languid, frozen draft, but even within his sack Arkady could feel it, and he began kicking and twisting. Too late. They threw him in.

The impact of landing snapped the belt. Arkady rose, but before he could pull off the sack he heard the door shut and the wheel lock turn. He found himself standing on a wooden case. When he untied his gag and unwound the rags from his mouth, the first breath burned the lungs. It was a joke; it had to be a joke. White, almost liquid steam seeped from the planking and rolled down the walls of the fishhold; within the planking he could see the cooling grid, the pipes cased in skeletal ice. Each of his feet stood in a separate pool of milky vapor. As he watched, the hairs on the back of his hands stood and turned white with frost. As it left his lips, his breath crystallized, glittered and snowed.

He stopped himself as he reached for the wheel of the door, because bare skin would adhere to the metal. He covered the wheel with the sack and then put his weight into it, but it wouldn't budge.

The men outside must be holding it shut, and there was no chance he was going to overpower three or more of them. He shouted. Around the cold store were ten centimeters of fiberglass wool insulation; even the inside of the door was padded. No one was going to hear him unless he walked right by. For the last week, fish from the flash freezers had been stowed in the aft hold to balance the ship's trim. If this was the midship hold, there was no reason for anyone to hear. Overhead and out of reach was an insulated, watertight hatch. No one was going to hear him through that, either. Two cases below was the false deck and access to a lower level and another door. There was no way he could think of to lift two cases, each weighing a quarter of a ton. On one case was a rumpled tarp stiff with ice. The stamp on the cases said, "Frozen Sole—Product of USSR." Not a joke, but there was something comical about it.

Veterans of the north knew the stages of exposure. He was shivering; shivering was good. The body could actually maintain its temperature for a while by shaking to death. Still, he lost a degree every three minutes. When he lost two degrees he would stop shivering and his heart would start slowing and shutting off the flow to skin and limbs to maintain core heat; that was the cause of frostbite. When he lost eleven degrees his heart would stop. Coma came midway. He had fifteen minutes.

There was another problem. He had the classic first signs of poisoning he'd seen in sailors who had imbibed vapors: blinking, dizziness, intoxication. Sometimes they howled like hyenas; sometimes they danced off the walls. He couldn't help laughing. He'd gone to sea to die in this ice? That was funny.

His arms jerked spasmodically as if a maniac were bending his bones. He'd worked in this kind of cold before—granted in quilted coveralls, felt boots and fur-lined hood. Frost made its own white fur over his shoes and cuffs. He swayed, trying to keep his balance and not step into the narrow space between the cases; he was sure if he slipped he wouldn't get his leg out again.

At his chest level was a perforated plate that covered the thermostat. He couldn't get the plate loose with his fingernails; it was another good example of the sort of emergency for which a fisherman should carry his knife at all times.

He jiggled the matches out of his pocket and dropped them. Since he was trying not to tip over, he picked up the book painfully with the sort of graceful bow a French dandy might execute as he swept up a lady's handkerchief from the ground. Again he dropped the matches and this time went down on all fours to retrieve them. The flame was a tiny yellow ball overwhelmed by the cold, but a precious dew formed on the thermostat plate as it warmed. The problem was that his hands were jerking so badly he couldn't keep the flame to the plate for more than a second at a time.

There was a certain cunning to killing him this way. Freezing him and, he assumed in thinking it through, moving his body one place to thaw, then taking it to another site to be found. It was now well established that Vainu was not the most expert of pathologists, and the most obvious evidence he would find would be signs of sniffing fumes, the tragic vice of petroleum-age man. With official approval, they'd slap his body back in the same cold store until they reached Valdivostok. He saw himself riding a block of ice back home.

These were excellent matches, wood tipped with phosphorus and wax especially for the foul weather that seamen encountered. On the box cover was the design of a ship's prow splitting a curling wave. On the ship's stack was a hammer and sickle. His whole body was shaking so badly that it was hard to even aim the flame at the plate. For no reason he suddenly remembered an even better case of suicide than the ones he'd cited to Marchuk and Volovoi. A sailor had hanged himself in Sakhalin. There was no investigation because the boy had secured the rope to the hammer and sickle on the smokestack. He was put in paper slippers and buried in a day because no one even wanted to ask questions.

At least he'd stopped shivering and could hold the match steady. Looking down, he saw that both his pants legs were covered in fleecy frost. A big fish like a halibut could be frozen rock-solid to the core in an hour and a half. The box squirted from his fingers. They were turning from white to blue and moved so slowly. When he knelt to pick up the box, his hands fumbled like a pair of hooks. As he struck another match the box dropped, bounced off the crate and fell between it and the wall. He heard it ticking off crates on its way down to the deck.

With all his concentration he brought the cool little glow again to the thermostat, marveling at how the dim heat spread visibly like dew upon the metal plate. It was his last match now. He held on while flames burned on his fingernails. There was still some gasoline left on his hands from taking the rags from his mouth. Secondary flames lit like candles on his palms. They didn't hurt. He stared because they were so remarkable, like a religious experience. Slowly his eyes moved to the rags. Was this how slowly fish thought? he wondered. As the match flame sank to a nub, he thrust it and his hands into the rags, which burst into a beautiful flowerlike fire. He kicked the burning rags closer to the planks beneath the plate.

The rags unfolded in hues of violet and blue that turned to rich black smoke. Around the fire, on the planks and on the crate, grew a ring of wet glaze, of ice melting, refreezing and melting again. Arkady sat at the edge of the flames, arms out to cup the heat. He remembered a picnic he'd once had in Siberia of frozen fish whittled into shavings, frozen reindeer sliced into strips, frozen berries formed into patties and Siberian vodka that had to be constantly turned, first this side and then that, toward the fire. The year before, an Intourist guide had taken a group of Americans into the taiga and laid out an even more splendid lunch but had forgotten to turn the bottle. After many toasts with warm tea to international friendship, mutual respect and closer understanding, the guide poured glasses of nearly frozen, almost congealed vodka and showed his guests how to drink it in one go. "Like this," he said. He tipped the glass, drank it and fell over dead. What the guide had forgotten was that Siberian vodka was nearly two hundred proof, almost pure alcohol, and would still flow at a temperature that would freeze the gullet and stop the heart like a sword. Just the shock was enough to kill him. It was sad, of course, but it was also hilarious. Imagine the poor Americans sitting around their campfire, looking at their Russian guide and saying, "This *is* a Siberian picnic."

It was an unequal battle between a mere rag fire and the glacial cave of a fishhold. The flames subsided to eyes of light, to a nest of wrestling glowworms, then to a last black gasp of smoke above a shell of ashes. The crate and planks were smudged, not even charred.

Gasoline was a bit like Siberian vodka. Moment by moment he felt more Siberian. Finally, sailing off the coast of America, he had achieved that blissful distinction. Frost advanced up his pants and sleeves again. He blinked to keep his eyes from icing shut and watched his breath explode into crystals that rose up, then eddied down in fine drifts. How else would a Siberian breathe? Wouldn't he have made a good guide? But who for?

Time to lie down. He tugged the tarp off the crate to use as a blanket. It slid off stiff with ice, revealing Zina Patiashvili in a clear plastic bag. Clear but covered within by wonderful patterns of crystalline frost like a coat of diamonds. She was white as snow and her hair was dusted with ice. One eye was open, as if she wondered who was joining her.

Arkady curled up in the corner farthest from Zina. He didn't believe the wheel really was turning until the door cracked open. Natasha Chaikovskaya filled the doorway, eyes and mouth agape at the remains of the fire and at Zina and then at him. She rushed into the hold and lifted Arkady, gently at first so his skin on the ice wouldn't tear, then like a weight lifter starting a press. He'd never been lifted by a woman before. Probably Natasha wouldn't take that as a compliment.

"I made a fire," he told her. Apparently it had actually worked. He had dropped the temperature at the thermostat and finely tuned monitors had sounded. "You heard an alarm?"

"No, no. There aren't any alarms. I was just walking by when I heard you inside."

"Shouting?" Arkady didn't remember.

"Laughing." Natasha shifted, getting a better grip to angle him out the door. She was frightened, but also disgusted, as anyone is with a drunk. "You were laughing your head off."

14 While Izrail Izrailevich gently massaged Arkady's fingers and Natasha ministered to his bare toes, their patient responded with hypothermic spasms. The factory manager looked with scorn and disappointment at Arkady's eyes, which were a brilliant pulpy red from gasoline fumes.

"Other men I expect to be drunkards or sniffers, not you," Izrail said. "It serves you right to wander into a fishhold and almost freeze to death."

The trouble was, feeling returned as a sensation of skin burning, of capillaries bursting and waves of shakes. Fortunately none of his cabin mates was home when Izrail and Natasha laid him out on the lower bunk. Buried in blankets when touch itself was torture, he felt as if he were wrapped in broken glass.

Fish scales glittered on the factory manager's sweater and beard; he had run from the slime line to help carry Arkady to the cabin. "Do we lock up all the gasoline, paint and thinner as if they were expensive foreign liquors?"

"Men are weak," Natasha reminded him.

Izrail gave his opinion. "A Russian is like a sponge; you don't know his true shape until he's soaked. I thought Renko was different."

Natasha blew her warm breath on each naked toe and then tenderly kneaded it, which felt like having red-hot needles stuck under the nails. "Maybe we should take him to Dr. Vainu," she suggested.

"No," Arkady managed to say. His lips were rubbery, another effect of the fumes.

Izrail said, "I let you off the line because you were going to perform some sort of investigation for the captain, not so you could go crazy."

"Zina was in the hold," Natasha told Izrail.

"Where else are we supposed to keep her? Did you say he started a fire?" Izrail was concerned. "Did he thaw any fish?"

"He didn't even thaw himself." Natasha attended to a toe that remained blue.

"If he damaged any fish—"

She said, "Fuck your fish, excuse me."

"All I'm saying is, if you want to kill yourself, don't do it in my fishhold," Izrail told Arkady. Vigorously he rubbed Arkady's other hand.

A thought occurred to Natasha and spread on her brow like a furrow on virgin snow. "Does this have to do with Zina?"

"No," Arkady lied. Go away, he wanted to say, but he couldn't slip more than one word at a time through a chattering jaw.

"You were looking for something? Someone?" she asked.

"No." How could he explain about a lieutenant who might or might not exist? He had to stop shaking and rest his traumatized nerve endings a little; then he could start asking questions again.

"Maybe I should get the captain," Izrail said.

"No." Arkady started to rise.

"Okay, okay, that seems to be the only word you remember," Izrail said. "But if this was an attack, I'm not surprised. I don't share their attitude, but I can tell you that the crew is unhappy about this rumor that because of you Dutch Harbor is off limits. Why do you think they come on this stinking barrel of shit? Fish? You want to jeopardize all their months of work to find out what happened to Zina? This ship is full of silly women. Why do you care so much?"

AS HIS SHAKES receded Arkady burrowed into a comatose state. He saw that he had been changed from his frozen clothes into dry ones, a task that must have been performed by Izrail and Natasha, an act about as erotic as dressing a fish. He had a vision of himself on a conveyor belt moving toward the saw.

Obidin and Kolya came into the cabin, fumbled quietly for one thing or another and left without paying any attention to Arkady or the fact that he was in the wrong bunk. It was etiquette on a ship to let other men sleep.

When he surfaced again, Natasha was sitting on the opposite bunk. As soon as she saw he was awake, she said, "Izrail Izrailevich wondered why you care about Zina. Did you know her?"

He felt comically weak, as if his body had been beaten and badly sunburned while he dozed. At least he could talk now, in a rush of words between the shakes. "You know I didn't."

"I thought I knew you didn't, but I wondered why you care." She looked at him, then away. "I suppose it helps to care, in a professional manner."

"Yes, it's a professional trick. Natasha, what are you doing here?"

"I thought they might come back."

"Who?"

She crossed her arms as if to say she wouldn't play games. "Your eyes are red slits."

"Thank you."

"Are all investigations like this?"

HE BURPED IN his sleep and the entire cabin reeked like a garageful of gasoline fumes. When Natasha opened the porthole to clear the air, a song mournfully crept in from outside:

> "Where are you, wolves, ancient wild beasts?
> Where are you, yellow-eyed tribe of mine?"

Another thieves' song, again about wolves, rendered in the most sentimental fashion by a hardheaded fisherman. Or, just as likely, by a mechanic in greasy coveralls, or even an officer as prim as Slava Bukovsky, because in private everyone sang thieves' songs. But especially workers sang. They strummed their guitars, always primitively tuned D-G-B-d-g-b-d.

> "I'm surrounded by hounds, feeble relatives,
> We used to think of as our prey."

Westerners thought of Russians as slow-moving bears. Russian men saw themselves as wolves, lean and wild, barely restrained. The song was another one by Vysotsky. To his countrymen much of Vysotsky's appeal lay in his vices, his drinking and wild driving. The story was that he'd had a "torpedo" implanted in his ass. A "torpedo" was a capsule of Antabuse that would make Vysotsky sick whenever he had alcohol. Yet still he drank!

"I smile at the enemy with my wolfish grin,
Baring my teeth's rotten stumps,
And blood-specked snow melts
On the sign: 'We're not wolves anymore!' "

As Natasha closed the porthole, Arkady came fully awake. "Open it," he said.

"It's cold."

"Open it."

Too late. The song had ended; all he could hear through the open porthole was the heavy sigh of water as it slid by below. The singer had been the same as on Zina's tape. Maybe. If he sang again, he could tell. Arkady started shaking, though, and Natasha closed the porthole tight.

AS THE CABIN door opened Arkady awoke and sat bolt upright, knife in hand. Natasha turned on the light and regarded him with worry. "Who were you expecting?"

"No one."

"Good, because in your condition you couldn't scare a dormouse." She uncurled his fingers from the knife handle. "Besides, you don't need to fight. You have a brain and you can outthink anyone else."

"Can I think myself off this ship?"

"The brain is a wonderful thing." She put the knife aside.

"I wish the brain were a ticket. How long have I been asleep?"

"One hour, maybe two. Tell me about Zina." She wiped the sweat from his brow and eased him back onto his pillow. His hand was still cramped from holding the knife, and she began massaging the fingers. "Even when you're wrong, I like to hear how you think."

"Really?"

"It's like listening to someone play the piano. Why did she come on the *Polar Star*—to smuggle those stones?"

"No, they were too cheap. Natasha, I want the knife."

"But just for herself the stones might have been enough."

"A Soviet criminal rarely operates alone. You don't find a Soviet criminal alone in the dock. There are ten, twenty of them there at a time."

"If it wasn't an accident—and not for one second am I saying that it was anything but—maybe it was a crime of passion."

"It was too clean a murder. And planned. For her blood to pool the way it did she must have been stowed for at least half a day before she went into the water. That means moving her to hide her, then moving her again to throw her overboard. We were fishing harder then; people were on deck."

Arkady stopped for breath. A therapeutic massage was not easy to distinguish from torture.

"Go on," Natasha said.

"Zina fraternized with Americans, which she could have done only with the permission of Volovoi. She informed for Volovoi. There wouldn't be any reprimand from the galley staff because they were told to let her roam, and she probably kept Olimpiada happy by feeding her chocolates and brandy. But why did Zina always go to the stern deck when the *Eagle* delivered fish? And *only* when the *Eagle* delivered fish—not any other boat? To wave to a man she might dance with one night out of every two or three months? Is Slava's band that good? Maybe the question should be asked the other way. What were the Americans looking for when they delivered fish?"

Arkady didn't mention the possibility that there was an intelligence station on the *Polar Star*. On the tape the lieutenant had invited Zina into the station when fish were coming on board. Did the station operate only between incoming nets? Was it a matter of nets or the Americans?

"Anyway," he said, "Americans, various lovers, Volovoi—a lot of people used Zina or were used by her. We don't have to be brilliant; we just have to see the pattern."

He remembered her voice on the tape: "He thinks he tells me what to do. A second thinks he tells me what to do." Arkady counted the he's. Four significant men, one of whom she knew was a killer.

"What people?" Natasha asked.

"An officer, for one. He could be compromised."

"Which?" She was alarmed.

He shook his head. His hands were pink, as if they'd come out of boiling water. They felt that way.

"What do you think?" he asked her.

"About First Mate Volovoi, I don't agree. About the Americans, they must answer for themselves. About Olimpiada and the chocolates, you may be right."

WHEN HE AWOKE again Natasha had returned with a giant samovar, a silver urn with a spigot for a nose and cheeks shining with good-natured heat. While they took tea, each drinking from a steaming glass, she sawed a round loaf of bread.

"My mother drove trucks. Remember how we built trucks then, when the factories fulfilled their plan according to gross weight? Each truck weighed twice as much as trucks anywhere else in the world. Try to steer one of those in the snow.

"The route was across a frozen lake. My mother was a shock-worker of Communist Labor; she was always in the first truck. She was popular. She had a photo album, and she showed me a picture of my father. He drove too. Maybe you wouldn't think it, but he looked surprisingly intellectual. He read anything, could argue with anybody. Wore glasses. His hair was light, but actually he looked a little like you. She said he was too romantic was his problem; he was always in trouble with the bosses. They were going to be married, but in the spring, in the thaw, his truck went through the ice.

"I grew up around dams. I always loved them. There's nothing on earth as beautiful and beneficial to mankind. Other students were interested in special institutes, but I got out of school as fast as I could and up on a scaffold with a mixer. A woman can mix cement as well as any man. The most exciting time is working at night under lights powered by the last dam you helped to build. Then you know you're someone. A lot of the men, though, are drifters because they make so much money. That's their dilemma. They make so much money that they have to drink it up or spend it going to the Black Sea or on the first girl like Zina. They don't make homes. It's not their fault. It's the site directors who are shameless, who offer anything to get their project finished first. Naturally the men say, 'Why stay in one place when you can sell yourself for more money somewhere else?' That's Siberia today."

THE NET SLID up the stern ramp into a circle of sodium lamps, rose on boom cables and swayed as if alive, seawater weeping from chafing hair and flowing over the deck in shallow waves. Forty tons or fifty tons of fish, maybe more! Half a night's quota in one tow. Crabs danced over wooden planks. Taut cables moaned from the weight as the trawlmaster flashed his scalpel and on the run sliced the belly of the bag from one end to the other. The whole net seemed to split open at once, flooding the deck up to the gunwale rail and boat-deck stairs in a rich, live, twisting mass of slime eels, milky blue in the light. . . .

Arkady awoke with a start, heaved off his blankets, pulled on his boots, found his knife and fought the door to get out of his cabin. It wasn't just claustrophobia but a sense of being buried alive; leaving the bed didn't help if he was still below steel decks.

Outside, the lights were smothered in an underlit night fog no worse than the smoke of a fire. He'd slept through the entire afternoon. It was only a day and a half since he was introduced to Zina Patiashvili's corpse, and he was feeling rather that way himself. And in less than twelve hours he was supposed to uncover some startling revelation that would resolve to everyone's satisfaction the mysterious death of Zina Patiashvili and allow the ship's crew to go into port. He stumbled against the rail, inching away from the trawl deck toward the bow. The catcher boats had disappeared, so there were neither stars nor other lights to lead the eye away from the dull glow of the *Polar Star*'s lamps.

The deck was empty, suggesting that it was dinnertime. Everyone was falling into a single schedule now that the factory ship had stopped taking fish and was steaming to port. He hooked an elbow over the rail for support. This was not going to be the usual brisk perambulation around the deck. It would be a stroll with ample time to think about drowning, about fear that wrapped like a wet shroud around his heart. He marked his progress by the machine shop. The bridge house was a goal far in the distance, dissolving in the mist.

"The poetry lover."

Arkady turned toward Susan's voice. He hadn't heard her approach.

"Taking a break?" she asked.

"I like the sea air."

"You look it." She leaned on the rail next to him, pushed her hood back and lit a cigarette, then held the match up to his eyes. "Christ!"

"Still pink?"

"What happened to you?"

His muscles were still cramping, going from numb to hot to numb again. As casually as possible he gripped the handrail. He would have walked away if he could have trusted his legs to make a dignified exit. "I was just trying to See in New Ways. It was a strain."

"Oh, I get it," Susan said as she glanced around the deck. "This is the scene of the accident; that's why you're here. It's still an accident, isn't it?"

"Of the unexplained sort," Arkady granted.

"I'm sure you'll come up with the right explanation. They wouldn't have picked you unless they knew you would."

"Thank you for your confidence." He felt his knees sag treacherously. If she disdained him so much, why didn't she leave?

"I wondered," she said.

"Now you're wondering?"

"Well, you questioned the fishermen on the catcher boats. Weren't they all off the *Polar Star* before anything happened to Zina?"

"It appears so." She wants to know, he thought.

"You're almost for real, aren't you? I hear Slava is running everywhere looking for a suicide note, but you stagger around as if you actually want to know what happened. Why?"

"That's a mystery to us all." Although his mouth tasted like a gas tank, he felt the urge for a smoke. He patted his pockets.

"Here." Susan put her cigarette between his lips and then pulled back from the rail. At first he thought that it was from him; then he saw that the *Eagle* had come alongside out of the fog. As the trawler edged nearer, he could make out the form of George Morgan on the darkened bridge. In the lights of the deck, two fishermen in slickers were tying torn mesh and garbage to dump at sea. Arkady recognized Coletti's sullen glare and Mike's open grin. The Aleut's picture was the same as in Zina's photo: innocent and without shading.

The deck around the men was wet and littered with flatfish and crabs, and though the trawler was pitching more than the *Polar Star*, the Americans seemed rooted where they stood in forward-leaning, lock-kneed stances. Between the two boats was a shifting screen of birds that materialized out of habit. Perhaps a hundred birds hovered on outstretched wings: black-capped terns with swallowtails, masked petrels and milk-white gulls seesawing overhead. They looked as if someone had emptied a basket of papers off the ship and the pages had flown and kept pace. The slightest dip of one bird created a ripple of adjustments, so that the flock shimmered and squawked.

Mike waved again, and it took Arkady a moment to realize that a third person had joined him and Susan at the rail. Natasha spoke into Arkady's ear. "I found someone who wants to talk to you. I went to your cabin and you were gone. Why did you get out of bed?"

As he started to describe the benefits of fresh air Arkady began to cough, which set off a chill that doubled him over. There seemed to be frozen bits inside him, which, as they melted, spread currents of debilitating cold.

With one eye on Susan, Natasha went on talking as if they were taking tea at the rail. "Now it's time for my lecture. Afterwards, we'll go meet my friend."

"Your lecture?" Susan made it clear she was trying not to smile.

"I am the ship's representative of the All-Union Knowledge Society."

"How could I have forgotten?" Susan asked.

It would have been less cruel for her to laugh out loud, because Natasha only had the sense that she was being mocked, the way a woman whose slip shows only at the rear is vaguely aware that she

is the subject of humor without knowing why. Out of sheer nervous-
ness she took the cigarette from Arkady's mouth. "In your condition
the last thing you need is this." She turned to Susan. "This is the
most disgusting habit of Soviet men. Smoking is man's most unnatural act."

She snapped the cigarette at the birds. A gull tipped its wings,
caught it, then dropped it. A petrel slid forward, caught the tum-
bling cigarette, ate half and rejected the rest. The filter landed in
the water, where it was studied by a tern.

"They must be Russian birds," Susan said.

An idea struck Arkady while he coughed. Susan was wearing a
fishing jacket and Natasha was wearing a fishing jacket; it was about
all that the two of them had in common. Where was Zina's fishing
jacket? He hadn't thought about it before because no one took a
jacket to a dance, and during intermissions when people went on
deck they could stand a few minutes of sub-Arctic air. Soviet women
especially wouldn't bother with any jacket that might encumber an
embrace. In their stolid frames were souls so romantic that they
lifted like doves on the slightest breeze.

As Arkady finished his last rasp and straightened up, Susan lit
another cigarette and kept it for herself.

"Renko, are you the investigator or the victim?"

"He knows what he's doing," Natasha said.

"That's why he looks like the shark's lunch?"

"He has a system."

What is it? Arkady wondered.

Morgan's voice came from the radio in Susan's pocket: "Ask
Renko what happened to Zina. We all want to know."

On the deck of the *Eagle*, Mike waved again and gestured to
Natasha as if inviting her down for a visit. Her cheeks reddened, but
she gave the fisherman her shoulder to indicate that fraternization

was an item strictly in her past. "We have to go to the lecture," she said firmly.

"They want to know what happened to Zina," Susan said.

Unsure of his legs, Arkady tested them with a casual shuffle.

"What do you want me to tell them?" Susan asked.

"Tell them . . ." Arkady stalled. "Tell them they still know more than I do."

The inspirational lecture on scientific atheism given in the cafeteria by Natasha Chaikovskaya, corresponding member of the All-Union Knowledge Society, was well attended by the off-duty crew because Volovoi stood at the back, his raw face scanning not only the presence but the enthusiasm of the audience. Skiba and Slezko were in the last row of benches, giving the Invalid an extra four eyes. The day before a port call was always the most anxious, when it could be canceled for any number of reasons: time did not permit; money transfers had not been completed; the political climate wasn't right.

The anticipation of Dutch Harbor had gripped everyone. It was not only the first land in more than four months; it was the point of the entire voyage, those blessed few hours with foreign currency in an American store. If a man wanted to catch fish or a woman wanted simply to clean them, they could trawl the Soviet coast rather than spend half a year in the Bering Sea. The women were wearing freshly laundered blouses with flower prints coming into bloom, their hair spiked with pins. The men were more divided. The ship had gathered speed for the long run to the Aleutians, incidentally firing its boilers for showers, and half the men were scraped clean and sporting the knit shirts of men at ease. The other half, skeptics, still wore a crust of beard and dirt.

"Religion," Natasha read from a pamphlet, "teaches that labor is not a freely given contribution to the state, but an obligation imposed by God. A citizen who holds this view is unlikely to economize on materials."

Obidin spoke up from the middle row of tables. "Did God economize when He made heaven and earth? When He made the elephant? Maybe God doesn't care about economizing on materials."

"Materials of the state?" Natasha was outraged.

"Why are you trying to subvert her?" Volovoi had sidled up to Arkady. "She's a simple worker. Why drag her into this dirty work of yours?"

Natasha had dragged Arkady to the lecture. Not that he could have resisted; he was standing because he was afraid if he sat he wouldn't be able to rise. His arms were crossed over feverish tremors.

People shouted at Obidin, "Shut up! Listen and learn!"

"Two days ago half the ship didn't know who you were," Volovoi went on. "Now you're the most hated man on board. You've outsmarted yourself. First you say Zina Patiashvili was murdered. Now you can't let these people, your own shipmates, have their port call without saying she wasn't."

"Someone's been spreading the story that it's up to me," Arkady said.

"Rumor always has a thousand tongues," Volovoi observed. He looked at his watch. "Well, you have eleven hours before your great decision: Dutch Harbor or no Dutch Harbor? Will you admit to error or put yourself above your entire ship? Others might say you will compromise. I don't know you in particular, but I know your type. I think you'd keep this whole crew anchored off Dutch Harbor and not let a single man on shore rather than confess that you're wrong."

"Science has shown," Natasha was saying, "that the flame of a church candle induces a hypnotic effect. In comparison, science is the electrification of the mind."

"After all," Volovoi asked, "what do you have to lose? You have no Party card, no family."

"You have a family?" Arkady was interested. He saw the Invalid's apartment in a Vladivostok high rise: a spiritless wife, a litter of little Volovois in red Pioneer scarves gathered at the glow of a television set.

"My wife is second secretary of the City Soviet."

Erase the spiritless wife, Arkady thought. Enter a match for Volovoi, the hammer and anvil from whom the next generation of Communists would be pounded out.

"And a boy," Volovoi added. "We have a stake in the future. You don't. You're the bad apple, and I don't want you infecting Comrade Chaikovskaya."

Natasha progressed from the electrification of the mind to the evolution of the flesh, from *Homo erectus* to Socialist Man. Her refresher course in atheism had been ordered up because of the old Orthodox church in Dutch Harbor, pitting science against ghosts.

"What makes you think I can infect her?"

"You're glib," Volovoi said. "You had an important father, went to special schools in Moscow, had everything the rest of us didn't. You may impress her—you may even impress the captain—but I see you for what you are. You're anti-Soviet. I can smell it on you."

"There's no difference," Natasha was saying, "between belief in a 'supreme intelligence' and the faddish interest in aliens from other galaxies."

Someone protested. "Statistically there has to be life in other galaxies."

"But they're not visiting us," Natasha said.

"How would we know?" It was Kolya; who else? "If they have achieved intergalactic flight, then they certainly have the ability to disguise themselves."

No one annoyed Natasha more than Kolya Mer. It didn't matter that they worked side by side on the factory line. Even the fact that she'd come to his aid when he sawed off his finger seemed to have made her more his enemy than his friend.

"Why would they come to visit us?" she demanded.

"To see scientific socialism in action," Kolya said, and drew some approving murmurs around the cafeteria, though to Arkady the idea was the equivalent of walking around the world to see an anthill.

"I notice you haven't visited me yet," Volovoi said. "You haven't cared to inform me of your progress."

"I think you're sufficiently informed," Arkady said, thinking of Slava. "Anyway, I'd only ask to see your file on Zina Patiashvili, and you wouldn't show it to me."

"That's right."

"But I can guess what it says: 'Reliable toiler, politically mature, cooperative.' She didn't do her work, she was a giddy girl who slept with everyone, and you must have known all this, which means she was an informer—not a Skiba or a Slezko, but an informer. Either that or she was sleeping with you."

"Have you read the Bible?" Obidin asked.

"It is not necessary to read the Bible. That's like saying you have to have a disease to be a doctor," Natasha said. "I know the structure of the Bible, the books, the authors."

"The miracles?" Obidin asked.

"Shame! Shame!" The audience around Obidin rose to denounce him. "She's the expert! There are no miracles!"

Obidin shouted in return, "A woman is murdered, lies on the ocean floor and returns to the very ship where she was killed and you say there are no miracles!"

More people stood, infuriated, shaking their fists. "Liar! Fanatic! That's the kind of talk that will keep us out of Dutch Harbor!"

Slezko rose and pointed at Arkady; it was like looking into the barrel of a sniper. "There's the provocateur who's keeping us out of Dutch Harbor!"

"Miracles are real!" Obidin shouted.

"It will be a miracle if you get off this ship alive," Volovoi told Arkady. "I hope you do. I look forward to your return to Vladivostok and your walk down the ladder to the Border Guard."

LIDIA TARATUTA POURED Arkady a glass of fortified wine. A *bufetch-itsa,* the woman in charge of the officers' mess, rated a two-berth cabin, but she seemed to have this one all to herself. Red was clearly her favorite color. A maroon Oriental rug of intricate design was pinned like a huge butterfly to the bulkhead. Red candles sat in brass holders. Red felt boots stood by the bunk. The cabin had the aura of an actress who had become a touch too voluptuous with age. There was an overfullness to Lidia's hennaed hair and to her lips. An amber pendant hung in the warmth of a blouse that was half unbuttoned. The blouse expressed recklessness and generosity, as if it had unbuttoned itself. In the Soviet fishing fleet a captain did not choose—he was given his ship, his officers, his crew—with one exception: his *bufetchitsa.* Marchuk had used his option well.

"You want to know what officers Zina was sleeping with? You

think she was a slut? Who are you to judge? It's good you have Natasha to work with because I see that you don't understand women. Maybe in Moscow you dealt with nothing but whores. I don't know what Moscow is like. I only went once as a union representative. On the other hand, you don't know what life on a ship is like. So which is worse, that you don't understand women or that you don't know this ship? Well, you may never want to be on another ship. More wine?"

Since Natasha was standing in front of the door in case Arkady tried to escape, he accepted the glass. He was the first to admit he didn't understand women. He certainly didn't know why he had been brought here.

"He can't leave the ship," Natasha said. "He's an investigator, but he's in some kind of trouble."

"A man with a past?" Lidia asked.

"A spell of political unreliability," Arkady said.

"That sounds like a head cold, not a past. Men have no past. Men move on from place to place like leaves. Women have pasts. I have a past." Lidia's eyes flicked to a framed wardrobe picture of two little girls sitting like a pair of cockatoos on a single chair, wearing white dresses, with white bows in their hair. "That's a past."

"Where's the father?" Arkady asked, to be polite.

"What a good question. I haven't seen him since he kicked me, six months pregnant, down the stairs. So now I have two children in a day-care center in Magadan. There's a nurse and an aide for thirty kids. The nurse is an old woman with consumption; the aide is a thief. That's who's raising my angels. All winter the girls have coughs. Well, those women are paid ninety rubles a month, they're forced to steal, so I send extra every time I'm in port just to make sure my girls don't starve or die of pneumonia before I see them again. Thank God I can go to sea and make money for them, but if I ever saw their father again I'd cut off his prick and use it for bait. Let him dive for it, right, Natasha?"

A giggle rose like a bubble from the Chaika, who caught herself and stared soberly again at Arkady. "Be careful, he's a mind reader."

"Believe me," Arkady said, "I can't remember when I've understood a situation less."

Lidia smoothed her lap. "Well, what do you know about your crew mates? For example, what do you know about Dynka?"

He was taken by surprise again. "A nice—" he began.

"Married at fourteen to an alcoholic," Lidia said. "A cab driver. But if her Ahmed goes to an alcohol clinic, as soon as he registers he loses his driver's license for five years, so she has to get him Antabuse on the black market. She's not going to make that kind of money in Kazakhstan, so she has to work out here. The old lady in Natasha's cabin, Elizavyeta Fedorovna Malzeva, sits and sews all day. Her husband used to be a purser on the Black Sea Fleet until his pecker wandered up a passenger, who charged him with rape. He's been in a camp for fifteen years. She gets by with her daily dose of Valeryanka. Watch her in Dutch Harbor; she'll try to get some Valium. Same thing. So, Comrade Renko, you're surrounded by frailty, by women with pasts, by sluts."

"I never said that." Actually, it had been Natasha who had first called Zina a slut, but Arkady thought it probably wouldn't help to protest on grounds of consistency. Anyway, he wasn't fighting the situation anymore. He'd always suspected that while men might make the best police, women would make the best investigators. Or at least a different kind of investigator, picking up different sorts of clues in a different manner, searching sideways or backwards, as compared with the straightforward, pig-in-a-rut method of men.

"He's more interested in Americans," Natasha said. "We left Susan smirking up on deck."

"He's sick?" Lidia asked.

Arkady was so used to trembling that he no longer noticed it.

Natasha said, "He doesn't take proper care of himself. He goes places he shouldn't go and asks questions he shouldn't ask. He wants to know about Zina and officers."

"Which officers?" Lidia asked.

Defensively Arkady said, "I only mentioned to Natasha the question of officers sleeping with crew."

"That's a broad brush." Lidia refilled his glass. "On a ship we live together for six months at a time. We spend more time here than we do with our families. Of course relationships develop because we're human. We're normal. But if you start putting things like that in your report, you can ruin people. A name gets written down in a report and never gets erased. From the outside it can look bad. An investigation about Zina suddenly becomes an investigation of the whole ship, of philanderers and sluts. See what I mean?"

"I'm starting to," Arkady said.

"He is." Natasha nodded.

"You mean *your* name," Arkady said.

"Everyone knows what the *bufetchitsa* does," Lidia said. "I direct the officers' mess, I clean the captain's cabin, I keep the captain happy. It's customary and I knew it the day I applied. The Ministry of Fisheries knows it. His wife knows it. If I didn't take care of him on board ship, he'd rape her at the door, so she knows. Other senior officers have other arrangements. You see, it makes us human, but it doesn't make us criminal. If you put even a hint of that in your report, it forces the Ministry and all those wives back on shore, who would much rather kiss their husbands' pictures than come sail on the *Polar Star,* to demand our heads."

Lidia took a ladylike sip of wine. "Zina was different. It wasn't that she was a tramp, necessarily; it was just that sleeping with a man

meant nothing to her. There was no affection in her. I don't think
that she ever slept with anyone more than once; that was the way
she was. Of course, once I was aware of what was going on, I took
steps to remove the temptation."

"Such as?" Arkady asked.

"She was working in the officers' mess. I moved her to the crews'."

"That sounds more like spreading temptation."

"Anyway," Lidia said, "she became obsessed with Americans, so
you see that there's no need to even mention our good Soviet men
at all."

Arkady asked, "Obsessed with Americans or with one American
in particular?"

"See how sharp he is!" Natasha said proudly.

Lidia answered evasively, "With Zina, who could say?"

Arkady tapped his head as if it might stir an idea. He had received
the message Lidia was sending—don't name the ship's officers in any
report—but he didn't understand her reason for sending it.

"He's thinking," Natasha said.

He seemed to have dislodged a new headache. "Did you go to the
dance?"

"No," Lidia said. "That night I had to prepare a buffet in the
officers' wardroom for the Americans. Sausages, pickles, delicacies
they don't have on their own boat. We were too busy to dance."

" 'We' "?

"Captain Marchuk, Captain Morgan, Captain Thorwald and myself. The American crews went on to the dance, but the captains
were going over charts and I was serving and cleaning."

"All evening?"

"Yes. No, I did take one break, a cigarette on deck."

Arkady remembered that at 11:15 Skiba saw her walking forward
at midships. "Someone saw you."

Lidia put a lot of work into hesitating, batting her eyelashes, even delivering a sigh from the bosom. "It doesn't mean anything, I'm sure. I saw Susan at the stern rail."

"What was she wearing?"

The question took Lidia by surprise. "Well, a white shirt and jeans, I suppose."

"And Zina, what was she wearing?"

"A white shirt, I think, and blue pants."

"So you saw Zina too."

Lidia blinked, like a person walking off an unexpected step. "Yes."

"Where?"

"The stern deck."

"Did they see you?"

"I don't think so."

"You were close enough at night to know what two different women were wearing and neither of them saw you?"

"I have excellent eyes. The captain often says he wishes he had an officer with eyes as good as mine."

"How many times have you sailed with Captain Marchuk?"

Lidia's excellent eyes brightened like a pair of candles. "This is my third voyage with Viktor Sergeievich. He became a leading captain of the fleet on our first trip. On the second, he overfulfilled the quota by forty percent and was named a Hero of the Soviet Union. He was also named a delegate of the Party Congress. They know him in Moscow; they have big plans for him."

Arkady finished the wine and got to his feet, which felt not excellent or even good but serviceable. His brain was finally working. "Thank you."

"I can get us some smoked fish," Lidia offered. "We can have more wine, a little something to eat."

He tried a tentative step or two. It looked as if he'd make the door.

"Arkady," Natasha said, "be careful where you throw the first stone."

THE BRIDGE WAS dark except for the green glow of radar and loran screens, of VHF and side-band radio displays, of the glass ball of the gyrocompass, of the lunar face of the engine telegraph. The twin figures of left- and right-rudder controls stood at either side of the deck. Marchuk was at the starboard window; a helmsman was at the wheel. Arkady realized how much the *Polar Star* ran itself. With meditative clicks the automatic pilot hewed to a course already set. The luminous numbers that seemed to hang in the air were largely information after the fact, dispensed by the factory ship as it plowed into the night.

"Renko." Marchuk noticed Arkady. "Bukovsky is looking for you. He says you haven't reported."

"I'll get to him. Comrade Captain, can we talk?"

Arkady could feel the helmsman stiffen. Factory workers did not come onto the bridge uninvited.

"Leave us," Marchuk told the man.

"But—" Regulations were that two officers or an officer and a helmsman had to be on the bridge at all times.

"It's all right," Marchuk assured him. "I'll take over. Seaman Renko will scan the heavens and seas and keep us safe from harm."

After closing the door behind the helmsman, Marchuk checked the navigation room to be sure no one was there, then took his position behind the wheel. The bulkhead behind him held a fire-control panel and a closed box of radiation meters; these were in case of war. Whenever the autopilot clicked, adjusting to a swell, the wheel made a barely perceptible turn.

"Did you sleep with Zina Patiashvili?" Arkady asked.

For a while Marchuk said nothing. Oversized wipers spread snow on the windshield, and through the streaks Arkady could see anchor winches riding the bow deck and little arabesques that were counterclockwise coils of rope on either side of the winches. Beyond, in the wide beam of the searchlight, was a seemingly solid wall of snow. It was cold on the bridge, and his shakes started again. The radar monitor in the windshield counter was a Foruna—Japanese. Its ever-moving beam, a little fragmented by the snow, showed two blips keeping pace—the *Eagle* and the *Merry Jane,* he assumed. At least the echo sounder was Soviet, a Kalmar; it said the *Polar Star* was making fifteen knots over the bottom, which meant that the old ship had the aid of a following sea. According to the terms of the joint fishery, Soviet ships weren't allowed to use their echo sounders in American waters, but no captain would sail blindly while Americans were off the bridge.

"This is the way you run an investigation?" Marchuk asked. "With wild accusations?"

"With the time limit I have, yes."

"I hear you took Chaikovskaya as your assistant. A strange choice."

"No stranger than your picking me."

"There are cigarettes on the counter. Light one for me."

Marlboros. As Arkady lit one for him the captain stared across the flame at his face. It was an intimidation that strong men practiced to catch a flinch. "You have a fever?"

"A chill."

"Slava calls you and Natasha his 'pair of deuces.' What do you think about that?"

"Slava could use a pair of deuces."

"Natasha said something about me?"

"She introduced me to Lidia."

"Lidia told you?" Marchuk was startled.

"Not meaning to." Arkady blew out the match, then wandered back to the windshield and the lethargic rhythm of the wipers. The fog had been brooding up to this snow. If fog was thought, snow was action. "She heard I was asking about Zina and officers. She was concerned about your reputation and confided to me that you already had a lover—herself. Why? As she says, everyone, including your wife, knows that you sleep with your *bufetchitsa.* Even I knew it. She was trying to stop a line of questioning, to throw herself in front of a train for you."

"Then you're guessing."

"I *was* guessing. When?"

The wheel clicked right, left, left, held course. On the counter, the echo sounder displayed the depth: ten fathoms. Such a shallow sea.

Marchuk either cleared his throat or laughed. "In port. I was there for so long while the ship was hauled out. Generally, you know, I'm busy during repairs because the yards outfit you with such shit—inferior plates, bad welding, cracked boiler mounts. The navy gets the quality goods, so it's a full-time job to wheedle any decent brass, copper, alternators. This time it was all taken care of.

"In short, I was bored, and the wife had been in Kiev for a month. Look, this is a typical maudlin story. I took out some navy men who wanted to eat at a real sailors' restaurant. The Golden Horn. Zina was a waitress there. We all made a pass at her. After my guests were drunk enough to be put to bed, I went back. That was the one and only time. I didn't even know her last name. You can imagine my surprise when I saw her on board."

"Did she ask to sail on the *Polar Star?*"

"She asked, but a captain doesn't have that authority."

It sounded like the truth, Arkady thought. Even if Marchuk had arranged her berth, he certainly wouldn't have placed her under the eye of Lidia Taratuta. "Did you see Zina the night of the dance?"

"I was in the wardroom. I had a buffet set out for the American fishermen."

"From?"

"From the *Eagle* and the *Merry Jane.* The crews went to the dance and the captains stayed to argue over sea charts."

"Captains have different opinions?"

"Or they wouldn't be captains. Of course there are different qualifications. A Soviet captain must study six years in a maritime academy, then have two years as a coast mate, then two years as a deepwater mate to finally qualify as a deepwater captain. There are always a few—let them be nameless—who think a father in the Ministry can make them an officer, but they're rare. A Soviet captain has degrees in navigation, electronics, construction and law. If an American *buys* a boat, he becomes a captain. The point is, when we leave Dutch Harbor we're going to the ice sheet. That's good fishing, but you have to know what you're doing."

"Was Lidia with you the night of the dance?"

"The entire time."

Arkady didn't like the idea of the ice sheet. The sky was already covered with fog. Covering the sea with ice, paving the water white, would remove what little dimension was left. Also, he hated the cold. "How far is it from the wardroom to the stern?" he asked.

"About a hundred meters. You should know that by now."

"It's just that I don't understand something. Lidia says she stepped out of the wardroom here in the wheelhouse and happened to see Zina on the stern deck. But you can't see the stern deck from here, not even with her keen eyes. You have to walk there. That's two hundred meters altogether, back and forth the length of the ship, that Lidia traveled in the cold to have a cigarette and happen to see a young rival who dies that same night. Why would Lidia do that?"

"Maybe she's stupid."

"No, I think she loves you."

Marchuk was silent. The snow impacted on the windshield into wet craters, so it wasn't freezing outside. The heavy snow settled the water too, and the *Polar Star* seemed to be easing through the night.

"She followed me," Marchuk said. "I got a note under my door that Zina wanted to talk to me. 'Meet me at the stern at eleven' was all it said."

"It was from Zina?"

"I recognized the handwriting."

"So you'd received other notes."

"Yes, once or twice. Lidia caught on. Women sense these things; they just know. Lidia is more jealous than my own wife. Anyway, all that Zina wanted to know was who she was going into Dutch Harbor with. She didn't want to be stuck with any old women. I told her that Volovoi drew up the list, not me."

"In Vladivostok, the night you were with Zina, you went to her place?"

"I certainly wasn't going to take her to mine."

"Describe it."

"An apartment on Russkaya Street. Pretty nice, actually: African figures, Japanese prints, a lot of guns. She shared it with some guy who was away. I'd have turned him in for the guns, but how could I explain how I'd seen them? It wouldn't sound good at fleet head-quarters, a leading captain informing on a man whose woman he'd shared. I don't know why I'm telling you."

"Because you can deny everything later. That's why you chose me in the first place, so you can dismiss everything I discover if you don't like it. What I don't understand is why you wanted any investigation at all, knowing the stories that could come to the surface. Were you crazy, or just stupid?"

Marchuk was silent for so long that Arkady thought he might not have heard the question. In any case, the captain wasn't the first man with a sexual appetite.

When Marchuk finally spoke, his voice choked with self-disgust. "I'll tell you why. Two years ago I had a trawler in the Sea of Japan. It was night, bad weather, a Force Nine wind. I was trying to fill the quota because I'd just been named a leading captain. Anyway, I put my men on deck. A wave hit us broadside. It happens. When it's past, you count heads. We were missing one man. His boots were on deck, but he was gone. The wave took him over the side? Down the ramp? I don't know. Naturally, we stopped fishing and looked. At night, in waves like that, in water that cold, he must have died of hypothermia in a matter of minutes. Or else he took a mouthful and went right to the bottom. We never saw him. I radioed Fleet Command in Vladivostok and reported the death. They ordered me to continue searching, and also to check the ship to be sure no life vests or anything floatable was missing. We steamed back and forth for half a day searching the water, tearing the ship apart and counting vests, buoys, barrels. Only when we could declare nothing missing did Fleet Command say that we could go back to fishing. Fleet Command never said it directly, but everyone knew why; it was because Japan was only twenty nautical miles away. To the minds at Command, it was possible that this fisherman had conceived the idea of defection and had set out to cross near-freezing heavy seas in the dark. How grotesque. I had to make this dead man's friends search for him not in order to find him, not to return his body to his family, but as if he were a prisoner escaping, as if we were all prisoners. I did it, but I told myself that I would never again leave my crew to the mercy of Vladivostok. So Zina wasn't perfect? Neither am I. *You* find out what happened."

"For your crew's sake?"

"Yes."

There was something both comforting and suffocating about the snow. The radar had buttons for brightness, color, range. On the screen nothing lay ahead but the scattered green dots of wave return.

"How long to Dutch Harbor?"

"Ten hours."

"If you want to do something for your crew, give them their port call. I'm not going to learn anything in ten hours."

"You were my compromise with Volovoi. He's the first mate. You heard what he said."

"You're the captain. If you want your crew to go ashore, do it."

Marchuk fell silent again. The cigarette burned down to a coal between his lips. "Keep looking," he said finally. "Maybe you'll find something."

Arkady left by the outer bridge. From outside, Marchuk looked like a man chained to the wheel.

16 By the time Arkady reached his cabin he was shaking so hard he decided to confront the spasms and kill them. From his room he took a towel and descended one deck to a small shower room with pegs and a sign that said A GOOD CITIZEN RESPECTS THE PROPERTY OF OTHERS. A handwritten sign advised TAKE YOUR VALUABLES WITH YOU.

With his knife tucked into the back of his towel, he entered the greatest luxury on the *Polar Star,* the sauna. It had been built by the crew, and though not much larger than a stall, it was all of red cedar. A cedar box held smooth river stones heated by pipes that carried live steam from the laundry. A cedar bucket held water and a cedar ladle. A satisfactory mist already hung in the air. Two pairs of legs dangled from the upper bench, but they looked too spindly to be the legs of killers.

Whether at a palatial spa in Moscow or a cabin in Siberia, it was a Russian credo that nothing cured more ills than a sauna. Chills, arthritis, nervous and respiratory diseases, and especially hangovers were helped by the balm of steam, and since the *Polar Star*'s little sauna was in constant use, it was always hot. The pores of Arkady's skin opened wide and he felt prickly sweat on his scalp and chest. Though his hands and feet stung, they hadn't turned white, the first warning sign of frostbite. Once he'd driven the shakes out, he'd be able to think straight. As he ladled more water onto the stones they turned a glossy black and then as quickly dried to gray. The superheated mist became more dense. There was a birch lash in the corner for driving out the poisons of a bad drunk, but he had never believed in whipping himself, even under the guise of medical attention.

"You going to pick up any stuff?" a voice asked in English from the cloud. It was the American fisheries observer, Lantz. "Dust or shit, Dutch is on the route. A lot of those fishing boats make funny runs all the way to Baja, even to Colombia."

"I'll stick with beer." The other voice was the rep called Day.

"Ever try rocks? Smoke it in a pipe. Very intense. That'll unwind you fast."

"No, thanks."

"Worried? I'll get you a cocktail; it looks like a regular cigarette."

"I don't even smoke. After this, I'm going back to school. I'm not going to do crack in the Yukon. Lay off."

"What a wimp," Lantz said as Day stepped down from the mist and out the door. There was a sound of Lantz blowing his nose on his towel; then he slowly slid off the bench. He was skin and bones, like a pale, long-limbed salamander. His eyes finally took in who was sitting on the lower bench. "Well, look who's sneaking around and listening to other people. How about you, Renko? Are you going to get your American dollars and run into Dutch Harbor?"

"I don't think I'll be going in," Arkady said.

"No one will. They say you fucked it up for everyone."

"That could be."

"And I hear that even if everyone else does, you won't. So what are you, Renko, a policeman or a prisoner?"

"This is coveted employment, to work on an oceangoing ship."

"If you can make port calls, not if you're trapped on board. Poor Comrade Renko."

"It sounds like I'm missing a lot."

"It looks like you need a lot. So you're just going to be walking up and down the deck hoping someone's going to bring you back a pack of smokes. Pathetic."

"It is."

"I'll bring you back a candy bar. It'll be the fucking highlight of your trip."

The door sucked steam out as Lantz left. Arkady threw more water in on the box and collapsed on the bench again. He was scared when even an American saw how much trouble he was in.

He was also scared by how little he understood. It didn't make sense that Zina would leave the dance just to ask Marchuk who her shopping companions in Dutch Harbor would be. But then she stayed on the stern deck. According to the notes kept by Skiba and Slezko, Lidia crossed the midship deck at 11:15, at which point Zina was still alive at the stern rail. That was fourteen minutes before Ridley returned to the *Eagle* and fifty-five minutes before the trawler cast off. Zina was too smart to try defecting when an American boat was tied up to the factory ship. Vladivostok would demand and the company, half Soviet-owned, would agree that the *Eagle* and the *Merry Jane* be searched. The two conditions for a successful disappearance, from what Marchuk had said, were that the Americans be beyond conceivable swimming distance and that not a single item of lifesaving gear be missing from the *Polar Star*. If defection was impossible, what *did* Zina want?

The suggestion of a beer stuck in his throat. Sakhalin trawlers had made extra money by picking up cases of Japanese beer tied to crab pots and leaving in exchange sacks of salmon roe. He could use one of those beers, as cold as the sea, not the warm, liquid headache that Obidin brewed.

The sauna door opened, and in the thick steam the new arrival seemed to be wearing shoes. He was a large man, naked except for a towel tied at the waist, and he was not wearing shoes; his feet were dark blue, almost purple. They were tattooed in a design of florid curls, each toe standing out as a green claw. This leonine design, like a griffin, reached up his legs to his knees. He was what a scientist would call a mesomorph, muscular and nearly as deep through the chest as he was broad. Some of the older tattoos had smudged and blurred, but Arkady could make out chained buxom women climbing each thigh to the red flames that spread around the edge of the towel. The stomach was scalloped with blue clouds. On the right side of the rib cage was a bleeding wound with the name of Christ; on the left side a vulture held a heart. The man's breast was smeared with scar tissue. Administrators did that in labor camps; if a prisoner tattooed something they didn't like, they burned it off with permanganate of potash. The man's arms were green sleeves, the right covered in fading dragons, the left with the names of prisons, labor camps, transit camps: Vladimir, Tashkent, Potma, Sosnovka, Kolyma, Magadan and more, a roster of wide personal experience. The tattoos stopped at the wrists and neck; the total effect was of a man wearing a tight dark suit, or of a pale head and hands levitating. Another effect was that a person knew just what this tribesman was: an urka—in Russia a professional criminal.

It was the trawlmaster, Karp Korobetz. He smiled at Arkady broadly and said, "You look like shit."

"I know you." Arkady realized and said it at the same time.

Karp said, "It was a dozen years ago. In the hall when you started asking questions, I said to myself, 'Renko, Renko, I know that name.' "

"Article 146, armed robbery."

"You tried to hang me for murder," Karp reminded him.

Now Arkady's memory worked fine. Twelve years before, Korobetz had been a big, soft kid who worked whores twice his age out of the tough Maria's Grove section of Moscow. Usually an arrangement was maintained between pimps and the militia, especially at that time, when prostitution was not supposed to exist, but the boy took to robbing victims when their pants were down. One old man, a veteran with a chest of medals, resisted, and Karp shut him up with a hammer. His hair had been lighter and longer then, with fanciful plaits around the ears. Arkady had appeared at the trial only to testify as the senior investigator for homicide. But there was another reason he hadn't recognized Korobetz. Karp's face had changed; his hairline actually was lower than before. If prisoners tattooed something on their brow like "Slave of USSR," camps had the skin surgically removed, so that the whole scalp shifted forward.

"What did you write there?" Arkady pointed to the trawlmaster's forehead.

" 'Communists Drink the Blood of the People.' "

"All that on your forehead?" Arkady was impressed. He looked at Karp's chest. "And there?"

" 'The Party Equals Death.' They took that off with acid in Sosnovka. Then I wrote, 'The Party Is a Whore.' After they burned that off, the skin was too rough to use anymore."

"A short career. Well, Pushkin died young."

Karp brushed away a wisp of steam. His slate-blue eyes lay in a crease that ran across the bridge of his nose. He combed his damp hair with his fingers. Now his hair was full at the top and short on the sides, Soviet style, while the body had become Neanderthal. An inked Neanderthal.

"I ought to thank you," Karp said. "I learned a trade at Sosnovka."

"Don't thank me. Thank the people you robbed and beat; they're the ones who identified you."

"They taught us how to make television cabinets. Did you ever have a Melodya set? I might have made it. Of course, that was long ago, before my social rehabilitation. See how strange life is? Now I'm a seaman first class and you're a seaman second class, so I'm on top of you."

"The sea is a strange place."

"You're the last person I ever expected to meet on the *Polar Star.* What happened to the high and mighty investigator?"

"The land is a strange place."

"Everything's strange to you now. That's what happens when you lose your desk and your Party card. Tell me what you're doing for this so-called fleet electrical engineer."

"I'm doing something for the captain."

"Fuck the captain. Where do you think you are, the middle of Moscow? There are about ten officers on the *Polar Star;* the rest is crew. We have our own system; we sort things out between ourselves. Why are you asking about Zina Patiashvili?"

"She had an accident."

"I know that, I found her. If it's just an accident, why bring you in?"

"My experience. You know my experience. What do you know about Zina?"

"She was an honest toiler. The ship is poorer for her loss." Karp broke into a smile, showing gold molars. "See, I learned how to say all that shit."

Arkady stood. Their eyes were on a level, though Karp outweighed him. He said, "I was stupid not to recognize you. You're twice as stupid to tell me who you are."

Karp looked hurt. "I thought you'd be pleased to see how I'd reformed and become a model worker. I hoped we could be friends, but I see you haven't changed at all." Forgiving, he leaned closer to offer advice. "We had a guy in one camp who reminded me of you. He was political. He was an army officer who wouldn't take his tanks into Czechoslovakia against the counterrevolutionaries—something like that. I was his section leader and he couldn't follow orders; he thought he was still in charge. You know, they'd take us out on a railroad spur and we'd drop trees and load them. A timber collective. Healthy reconstructive labor at about thirty degrees below. The dangerous part is when you've got the trees on the flatbed; you don't want them rolling off. It's funny that the one guy with the education, this officer, is the one who had the accident, and he didn't even get his accident straight. What he said was he was held down on the track and somebody busted his bones with an ax handle. I mean upper arms, lower arms, hands, fingers—the works. Imagine. You've seen stiffs; the body has a lot of bones. But I was there and I didn't see anything like that. It's what happens when you make a mistake and a whole flatbed of logs rolls on you. He went crazy. He finally died of a ruptured spleen. I bet he wanted to at that point, or spend the rest of his life like a broken egg. The only reason I mention him is because you remind me of him, and because a ship way out at sea is such a dangerous place. That's what I wanted to tell you. You should be careful," Karp said as he left. "Learn how to swim."

Arkady's shakes came back twice as bad. Did he ever get so scared when he was an investigator? Maybe it was fitting that he'd come all the way from Moscow to sail with Karp Korobetz. Why hadn't he recognized him? The name wasn't that common. On the other hand, would Karp's own mother recognize him now?

The trawlmaster was the one who had thrown him into the fishhold; that was what his shakes were telling him. Three men had carried him and probably one had gone ahead and one had followed; that would be Karp and his deck team, the well-organized winners of the socialist competition.

Sweat poured off Arkady, giving him a sheen of fear. Karp was crazy; no mere case of "sluggish schizophrenia" here. Not dumb, though, so why would he draw attention to himself while Arkady had some temporary authority?

What had Karp said and what had he omitted? He hadn't mentioned the fishhold; why would he? But he hadn't mentioned Dutch Harbor, either. Everyone else was worried about the port call, but not Karp; he wanted to know about Hess. Most of all he'd wanted to spread some terror, which he'd done.

Again the sauna door opened. Arkady saw a dark foot and immediately reached behind him for his knife. As cool air from the open door lifted the mist, however, he saw that the foot was a shoe, a blue Reebok. "Slava?"

The third mate was irritably sweeping steam aside. "Renko, I've been looking everywhere for you. I found it! I found the note!"

Arkady still couldn't get Karp out of his head. "What? What are you talking about?"

"While you've been sleeping and taking saunas, I found the note from Zina Patiashvili. She wrote one." Slava's face poked through a wreath of mist. "A suicide note. It's perfect. We're going into port."

II.

eArth

17

Dutch Harbor was surrounded by a green ring of cliffs covered by thick subarctic grasses. There were no trees, nothing bigger than a bush, but as the wind moved over the grass the effect was magical, as if the hills were a wave.

The island was actually called Unalaska, and on one side of the bay there was an Aleut village by that name, a beachside line of cottages that led to a white wooden Russian Orthodox church. The town of Dutch Harbor, however, was out of Arkady's sight, past a tank farm and beyond the breakwater that protected a loading dock with slag heaps of rusting trawl doors and rotting snow, and gas pumps and rows of the half-ton cages called crab pots. Beyond lay a pier of catcher boats and one large ship that had become a dockbound cannery with a fence of pilings around its hull. Behind all this, the hills of Unalaska rose rapidly to volcanic peaks edged in black stone and snow.

It was odd, Arkady thought, how the eye became starved for color.

The clouds were broken, so that sunspots moved around the bay. Off the lower cliffs, puffins dropped like rocks to the water. Eagles lifted from the higher cliffs and soared to inspect the *Polar Star;* they were enormous birds, bear-brown with imperious white heads. It was like being at the top of the world.

The Americans had already gone ashore in the pilot boat. Soo-san was going home in a gift fishing jacket decorated with souvenir pins. On her way off the ship she'd distributed farewell kisses with the generosity of someone leaving jail. On the pilot boat as it came out had been a new head rep carrying a suitcase with one hundred thousand dollars in it, the *Polar Star*'s port-call foreign currency. The entire crew had waited while the bills were counted and re-counted in the captain's cabin.

Now, after four months' fishing, Arkady's co-workers were lined along the starboard rail and moving down the steps of the gangway to a lifeboat that would bear them and their allotted American dollars to the port they had dreamed of all this time. Not that they showed it. A Soviet seaman dressed for special occasions did not necessarily shave. He did shine his shoes, slick his hair back and wear his sports jacket even if the sleeves were too short. He also wore his most unimpressed face, not only for Volovoi's sake but for his own, so that his anticipation showed only as a wary narrowing of the eyes.

With exceptions. Under the brim of a squat peasant's cap, Obidin's gaze was fixed on the church across the water. Kolya Mer had stuffed his coat with cardboard pots; he eyed the hills like Darwin approaching the Galapagoan shore. Women wore their nicest cotton dresses under the usual layers of sweaters and rabbit-fur coats. They had their grim tourist faces too, until they looked at one another and broke into nervous giggles, then waved up at Natasha, who stood on the boat deck with Arkady.

Natasha's cheeks were almost as red as her lipstick and she wore not one but two combs, as if she would need extra ammunition ashore. "It's my first time in the United States," she told Arkady. "It doesn't seem so different from the Soviet Union. You've been before. Where?"

"New York."

"That's different."

Arkady paused. "Yes."

"Well, so you came to see me off?"

Natasha looked ready to fly from sheer excitement over the water to the waiting shops. In fact Arkady had come to see whether Karp was going ashore. So far the trawlmaster hadn't. "To thank you and see you off," he said.

"It will just be for a few hours."

"Even so."

Her voice and eyes dropped. "It was a stimulating experience for me to work with you, Arkady Kirilovich. You don't mind that I call you Arkady Kirilovich?"

"Whatever you like."

"You're not the fool I thought you were."

"Thank you."

"We came to a successful conclusion," Natasha said.

"Yes, the captain has declared the inquiry officially over. There may not even be an investigation in Vladivostok."

"It was good of Third Mate Bukovsky to find that note."

"Better than good, unbelievable," Arkady said, considering he had looked under Zina's mattress well before Slava had found her note there.

"Natasha!" As her friends moved along the rail they waved frantically at her to claim her place in line.

Natasha was ready to run, to sail, to fly, but there was a line on her brow because she had witnessed Arkady's earlier search of the bed.

"At the dance she didn't seem so down in the mouth."

"No," Arkady had to agree. Dancing and flirting were not the usual symptoms of depression.

Natasha's last question was the hardest one for her. "You really think she killed herself? She could have done something that rash?"

Arkady gave his answer thought because he knew Natasha had lived months for this one day's excursion, yet would stay loyally on board with him if he gave her any reason to. "I think it's rash to write a suicide note. I refuse to, myself." He pointed to the lifeboat. "Hurry, you're going to miss your ride."

"What can I get you?" Natasha's brow was clear again.

"A complete set of Shakespeare, a video camera, a car."

"I can't get those." She was already on the steps leading down to the deck.

"A piece of fruit will do."

Natasha elbowed her way to her friends just as they were going down the gangway. They were like children, Arkady thought, the kind of Moscow children you see stamping their feet outside school on dark December mornings, bundled up to their hard little faces until the warm door is opened and their eyes light up. He wished he were going with them.

The lifeboat looked like a surfaced submarine; it could seal up forty passengers fleeing a sinking ship and was colored that crayon hue called "international orange." For this holiday jaunt, the hatches were open so that the helmsman and passengers could stand in the fresh air. Natasha waved again before assuming a pose of resolute Soviet sobriety. They cast off, and the entire party appeared in their drab clothes on their orange boat to be headed for either a funeral or a picnic.

The *Merry Jane* was approaching to take more people ashore, and a whole new line had formed along the rail. Among those waiting was Pavel from Karp's deck team. Looking at Arkady, he drew a finger across his throat.

Land did smell, Arkady thought. Unalaska smelled like a garden and he wanted to walk on dry land and leave the scow on which he'd lived for ten months, if only for an hour.

So far, he hadn't told anyone about the attack. What could he say? He hadn't seen Karp or the other men. It would be his word against six politically reliable and socially responsible seamen first class. The only provable fact was that he had been inhaling fumes and inducing hallucinations, not to mention attempting to set fire to the fishhold.

Smoke smudged the air above where Dutch Harbor must be. How large was the town? Cleaner wisps hung from the sides of the mountains. That's what they were, mountains that rose directly from the ocean floor. He imagined soaring over them and descending into a green valley, close enough to see those precious bog orchids of Kolya Mer's, close enough to pick up earth in his hand.

The lifeboat was now traversing the water in front of the Aleut houses: a pretty picture, the orange boat putt-putting by the white church. He imagined Zina on it.

"It's ironic," Hess said as he joined Arkady.

The fleet electrical engineer was resplendent in a shiny black parka, jeans and Siberian felt boots. Arkady hadn't seen him since yesterday morning. Of course, Hess was small—maybe even small enough to move invisibly around the ship through funnels and ventilator shafts.

"What is?" Arkady asked.

"That the only member of the crew who ever could have defected, the only man whose loyalty has really been tested, is the only one not allowed off the ship."

"In irony we lead the world."

Hess smiled. His stiff hair leaned in the breeze but he stood with the wide, solid stance of a sailor as he gazed around.

"A handsome harbor. During the war the Americans had fifty thousand men here. If we'd had Dutch Harbor there'd still be that many, instead of a few natives and fishing nets. Well, the Americans can be choosy. The Pacific Ocean is an American lake. Alaska, San Francisco, Pearl Harbor, Midway, the Marshalls, Fijis, Samoa, the Marianas. They own it."

"You're going ashore?"

"To stretch my legs. It might be interesting."

Perhaps not to a fleet electrical engineer, Arkady thought, but to an officer of naval intelligence, yes, a stroll around the major port of the Aleutians might be informative.

Hess said, "Let me congratulate you on resolving the case of that poor girl."

"Your congratulations should go entirely to Slava Bukovsky; he found her note. I searched the same place and never saw it."

Arkady had examined the note once Slava had stopped flourishing his discovery. It had been written on half a lined page that appeared to have been torn from Zina's spiral notebook. The handwriting was hers; the prints were hers and Slava's.

"But it was suicide?"

"A suicide note definitely is evidence of suicide. Of course, being fatally hit on the back of the head and being stabbed after death is evidence of something else."

Hess seemed to be studying the trawler as it swung alongside the

Polar Star. Was he a line officer? Arkady wondered. Considering the slow promotions that Germans generally got, he might be no more than a captain second rank. If he stayed near Leningrad, though, close to naval headquarters, maybe taught at one of the officers' academies, he could have the title of professor. Hess looked professorial.

"The captain was relieved to hear that you agreed with Bukovsky's conclusions. You were sick in bed or he would have asked you himself. You seem better now."

The shakes had chased Arkady back to his cabin, it was true, and he *was* better now, well enough to light a Belomor and start poisoning himself again. He tossed the match away. "And you, Comrade Hess," he asked, "were you relieved?"

Hess allowed himself another smile. "It sounded too convenient for you to have anything to do with it. But you could have corrected Bukovsky and gone to the captain."

"And stopped this?" Arkady watched as a Portuguese crewman helped Madame Malzeva off the gangway onto the trawler deck. She stepped down daintily, shawl over her shoulders, as if onto a gondola. "This is the reason for their whole voyage. I'm not going to ruin their two days here. Is Volovoi ashore?"

"No, the captain is. You know the regulations: either the captain or the commissar has to be on the ship at all times. Marchuk went in on the pilot boat to make sure the merchants of Dutch Harbor are ready for our invasion. I hear they are not only ready but eager." He looked at Arkady. "Murder, then? When we're back at sea, will you start asking questions again? Officially the inquiry is over. You won't have the support of the captain; you won't even have the assistance of Bukovsky. You'll be entirely alone, one factory worker in the bottom of the ship. It sounds dangerous. Even if you knew who was responsible for the girl's death, it might be better to forget."

"I could." Arkady thought about it. "But if you were the killer and you knew that I knew, would you let me live until we returned to Vladivostok?"

Hess considered the idea. "You'd have a long voyage home."

Or short, Arkady thought.

"Come with me," Hess said.

He motioned and Arkady followed him into the aft house. He assumed they were going to some quiet spot to talk, but Hess led him directly out to the boat deck on the port side of the ship. A Jacob's ladder hung from the rail to another lifeboat already in the water. A lone helmsman waved up. Not for a fleet electrical engineer the crowded deck of a trawler.

"Ashore," Hess said. "Come with me to Dutch Harbor. Everyone else is enjoying a port call, thanks to you. You should have some reward."

"I don't have a seaman's first-class visa to go in, as you know."

"On my authority," Hess said lightly, but also as if he meant what he said.

Even thinking about going ashore had the effect of a glass of vodka. Perspective changed, bringing houses, church and mountains closer. The wind freshened on his cheek and water lapped more audibly against the hull. As Hess pulled on black calfskin gloves Arkady looked down at his own bare hands, stained canvas jacket, rough pants and rubber boots. Hess caught the self-scrutiny. "You've shaved," he reassured Arkady. "A man who's shaved is ready to go anywhere."

"What about the captain?"

"Captain Marchuk knows that initiative is the new order of the day. Also, trust in the loyalty of the masses."

Arkady took a deep breath. "Volovoi?"

"He's on the bridge watching the other direction. By the time he sees you going ashore you'll be there. You're like a lion who finds his cage door open. You hesitate."

Arkady held the rail as if for balance. "It's not that simple."

"There is one little thing," Hess said, and brought from his parka a sheet of paper that he spread on the bulkhead. The page bore a two-sentence acknowledgment that defection from a Soviet ship was a state crime for which an offender's family would suffer in his absence. "Everyone signs it. You have a family? A wife?"

"Divorced."

"She'll have to do." When Arkady signed, Hess said, "One other thing. No knives, not in port."

Arkady took his knife from his jacket pocket. Up until yesterday it had lived in the closet. Now he and his knife felt inseparable.

"I'll keep it for you," Hess promised. "I'm afraid no foreign currency has been allotted for this unanticipated port call of yours. You don't have American dollars?"

"No, nor francs nor yen. There hasn't been the need."

Hess neatly folded the paper and slipped it back inside his parka. Like a host who enjoys impromptu parties most, he said, "Then you must be my guest. Come, Comrade Renko, I will show you the famous Dutch Harbor."

THEY STOOD IN the open hatches and breathed the sharp fumes of water that was silky with oil. Arkady hadn't even been so near the surface of the water in ten months, let alone on land. As the lifeboat drew across the harbor he saw how the Aleut houses edged between mountain and bay, and how proudly they all seemed to march behind their white church with its onion dome. There were lights in the windows and human forms in the shadows; the very existence of shadows seemed miraculous after a year of staring into fog. And the smell was overwhelming: the briny tang of the beach's gray sand and, powerful as gravity, the sweet breath of green grass and mosses. There was even a graveyard with Orthodox crosses, as if people could be buried without sinking directly to the ocean floor.

The lifeboat was built with a miniature bridge, but the helmsman, a blond-haired boy in a heavy sweater, used the outside wheel. Behind him, from a short pole, a Soviet ensign fluttered like a red hankie.

"Built for the war and then allowed to fall apart," Hess said and pointed to a house on the crest of a cliff. Half the house had fallen in, exposing stairs and rails like the inner workings of a seashell. Looking around, Arkady saw half a dozen more army-gray structures on other hills. "That was the war when we were allies," Hess added for the sake of the young helmsman.

"As you say, chief," the helmsman said.

Protected by encircling land, the inner bay was calm. A mirrored, inverted ring of undulating green surrounded the lifeboat.

"That was before you were born," Arkady said to the boy. He recognized him now, a radio technician named Nikolai. He looked like a recruiting poster—corn-silk hair, cornflower-blue eyes, and the big shoulders and indolent smile of an athlete.

"That was my grandfather's war," Nikolai said.

Immediately Arkady felt ancient, but he pressed the conversation. "Where did he serve?"

"Murmansk. He went to America and back ten times," Nikolai said. "Two boats were sunk under him."

"But it's hard work, too, what you do."

Nikolai shrugged. "Mental work."

By now Arkady had recognized the voice of Zina's lieutenant. He could see the young man confidently navigating among the waitresses at the Golden Horn, the stars on his shoulder boards glittering, his cap askew. It occurred to Arkady, not for the first time, that he hadn't been attacked until he'd gone searching for Hess's assistant.

"Such a handsome harbor." Hess's eyes wandered from the tank farm to the mile-long concrete dock to the radio tower on the hill, as if he were reviewing the charms of an uncharted tropical isle.

Perhaps no one had seen him climb down to the boat, Arkady thought. How simple it would be to dispose of him. It was a common enough practice for ships to dump their weighted garbage as they entered port. There was an extra anchor and chain inside every lifeboat.

But the lifeboat continued to slide over the iridescent surface, past the wet primary colors of catcher boats that Arkady had never seen before, near enough to watch men hosing decks and hoisting nets to repair, and to hear calls from docks previously hidden behind the slate-blue hull of the cannery ship.

As the hills closed in and the harbor narrowed to an inlet, Arkady glimpsed pinpoints of Arctic flowers and seams of snow hidden in the grass. The air carried the throaty taste of woodsmoke. After the boat cleared the cannery ship, the inlet tailed into a stream and he saw docks of smaller boats, including purse seiners no bigger than rowboats, a couple of single-engine seaplanes and the unmistakable orange of the first lifeboat from the *Polar Star*. Slava Bukovsky was on guard, watching with surprise that folded into dismay as their lifeboat approached. Beyond Slava were dogs nosing around refuse heaps, eagles roosting on roofs and, most miraculous of all, men walking on dry land.

18 Forgotten were Siberian orchids. Kolya stood at the end of the aisle like a traveler faced with three signposts. To his left was a stack of stereo receivers with digital tuning and chrome five-band graphic equalizers and black hi-tech speakers. To his right was a tier of twin-deck, Dolby-equipped cassette players that not only could play but could propagate tapes like rabbits. Straight ahead was a veritable tower of suitcase-sized receivers with cassette decks in a variety of pink, turquoise and ivory high-impact plastics for recording Western music right off the air. Kolya dared not look behind because there were racks of pocket cassette players, key chains that beeped when you clapped, cassette-fed toy bears that talked, calculator watches that recorded your mileage and took your pulse—the dizzying and proliferating armory of a civilization based on the silicon chip.

Kolya dealt with this alien situation with time-honored Soviet technique, stepping back and with snake eyes examining each article as if it were a tub of rancid butter, an excellent attitude in the

Soviet Union, where the shelf for items "broken when bought" was sometimes fuller than the display case; no experienced Soviet shopper left a store with his purchase until he'd taken it out of its box, turned it on and made sure it did *something*. Soviet shoppers also searched for the date of completion on the manufacturer's tag and hoped for a day in the middle of the month, rather than at the end, when the factory management was trying to meet its quota of TV's, VCR's, or cars with or without all the necessary parts, or at the beginning of the month, when the workers were in a drunken stupor from having met the quota. Here no shelf overflowed with defective goods, nor were there any dates on the manufacturers' tags, so having finally reached their destination, Kolya and a hundred other Soviet men and women now stood numbed before the foreign radios, calculators and other electronic exotica they had dreamed of.

"Arkady!" Kolya was overjoyed to see him. "You've traveled before. Where are the clerks?"

It was true there didn't appear to be any. A Soviet store is amply staffed because a shopper must buy in three stages: securing a chit from one clerk, paying a second, exchanging the receipt with a third—all of whom are far too interested in personal conversations or the telephone to take kindly the interruption of some stranger who has come in off the street. Besides, Soviet clerks hide any quality stuff—fresh fish, new translations, Hungarian bras—under the counter or in the back of the store, and they're people with pride who are in no hurry to sell inferior goods. The entire business is distasteful to them.

"Try her," Arkady suggested.

A grandmotherly woman smiled from a counter. She wore a mohair sweater as white as an Arctic fox, and her hair was an astonishing silver-blue. Spread out on the counter before her were sliced oranges, apples and crackers smeared with pâté. A card on an electric urn said in Russian COFFEE. There was also a cash register, and she was taking money from some sophisticated seamen who simply carried their stereos to her. At her back a large sign announced, again in Russian, DUTCH HARBOR WELCOMES THE POLAR STAR!

Kolya seemed relieved until another thought struck him. "Arkady, what are you doing here? You don't have the right visa."

"I have special dispensation."

Arkady was still trying to get his land legs. There was roll and pitch even on a factory ship, and after ten months his body didn't trust level, motionless ground. The fluorescent lights and shiny colors of the store displays seemed to swim around him.

"I thought you were a factory worker, and you become an investigator," Kolya said. "I thought you couldn't go ashore, and suddenly you're here."

"I'm confused myself," Arkady admitted.

Although Kolya had more questions, his eyes had lit on a rack of blank low-bias cassette tapes, which held a magnetic attraction for him. Arkady had caught a few other astonished glances in his direction, but everyone was too busy in this brief paradise to ask questions. One figure did stop; from the end of an aisle, the informer Slezko gawked in alarm, a gold tooth brightening his gray face. In his hands was a box of electric rollers—evidence that somewhere there was a Mrs. Slezkova.

"Ugggh." A machinist recoiled from his first bite of a cracker. "What kind of meat is in this pâté?"

"Peanuts," Izrail told him. "It's peanut butter."

"Oh." The machinist took another nibble. "Not bad."

"Renko, you're a regular Lazarus," Izrail said. "You keep popping up. This business with Zina, it's not over, is it? I see your look of determination and my heart sinks."

"Arkady, you came!" Natasha seized his arm as if he had appeared at a ball. "This proves it. You are a trustworthy citizen or they wouldn't have let you. What did Volovoi say?"

"I can't wait to hear," Arkady said. "What have you bought so far?"

She blushed. The only purchase in her net bag was two oranges. "Clothes are upstairs," she said. "Jeans, jogging gear, running shoes."

"Bathrobes and slippers," Madame Malzeva butted in.

Gury had strapped on a heavy safari watch with a compass built into the strap. He turned in different directions as he moved to the counter, like a man dancing alone. "Apple?" The woman with blue hair offered him a slice.

"Yamaha." Gury tried his English. "Software, programs, blank disks."

Without money, Arkady felt like a voyeur. As the two women swept toward the stairs he retreated in the opposite direction. Passing by the food aisles, he saw Lidia Taratuta cramming her bag with instant coffee. Two mechanics shared a box of ice cream popsicles; they leaned against a freezer, popsicles in hand, like a pair of drunks. How could they resist? Soviet advertising consisted of the directive "Buy . . . !" The package might bear a star, a flag or a factory's profile. In contrast, American packaging was promiscuously splashed with color pictures of untouchably beautiful women and winsome children enjoying "New and Improved" products. Lidia had moved on to detergents and was starting to fill a shopping cart.

Even Arkady stopped at the produce section. Yes, the lettuce was browning and wrapped in cellophane, the bananas were liver-spotted with age, and many of the grapes were split and weeping, but they were the first uncanned, unsyruped fruit he had seen in four months, so he paused to pay his respects. Then the only member of the *Polar*

Star's crew able to resist the blandishments of capitalism went out into the road.

The northern afternoon had settled into a slowly dimming light that gently revealed the wide plaza of mud that was the center of Dutch Harbor. On one side was the store, on the other the hotel. Both were prefabricated shells of ribbed metal walls and sliding windows, and were so long they suggested that some lower floors had sunk into the mud and disappeared. A score of smaller prefabricated houses took shelter on the lower ridge of a hill. There were shipping containers and dumpsters for storage and trash, and stray unraveling heaps of suction hose used for off-loading fish. Mostly there was mud. The roads were frozen waves of mud; panel trucks and vans rocked like boats as they moved across the plaza, and each vehicle wore a skirt of mud. Every man-made structure was earth-toned, ocher or tan, a calculated surrender to mud. Even the snow was stained with it, yet Arkady could have lain down and wallowed in it, in the unyielding, toothy grip of cold mud.

A dozen Soviets stood outside the store, either because they were putting off the climactic act of shopping or because sheer excitement had impelled them to take a break and step out for a cigarette. They stood in a circle, as if it were safer to look at the town over another man's shoulder.

"It's not so different from home, you know," said one. "This could be Siberia."

"We use preformed concrete," said another.

"The point is, it's just like Volovoi said. I didn't believe him."

"This is a typical American town?" asked a third.

"That's what the first mate said."

"It's not what I expected."

"We use concrete."

"That's not the point."

Looking around, Arkady saw three roads leading from the square: one along the bay to the tank farm, a second to the Aleut side of the bay and a third headed inland. Earlier, from the ship, he had noticed other anchorages and an airport on the island.

The conversation continued. "All those foods, all those radios. You think it's normal? I saw a documentary. The reason their stores have so much food is that people don't have any money to buy it."

"Come on."

"True. Posner said it on television. He likes Americans, but he said it."

Arkady took out a Belomor, though a *papirosa* seemed out of place. He noticed that the store also housed a bank on the first floor and some offices on the second. In the early dusk their lights had a stove-grate warmth. Across the road, the hotel had smaller, blearier windows, except for the blazing plate-glass front of a liquor store, which the crew had been warned to avoid.

"There's a place like that at home. A seamen's hostel, ten kopeks a night. I wonder how much that is?"

"I wonder how many men to a room?"

The second floor of the hotel overhung the first, making a protected walkway that must have served during the rainy season or when snow piled high during the winter. On the other hand, the population of Dutch Harbor would halve in November when the fishing season ended.

"The point is, all your life you hear about a place and it becomes fantastic. Like a friend of mine went to Egypt. He read up on pharaohs and temples and pyramids. He came back with diseases you wouldn't believe."

"Sshh, here comes one now."

A woman about thirty was headed for the store. Her hair had been teased into a yellow froth and her face was made up into a pout. In spite of the cold, she wore only a short rabbit-skin jacket, jeans and cowboy boots. The circle of Soviet cosmopolitans admired the view of the bay. An African warrior with a spear could have walked by them without their attention wavering from the water. Not until she was past did they glance after her.

"Not bad."

"Not so different."

"That's my point. Not better." This one kicked at the mud appreciatively, inhaled deeply and gave the dour hotel, hills and bay an authoritative sweep of his eyes.

"I like it."

One by one they killed their cigarettes, tacitly arranged themselves into the prescribed groups of four and, working up their courage with an interchange of shrugs and nods, began moving back into the store. "I wonder," one asked on the way, "can you buy those boots here?"

Arkady was thinking of the end of *Crime and Punishment,* of Raskolnikov redeemed on the bank overlooking the sea. Maybe he had been seduced in part by Dostoyevsky's portrait of the intelligent interrogator into becoming an investigator himself; yet here, at this midpoint in life, by some twist he wasn't the police but the criminal, a kind of unconvicted convict standing by the Pacific just like Raskolnikov, but on the other side of the ocean. How long before Volovoi had him dragged back to the ship? Would he cling to the ground like a crab when they came for him? He knew he didn't want to go. It was so restful to stand still in the shadow of a hill and to know that the hill, fixed, unlike a wave, was not going to slide underfoot. The grass trembling in the breeze would still be on that same slope tomorrow. Clouds would collect at the same peaks and light like flames at sunset. The mud itself would freeze and melt according to the season, but it would still be there.

"I saw you and couldn't believe it." Susan had come out of the hotel and crossed the road. Her jacket, the one she had worn from the boat, was askew, her hair was rumpled and her eyes were wild, as if she'd been crying. "Then I said to myself, Of course he's here. I mean, I had almost believed that someone on the slime line might just possibly have been, long ago, a detective. And spoke English. After all, that's the sort of man who would have gotten into so much trouble that he wouldn't have a visa to come ashore. It was just possible. Then I look out the lobby door and who do I see? You. Standing here like you own the island."

At first he thought she was drunk. Women drink, even Americans. He saw Hess and Marchuk emerge from the hotel, followed by George Morgan. All three were in shirt sleeves, though the captain of the *Eagle* still wore his cap.

"What is today's story?" Susan asked. "What is the operative fairy tale?"

"Zina killed herself," Arkady said.

"And as your reward you come ashore? Does that make sense to you?"

"No," Arkady confessed.

"Let's try it a different way." She aimed her finger at him as if it were a sharp stick extended at a snake. "You killed her and as your reward you come ashore. Now *that* makes sense."

Morgan grabbed the sleeve of Susan's jacket and pulled her away from Arkady. "Will you think about what you're saying?"

"You two bastards." She swung her arm free. "You probably cooked it up together."

"All I'm asking," Morgan told her, "is that you think about what you're saying."

She attempted to return to Arkady by going around Morgan, but he held his arms out.

"What a pair you make," she said.

"Calm down." Morgan tried a soothing voice. "Don't say anything that we're all going to regret. Because it can get very messy, Susan, you know that."

"What a perfect pair of bastards." She turned away in disgust and stared at the sky—a trick, Arkady knew, to hold in tears.

When Morgan began, "Susan—" she silenced him by holding up her hand, and without another word started back to the hotel.

Morgan turned a bent smile toward Arkady. "Sorry, I don't know what that was about."

Susan pushed between Marchuk and Hess as she went into the hotel. They joined Morgan and Arkady in the road. The Soviet captain already had the glitter of a man who has had a drink or two. It was cold enough now for breath to show. There was an air of male embarrassment about Susan's behavior.

"Of course," Morgan said, "she has just learned that her replacement had to go back to Seattle. She's going to have to stay on the *Polar Star.*"

"That could do it," Arkady said.

19 Arkady and the two other Soviets had beers at a table that was redwood caramelized in plastic. As a body bounced against the shoulder-high partition that separated them from the bar, Marchuk observed, "When Americans get drunk they get loud. A Russian gets more serious. He drinks until he falls with dignity, like a tree." He pondered his beer for a moment. "You're not going to run on us?"

"No," Arkady said.

"Understand, it's one thing to take a man off the slime line and let him loose on the ship. It's another to let him off the ship. What do you think happens to a master whose seaman defects? A master who allows a man with your visa to go ashore?" He leaned forward, as if pinning Arkady's eyes. "You tell me."

"They probably still need a watchman in Norilsk."

"I'll tell you. I'll come after you and kill you myself. Of course you have my wholehearted support, but I thought you should know."

"Cheers." Arkady liked an honest man.

"Congratulations." George Morgan pulled up a chair and touched his bottle to Arkady's. "I understand you solved your mystery. Suicide?"

"She left a note."

"Lucky." Morgan was the unruffled man in control again. Not a black-bearded tiger like Marchuk or a gnome like Hess, but a professional's smooth face pierced by two blue eyes.

"We were just saying what an unusual place Dutch Harbor is," Hess said.

"We're closer to the North Pole than to the rest of the States," Morgan said. "It's strange."

Different, Arkady thought. A Soviet bar was quiet, a gathering place for sedated men; this one was explosive with sound. Along the counter was a crowd of big men in plaid shirts and caps, with long hair and beards and a physical ease that seemed to lead naturally to backslapping and drinking from the bottle. The crowd and noise was doubled by a long mirror above a gemstone row of bottles. In a corner, Aleuts played pool. There were women at the tables, girls with drawn faces and extravagantly blond hair, but they were mostly ignored, except for a circle of them where Ridley held court. Morgan's engineer also distinguished himself from the crowd by wearing a velvet shirt and a gold chain; he looked like a Renaissance prince mingling with peasants.

He came over to Arkady. "The ladies want to know if you have a two-headed prick."

"What is normal here?" Arkady asked.

"Nothing is normal here. Look at it, all these seagoing American entrepreneurs completely dependent on you Communists. It's true. The banks had the fishermen's balls in the drawer because they'd all borrowed during the king-crab boom. That's why even Gulf boats like ours are up here. When the crabs disappeared, everyone was losing boats, gear, cars, homes. We'd be pumping gas if we weren't fishing. Then the Russians come along in '78 and buy anything we catch. Thank God for international cooperation. We'd be on our asses if it were up to the United States. You want strange? That's it."

"How much do you make?"

"Ten, twelve thousand a month."

Arkady figured he himself made about one hundred dollars at a realistic black-market exchange.

"That's strange," he had to admit.

In their corner, under a hanging fluorescent light, the Aleuts played pool with somber concentration. They wore caps, parkas and dark glasses, all but Mike, the deckhand off the *Eagle.* He whooped as the cue ball rolled toward a pocket, nudged another ball in and stopped short of a scratch. Three Aleut girls in pastel quilted coats sat along one wall, their heads together, talking. A white girl sat alone by the other wall, her jaw working on gum, her eyes following Mike's shots, ignoring the others.

"The Aleuts own the whole island," Ridley said to Arkady. "The navy threw them off during the war, then Carter gave them the whole place back, so they don't need to fish. Mike, he just loves the sea."

"And you?" Arkady asked. "You love it too?"

Ridley had not only brushed his hair into a ponytail and tied braids by his ears, but seemed to have supercharged his eyes and sharp smile. "Fucking hate it. It's an unnatural act to float steel on water. Salt water is our mutual enemy. Life is short enough."

"Your shipmate Coletti was in the police?"

"A patrolman, not a bilingual investigator like you. Unless you count Italian."

The scotch came and Morgan poured.

Ridley said, "What I miss at sea is civilization, because civilization is women, and that's where the *Polar Star* has us beat. Take Christ and Freud and Karl Marx, put them in a boat for six months and they'd be just as foulmouthed and primitive as us."

"Your engineer is a philosopher," Hess told Morgan. "In fact, in the fifties, we used to have cannery ships off Kamchatka that had about seven hundred women and a dozen men. They canned crabs. The process demanded that no metal be in contact with the crab, so we used a special lining produced in America. However, as a moral point, your government ordered no more lining for those Communist cans, so our crab industry collapsed."

Arkady remembered the stories. There had been riots on board the ships, women raping the men. Not a lot of civilization.

"To joint ventures." Morgan raised his glass.

Pool wasn't played in the Soviet Union, but Arkady remembered the GI's in Germany and their obsession with the game. Mike seemed to be winning, and gathering good-luck kisses from his gum-chewing girlfriend. If the czar hadn't sold Alaska, would the Aleuts be pushing pawns on a chessboard?

Ridley followed Arkady's eyes. "Aleuts used to hunt sea otters for Russia. They used to go after sea lions, walrus, whales. Today they're busy renting docks to Exxon. A bunch of Native American capitalists now. Not like us."

"You and me?"

"Sure. The truth is, fishermen have more in common with each other than with anyone on land. For example, people on land love sea lions. When I see a sea lion I see a thief. When you go by the Shelikoff Islands they're lying in wait for you—gangs of them, forty, fifty at a time. They're not afraid; they come right up to the net. Hell, they weigh six hundred, seven hundred pounds each. They're like goddamned bears."

"Sea lions," Hess explained to Marchuk, who rolled his eyes in understanding.

"They do two things," Ridley said. "They don't just grab a single fish from the net and jump. No, they take one bite out of the belly of each fish. If it's salmon in the net, they're stealing fifty dollars a bite. Second, when he's tired of that, the son of a bitch grabs one last fish and dives in the water. Then he does something real cute. He comes to the surface with the fish in his mouth and waves it at you—like saying, 'Fuck you, sucker.' That's what Magnums were made for. I don't think anything less than a Magnum will even slow a big male. What do you use?"

Hess carefully translated what Marchuk said. "Officially they are protected."

"Yeah, that's what I said too. We have a whole armory for them on the *Eagle.* They should be protected." Ridley nodded.

Ridley had an ambidextrous quality, it seemed to Arkady, an ability to play both the charmer and the thug, all the while looking like a poet. The engineer had fixed on him as well. "From your expression," he said, "you think it's murder."

"Who?" Arkady asked.

"Not who. What," Ridley said. "Sea lions."

Marchuk raised his glass. "The main thing is that whether we're Soviets or Americans, we're all fishermen and are doing what we like to do. To happy men."

" 'Happiness is the absence of pain.' " Ridley drained his glass and set it down. "Now I'm happy. Tell me," he asked Arkady, "working down on the slime line all wet and cold and covered with fish guts, are you happy?"

"We use a different adage on the slime line," Arkady said. " 'Happiness is the maximum agreement of reality and desire.' "

"Good answer. I'll drink to that," Morgan said. "That's Tolstoy?"

"Stalin," Arkady said. "Soviet philosophy is full of surprises."

"From you, yes," Susan said. How long she'd been standing by the table Arkady didn't know. Her hair was combed back wet and her cheeks were damp and pale, making her mouth redder and her brown eyes darker, the contrast lending her a new intensity.

RIDLEY HAD GONE off with Coletti in search of a card game. Marchuk had returned to the ship to give Volovoi his turn ashore. Once the first mate learned that Arkady was on shore he would fly like a winged hangman. Still, two hours on land was better than none. Even in a bar, every minute on shore was like breathing air again.

Though the noise level continued to rise, Arkady noticed it less and less. Susan sat with her legs tucked underneath her. Her face was in shadow within a ring of golden hair. Her usual veneer of animosity had split, revealing a darker, more interesting plane.

"I detest Volovoi, but I can believe in him easier than I can believe in you."

"Here I am."

"Dedicated to truth, justice and the Soviet way?"

"Dedicated to getting off the ship."

"That's the joke. We're both going back and I'm not even Russian."

"Then quit."

"I can't."

"Who's forcing you to stay?" Arkady asked.

She lit a cigarette, added scotch to her ice, didn't answer.

"So we'll suffer together," Arkady said.

George Morgan and Hess shared their bottle. "Imagine," Hess suggested, "if we did everything as a joint venture."

"If we really cooperated?" Morgan asked.

"Did away with suspicion and stopped trying to pull each other down. What natural partners we would be."

"We take the Japanese, you take the Chinese?"

"Split the Germans while we can."

"How would you describe hell?" Susan asked Arkady.

He thought about it. "A Party Congress. A four-hour speech by the Secretary General. No, an eternal speech. The delegates spread out like flatfish listening to a speech that goes on and on and on."

"An imaginary evening with Volovoi. Watching him lift weights. Either he's naked or I'm naked. Whichever, it's horrible."

"He calls you 'Soo-san.' "

"So do you. What's a name you say better?"

"Irina."

"Describe her."

"Light brown hair, very dark brown eyes. Tall. Full of life and spirit."

"She's not on the ship."

"No."

"She's home?"

Arkady changed the subject. "They like you on the *Polar Star.*"

"I like Russians, but I don't like having my cabin bugged. If I mention there's no butter, suddenly I'm served a plate of butter. Bernie has a political discussion with a deckhand and the man is taken off the ship. At first you try not to say anything offensive, but after a while to keep your sanity you start talking about Volovoi and his slugs. The *Polar Star* is hell to me. You?"

"Only limbo."

"It can all be joint venture," said Hess. "The shortest sea route between Europe and the Pacific is through the Arctic, and we could provide the icebreakers the same way the *Polar Star* leads the *Eagle* through the ice sheet."

"And depend on you?" Morgan asked. "I don't think things have changed *that* much."

"You liked Zina," Arkady said. "You gave her your swimsuit, you let her borrow your sunglasses. In return, she gave you—what?"

Susan took a long time to answer; it was like holding a conversation in the dark with a black cat. "Amusement," she said finally.

"You told her about California, she told you about Vladivostok, an even trade?"

"She was a combination of innocence and guile. A Russian Norma Jean."

"I don't understand."

"Norma Jean bleached her hair and became Marilyn Monroe. Zina Patiashvili bleached her hair and remained Zina Patiashvili. Same ambition, different result."

"You were friends."

Susan refilled his glass so full that the scotch swelled like oil above the rim, then did the same for herself. "This is a Norwegian drinking game," she said. "The first one to spill has to drink. Lose twice and you sit in a chair while the other person hits you on the head and tries to knock you over."

"We'll do it without the hitting. So you and Zina were friends," Arkady repeated.

"The *Polar Star* is like a deprivation tank. You know how rare it is to meet someone who actually seems to be alive and unpredictable? The problem is that you Soviets have a peculiar idea of friends. We're all peace-loving peoples of goodwill, but God forbid that an American and a Soviet get too close. Then the Soviet is next heard of on a ship off New Zealand."

"Zina wasn't shipped off."

"No, so we knew she was informing on us, at least to some degree.

I was willing to accept that because she was so alive, so much fun, so much smarter than any of the men knew."

"Which of your men did she sleep with?"

"How do you know she slept with someone?"

"She always did; it was the way she operated. If there were four American men on board she slept with at least one of them."

"Lantz."

Arkady remembered Lantz, the thin, languid observer from the sauna. "After that you warned her off? It wouldn't have been Volovoi." Arkady took a sip. "Good scotch."

Overfilled, the surface of her drink trembled but didn't break. Neon light lay on it like a moon.

"Who do you sleep with on the *Polar Star*?" she asked.

"No one."

"Then the *Polar Star* is a deprivation tank for you too. I drink to you."

For the first time Morgan raised his head in her direction, then returned to a description by Hess of the latest invasion of Moscow. "The Japanese are everywhere, at least in the best hotels. The best restaurant in Moscow is Japanese, but you can't get in because it's full of them."

Arkady said, "Zina told you about herself and Captain Marchuk, didn't she? Is that why you didn't tell me you saw them at the stern rail during the dance, so that you wouldn't embarrass him?"

"It was dark."

"He didn't think she was suicidal. You talked to her; did you think she was depressed?"

"Are you depressed?" Susan asked. "Are you suicidal?"

Arkady was thrown off track again. He was out of practice at interrogation—too slow, too swayed by the counterflow of her questions.

"No, I would describe myself as a carefree reveler in life. I was more carefree when I was a Party member, of course."

"I bet."

"It's harder to get in trouble if you have a card."

"Really. Like how?"

"Take smuggling. Without a Party card, tragedy. With a Party card, comedy."

"How is that?"

"A drama. Say the second mate gets caught. He goes before the other officers and sobs, 'I don't know what came over me, comrades. I have never done anything like it before. Please give me a chance to redeem myself.' "

"So?" Susan had been lured into the light.

Hess and Morgan had fallen silent, listening.

"A vote is taken," Arkady said, "and a decision is reached to place a severe reprimand on his Party record. Two months pass and another meeting is held."

"Yes?" Susan said.

"The captain says, 'We were all disappointed in the conduct of our second mate and there were times I felt I could never sail with him again, but now I see a sincere effort to redeem himself.' "

"The political officer says—" Susan prompted him.

"The political officer says, 'He has drunk again from the clear wellsprings of Communist thought. I suggest that, taking into consideration his spiritual rebirth, the severe reprimand be removed from his Party record.' What could be more comic?"

Susan said, "You're a funny man, Renko."

"He's an angry man," said Hess.

"That's how it ends if you're a Party member," Arkady said, "but if you're not a Party member, if you're just a worker and are caught smuggling videotapes or gems the outcome is five years in a labor camp."

"Tell me more about Irina," Susan said. "She sounds interesting; where is she?"

"I don't know."

"Somewhere"—she spread her arms—"out there?"

"Some people are like that," Arkady said. "You know, there's a North Pole and a South Pole. There's another place called the Pole of Inaccessibility. Once it was thought that all the ice in the Arctic Sea turned around one point, a mythical pole surrounded by wheeling floes impossible to cross. I think that's where she is." Without a pause he asked, "Was Zina depressed the night of the dance?"

"I didn't say I talked to her."

"If you'd warned her off the Americans on the *Polar Star*, then wouldn't you warn her off the Americans on the *Eagle*?"

"She said she'd found true love. You can't stop that."

"What exactly were her words?"

"That no one could stop her."

"If you're talking about Mike"—Morgan spoke up—"they only met at a couple of dances. Otherwise all they did was wave at each other. Anyway, all my men were back on my boat, so what does it matter?"

"Unless she was murdered," Susan said.

Morgan reacted with the thin smile of a man whose patience for the simpleminded was wearing thin. He seemed to find everyone but Hess in that category, Arkady thought.

"I'm out of cigarettes," Susan said. "There's a machine in the lobby. Are you allowed to come?" she asked Arkady.

He looked toward Hess, who slowly nodded. Morgan shook his

head at Susan, but she ignored him. "We'll just be a second," she said.

The machine offered a dozen brands, like flavors. Susan, though, didn't have the correct change.

"I know you don't have any."

"No," Arkady said.

"I have cigarettes in my room. Come on."

Susan's room was on the second floor at the far end of the hall, a gamut of sounds. Each room had a different argument or played a different tape. She touched the walls twice for balance's sake and Arkady wondered how drunk she was.

She unlocked the door to a room that was not much larger than her cabin on the *Polar Star* but offered twin beds, shower, telephone and, instead of a built-in Soviet radio with two stations, a television on a desk. The bureau held a disarray of scotch, a plastic ice bucket, a gooseneck lamp. The beds were by the window, and though it was thin and dirty, not even double-paned, Arkady felt bathed in utter luxury.

Outside, the sun was gone and Dutch Harbor drifted in the dark. From above Arkady watched his shipmates emerge from the store and gather on the road, reluctant to walk to the dock even though their arms were weighed down with plastic and string bags stuffed with their purchases. They were used to standing in line for hours to buy a single pineapple or a pair of stockings. This was nothing; this was heaven. Polaroid cameras flashed, capturing a closed rank of friends, blue-white in an American port. Natasha and Dynka. Lidia and Olimpiada. On a hill above the tank farm a fire burned like a beacon. Ridley had said there were fires all the time, kids torching the wooden structures left from the war. Fog had thickened around the hill, turning the flames into a soft furze of light.

Arkady found the light switch and turned it on. "What did you mean when you said that Morgan and I had 'cooked up' something together?"

"Captain Morgan is not too careful about the company he keeps." Susan turned the switch off. "I guess I'm not either."

"Someone tried to kill me two days ago."

"On the *Polar Star*?"

"Where else?"

"No more questions." Her hand was on his mouth. "You seem to be for real," she said, "but I know you have to be a fake because everything is fake. Remember the poem?"

Her eyes seemed so dark that he wondered how much he'd had to drink. He could smell the dampness in her hair. "Yes." He knew which one she meant.

"Say it."

" 'Tell me how men kiss you.' "

Susan leaned into him and rose at the same time, bringing her face up to his. Strange. A man considers himself nearly dead, cold, inert; then the right flame appears and he flies into it like a moth.

Her lips opened to his. "If you were real," she said.

"As real as you."

He lifted her and carried her to the bed. Through the window he saw that the plaza outside was as bright with camera flashes as a celebration of silent firecrackers, a last wave of picture taking before the happy visitors, his shipmates, decamped for the dock. Out on the road, a camera's bright flash illuminated Natasha as she posed coquettishly, jacket open to a glass necklace, her head tossed in profile to display crystal earrings. Arkady felt oddly like a traitor seeing her from a hotel window.

He stood poised above the bed, at one of those points that make all the difference in the rest of a lifetime. On the road a blue flash illuminated Gury and Natasha, and incidentally froze Mike, the Aleut, as he was leaving the hotel.

"What's the matter?" Susan asked.

Another flash bathed a happy Madame Malzeva holding a bolt of satin, and also caught Volovoi rushing in the hotel door.

"I have to go," Arkady said.

"Why?" Susan asked.

"Volovoi's here. He's looking for me."

"You're going with him?"

"No."

"You're going to run?" She sat up.

"No. I couldn't on this island even if I wanted to. You depend on us too much. Who else would the fishermen here sell their fish to? Who else comes all this way to buy stereos and shoes? If any Soviet tried to run here, you'd throw him back as fast as you could catch him."

"Then where are you going?"

"I don't know. Not back. Not yet."

20 As he climbed the hill Arkady felt the thick grasses softly yielding, then springing up behind his step. Below him, the hotel lay bathed in electric light, its bright windows banked in midair above the walkway, which was a shaft of still white light. A figure on the walkway seemed to move in slow motion: Volovoi looking right, then left.

The last few Soviets were joining the crowd on the road, and some of them were already moving toward the docks, like the vanguard of a herd. Some of the men lingered while Lantz visited the liquor store. Returning, he distributed pints of vodka, which they stuffed in their pants. Natasha and Lidia lingered too, as if to give the evening a last embrace. America? With so many Soviets in the street it could have been a Russian village, with Russian dogs barking in the yards, Russian grass blanketing the hills. Arkady imagined Kolya off in the dark digging up tender orchids, and Obidin entering the doorway of the church.

He had crossed the road away from the hotel and worked his

way through the dumpsters beside the store. The building had windows only in front, so he had slipped into the shadows in back, then maneuvered between the prefab housing on the ridge, long metal homes with aluminum windows bathed in the shifting colors of television sets. A couple of dogs, black-and-white animals with pale eyes, challenged him, but no owner appeared. The yards had pitfalls, auto parts and suction hoses covered by snow, but he slipped only once before reaching the hill. Mike was well ahead, keeping the beam of the flashlight on a path. So far he hadn't looked back.

Land was so seductive, dark but firm underfoot. Sometimes Arkady stepped on cushions of waterleaf or moss. Dried lupin brushed his hands. He couldn't so much see as sense the volcanic mountains rising like walls in the mist. Ahead, a fire lit one peak. Out in the harbor the lights of the ships at anchor were more distinct; the lamps of the *Polar Star* floated on a tilted sheet of black.

What if he did run? There were no trees to hide behind, few houses to beg at. There was an airport on the other side of the island. What could he do, jump onto a wheel as a plane took off?

Hummocks made climbing easy. Snow was cupped into the northern slope; there was just enough light to turn the drifts blue. After ten months at sea, it was like mounting heaven. A cold wind, a harbinger of the winter to come, stirred earthy vapors of berry bushes, parsley and moss. Mike seemed to be enjoying himself, too, following his flashlight at a leisurely pace.

Where the path joined a dirt road the fog grew more intense. At points the ground dropped away on either side, and Arkady could make out the difference between firm footing and air mainly by the sound of the sea breeze as it rushed up the face of the cliff. He knew which way to walk because the fire, though obscured, was closer and brighter, like a beacon.

Then, in a matter of steps, the fog dissipated and fell away. It was as if he had climbed to the surface of a second ocean and set of mountains. The fog lay heavy, still and foamy white under a night sky as brilliantly clear as deep space. The mountain peaks floated like smaller islands, hideaways of sheer black rock and starlit ice.

The road ended at the fire. Around its glow Arkady saw signs of an abandoned military battery: earthworks turned to grassy knoll, gun plates now rings of rust, a mare's nest of barbed wire. In the muffled tussling of the flames were boards, bedsprings, oilcans and tires. On the far side of the fire, Mike pulled open a heavy door built into the hill. For the first time, Arkady noticed that he carried a rifle.

The stars were so near. The Little Bear was still chained to Polaris. Orion's arm reached over the horizon as if tossing stars. In his ten months on the Bering Sea, Arkady had never seen a night so clear, yet they'd always been there, just above the fog.

He walked around the fire to the door. It was iron, set in a concrete frame, an entrance to a wartime bunker. The concrete was chipped and stained with rust, but it had resisted both years and vandals. A new padlock hanging open on the hasp showed that someone had taken ownership, and the door swung easily on oiled hinges.

"Mike!" he yelled.

A kerosene lamp burned on the floor, and in its light Arkady saw that someone had done his best to turn the bunker into a fisherman's loft. A trawl net billowed artistically from the ceiling. On the walls were shelves of starfish, abalone shells and jawbones of baby sharks. There was a cot and fruit-box bookcases stuffed with paperbacks and magazines, and barrels of salvaged webbing, twisted tow shackles and split corks.

When he saw the rifle on the cot, Arkady relaxed. "Mike?"

On a stand, and filling the entire middle of the bunker, was the largest kayak Arkady had ever seen. It was at least six meters long, low and narrow, with two round hatches, and although it was only half finished an intrinsic sleekness and grace were evident. Arkady remembered the voice on Zina's tape describing a native boat, a baidarka, that the speaker would paddle around the *Polar Star*. The more he examined the boat, the more impressed he was. The keel was wood, jointed with bone. The ribs were bent wood, lashed with sinew. He didn't see a nail in the whole construction. Only the sheath of the craft was a compromise with the modern age: a covering of fiberglass fabric sewn up to the rear-hatch coaming by nylon thread held in place with a hemostat. On a workbench was an assortment of whittling knives and files, sail needles and twine, paintbrushes, gas mask, electric hair dryer and half-gallon cans of epoxy resin. Epoxy was volatile material; pails of sand bracketed the bench, and there was a toxic bite to the air from a sample that had been painted on the skin.

"Come on out," Arkady called. "I just want to talk."

The way the bow of the craft split and curled backward, Arkady could easily imagine the baidarka bending, riding lightly on the waves. He could also see why Zina was attracted to Mike. A merman, she had called him, a romantic who dreamed of sailing with her to all the points of the Pacific. How different from himself, who just wanted to stay on land.

The hair dryer meant there had to be power. Arkady found an extension cord on the floor and followed it to a blanket hanging on the end wall, pulled it aside and discovered a second, smaller room. There was a gasoline generator with an exhaust pipe to a duct. A gasoline can lay on its side and a flashlight spilled its own light.

Just inside the doorway, Mike sprawled as if hugging the rough floor. The Aleut's left eye was open and had the sheen of a dark wet rock. Arkady couldn't feel any breath or pulse. On the other hand, he didn't see any blood. Mike had walked into the bunker only steps ahead of him, had lit the kerosene lamp and then gone to the generator. Young men had heart attacks. He turned the Aleut over, unbuttoned his shirt and hit his chest while Mike watched with one eye.

"Come on," Arkady urged.

Mike wore a religious medal on a chain of metal beads; it clinked at the back of his neck each time Arkady hit his chest. He was too warm to be dead, too young and strong, with a boat half built. "Mikhail! Come on!"

Arkady opened Mike's mouth, blew in and inhaled the taste of beer. He beat the chest again as if anyone inside could be roused. The medal clicked as Mike stared with a fading eye.

Or a stroke, Arkady thought, and put his fingers inside the mouth to clear the tongue. He touched something that felt improbably hard, and when he pulled his hand out, his fingertips were smeared red. He opened Mike's mouth as wide as he could, looked in with the flashlight and found a point emerging from the tongue like a silver thorn. Gently he turned the boy's head to the side and brushed the thick black hair at the base of the skull away from two steel ovals that looked like an old-fashioned lorgnette tangled in the hair. American males had affectations: earrings, heavy finger rings, leather cuffs on long braids. But these two bright ovals were embedded in the head, the handles of a pair of scissors that had been neatly driven like an ice pick, with hardly a drop of blood, halfway through the cranium. They were what Mike's medal had been hitting. One hand doesn't clap; one medal doesn't click. The body sagged gratefully as Arkady let it down.

Volovoi stepped into the bunker. After him came Karp.

"He's dead," Arkady said.

The first mate and trawlmaster seemed more interested in the bunker than in the body. "Another suicide?" Volovoi asked as he looked around.

"You could say so." Arkady stood. "It's Mike from the *Eagle*. I followed him, and he was in here no more than a minute before me. No one came out. Whoever killed him could still be here."

"I'm sure," Volovoi said.

Arkady flashed the beam around the second room of the bunker. Except for the generator all it contained was bare walls scribbled with graffiti. There was a pool of water in one corner, and above it a shaft russet-striped with stains that led up through the bombproof ceiling to a closed hatch. The hatch was out of reach, though there were two broken flanges that had once supported steps.

"There must have been a rope here or a ladder," Arkady said. "Whoever got out probably pulled it up with him and then closed the hatch."

"We were following you." Karp took the rifle off the bed and admired it. "We didn't see anyone leave."

"Why were you following an American?" Volovoi asked.

"Let's look outside," Arkady said.

Karp blocked his way. "Why were you following him?" Volovoi asked again.

"To ask him about Zin—"

"The inquiry is over," Volovoi said. "That's not a permissible reason to follow anyone. Or to leave the ship against orders, to disappear from your compatriots, to sneak alone at night out of a foreign port. But I'm not surprised; I'm not surprised by anything you do. Hit him."

Karp jabbed the barrel like a spear into Arkady's back between the shoulder blades, then took a measured swing, like a farmer with a scythe, and drove the side of the barrel into the back of his knees. Arkady dropped to the floor, gasping.

Volovoi sat on the cot and lit a cigarette. He plucked a well-thumbed magazine from the bookcase, opened the centerfold and tossed it aside, a flush of disgust spreading over his pink face.

"This proves my point. You've killed before, according to your file. Now you want to defect, to go over to the other side, to dishonor your shipmates and your ship the first chance you had. You picked the weakest of the Americans, this native, and when he wouldn't help, you killed him."

"No."

Volovoi glanced at Karp and the trawlmaster swung the rifle down onto Arkady's ribs. His jacket absorbed some of the force, but Karp was a powerful man and an enthusiastic assistant.

"The suicide note that Zina Patiashvili wrote," Volovoi said, "was found in the dead girl's bed. I myself asked Natasha Chaikovskaya why you didn't search there. She told me you had, yet you didn't report a note."

"Because it wasn't there."

In spite of the bunker's dank cold, the first mate was sweating. Well, there was the climb, and Arkady had noticed in the past how interrogation was hard work for everyone involved. In the glare of the lamp, Volovoi's crew cut was a crown of radiant spikes. Of course, Karp, who was doing all the heavy labor, perspired like Vulcan at his forge.

"You followed me together?" Arkady asked.

"I'm asking the questions. He still doesn't understand," Volovoi complained to Karp.

Karp kicked Arkady in the stomach. So far it was all routine police work, Arkady thought, a good sign, still just intimidation, nothing irreversible. Then the trawlmaster pinned Arkady's neck to the floor

with the rifle stock and landed a more serious kick, one that endeav-
ored to enter the stomach and come out at the spine.

"Stop," Volovoi said.

"Why?" asked Karp. His boot was cocked for a third go.

"Wait." Volovoi smiled indulgently; a leader could not explain
everything to an associate.

Arkady rose to one elbow. It was important not to be totally inert.

"I expected something like this," Volovoi said. "Restructuring
may be necessary in Moscow, but we're far from Moscow. Here we
know that when you move rocks you stir up snakes. We're going to
make an example."

"Of what?" Arkady asked, trying to hold up his end of the conversation.

"An example of how dangerous it can be to encourage elements
like you."

Arkady dragged himself against the workbench. He didn't sit up;
he didn't want to appear too comfortable. "I don't feel encouraged,"
he said. "You were thinking of a trial?"

Karp said, "Not a trial. You haven't seen him in front of a judge,
the way he twists words."

"I didn't kill this boy," Arkady said. "If you didn't, then whoever
did is walking down the hill right now."

He ducked because he saw the rifle stock coming, so instead of
crushing his face it swept the cans off the workbench. Now he was
frightened, because while he could tolerate an officially authorized
beating kept within certain rough bounds, this was getting out of
control.

"Comrade Korobetz!" Volovoi warned Karp. "That's enough."

"He's just going to lie," Karp said.

Volovoi said to Arkady, "Korobetz is not an intellectual, but he is an outstanding worker and he accepts the direction of the Party, something you never did."

Except for a white seam across the middle of his narrow forehead where the skin had been removed, Karp's face was red.

"Your direction?" Arkady hunched closer to a whittling knife that had fallen with the cans.

"We caught him running, we caught him killing someone," Karp insisted. "He doesn't have to be alive."

"That's not your decision," Volovoi said. "There are hard questions to be asked and answered. Such as who, knowing how dangerous and unstable a personality Renko is, persuaded the captain to set him loose in a foreign port? What was Renko planning with this ring of Americans? New Thinking is necessary to increase the productivity of labor, but in terms of political discipline our country has become slack. A year ago he never would have been allowed ashore. That's why an example is so important."

"I haven't done anything," Arkady said.

Volovoi had thought about this. "There's your provocative investigation, your attempt to sway the trusting captain and crew of the *Polar Star,* your defection as soon as your feet hit foreign soil. Who knows what else you've been involved in? We'll tear the entire ship apart, rip out every bulkhead and tank. Marchuk will get the message. All the captains will get the message."

"But Renko's not a smuggler," Karp said.

"Who knows? Besides, we always find something. When I'm done the *Polar Star* will be in small pieces."

"You call that restructuring?" Karp asked.

Volovoi lost patience. "Korobetz, I'm not going to debate politics with a convict."

"I'll show you a debate," Karp said. He picked up the knife on the floor before Arkady could grab it, turned to the cot and stuck the blade up to the hilt in Volovoi's throat.

"That's how convicts debate," Karp said, cradling the back of Volovoi's head and pressing it forward against the knife.

While Volovoi struggled a jet of blood sprayed the wall. His face swelled. His eyes inflated with disbelief.

"What? No more speeches?" Karp asked. "Restructuring answers the demands of—what? I can't hear you. Speak up. Answers the demands of the working class! You ought to know that."

A man lifts weights, keeps himself in shape, but it's not the same as real labor, and it was obvious that Volovoi's muscles were putty compared with Karp's. The first mate thrashed, but the trawlmaster kept the knife tight in his throat as lightly as a hand on a lever. This was how they did it in the camp, when the urkas discovered an informer. Always the throat.

"Demands for more work? Really?" Karp said.

As Volovoi's face became darker, his eyes grew whiter, as if all the lectures still inside him had been choked off and the pressure of them was building up. His tongue unrolled.

"You thought I was going to kiss your cock and ass forever?" Karp asked.

As Volovoi's face went black he rocked the cot against the wall and his hands shot out. His eyes looked full of wonder, as if he had to be watching someone else, as if this couldn't be happening to him.

No, Arkady thought, Volovoi's not surprised any longer. He's dead.

"He should have just shut up," Karp said to Arkady and jerked the knife first one way and then the other before pulling it out.

Arkady wanted to fly through the door, but the best he could do was push himself to his feet with a can of epoxy to swing in defense. "You got carried away."

"Yeah," Karp admitted. "But I think they're going to say *you* got carried away."

Volovoi still sat upright, as if he could rejoin the conversation. From neck to chest he seemed to have burst under the weight of blood.

Arkady asked, "Have you ever spent any time in a psychiatric ward?"

"Have you? See?" Karp smiled. "Anyway, I've been cured. I'm a new man. Let me ask you a question."

"Go ahead."

"You like Siberia?"

"What?"

"I'm interested in your opinion. Do you like Siberia?"

"Sure."

"What kind of a fucking answer is that? I *love* Siberia. The cold, the taiga, the hunting, everything, but most of all the people. Real people, like the natives. People in Moscow look hard, but they're like turtles. Get them east, out of their shells, you can just step on them. Siberia's the best thing that ever happened to me. Like home."

"Good."

"Just the hunting." Karp wiped his blade on Volovoi's sleeve. "Some guys go out in helicopters and blast away with Kalashnikovs. I like the Dragunov, a sniper rifle with a scope. Sometimes I don't even bother shooting. Like, last winter a tiger wandered into Vladivostok killing dogs. A wild tiger in the center of the city. The militia, naturally, shot it. You know, I wouldn't have killed it; I'd have taken it back out of town and let it go. That's the difference between you and me: I wouldn't have killed the tiger." He propped Volovoi against the wall. "How long do you think he can stay like that? I was thinking of making a matched set. You know, symmetry."

Symmetry was always an interesting fetish, Arkady thought.

There was a padlock hanging on the bunker door, he remembered; if he could get outside he could lock Karp in.

"But it wouldn't look right," Arkady said. "You don't want to leave three murders here. It's a matter of arithmetic. I can't be a victim too."

"This wasn't my first plan," Karp confessed, "but Volovoi was such a prick. All my life I've listened to pricks like him and you. Zina—"

"Zina?"

"Zina said words freed you or fucked you or turned you inside out. Every word, every single one, was a weapon or a chain or a pair of wings. You didn't know Zina. And *you* didn't know Zina," he added, turning to Volovoi. The political officer, his head tipped, seemed to be listening. "An Invalid doesn't want to debate with someone from the camps? I could tell you about the camps." He turned to Arkady. "Thanks to you."

"I'm going to send you there again."

"Well, if you can," Karp said and spread his arms as if to say, Now we've finally come to the point, a point past words and into his domain. He added, as his personal conclusion, "You should have stayed on the boat."

When Arkady threw the epoxy, Karp casually lifted a forearm and let the can bounce off. In two steps Arkady was across the room and pushing open the door, but Karp's hand reached out and dragged him back in. Arkady ducked under the knife and grabbed Karp's wrist in the "Come along" grip he had been taught by a militia instructor in Moscow, which brought an appreciative laugh from Karp. He dropped the knife but swung Arkady into the bookcase. Paperbacks fluttered out like birds.

As Arkady started for the door again Karp lifted him and threw him over the baidarka into the opposite wall, rattling shark jaws and iridescent shells onto the bunker floor. He swept the boat aside. For all his power, he crouched in the favorite urka stance, with two fingers extended toward the eyes, a style Arkady had seen before. He moved inside the stabbing hand and hit Karp flush on the mouth, which didn't stop the trawlmaster's forward motion, so Arkady hit him in the stomach, which was like probing concrete, then brought an elbow back to the chin and dropped Karp to one knee.

Roaring, Karp tackled Arkady and drove him into one wall and then another, until Arkady reached up and clung to the fishnet hanging from the ceiling. As Karp ripped him down, Arkady brought a fold of net with him, smothered the trawlmaster's head in it and kicked his legs out from under him. Going for the door a third time, Arkady tripped on the open ribs of the boat, and before he could rise Karp had him by the ankle. On the floor, he had no chance against the trawlmaster's weight, and Karp climbed up his body, ignoring blows until Arkady brought a barrel of shackles down on Karp's head.

Arkady twisted free. He was trying to open the door when the barrel shot by his ear and slammed it shut. Karp tore him off the handle and threw him on the cot next to Volovoi. As if to commiserate, the dead man sagged against Arkady's shoulder. From his jacket, Karp took his own knife, the double-edged one that fishermen were urged to carry at all times in case of emergency. On the cot, Arkady found the knife that Karp had dropped earlier.

Karp was faster, and his stroke should have sliced Arkady from the navel up, but the dead Volovoi finally lost equilibrium and slumped sideways in front of Arkady. The knife thudded into the first mate, and for a moment, leaning forward, his blade embedded in the wrong target, Karp was vulnerable from heart to neck. Arkady hesitated. Then it was too late. Karp kicked the bed over, trapping him against the wall. Trying to rise, Arkady lost his knife.

Karp lifted him up from behind the cot and tossed him over Mike's body into the smaller room. The trawlmaster paused to liberate his knife from Volovoi before following. Arkady could barely budge the generator, but he did manage to heave the gasoline can. Expecting it, Karp ducked until the can had flown by before he stepped over Mike.

There was a chimelike ring of glass breaking. The sound must have come before Karp entered the room, but afterward Arkady remembered the man's surprise backlit by a white glare, as if the sun had suddenly risen behind him. The explosion of the kerosene lamp and gas can was followed by a whoosh of spilled epoxy igniting. As gasoline spread, the scattered books caught fire, the tangled sheet of the cot, the corner of the bench. Karp jabbed at Arkady, but half-heartedly, in a disconcerted way. There was a second explosion as the full bucket of epoxy blew and a flame shot to the ceiling. Thick brown, acrid fumes spread up the walls.

"Even better," Karp said. He waved the knife one last time and ran back through the burning room; he looked like a demon retreating from hell. After opening the bunker door he stopped to give Arkady a last glance, his eyes lit by the flames. Then he darted out and the door shut.

The baidarka ignited, its ribs black in the boat's translucent skin, which sweated burning beads of epoxy. Already the ceiling was concealed by poisonous smoke that rolled forward like a storm cloud. Arkady stood over Mike. A remarkable scene, he thought. Storm, fire, the Aleut stretched out toward his burning boat, Volovoi on his upended funeral pyre, one sleeve covered in flame. He thought of a phrase he had once read in a French guidebook: "worth a visit." Sometimes the mind did that in a panic, going off on its own last-minute trips. There were two choices: burn in one room or choke to death in the other.

His hand over his mouth, Arkady darted through the burning room and flung himself against the door. It gave; it wasn't padlocked, only blocked by Karp on the outside. The same as the fishhold. Simple ideas were the best. Flames marched toward Arkady's feet. He bent beneath the smoke, wheezing between coughs. It wouldn't take five minutes, ten at the most; then Karp could open the door wide and check his success.

Arkady shot the door's inside bolt. He had once known a pathologist who had claimed that Renko's greatest talent lay not in escaping disastrous situations but only in complicating them. Holding his breath, he waded back through the fire and focused on a barrel that he rescued and carried into the second room. Inside the barrel was trash, Mike's collection of loose netting. With a fisherman's eye, he picked the longest strip of nylon mesh. Illuminated by the flames at the door, the water in the corner had become a golden pond, and he could just see the broken flanges, two rusting tips of iron, under the closed hatch. He set the barrel upside down in the water and stood on it. On his toes he could just swing the strip of mesh high enough to reach. The hatch was not airtight, and by now smoke was lapping into the room, creeping along the ceiling, following the draft to where Arkady balanced. As he hooked a flange, the barrel tipped over and rolled away. While he climbed the net, he heard bottles breaking amid the growing, surflike sound of fire. He pushed open the hatch. Smoke rushed up, as if trying to drag him back, but by then he was outside and over the earthworks, rolling over mist-slicked grass and falling back toward the sea.

III.

ICe

21 The first sign of the ice sheet was a few broken pieces of ice as slick and white as marble floating on black water, and though the *Polar Star* with its company of four catcher boats moved easily into a north wind, there was a general sense of heightened apprehension and isolation. Below-decks was the new sound of ice scraping the waterline. On deck the crew leaned back to study the gear that surmounted the bridge house and gantries: the slowly turning bars, the interlocked rings, the star-shaped whip and line antennas that provided radar, VHF, short-wave, radio and satellite direction. The sense of a distant reality was increasingly important as scattered ice turned to an endless maze of ice rafts, circular and smooth. More and more the trawlers fell in line behind the *Polar Star,* especially the *Eagle,* built for the warm waters of the Gulf of Mexico, not for the Bering Sea.

By evening the wind had increased, as if sliding faster over ice than over water, and brought a fine rain that froze on the windshield of the bridge. Through the night, crewmen hosed ice off the *Polar*

Star's decks with water from the boilers. The trawlers, even more vulnerable to the destabilizing weight of ice, did the same, and so they moved as a steaming parade through the dark.

The *Alaska Miss,* its screws dented by a floe, turned back at dawn. The others stayed because the fish were there. In the morning light the boats found that the ice had melded into one solid sheet. Ahead lay a white and featureless shell under a blue arch; in the *Polar Star*'s wake stretched a fairway of carbon-black water into which the trawlers, spaced a mile apart, dipped their nets. For some reason ground-fish, particularly sole, chose the ocean floor just inside the ice sheet to mass practically in tiers. Nets thirty and forty tons heavy rose from the water, fish and mesh and plastic chafing hair immediately covered in dazzling crystals of ice, so it appeared that the trawlers were literally hauling gems from the sea. In a way it was true. The Americans were getting rich and the Soviets were doubling their daily plan.

All the same, the *Polar Star*'s flag hung at half-mast. The voyage's entire quota had been dedicated to the memory of Fedor Volovoi. Messages of sympathy were sent to the dead man's family; messages of support were received from fleet headquarters in Vladivostok and the company offices in Seattle. The Party cell had nominated a gloomy Slava Bukovsky to carry out the duties of political officer. Volovoi would be riding home in the No. 2 food store in a plastic bag next to the one containing Zina Patiashvili, who had been transferred; all the space in the fishhold would be needed. It was whispered on board that the first mate's throat was more than simply charred. In his capacity as trade union representative charged with writing death forms, Slava denied the rumors, but with all his new duties, the third mate seemed to be more afflicted with depression than inspired by opportunity. Arkady himself ached after the beating from Karp, but no worse than if he had fallen down a very long staircase.

On the slime line a half-ton of yellowfin sole poured like a quickening flood down the chute every ten minutes to be gutted, cleaned and trimmed. The fish were so laced with ice that Obidin, Malzeva, Mer and the others were numb from fingers to shoulders. Over the sound of the saws and the incessant murmuring of cheerful tunes from the radio came the thumping of ice along the hull. The ice-breaking bow of the *Polar Star* had been designed to ride up and crash through ice a meter thick. Still, the hull protested. The whole bulkhead would shudder, and individual plates bowed in and out like drums.

As she steered fish through the saw Natasha again and again raised a questioning look at Arkady, but he was listening to the progress of the ship, to the ice resisting and then exploding under the bow, a sound like the earth splitting.

MARCHUK LOOKED AS if he had been climbing mountains. Fog, never far away, had returned as a mist that froze on the windshield of the bridge, so the captain had gone out on the flying bridge. His great-coat, boots, open-finger gloves and captain's cap were lined in every fold with ice, and his beard had the shimmer of rime. As he stood now behind his desk, water began to pool on the floor. By the evidence of his red ears it was plain that Marchuk had not traded his cap for the flapped woolen cap of lesser men. Anton Hess had not been out on deck; still, he was padded with two sweaters and the same sort of gloves as Marchuk's. A Soviet ship is over-heated—the glory of a Russian home is heat—but nothing stayed warm on the ice sheet. Under his forehead and wild hair, Hess's eyes were hollowed by exhaustion. Two strong men, yet each seemed uncertain, even frightened. For the first time in their lives they were sailing without a watchdog of the Party—worse, with a dead watchdog in the freezer.

Standing on the carpet next to Arkady, but not with him, as far as he could suggest by expression, was Slava Bukovsky. It was the same group that had assembled in the captain's cabin before, with one obvious exception.

"I apologize for not meeting when we raised anchor," Marchuk said. "Matters were unclear. Also, my attention is taken with the radio whenever we approach ice. Americans are not used to ice, so I have to hold their hands. Now, Comrade Bukovsky, I have read your report, but the others might like to hear it."

Slava took the opportunity to move forward, a step farther away from Arkady. "My report is based on the American report. I have it here."

As soon as Slava opened his briefcase his papers escaped onto the carpet. It occurred to Arkady that if Marchuk had a tail it would be twitching.

The third mate found the paper he wanted. He read, "The competent authorities in Dutch Harbor—"

"Who are the competent authorities?" Hess interrupted.

"The local fire chief. He said it appeared to be an accidental fire," Slava went on. "The native called Mikhail Krukov had been warned many times about the danger of using volatile materials in the construction of his boats, and there was evidence of a kerosene lamp, of gasoline and of alcohol. The accident occurred in a concrete construction dating back to the war, a bunker without sufficient ventilation and without safeguards for the generator that Krukov used. Apparently the natives have taken over a number of abandoned military structures without permission. Krukov was well known locally as some sort of boatbuilder. The Americans assume that he was showing one to Volovoi, that the two men shared a bottle and that in that closed space there was somehow an accident that broke a kerosene lamp, igniting toxic materials, which, in turn, exploded. Fedor Volovoi, apparently, was killed immediately by flying glass. The native, it seems, died of burns and inhalation."

"Mikhail Krukov?" Marchuk raised his eyebrows. "A Russian name?"

"He was called Mike," Slava said.

"They were drunk?" Hess asked. "Is that what the competent authorities suggest?"

"Like our own, their natives are known to be abusers of alcohol," Slava said.

Marchuk smiled like a man who had heard a joke on the way to the gallows. He turned the smile toward Arkady. "Volovoi didn't drink and he hated boats. But that's the report; that's what I'm supposed to tell Vladivostok. Somehow I have the feeling that you have something you could add."

The ship trembled as it hit a larger ice floe. Arkady waited until the grinding slid past. "No," he said.

"Nothing?" Marchuk asked. "I think of you as such a reliable source of surprises."

Arkady shrugged. As an afterthought he asked Slava, "Who found the bodies?"

"Karp."

"Karp Korobetz, a trawlmaster," the captain explained to Hess. "He was searching for Volovoi in the company of an engineer from the *Eagle.*"

"Ridley," Slava said. "He showed Karp the way to the bunker."

"What time did they discover the bodies?" Arkady asked.

"About ten," Slava said. "They had to break the door in."

"You hear that?" Marchuk underlined the words for Arkady. "They had to *break in.* It was locked from the inside. That's the touch I like."

"Karp and Ridley entered the bunker?" Arkady asked Slava. "They looked around?"

"I suppose."

Slava jumped as Marchuk slapped his cap against a boot and shook off water. The captain replaced the hat on his head and lit a cigarette. "Go on," he encouraged Slava.

"Volovoi was found in the main room of the bunker and the American was found in a second room," Slava said. "There was a trapdoor of sorts in the second room, but no ladder was found."

"There was no way up from the inside," Marchuk said. "It's like a mystery."

"I didn't see much of Dutch Harbor," Arkady said.

"Really?" Marchuk said.

"But I didn't notice much in the way of medical facilities," Arkady continued. "Did a doctor examine the bodies?"

"Yes," Slava said.

"In a laboratory?"

"No." Slava became defensive. "There was clearly a fire and explosion, and the bodies were almost too badly burned to be moved."

"The Americans accept that?" Arkady asked.

Marchuk said, "They would have to fly the bodies to the mainland, and we're not going to let them have Volovoi. His body will be examined in Vladivostok. Anyway, Captain Morgan has accepted the report."

"Just out of curiosity," Arkady said, "who was next at the scene, after Korobetz and Ridley?"

"Morgan," Slava read.

"You accept the report, too?" Arkady asked Marchuk.

"Of course. Two men die, one of theirs and one of ours, and nearly every sign indicates that they got drunk and burned themselves to death. That's the kind of stink the Americans and we can mutually put behind us. Cooperation is the byword of a joint venture."

The captain swung his attention to Slava. "Volovoi was a real shit. I hope you can fill his shoes." He leaned forward, turning again to Arkady. "But how do you think this will look for me, returning to Vladivostok with two of my crew in bags? Do you know what a circus it will be? What will my next command be? A garbage scow in Magadan? They still float logs along Kamchatka. Maybe they'll save a log for me."

"You went ashore on my authority," Hess said to Arkady. "Supposedly you were still gathering information about the dead girl, Zina Patiashvili."

"Thank you," Arkady said. "It was invigorating to be on land again."

"But now we have three dead instead of one," Hess pressed on, "and since one was the vigilant defender of the Party, the Party will have its questions when we return home."

"Somehow"—Marchuk stared at Arkady—"somehow I connect it all to you. You come on board; there's one dead. You go ashore; there are two more dead. Compared with you, Jonah was a ray of sunshine."

"You see, this is the question: where were *you*?" Hess asked. "Volovoi left the hotel searching for you. No one could find either of you, and the next time we see the commissar he's up on top of a hill burned to death with an Indian—"

"An Aleut," Slava said. "It's in my report."

"A native, whatever, to whom Volovoi had hardly ever spoken before. What was Volovoi doing drinking, which he never did, with a boatbuilder on top of a hill? Why would he be there when he was looking for you?" Hess asked Arkady.

"Do you want me to try to find out?"

Hess smiled at the answer from sheer professional appreciation, as if he had seen a goalie stop a difficult kick, then boot the ball into the opposite net.

"No, no," Marchuk said. "No more help from you. I can just see their faces in Vladivostok if we tried to explain why we assigned you to investigate the death of Volovoi. Comrade Bukovsky is in charge."

"Again? Congratulations," Arkady said to Slava.

"I have already questioned Seaman Renko," Slava said. "He claims that after leaving Susan, being drunk and feeling ill, he went out behind the hotel and passed out. Then he remembers nothing until he found himself in the water, having fallen off the dock."

Marchuk said, "Izrael, the factory manager, tells me that you were drunk in a fishhold the other day and almost froze yourself. No wonder you lost your Party card."

"The hidden drunks are the worst," Arkady agreed. "But, Captain, you just said you accepted the American report that there was an accidental fire. Then what is Comrade Bukovsky investigating?"

"I'm assembling our own findings," Slava said. "I'm not necessarily asking questions."

"The best kind of investigation." Arkady nodded. "A straight line with no dangerous curves. Incidentally," he said to Hess, "could I have my knife back? You took it before we went ashore."

"I'd have to look for it."

"Please do. It's property of the state."

Marchuk crushed his cigarette into an ashtray and glanced at the porthole, heavy-lidded with ice. "Well, your days as an investigator are over once again. The death of Zina Patiashvili is a closed matter

until we reach home. Gentlemen, the fish await." He rose, pulled
the beak of his cap forward, picked up the twisted butt and used it
to light another cigarette. Everyone had been smoking Marlboros
since Dutch Harbor. "I like you, Renko, but I have to say this: if
our comrade Volovoi didn't die in the fire—if, for example, his
throat was cut—I would suspect you first. We can't figure out how
you could kill two men or escape the fire. I like the way you fell in
the water. That would dampen the smell of the smoke and wash the
grass off your boots." He pushed up the collar of his coat. "My
Americans await. It's like leading little girls across a frozen pond."

22 From the stern rail Susan focused binoculars on the wake of the *Polar Star.* Her jacket was buttoned to her chin and, like a girl on skis, she wore mittens and a woolen cap.

"See anything?" Arkady asked.

"I was watching the *Eagle.* A Gulf boat shouldn't be here."

"I've been looking for you."

"Funny," she said, "I've been avoiding you."

Out of habit, Arkady checked over his shoulder to see whether Karp was near. "That's hard on a ship."

"Apparently."

"Can I look?" he asked.

She handed him the glasses. Arkady focused first on the water reaching up the *Polar Star*'s ramp, the waves almost a tropical blue as they flowed in and out of the rusty gullet. Water so cold seemed molten. Seawater started to crystallize at 29 degrees Fahrenheit, and because it carried so much brine it formed first not as a solid but as a transparent sheen, undulating on black swells, going gray as it congealed.

The trawlers had to stay close to mother. Through the glasses he could see the *Merry Jane* slip by the *Eagle* as the first ship brought in a bag that lay fat and wet on its deck. The *Eagle* was just setting its net, and as it rose on a swell he had a clear view of two deckhands in yellow slickers. Americans didn't use safety gates. Water surged freely up and down the ramp, and the men expertly timed their every move, jumping onto gantry rungs when larger waves broke over the gunwales. The binoculars were 10×50, so Arkady could see that it was the former policeman Coletti who was working the hydraulic levers on the gantry. The second fisherman threw loose crabs over the side, and only as the man turned did Arkady recognize the peaked brows and grin of Ridley.

"Just a two-man crew?" Arkady asked. "They didn't replace Mike?"

"They're capitalists. One less share to give up."

Setting a net was a delicate operation in the best of circumstances, which was a calm sea with room to maneuver. The *Aurora* had already tangled its trawl wires on a propeller and left, at a limp, for Dutch Harbor. In the wheelhouse, Morgan, in a baseball cap and parka, alternately worked the *Eagle*'s throttle and tended the controls of the winch behind him.

"Why didn't you stay at the hotel with me?" Susan asked.

"I told you that Volovoi was coming to take me back to the ship."

"Maybe he should have. There'd be more people alive now."

Arkady, always slow on the uptake, finally put the glasses down and noticed that Susan's cheeks weren't burning merely from the cold. What had he looked like when he suddenly left her? A coward, a seducer? More likely a buffoon.

"I'm sorry I left," he said.

"Too late," Susan said. "You weren't just running from Volovoi. I watched from the window when you crossed the road. You were following Mike." The steam of her breath seemed like visible contempt. "You followed Mike, Volovoi followed you. Now they're both dead and you're taking an Arctic cruise."

Arkady had come to apologize, but as always there seemed to be a barrier between the two of them he couldn't cross. Anyway, what could he say? That Mike was dead when he found him? That a model trawlmaster had sliced the first mate's throat, though he had witnesses for where he supposedly was and Arkady did not? Or, what were you looking for in the water?

"Can you tell me what happened?"

"No," he admitted.

"Let me tell you what I think. I think you really were an investigator of some sort at some time. You're pretending to try to find out about Zina, but you've been offered a chance to get off the boat if you can blame an American. It would have been Mike, but now that he's dead you have to find another one. What I don't understand," she said, "is me. Back at Dutch Harbor I actually believed you. Then I saw you running across the road after Mike."

Arkady found himself getting warm. "Did you tell anyone I was following him?"

In spite of her anger she looked back at the *Eagle.* Arkady looked through the glasses again. The boat went hull down, then disappeared behind a swell, and when it rose, both Ridley and Coletti had climbed the gantry to stay out of water that would have been up to their knees. In the wheelhouse Morgan had picked up his own binoculars and was watching Arkady in return.

"He'll stay close to us, won't he?"

"Or get iced in," Susan said.

"Is he a dedicated man?"

A swell like a smooth rock streaked with foam grew between the two men, gathered momentum as it rolled to the *Polar Star* and then plunged up the factory-ship ramp. Morgan held his binoculars steady on his target.

"He's a professional," she said.

"Did you make him jealous?" Arkady asked. "Was that why you asked me to your room?"

Susan's hand rose to slap him, then stopped. Why? Arkady wondered. Did she think a slap would be too banal, too bourgeois? Nonsense. On a Saturday night the Moscow metro resounded with slaps.

The ship's speakers squawked. It was 1500, time for light musical selections from Fleet Radio, beginning with a rumba suggesting Cuban beaches and waving palms. Socialist maracas struck up a Latin rhythm.

Arkady said, "This music reminds me: before Dutch Harbor you were leaving us for a vacation. Soo-san, why did you come back to this Soviet ship you hate so much? The fish? The excitement of filling the quota?"

"No, but it might be worth it to see you rotting on the slime line again."

THE RADIO ROOM was the first port-side cabin behind the bridge. Nikolai, the young man who had piloted the lifeboat that had taken Hess and Arkady into Dutch Harbor, was idly working the crossword puzzle in *Soviet Sport* when Arkady entered. His desk was occupied by stacked radios, amplifiers and a row of binders, one with the red stripe of classified codes, but there was room left for a hot plate and pot. Cozy. The rumba trotted in and out of the speaker. Not bad duty. Junior lieutenants with training in electronics were often assigned to fishing fleets to take an ostensibly civilian tour of foreign ports. Even in his warm-up suit and slippers Nikolai had the air of a freshly minted officer whose future was lined with gold braid. He raised his eyes lazily toward Arkady.

"Whatever it is, old-timer, I'm busy."

Arkady checked to make sure no one was in the passage, then closed the door, kicked over the radioman's chair and planted a foot on his chest.

"You screwed Zina Patiashvili. You took her into an intelligence station in this ship. If your chief finds out, you'll go to a military labor camp, and by the time you get out you'll be lucky if you still have teeth and hair."

On his back, Nikolai still held his pencil, his eyes two perfect pools of blue. "That's a lie."

"Then let's tell Hess."

Arkady looked down at a young man who was experiencing all the terrors of free fall, for whom a comfortable and promising world had suddenly become an abyss.

"How do you know?" Nikolai asked.

"That's better." Arkady removed his foot and helped him up. "You can pick up the chair. Sit."

Nikolai promptly did as he was ordered, always a good sign. Arkady turned up the speaker a notch as the rumba faded and was replaced by a Bulgarian folk song.

While the lieutenant sat at attention Arkady considered the different ways to handle this interrogation: as a former lover of Zina himself, as a blackmailer, as someone still carrying out a ship's inquiry. But he wanted an approach that would throw an aggressive naval intelligence officer into a pit of despair, as if the young man were already in the hands of the military's most despised enemy. He deliberately chose the unlikely words with which the KGB always began its more informal chats.

"Relax. If you're honest, you have nothing to worry about."

Nikolai shrank in his chair. "It was one time, that's all. She recognized me from Vladivostok. I thought she was a waitress; how did I know she was going to be on board? Maybe I should have told someone, but she begged me not to because she would have been sent back home on an off-loader. I had mercy on her, and then one thing led to another."

"It led her to your cot."

"I didn't plan it that way. There's no privacy on a ship. That was the only time."

"No."

"It was!"

"Vladivostok," Arkady prompted him. "The Golden Horn."

"You were watching her then?"

"Tell me about it."

Nikolai's story wasn't much different from Marchuk's. He'd gone to the Golden Horn with friends from the base and they'd all noticed Zina, but she seemed to be most attracted to him. When she got off work, the two went to her place, listened to music, danced, made love, and then he left and never saw her again until the *Polar Star.* "I thought the investigation about Zina was over," he said. "I heard you were back in the factory."

"She was a good waitress?"

"The worst."

"What did you talk about?"

Arkady could feel the radioman's mind freeze like a rabbit wondering which way to run next. Not only was he implicated in the betrayal of his service on the ship, but the interrogation had dangerously expanded into the past, implicating him again, if only through coincidence. The worst construction was that Zina had infiltrated the Pacific Fleet not once but twice, both times through him. Not necessarily as a foreign agent, to be sure; the KGB was always and obsessively trying to worm into the military, and naval intelligence was always and paranoically testing the vigilance of its own officers to see if it could breach its own security.

Like other men in similar dilemmas, Nikolai decided to plead guilty to a smaller crime as evidence of his honesty. "I have the best receivers in the world in Vladivostok. I can get American Armed Forces Radio, Manila, Nome. Sometimes I have to monitor them anyway, so I tape—just music and just for myself, never for profit. I offered one to Zina as a friend and said we ought to go someplace where we could play it. Okay, it was a come-on, but we never talked about anything but music. She wanted me to duplicate the tapes and sell the copies through her. Zina was Georgian through and through. I told her no. We went to her place and listened to the tapes, but that was all."

"Not quite all. You got what you wanted; you slept with her."

Arkady asked what Zina's apartment was like, and again Nikolai's description resembled Marchuk's. A private flat in a relatively new building, maybe a co-op. Television, VCR, stereo. Japanese prints and samurai swords on the wall. Doors and bar upholstered in red plastic. A rifle collection in a locked case. Though there were no photographs, clearly a man lived there too, and Nikolai had assumed that Zina's friend was powerful and wealthy, either a black-market millionaire or someone high up in the Party.

"You're a Party member?" Arkady asked.

"Young Communist."

"Tell me about the radios here."

Nikolai was happy to leave the subject of Zina Patiashvili and expound on more technical matters. The *Polar Star*'s radio cabin had a VHF radio with a range of about fifty kilometers for communicating with the catcher boats, and two larger, single side-band radios for longer range. One single side band was usually tuned to the fleet radio. The second single side band was for radio conferences with other Soviet ships spread across the Bering Sea, or for contact with fleet headquarters in Vladivostok and the company office in Seattle. In between, the radio monitored an emergency channel that all ships kept open.

The cabin also had a shortwave for Radio Moscow or the BBC. "I'll show you something else." Nikolai brought from under the desk a receiver no larger than a historical novel. "A CB radio. Very short range, but this is how the catcher boats talk to each other when they don't want us to listen in. All the more reason for us to have it." He turned it on to the voice of Thorwald, the captain of the *Merry Jane*, droning in a Norwegian accent, ". . . fucking Russians pounded the fucking Georges Bank to death and pounding the fucking African coast until there's no fucking fish there. At least we'll get some fucking money—"

Arkady turned the CB off. "Tell me more about Zina."

"She wasn't a real blonde. She was pretty wild, though."

"Not sex. What you talked about."

"Tapes. I told you." Nikolai had the confused expression of a student who was trying to cooperate but didn't know what his new teacher wanted.

"The weather?" Arkady prompted.

"For her, anywhere but Georgia was too cold."

"Georgia?"

"She said Georgian men would screw anything that bent over."

"Work?"

"She expressed an un-Soviet philosophy about labor."

"Fun?"

"Dancing."

"Men?"

"Money." Nikolai laughed. "I don't know why I say that because she didn't ask me for any. But she had a way of looking at you one moment as if you were the most handsome, desirable man on earth, which is a very erotic sensation, and then a minute later dismissing you with her eyes as if you couldn't possibly meet her expectations. I'd say, 'Why are you looking at me so coldly?' and she'd say, 'I'm imagining you're not a little sailor boy, that you're an *Afghantsi*, a soldier sent off to fight against Allah and his madmen, and you've just come home in a zinc-lined coffin and it makes me sad.' Cruel things like that—and right in the middle of love, too."

"What about the guns in the apartment? Did she talk about them?"

"No. I had the feeling I'd be some sort of softie in her eyes if I asked. She did say that the guy, whoever he was, slept with a gun under his pillow. I thought, Well, that's typically Siberian."

"Did she ask you questions?"

"Just about my family, my home, did I write often like a good son and send proper packages of coffee and tea?"

"Doesn't the navy have its own system so that parcels don't arrive ripped apart months after they're sent?"

"The navy takes care of its own."

"And she asked you to send a parcel for her?"

There was something increasingly calflike about the radioman in the widening of his eyes. "Yes."

"Tea?"

"Yes."

"Already wrapped for you to take?"

"Yes. But at the last minute she changed her mind and I left without it. That was another time when she gave me one of those looks as if I couldn't measure up."

"When you met on the *Polar Star,* did she tell you how she came to be on board?"

"She just said she'd got bored back at the restaurant, bored with Vladivostok, bored with Siberia. When I asked how she got a seaman's union card, she laughed in my face and said she'd bought it, what else? The rules about that are well known, but they didn't seem to apply to Zina."

"She was different?"

Nikolai struggled with words, then admitted failure. "You had to know her."

Arkady changed the subject. "Our single side-band radios, what's their range?"

"It varies with the atmospherics. The captain can tell you; one day we can get Mexico and the next day nothing. But members of the ship's crew often call home all the way to Moscow through a radio-telephone link. It's a morale builder."

Arkady asked, "Can other ships listen to those conversations?"

"If they happen to be monitoring the right channel they can hear the incoming part of the conversation, but not what we say."

"Good. Place a call for me to Odessa militia headquarters."

"No problem." Nikolai was eager to please. "Of course, all calls have to be cleared with the captain."

"You don't want to clear this call; you don't even want to log it. Let's review the situation," Arkady said, because the radio technician was a young man who needed careful instruction. "As a naval officer, simply for admitting Patiashvili into your station on the *Polar Star* you can be charged with betraying your sacred trust. Since this was an ongoing relationship the question of conspiracy to commit the state crime of treason comes up. Even if you were merely innocently attempting to seduce a citizen, you can still be charged with activities detrimental to the high standing of Soviet womanhood, failure to report illegal firearms, theft of state property—the tapes—and dissemination of anti-Soviet propaganda—the music. In any case, your life as a naval officer is at an end."

Listening, Nikolai looked like a man swallowing a fish whole. "No problem. It may take an hour or so to get through to Odessa, but I'll do it."

"Incidentally, since you are a music lover, where were you during the ship's dance?"

"My other duties." Nikolai lowered his eyes to indicate, below-decks, the intelligence station Arkady had yet to find. "It's funny you mention music. The tapes that Zina had in the apartment in Vladivostok? Some was rock, but most were magnatizdat. You know, thieves' songs."

" 'You can cut my throat, but don't cut my guitar strings'?"

"Exactly! You did know her."

"I do now."

On the way out, Arkady had to admit to himself that he'd been harder on the radioman than he'd really needed to be. It was the dig "old-timer" that had been Nikolai's mistake. He found himself running his hand over his face. Did he look old? He didn't feel old.

23 Under Gury's bunk was a new nylon bag stuffed with plastic booty: Sony Walkmen, Swatch watches, Aiwa speakers, WaterPiks, Marlboros and a Mickey Mouse telephone. Taped on the wardrobe were Polaroid snapshots of Obidin, his beard cleaned and combed, standing before the wooden church in Unalaska like a man modestly posing on a cloud beside his Lord. Inside, the wardrobe was redolent with the exhalation of rows of jars of home brew flavored with fresh and canned fruit from the Dutch Harbor store. Anyone reaching for his jacket was assaulted by the sugary fumes of peaches, cherries and exotic mandarin oranges. The most botanical corner of the cabin, however, was Kolya's shelves of specimens gathered on the island and brought back in cardboard pots: furry moss clinging to a rock bedded on a moist page from *Pravda;* a miniature bush with minute purple berries; the sickle-shaped, papery leaves of a dwarf iris; a paintbrush that still claimed one fire-red petal.

Kolya was giving Natasha the tour; with the porthole laced by frost, his corner of the cabin resembled a greenhouse. It was the first time he'd ever impressed her. "Any scientific voyage returned like this," he explained. "Cook and Darwin filled their small ships with botanical specimens in the holds, bulbs in the chain lockers, bread-fruit trees on deck. Because life is everywhere. The underside of the ice sheet around us is covered with algae. That's what brings the tiny creatures that, in turn, attract the fish. Naturally, predators follow: seals, whales, polar bears. We're surrounded by life."

Arkady's mind was on botany of a different sort. He sat at the narrow table, enjoying one of Gury's cigarettes and thinking of wild hemp, thousands of square hectares of luxuriant wild Manchurian hemp heavy with narcotic pollen, flowers and leaves growing like free rubles across the rugged Asian landscape. Every autumn what Siberians called "grass fever" broke out as people flocked like Party volunteers—better than Party volunteers—to the countryside for the harvest. Often no travel was necessary because the weed grew everywhere—along the road, in the potato field, in the tomato patch. Called *anasha,* it was trucked in bags west toward Moscow, where it could be smoked loose like cigarettes or tamped into pipes.

There was also *plan.* Hashish. *Plan* came in kilo bricks from Afghanistan and Pakistan, then traveled by different routes, some on army lorries, some on ferries over the Black and Caspian seas across Georgia, then north to Moscow.

"Polar bears wander for hundreds of kilometers out on the ice sheet," Kolya was telling Natasha. "No one knows how they find their way. They hunt two ways, by waiting at the holes where seals come up to breathe and by swimming under the ice and watching for a seal shadow above."

Or poppies, Arkady thought. How many Georgian collectives overfulfilled their quota for the magic flower? How much was swept from the threshing floor, how much dried, how much baled, how

much processed into morphine, then seemingly blown by the wind
to Moscow?

From an investigator's point of view, Moscow appeared to be an
innocent Eve, surrounded by dangerous gardens, constantly seduced
by oily Georgian, Afghan and Siberian snakes. The "tea" that Zina
had asked Nikolai to send was undoubtedly a block of hemp, *anasha*.
She'd changed her mind, probably because it was such small change,
but it meant that there was at least part of a network in place.

"You found all these flowers just around the road and the store?"
Natasha asked.

"Well, you have to know where to look," Kolya said.

"The seed of beauty is everywhere." Natasha wore her hair back
to show off the crystal earrings she'd bought in Dutch Harbor.
"Wouldn't you agree, Arkady?"

"It's undeniable."

"You see how much more constructively Comrade Mer spent his
time on shore, instead of getting disgustingly drunk and falling in
the water."

"Kolya, I bow to your scientific zeal." Arkady noticed that his
cabin mate's spiral notebook, with its gray crocodile-textured binding, was the kind sold in the ship's store, the same as Zina's. "May
I?" He flipped through the pages. On each Kolya had noted a
different plant by common name, Latin name, when and where
picked.

"Were you alone when you fell in?" Natasha asked.

"It's less embarrassing that way."

"Susan wasn't with you?"

"No one."

"You could have been hurt." Kolya was upset. "A little tipsy, in
the water, at night."

"I was wondering," Natasha said to Arkady, "what you plan to do when we return to Vladivostok. When he was alive, Comrade Volovoi suggested that you might have difficulties with the Guard. Positive statements from your co-workers, from Party members, might be helpful. Then you might want to go elsewhere. There are some very nice hydroelectric projects starting on the Yenisei. Arctic bonuses, a month's vacation anywhere. With your abilities, you'd learn how to run a crane in no time."

"Thanks, I'll consider that."

"How many former investigators from Moscow can say they built a dam?" she asked.

"Not many."

"We could keep a cow. I mean, *you* could keep a cow if you wanted. Anyone who wanted to keep a cow could keep a cow. In a private plot. Or a pig. Or even chickens, though you have to have someplace warm for fowl in the wintertime."

"Cow? Chickens?" Arkady shook his head. What was this about?

"The Yenisei is interesting," Kolya said.

"It's *very* interesting," Natasha emphasized. "Beautiful taiga of pines and larches. Deer and grouse."

"Edible snails," Kolya said.

"But you'd have a cow if you wanted. Room for a motorcycle too. Picnics on the riverbank. A whole town full of young people, children. You—"

"Did Zina know anything about ships?" Arkady interrupted. "Did she understand terminology, what different parts of a ship are called?"

Natasha couldn't believe her ears. "Zina? Again?"

"What would she mean by 'fishhold'?"

"She's dead. That's all over."

"The hold or anything near to it?" Arkady asked.

"Zina knew nothing about ships, nothing about her work, nothing except her own self-interest, and she's dead," Natasha said. "Why this fascination? When she was alive you cared nothing about her. It was one thing when the captain ordered you to carry out an investigation. Now your interest is morbid, negative and disgusting."

Arkady pulled on his boots. "You could be right," he said.

"I'm sorry, Arkasha, I shouldn't have said any of that. Please."

"Don't apologize for being honest." Arkady reached for his jacket.

"I hate the sea," Natasha said bitterly. "I should have gone to Moscow. I could have gotten work in a mill and looked for a husband there."

"The mills are sweatshops," Arkady said, "and you'd have lived in a dorm with a curtain between your bed and the next. It's too cramped; you'd hate it there. A big flower deserves a lot of space."

"True." She liked that.

BELOWDECKS IN THE bow it sounded as if the *Polar Star* weren't so much breaking ice as plowing through an unseen landscape, over-turning houses and trees, unearthing boulders. Arkady wouldn't have been surprised to see beds or branches puncture the rusty skin of steel. What did the rats think? They had left land generations before. Did this din evoke memories and odd dreams in rodent sleep?

Zina had said "fishhold," but what she must have meant was the chain locker next to the hold. The lowest and most forward point of the ship, the locker was an angular catchall space usually stuffed with hawsers and chains, a dark corner that might be visited twice on a voyage by a scrupulous bosun. Only a recessed peephole in the watertight hatch suggested that this door might be different from any other. Before he could knock, the hatch opened with a pop of air, like a bottle. As soon as he stepped in and the hatch closed behind him, he felt his eardrums compress.

A red overhead bulb revealed Anton Hess sitting in a swivel chair. In the light, his towering hair looked askew. He had turned from three monitors that were tapped into the bridge's echo sounder; on the screens three green seas flowed over three orange sea floors; he looked like a magician hovering over vats of fluorescent color. Stacked on one side were two loran monitors with luminous cross hairs that marked latitude and longitude on glowing charts that matched the paper plotters Arkady had seen on the *Eagle* and that far outstripped anything on Marchuk's bridge. On the other side was a blank oscilloscope and what looked like a sound engineer's acoustical mixer, complete with headset. Above this was a screen showing in gray halftones the passage between the locker and the fishhold, where Arkady had been standing a moment before. There was a small mainframe computer and racks of other equipment he couldn't make out clearly in the red haze, though all the gear, plus chair and cot, were crammed into an area not much larger than a closet. For a submariner, it must be just like home.

"I'm surprised it took you this long to find me," Hess said.

"Me, too."

"Sit." Hess indicated the cot. "Welcome to our little station. I'm afraid there's no smoking allowed because the air circulation is nonexistent, but it's like the paratroops: you pack your own parachute. I designed it, so I have no one else to blame."

One reason the space was so snug, Arkady realized, was the heavy soundproofing on every surface; there was even a false deck over insulation that muffled the grinding of ice and steel plate. As his eyes adjusted he saw another reason: built into the deck where the bulkheads met was a white hemisphere a full meter across. The dome seemed to be the lid of something much larger built into the bottom of the ship itself.

"Amazing," Arkady said.

"No, it's pathetic. It's a desperate resort to redress the unfairness of geography and the burden of history. Every major Soviet port faces a choke point or is icebound six months of the year. Leaving Vladivostok, our fleet has to pass through either the Kuril or the Korea Strait. In a war we probably wouldn't get a single surface ship out. Thank God for submarines."

On the three screens Arkady watched an orange tracery mounting like a wave, the signals of groundfish rising to feed. Why fish enjoyed foul weather no one knew. Hess held out something glittering to Arkady: a flask, brandy at body temperature.

"Underwater we're equal?"

"Ignoring the fact that they carry twice as many warheads. And that they can keep sixty percent of their missile boats on patrol while we can barely manage fifteen percent. Also that their boats are quieter, faster and dive deeper. But this is where irony comes in, Renko. I know you appreciate irony as much as I do. The only place where our submarines can safely hide is under the Arctic ice, and the only way the Americans can come after us from the Pacific is across the Bering Sea and through the Bering Strait. For once *we* choke *them.*"

Host and guest drank to geography. As Arkady sat back the cot squeaked and he thought of Zina on the same blanket. There hadn't been any lectures then. "So you have a quota of fish too, in a sense," he said.

"Not to catch, just to hear. You know that the *Polar Star* was in dry dock."

"I did wonder what work was done. No one has noticed any improvements that have to do with fishing."

"Extra ears." Hess nodded toward the white dome set into the deck. "It's called a towed array sonar. This is a passive system, a cable with hydrophones that plays out from an electric winch in that pod. On submarines we mount the pod over the stern. On the *Polar Star* we've mounted it near the bow to avoid getting it tangled in an American net."

"And you pull in the cable before a net is brought on," Arkady said. That was why Nikolai had time to dally with Zina, because a bag of fish was coming in.

"It's not a very effective system for deep water, but this is a shallow sea. Submarines, even theirs, hate shallow water. They race for the strait, and the faster they go, the louder they are and we hear them. Every boat sounds different." Hess swiveled toward a rack with a computer, monitor and a file of soft disks. "Here we have the signatures of five hundred submarines, theirs and ours. By matching, we sort out their routes and missions. Of course, we could do the same on one of our submarines or hydrographic boats, but they hide their subs from those. The *Polar Star* is only a factory ship in the middle of the Bering Sea."

Arkady remembered the map in the cabin of the fleet electrical engineer. "One of fifty Soviet factory ships along their coast?"

"Exactly. This is the prototype."

"It seems rather sophisticated."

"No," Hess said. "Let me tell you what is sophisticated in terms of electronic intelligence gathering. The Americans place nuclear-powered monitors off the Siberian coast. Those containers hold six tons of reconnaissance equipment and a supply of plutonium so they can transmit indefinitely right under our noses. Their submarines go into Murmansk harbor and place hydrophones right on our subma-rines. They like coming out with trophies. Of course, if they could get hold of our cable it would be displayed in Washington with one of those news events they do so well, as if they had never seen a can on a string before."

"That's what your cable is, a can on a string?"

"Microphones on a three-hundred-meter string, essentially." Hess granted himself half a smile. "The software is interesting; it was originally programmed in California to track whales."

"Do you ever mistake a boat for a whale?"

"No." Hess's fingers reached out and touched the round screen of the oscilloscope as if it were a crystal ball. There was a handcrafted quality to it, as there often was to the high technology produced by the Ministry for Electrical Apparatus. "Whales and dolphins sound like beacons in deep space. You can hear some whales for close to one thousand kilometers—deep bass notes with the long waves of low frequencies. Then there are the other sounds of fish, of seals pursuing the fish, of walrus digging up the floor with their tusks. Altogether it's like the sound of an orchestra constantly warming up. Then you hear a certain hiss that shouldn't be there."

"You're a musician?" Arkady asked.

"When I was a boy I thought the cello would be my career."

Arkady looked at the monitors and the repeated image of orange fish rising in an electric-green sea. The white dome had clamps; it was removable; if the winch had to be serviced, what else could Hess do, send down a diver?

"Why do you think I had you taken off the slime line?" Hess continued. "I heard something suspicious: that this dead girl, Zina Patiashvili, went to the stern every time the *Eagle* delivered a net. To wave at a native boy? Let's not be silly. The only possible answer is that she was signaling Captain Morgan whether we had played the cable out or not."

"Is it visible?"

"Not during tests, but she must have seen something besides Morgan's net."

"They say Morgan is a good fisherman."

"George Morgan has fished the Gulf of Thailand, off Guantánamo and Grenada. He should know how to fish. That's why I supported an investigation. Better to dig up the truth, to shake a traitor out of the tree sooner rather than later. But, Renko, I must tell you that too many bodies have been hitting the ground. First the girl, then Volovoi and the American? And you snake in and out, in and out of all this."

"I can find out about Zina."

"And our roasted first mate? No, we'll leave it to Vladivostok; there are too many questions now—including, how are you involved?"

"Someone's trying to kill me."

"That's not good enough. Zina–Susan–Morgan, that's the chain I want. Fit into that and you justify my interest. The rest is none of my concern."

"You don't care what happened to Zina."

"By itself, of course not."

"Would you be interested in evidence of smuggling?"

Hess laughed in horror. "My God, no. That's an invitation to the KGB to stick its nose into the affairs of intelligence. Renko, try to lift your eyes above petty crime. Give me something real."

"Like what?"

"Susan. I watched you in Dutch Harbor. Renko, you must be irresistibly charming in a wounded sort of way. She's attracted. Get closer. Serve your country and yourself. Find something on her and Morgan and I'll order an off-loader just for you."

"Incriminating notes, secret codes?"

"We'll rewire her cabin or we can put a transmitter on you."

"We can do it any number of different ways."

"Whatever you're comfortable with."

"Well, no, I don't think so," Arkady said after consideration. "Actually I came for something else."

"What did you come for?"

Arkady stood for a better view of the corners of the locker. "I just wanted to see if Zina's body was stowed here."

"And?"

The light was dim, but the space was close. "No," Arkady decided.

The two men looked at each other, Hess with the saddened expression of a man who has sung confidences and aspirations to a deaf ear.

"Petty crime is my passion," Arkady apologized.

The hatch popped open.

"Wait," Hess said as Arkady started to go. The little man searched in a drawer and came out with a shiny object. This time it was Arkady's knife. He handed it over. "Property of the state, right? Good luck."

Arkady glanced back on the way out. Under the black-and-white screen, Anton Hess was an exhausted man. The colored screens seemed inappropriately gay, tuned into some happier wavelength. Behind their glow the dome nesting in the insulated floor resembled the tip of a vulnerable egg that the fleet electrical engineer was shepherding around the world.

24 Rain beat the *Polar Star* with sharp horizontal drops that beaded into soft, spongy ice. The crew worked under lamps, hosing the ship off with live steam from the boilers so that the trawl deck smoked as if it were on fire. Ropes stretched across the deck and men clung to the lines, slipping as the deck rolled. Wearing their hard hats under fur-lined hoods, the team looked like a Siberian construction crew, all but Karp, who was still in a sweater as if the weather meant nothing to him.

"Relax." Karp grandly offered a hand as Arkady approached. A radio hung from a strap on his belt. "Enjoy the refreshing Bering weather."

"You haven't been after me." Arkady counted the deck team to be sure they were all in sight. On either side of the deck, pollack overflowed the bunkers. Surrounded by steaming mist, glazed by freezing rain, the fish sparkled like silvery armor in the lamps.

"It's not as if you had some other place to go." Karp pulled a block down by its rope to hammer ice from the sheave with the butt of his knife. The gantry operator was out of his cabin. Because of the ice sheet, no catcher boats were alongside. The entire deck was obscured by steam. "I could probably throw you overboard right now and nobody would notice."

"What if I hit the ice and didn't sink?" Arkady said. "You have to think things through. You're too impulsive."

Karp laughed. "You have brass balls, I'll give you that."

"What was it Volovoi said that made you stick him?" Arkady asked. "Was it that he swore he'd take the ship apart when we got back to Vladivostok? Knifing him didn't help. The KGB is going to be all over us when we return."

"Ridley will say I was with him all night." Karp picked out the last ice with his blade. "Say anything about Volovoi and it will come right back to you."

"Forget about Volovoi." Arkady shook out a *papirosa,* a cigarette that could stand up to rain, sleet or driving snow. "Zina is still who interests me."

Waist-high in a roar of clouds, Pavel worked his way along the rail with a hose of steaming water. Karp waved him off. "What about Zina?" he asked Arkady.

"Whatever she was doing she wasn't doing alone; that was never the way she operated. I look around this ship and the only one she would have operated with is you. You told Slava you hardly knew her."

"She was a fellow worker, that's all."

"Just another worker like you?"

"No, I'm a model worker." Karp enjoyed the distinction. He spread his arms. "You don't know about workers because you're not one, not at heart. You think the slime line's bad?" He tapped his knife on Arkady's chest to make a point. "Ever work in a slaughter-house?"

"Yes."

"A reindeer slaughterhouse?"

"Yes."

"Slipping around in guts with an oilskin on your shoulder?"

"Yes."

"Along the Aldan?" The Aldan was a river in eastern Siberia.

"Yes."

Karp paused. "The director of the collective's a Koryak named Sinaneft, went around on a pony?"

"No, he was a Buryat named Korin and he drove a Moskvitch with skis on the front wheels."

"You really worked there." Karp was amused. "Korin had two sons."

"Daughters."

"One with tattoos, though. Funny, isn't it? All the time I was in the camps, all the time in Siberia, I said if there was any justice in the world you and I would meet again. And all the time fate was on my side."

Overhead, the crane operator carried a mug into his cabin. Across the deck the American called Bernie made his way aft. Enveloped in a parka, he inched along the rope like a toddler. From Karp's radio came Thorwald's throaty voice announcing that the *Merry Jane* was approaching with a bag. The trawlmaster sheathed his knife and at once the work tempo changed. Hoses were shut off, cables were dragged to the ramp.

"You're not dumb, but you never think more than one step ahead," Arkady said. "You should have stayed in Siberia or smuggled videotapes or jeans—small stuff, nothing big."

"Now let me tell you about you," Karp said. He brushed ice from Arkady's jacket. "You're like a dog that's kicked out of the house. You live off scraps in the woods for a while and you think you can run with wolves. But really, in the back of your mind, what you want to do is bring down one wolf so they'll let you back in the house." He picked a crystal from Arkady's hair and whispered, "You'll never make it back to Vladivostok."

PEOPLE BECAME WINTER animals, wearing their jackets while they ate. In the middle of the long table was a pot of cabbage soup that smelled like laundry and was consumed with raw garlic offered on separate plates, along with dark bread, goulash and tea that steamed enough to make the cafeteria as foggy as a sauna. Izrail slipped onto the bench next to Arkady. As usual, the factory manager bore fish scales on his beard, as if he'd waded to the crew's mess. "You cannot ignore your socialist duty," he whispered to Arkady. "You must take your place on the work line with your comrades or you will be reported."

Natasha sat across from Arkady. She still wore her factory-line toque, the high white cap designed to keep her hair out of the fish.

"Listen to Izrail Izrailevich," she told Arkady. "I thought you must be sick. I went to your cabin and you weren't there."

"Olimpiada has a way with cabbage." Arkady offered to ladle soup for Natasha; she shook her head. "Where is Olimpiada? I haven't seen her."

Izrail said, "You will be reported to the captain, to your union, to the Party."

"Reporting me to Volovoi would be interesting. Natasha, you're not having any goulash?"

"No."

"At least bread?"

"Thank you, tea is sufficient." She poured herself a dainty cup.

"This is serious, Renko." Izrail helped himself to soup and bread. "You can't go around the ship as if you had special orders from Moscow." He bit into a clove and reflected. "Unless you do."

"You're dieting?" Arkady asked Natasha.

"Resisting."

"Why?"

"I have my reasons." With her hair pulled back inside her cap she was showing more cheekbone, and her dark eyes seemed larger and softer.

Obidin sat beside her and heaped his plate with goulash, which he examined for meat. "I understand there is a feeling we should never take fish again where we found Zina," he said. "Out of respect for the dead."

"Ridiculous." Natasha's eyes grew hard at the thought of Zina. "We're not all religious fanatics. This is the modern age. Have you ever heard of such a thing?" she demanded of Izrail.

"Have you ever heard of Kureyka?" Izrail asked in turn. A smile hid in his beard. "It's where Stalin was exiled by the czar. Then when Stalin ruled, he sent an army of prisoners to Kureyka to nail his old cabin back together and build around it a hangar filled with lights that shone twenty-four hours a day on the cabin and on a marble statue of himself. A giant statue. One night years after he died, they secretly dragged the statue out and dropped it into the river. All the boats detoured so they wouldn't sail overhead."

"How do you know about this?" Arkady asked.

"How do you think a Jew becomes Siberian?" the manager asked in turn. "My father helped erect the hangar." He bit into the bread.

"I won't report you right away," he told Arkady. "I'll give you a day
or two."

ON HIS WAY to the radio shack, Arkady heard a voice that sounded
like the one on Zina's tape. The voice and guitar, resonantly romantic, emanated from the infirmary door. It didn't sound like Dr.
Vainu.

> *"In a distant blustering sea*
> *a pirate brigantine is making sail."*

It was an old camper's song, though a camper had to be fairly
drunk and probably incapable of walking around a tree to enjoy such
weepy lyrics.

> *"The Jolly Roger flaps in the breeze.*
> *Captain Flint is singing along.*
> *And, our glasses ringing, we too*
> *Begin our little song."*

When Arkady entered the infirmary the song stopped.
"Shit, shit, I thought it was locked," Dr. Vainu said, rushing to
block Arkady's way. At the far end of the hall Arkady saw the broad
borscht-red backside of Olimpiada Bovina running into an examining room. The doctor was in a leisure suit and slippers and looked
only slightly rumpled, slippers on the wrong feet. Arkady would have
thought that Bovina and Vainu made a pair like a steamroller and
a squirrel.
"You can't just come in," Vainu protested.
"I'm in." Looking for the singer, Arkady led the doctor down the

hall to the operating room, where a sheet covered the operating table. Arkady noticed that the box with Zina's effects was still on a counter.

"This is a medical office." Vainu checked his zipper.

Beside the table was a steel tray with a beaker and, from the taste of varnish in the air, glasses of grain alcohol. Also, a half-eaten chocolate with a cream center. Arkady laid his hand on the sheet. Still warm, like the hood of a car.

"You can't just break in," Vainu said with evaporating conviction. He slumped against a counter and lit a cigarette to calm himself. On the counter beside the box was a new Japanese cassette player with its own miniature stereo speakers. Arkady pressed the player's "Rewind" button, then "Play." ". . . *Roger flaps in the breeze.*" Then "Stop." "Sorry," he said.

The voice really wasn't like the other singer's anyway.

COLONEL PAVLOV-ZALYGIN'S sonorous voice traveled the telephone path and airwaves all the way from Odessa. His unhurried rich baritone reminded Arkady that while the ice sheet might be moving south in the Bering Sea, in Georgia they were still pressing grapes, and on the Black Sea ferryboats were still filled with the last tourists of the year.

The colonel was happy to aid a colleague far at sea, though it meant digging through old files. "Patiashvili? I knew the case, but lately the bosses are sticklers about the law. Lawyers are getting into everything, accusing us of violence, appealing perfectly good sentences. Believe me, you're better off at sea. I should study the case and call you back."

Arkady remembered that if they happened to be monitoring the Soviet channel, other ships could hear the incoming half of the conversation. The fewer calls the better, even assuming he had a chance for another one. Nikolai studied the dials on the single side band; the needles swayed aimlessly. "It's the weather," he told Arkady. "Reception is deteriorating."

"There's no time," Arkady spoke into the receiver.

"Criminals are having their letters printed in the newspapers," Pavlov-Zalygin said. "In the *Literary Gazette*!"

"She's dead," Arkady said.

"Well," the colonel said, "let me think."

There was a four-second gap in each transmission that only added confusion. Instead of a microphone, the radio had a telephone receiver with a daisy pattern on the mouthpiece as an old-fashioned nicety. It struck Arkady that all the modern technology on the *Polar Star* was at the bottom of the ship with Hess.

"The trouble was we had no real case against her," Pavlov-Zalygin said reluctantly, "nothing we could take to court. We searched her apartment, we held her in custody, but we never had enough to charge her. Aside from that, the investigation was a great success."

"Investigation of what?"

"This was in the newspapers, in *Pravda*," the colonel said with pride. "An international operation. Five tons of Georgian hashish shipped from Odessa on a Soviet freighter to Montreal. Very high-quality goods, all in bricks, inside containers marked 'raw wool.' Customs discovered the narcotics here. Usually we make the arrests and destroy the illegal shipment, but this time we decided to collaborate with the Canadians and to make arrests at both ends."

"A joint venture."

"Just so. The operation was a great success, you must .... it."

"Yes. How was Zina Patiashvili involved?"

"The ringleader was a boyfriend of hers. She had worked six

months in the galley of the freighter; in fact, it was the only freighter she ever really worked on. She was seen on the dock when the ship was first loaded, but ...."

As static increased it pushed the needle in the radio's wattage meter.

"....... to the prosecutor. Nevertheless, we ran her out of town."

"The others involved are still in camps?"

"Camps of strict regimen, absolutely. I know there's been an amnesty, but it's not like the Khrushchev amnesty when we let everybody go. No, when ...."

"We're losing him," Nikolai said.

"You said that she worked on that freighter for six months, but her paybook shows that she worked in the Black Sea Fleet for three years," Arkady said.

"Not as a galley worker exactly. She .... with .... recommendations and the usual titles ...."

"Titles? What did she do?" Arkady asked again.

"Swam." Suddenly the colonel's voice was booming and clear. "She swam for the Black Sea Fleet at meets everywhere. Before that she swam for her vocational school. Some said she could have tried for the Olympics if she'd had any discipline."

"A small girl, dark hair bleached blond?" Arkady couldn't believe they were talking about the same woman.

"That's her, except then her hair was just dark. Attractive in a cheap .... foreign .... Hello? .... Re ...."

The colonel's voice faded like a boat sighted in a storm, moving from one fogbank of static to a thicker one.

"He's gone." Nikolai watched the needle bounce out of control.

Arkady signed off and sat back while the lieutenant watched him anxiously. With good reason. It was one thing for a virile young radioman to slip an honest citizen into a secret intelligence post to seduce her; it was quite another to reveal the post to a major criminal.

"I'm sorry." Nikolai couldn't stand the suspense any longer. "I wanted to get you up here to the radio shack earlier when the transmission was better, but there was a lot of fuss about the trawl we lost, with calls to Seattle and the fleet. It was the last net from the *Merry Jane.*"

"Thorwald?"

"The Norwegian, yes. He blames us, but we blame him because he tried to transfer more than the maximum load. He lost his trawl and gear. There's no way of grappling for it in this ice apparently, so he has to return to Dutch Harbor."

"We're down to the *Eagle?*"

"The company has already dispatched three more catcher boats to join us. They're not going to leave a factory ship like us depending on only one trawler."

"Did Zina tell you that she swam?"

Nikolai cleared his throat. "She just said she could."

"Back in the Golden Horn, the restaurant, was there anyone else you recognized, someone from the ship?"

"No. Look, I have to ask about your report. What are you going to say about me? Now you know everything."

"If I knew everything I wouldn't be asking questions."

"Yes, yes, but are you naming me in your report?" Nikolai hunched closer; he was the kind of boy, Arkady thought, who would try to read his marks upside down on his teacher's desk. "I have no right to ask, but I beg you to consider what will happen to me if there are adverse comments in your report. It's not for myself. My mother works in a cannery. I always send one bolt of navy cloth home, and she sews skirts and pants that she can sell to friends, that's how she gets by. She lives for me, and something bad like this would kill her."

"Are you suggesting that I'd be responsible if your betrayal of your duty caused your mother's death?"

"Of course not, nothing like that."

Vladivostok would listen to Zina's tapes no matter what happened to Arkady. On the basis of her trip to the chain locker alone the lieutenant faced the brig. "Before we reach home port you'd better talk to Hess," he said. He wanted to get out of the radio shack quickly. "We'll see what happens."

"I remember one other thing, on the subject of money," Nikolai said. "Zina never asked for any. What she wanted me to bring was a playing card, a queen of hearts. Not a payment, a . . ."

"A souvenir?"

"I went to the recreation officer and asked for a pack. Can you believe we have only one pack for the entire ship? And it didn't have a queen of hearts. The way he was smiling, he knew."

"Who was the recreation officer?" Arkady asked, though since the position was the lowest function an officer could have, only one name was likely.

"Slava Bukovsky."

Who else?

25 Arkady found Slava sitting in shadow on an upper bunk, wearing the headphones of a Walkman and playing the mouthpiece of a saxophone, his bare feet swinging with the beat. Arkady sat quietly at the cabin's table as if he'd arrived in the middle of a concert. Only the hooded light over the desk was on, but he could see the appointments that graced an officer's cabin: the desk itself, bookshelves, a waist-high refrigerator and a clock inside a waterproof case, as if Slava's were the cabin most likely to be flooded. He reminded himself not to be too disparaging; Slava had concealed successfully until now any involvement with Zina. The bookshelf held an entertainment officer's usual books on popular games and recommended songs, as well as forbidding tomes on Lenin's thought and on diesel propulsion; the second mate, Slava's cabin mate, was studying for his first mate's ticket.

As Slava's cheeks swelled, his eyes closed, his body swayed and soulful bleats emerged from the mouthpiece. There was a calendar on a pennant, a photo of a group of boys around a motorcycle, with

Slava in the sidecar, and a taped list of the year's May Day slogans; No. 14, *Toilers in the agro-industrial complex! Your patriotic duty is to fully provide the country with food in a short time!* was underlined.

The third mate pulled off his headphones, squeezed a last mournful note from the mouthpiece, let it drop and finally looked at Arkady. " 'Back in the U.S.S.R.,' " he said. "Beatles."

"I recognized it."

"I can play any instrument. Name an instrument."

"Zither."

"A regular instrument."

"Lute, lyre, steel drum, sitar, panpipes, Formosan chong chai?"

"You know what I mean."

"Accordion?"

"I can play that. Synthesizer, drums, guitar." Slava looked at Arkady suspiciously. "What do you want?"

"Remember that box of personal effects you took from Zina's cabin? Did you have a chance to go through her spiral notebook?"

"No, I didn't have time because I had to interview a hundred people that same day."

"The box is still in the infirmary. I just came from going over the notebook for fingerprints more completely than I did the first time. There are Zina's and yours. I compared them with the prints on the suicide note you found."

"So I looked in her dumb book. Too bad; you should have asked me in front of someone. Anyway, what are you doing running around the ship, not even bothering to show up in the factory?"

"We don't have that many fish to clean. The team isn't going to miss me."

"Why isn't the captain stopping you?"

Arkady had thought about this. "It's a little like the *Inspector General.* Remember that story about how a fool comes to town and is thought to be an official of the czar? Also, murder changes everything. Nobody knows quite what to do, especially with Volovoi out of the way. As long as I don't argue with orders, I can ignore them for a while. As long as people don't know how much I know—that's what scares them."

"So it's just a matter of calling your bluff?"

"Pretty much."

Slava sat up. "I could march right up to the bridge and tell the captain that a certain seaman second-class has been shirking work in order to pester the crew with questions he was ordered not to ask?"

"You can march better with your shoes on."

"Done."

Slava tucked the mouthpiece into his shirt pocket and hopped lightly from the bunk down to the deck. Arkady reached across the desk for an ashtray while the third mate pulled on his boots. "You're going to wait here?" he asked Arkady.

"Right here."

Slava threw on his running jacket. "Anything else I should tell him?"

"Tell him about you and Zina."

The door slammed and Slava was gone.

Arkady took a cigarette from his pants and found a book of matches in the desk's mug of pencils. He studied the design on the face of the book: the word "Prodintorg" was emblazoned on a ribbon. As he remembered, Prodintorg was in charge of foreign trade in animal goods: fish, crab, caviar, racehorses and animals for zoos, a wholesale approach to the wonders of nature. He had barely lit up when Slava returned, shutting the door with his back. "What about Zina?"

"Zina and you."

"You're guessing again."

"No."

A lifetime of bowing to authority shaped people. Slava sat on the lower bunk and put his face in his hands. "Oh, God. When my father hears about this."

"He may not, but you do have to tell me."

Slava raised his head, blinked and took the sharp breaths of a man hyperventilating. "He'll kill me."

Arkady prompted him. "I think you tried to tell me once or twice and I wasn't smart enough to hear you. What I couldn't solve, for example, was how Zina was assigned to this ship. To have that much influence in fleet headquarters is highly unusual."

"Oh, he tried to please, in his way."

"Your father?" Arkady held up the matchbook.

"Deputy minister." Slava was silent for a moment. "Zina insisted she had to be on this ship to be near me. What a joke! As soon as we left port, everything was over, as if we'd never known each other."

"He made the call that put you on the *Polar Star*, and then at your request ordered to have Zina assigned too?"

"He never orders; he just calls the head of the port and asks if there's any good reason someone can't be placed somewhere or something can't be done. All he says is that the Ministry is interested, and everybody understands. Anything: the right school, the right teacher, a Ministry car to bring me home. You know, the first sign of restructuring was when he couldn't get me into the Baltic Fleet, only the Pacific. That's why Marchuk detests me." Slava stared into the dark as if there were a ghost there at a desk with a battery of phones. "You never had a father like that."

"I did, but I disappointed him early and completely." Arkady reassured him. "We all make mistakes. You couldn't know that I'd already looked under the bed where you found the suicide note. Or, I should say, where you *put* the note, which came from her notebook that you took away from her cabin. I was slow not to figure that out right away. Was there anything else in the notebook that I didn't see?"

A nervous giggle overcame Slava. "More suicide notes—two or three on a page. I threw the rest away. How many times could she kill herself?"

"So there you were, leading the ship's band and watching a woman you'd helped get on board dancing with American fishermen and ignoring you."

"No one knew."

"You knew."

"I hated it. During the break I had a smoke in the galley just so I wouldn't see her. Zina came in and out and didn't give me a second glance. Because she couldn't use me anymore I didn't exist."

"That wasn't in your report."

"Nobody saw us. Once I tried to talk to her, one day in the wardroom, and she said she'd tell the captain if I ever bothered her again. That's when I saw what was going on between the two of them, the leading captain and Zina. What if he knew about me? I wasn't dumb enough to say that I might have been the last one to see her alive."

"Were you?"

Slava unscrewed the mouthpiece band and examined the reed. "Cracked. It's hard enough to find a sax to buy, and when you do own one it's impossible to find reeds. They control you either way." Gingerly he slipped the reed back on, like a man putting a ruby into a ring. "I don't know. She took a plastic bag from a soup pot. The bag was all taped up. She put it under her jacket and went out on deck. I've tried to figure it out over and over. I thought those people on deck saw her after I did, but they didn't say anything about a jacket or a bag. I'm not a good detective."

"How big was the bag? What color?"

"One of the big ones. Black."

"See, you remembered that. How is your report on Volovoi going?"

"I was just working on it when you came in."

"In the dark?"

"Does it matter? What can I say that anyone will believe? They have a way of checking the lungs, don't they, to tell whether he really died in a fire?" Slava laughed bitterly. "Marchuk says if I do a good job he'll second my move to a Party school, which is another way of his saying I'll never make captain."

"Maybe you shouldn't. What about the Ministry?"

"Working under my father?" The question answered Arkady's.

"Music?"

After a silence Slava said, "Before we moved to Moscow we lived in Leningrad. You know Leningrad?"

It hadn't struck Arkady so forcibly before how lonely Slava was. This soft young man sitting in the shadows was meant for a carpeted office with a view of the Neva, not a bridge in the North Pacific.

"Yes."

"The basketball courts near the Nevsky? No? Well, when I was five I was at the courts and there were some black Americans playing basketball. I'd never seen anything like them; they could have been from another planet. Everything they did was different—the way they shot, which was so easy, and the way they laughed, so loud that I put my hands over my ears. Actually they weren't even a team. They were musicians who had been scheduled to play at the House of Culture, but the performance had been canceled because they played jazz. So they were playing basketball instead, but I could imagine how they made music, like black angels."

"What kind of music did you make?"

"Rock. We had a high school band. We wrote our own songs, but we were censored by the House of Creativity."

"You must have been popular," Arkady said.

"It was pretty antiestablishment. I've always been a liberal. The idiots on this ship don't understand that."

"Is that how you met Zina, at a dance? Or at the restaurant?"

"No. Do you know Vladivostok?"

"About as well as I know Leningrad."

"I hate Vladivostok. There's a beach by the stadium where everybody swarms in the summertime. You know the scene: a pier covered with towels, air mattresses, chessboards, gobs of suntan lotion and all the anatomy you'd just as soon not see."

"That's not for you?"

"Thank you, no. I borrowed a sailboat, a six-meter, and sailed the bay. Because of the naval channel you have to stay fairly near the beach. Of course, most of the people don't go in the water any deeper than their waist, or any farther than the buoy lines, certainly not past the lifeguards in the rowboats. Just the sound drives you crazy, the yakking and splashing and lifeguards' whistles. Sailing was like escaping all of them. There was one swimmer, though, who swam so far out that I couldn't help noticing her. She must have swum underwater some distance just to get past the lifeguards. I was so distracted that I spilled the wind out of the sail and luffed. There was a rope trailing over the side and she grabbed it and pulled herself on board, just as if we'd planned it. Then she stretched out on deck for a rest and pulled her cap off. Her hair was dark then, almost black. You know how water beads in the sun, so she looked like she was covered in little diamonds. She laughed as if it was the most natural thing in the world for her to leap out of the water onto the boat of someone she'd never met. We sailed all afternoon. She said she wanted me to take her to a disco, but that she'd have to meet me there; she didn't want me to pick her up. Then she dived in the water and was gone.

"After the disco, we went hiking in the hills. She never let me pick her up or leave her off at her apartment. I assumed she was living in such poor conditions that she was embarrassed. I knew by her accent that she was Georgian, but I didn't hold that against her. I was able to tell her anything and she seemed to understand. With hindsight I realize she never talked about herself at all, except to say that she had a seaman's ticket and wanted to come on the *Polar Star* with me. She played me for a fool, which is exactly what I was. She played everyone for a fool."

"Who do you think killed her?"

"Anyone, but I was afraid a murder investigation would sooner or later point to me, which makes me a coward as well as a fool. Am I wrong?"

"No." Arkady couldn't disagree. "The water in the bay, was it cold?"

"Out where she was? Freezing." Sitting on the upper bunk, Slava seemed suspended in the dark.

Arkady said, "You told me earlier that this is your second voyage."

"Yes."

"Both voyages with Captain Marchuk?"

"Yes."

"Is there anyone else on the *Polar Star* whom you sailed with before?"

"No." Slava thought. "No officers, I mean. Otherwise, only Pavel and Karp. Am I in trouble?"

"I'm afraid you are."

"I've never been in real trouble before; I never had the nerve. It's new, a whole different range of possibilities. What are you going to do now?"

"Go to bed."

"It's early."

"Well, when you're in trouble, even getting to bed can be exciting."

ON DECK, ARKADY could feel the ship ride away from the wind, which meant that Marchuk had delivered the *Merry Jane* to the edge of the ice sheet and then turned north into the sheet again. Rain made the ice around the *Polar Star* shimmer like the blue of an electrical field. He hid in shadow until his eyes adjusted.

Slava hadn't known anything about the Golden Horn or about the apartment Zina had taken Nikolai and Marchuk to, so from the start she had treated Slava differently. No raucous seamen's restaurant, no apartment cum illegal arsenal to scare off the delicate third mate. She may never have seen Slava before that day she climbed onto his sailboat, but the trawlmaster had.

At any moment Karp could swing from a guy wire or pop out of a hatch. "Relax," he had said. Why hadn't Karp killed him yet? Arkady wondered. Not because of his intelligence or luck. Officers occupied the *Polar Star*'s wheelhouse, their realm of ignorance, and the rest of the factory ship's ill-lit passages and slippery decks were the trawlmaster's domain. Arkady could vanish whenever Karp wanted. Each day since Dutch Harbor had been a day of grace. He was alive, he realized, only because a third death was more than Vladivostok would be willing to accept. The *Polar Star* would immediately be ordered home. When a ship returned under a cloud, it was surrounded by Border Guard troops and the crew kept on board while the vessel was stripped down and searched. Yet Karp had to get rid of him. For the moment the trawlmaster's dilemma was the difference between Arkady wearing his head or not. Karp was still thinking, taking his time, since what could Arkady tell Marchuk that wouldn't point more at himself than at anyone else? Karp had an alibi and witnesses for where he was when the first mate died. Still, despite that "Relax," Arkady crossed the deck from pool of light to pool of light like a man connecting dots.

The crew was already packed away in their beds, and in Arkady's cabin only Obidin was awake.

"Some persons say there's an off-loader coming to get you, Arkady. Some say you're Cheka." Cheka was the old, honored name of the KGB. "Some say you don't know yourself." The smell of home brew rose from Obidin's beard like the scent of pollen from a thistle.

Arkady pulled off his boots and climbed into his bunk. "And what do you think?"

"They're fools, of course. The mystery of human action cannot be defined in political terms."

"You don't like politics." Arkady yawned.

"The black soul of a politician cannot be plumbed. Soon the Kremlin will join the other devil."

"Which devil?" Americans, Chinese, Jews?

"The Pope."

"Shut up," Gury's voice said. "We're trying to sleep."

Thank God, Arkady thought.

"Arkady," Kolya said a minute later. "You awake?"

"What?"

"Have you noticed Natasha lately? She's looking nice."

26 In his sleep Arkady watched Zina Patiashvili swim from the Vladivostok beach, which was exactly as Slava had described it except that the sunbathers were all seals, basking and craning their heads and long-lashed Oriental eyes up to the sky. She was in the same bathing suit she'd paraded in on deck that sunny day. The same dark glasses, and her hair blond, not even with telltale roots. It was a dazzling day. Long buoys were strung like candy sticks around a kiddie section. Timber had floated from the loading yards nearby, and boys rode stray logs like war canoes.

Farther into the bay Zina swam, even past the sailboats skating on the surface of the water so that she could turn on her back and look at the city's overlapping green trees, office blocks and the Roman arches of the stadium. Dynamo Stadium. Every town had its Dynamos, Spartaks or Torpedos. Why not names like Torpor or Inertia?

She dived to quieter, cooler water where light penetrated the water at an angle, as if through the blinds of a room, down to a level both translucent and black, pulling herself with sweeping strokes to the soft, silent floor of the bay. A fish darted in front of her face. Schools of fish flowed by on either side, herring as bright as a shower of coins, blue streams of sablefish, the floating shadow of a ray moving from two beams of light that approached with the sound of an onrushing train. Steel trawl doors plowed the sea floor on either side, sending up plumes of roiled mud. The lights attached to the headrope were blinding, but she could see the bottom exploding with the ground rope's advance, both geysers of silt and wave after wave of groundfish rising to try to escape the trawl, which roared as it engulfed them. A wall of water first pushed her away from and then sucked her into the maelstrom, into the deep bass chord of straining mesh, clouds of silt and glittering scales.

Awake, Arkady sat up in the dark as wet with sweat as if he'd climbed from the sea. He'd told Natasha it was simply seeing what was before your eyes; no genius was needed. How do you smuggle on open water? What went back and forth twenty times a day? And where would the trawlmaster hide what he'd received? Another obvious answer surfaced: where on the *Polar Star* had he been attacked?

THIS TIME ARKADY took a flashlight. Rats scurried from beams, slipping between planks, red pinpoints staring down as he descended the ladder in the forward hold. Cooling pipes swarmed with the adept clambering of the rats. At least the trip was shorter with a light.

He stepped gently down onto the bottom of the hold, remembering how last time he had picked up a loose plank and started beating on the walls in an attempt to drive out a lieutenant of naval intelligence, when all the while he had probably been standing on the lid of a treasure chest. The beam of the flashlight found the plank, the same paint cans and blanket, the same cat skeleton as before. Earlier, though, the cat had been in the center of the floor; this time it was curled up in a corner. There were heel and scuff marks on the floor planks. He touched them. Not scuff marks: water.

The hatch at floor level opened and Pavel, the deckhand on Karp's team, stepped halfway in. Wearing a helmet and jacket soaked with rain, he tried to squint over his hand through the glare of Arkady's flashlight. "Still here?" he asked. Then he saw who it was, slammed the hatch and locked it shut.

Arkady climbed the ladder to the next level. Its hatch was locked. He continued up to the top level, the one through which he'd entered the hold, his heart pounding like an extra prisoner willing his hands up the rungs. Kicking the hatch open, he ran to the stairs and down. When he reached the bottom level outside the hold, Pavel was gone, but wet prints on the metal deck pointed like arrows in the direction he'd taken. There was the damp traffic of other boots on the same path.

Arkady ran, trying to catch up. The path led aft, passed the No. 2 fishhold and then took the midship stairs to emerge by the forward crane of the trawl deck. There was no sign of Pavel or anyone else. Rain swept the boards of the deck, wiping them clean, and Arkady pocketed the flashlight and took out his knife. The main winch lamp was off; the gantry lamps were caked with ice. Across the deck the entrance to the stern ramp was black.

At this point he didn't need arrows. What was surprising was that it was the first time he'd ever been on the ramp. The gantry lights touched the rough hide of its walls and the overlapping folds of ice at the top of the slip. With each step down, though, the light faded and the angle of the ramp became more precipitous. Far forward, the prow of the *Polar Star* hit heavier ice and shuddered. Deep within the stern, in the sound box of the ramp, the shudder swelled into a moan. A following wave rushed up the ramp and subsided with a sigh, the way the audiomechanics of a seashell amplified and exaggerated sound, the way the inner ear gauged the pounding of the heart.

If Arkady slid there was nothing between him and the water but the safety gate. He held on as best he could to the side of the ramp as he felt its surface start to fall away. Overhead, at the well, was a second dim intrusion of light. He could see that the chain of the safety gate was taut on its hook on the wall of the ramp; the gate had been swung up and out of the way. Too late to grab the hook, he began to slide. Just a bit to begin with, the first millimeter that informs a falling man of his situation, then with momentum that grew as the curve of the ramp became steeper. Spread-eagled, face forward, his fingers digging into ice, he saw the white tracery of a wave rising toward him while his knife rattled ahead of him, free. At the lip the ramp opened to the black of the fairway and the sky, the sound of the screws and, to the sides, wings of ice. As the water rushed up, his hand found a rope along the side of the ramp and he twisted his wrist around it. When he came to a stop, he saw below him another man standing in boots at a steep angle like a mountain climber in the waves washing the bottom of the ramp. The lifeline was tied to his waist.

Karp wore a dark sweater and a wool cap pulled down to his heavy brow, and held what looked like a cushion. "Too late," he told Arkady. He threw the cushion backhanded into the water. From the way it hit and plunged, the package was weighted. "A fortune," he said. "Everything we had. But you're right; they'll tear this ship apart when we get back to Vladivostok."

Karp leaned back with both hands free and lit a cigarette, a man relieved and at ease. The wake had a luminescence that dissipated in the dark. Arkady pulled himself to his feet.

"You look scared, Renko."

"I am."

"Here." Karp shifted, gave the cigarette to Arkady and lit another for himself. His eyes shone as they searched the ramp above. "You came alone?"

"Yes."

"We'll find out."

Arkady's attention was fixed on the rain and on a light swaying in the distance like a lamp in a breeze. It was the *Eagle,* maybe two hundred meters back. "What you tossed in, what if the net picks it up?"

"The *Eagle* isn't towing now, they're busy enough hosing off ice. Pretty top-heavy in a boat like that. How did you know I'd be here?"

Arkady decided not to mention Pavel. "I wanted to see where Zina had gone into the water."

"Here?"

"She left her jacket and a bag either here or on the landing while she went to the dance. What did she look like in the net?" Arkady asked.

Karp gave his cigarette a long pull. "Ever see anyone drown?" he asked.

"Yes."

"Then you know." Karp turned to study the *Eagle*'s light fade in a sweeping gust of rain. He seemed unhurried, as if waiting for a friend. "The sea is dangerous, but I should be grateful to you for getting me out of Moscow. I was making, with pimping and shake-downs, what? Twenty or thirty rubles a day? To the rest of the world, rubles aren't even money."

"You're not in the rest of the world. In the Soviet Union a fisherman makes a lot of rubles."

"For what? Meat's rationed, sugar's rationed. Restructuring is a joke. The only difference now is that vodka is rationed too. Who's a criminal? Who's a smuggler? Delegations go to Washington and come back with clothes, toilets, chandeliers. The Secretary General collected fast cars, his daughter collected diamonds. The same in the republics. This Party leader has marble palaces; that one has suit-cases so full of gold you can't lift them from the floor. Another has a fleet of trucks that carry nothing but poppies, and the trucks are protected by the motor patrol. Renko, you're the only one I don't understand. You're like a doctor in a whorehouse."

"Well, I'm a romantic. So you wanted something else, but why drugs?"

Karp's shoulders wore frozen beads of rain; their outline made Arkady think of the mist in a cloud chamber that betrayed the dewy track of ions.

"It's the one way a worker can make real money as long as he has the nerve," Karp said. "That's why governments hate drugs—be-cause they can't control them. They control vodka and tobacco, but they don't control drugs. Look at America. Even blacks are making money."

"You think it will happen in the Soviet Union, too?"

"It already is. You can buy ammo off a Red Army base, run it right over the border and sell it to the Afghans fighting us. The *dushmany* have warehouses with cocaine piled to the roof. It's better than gold. It's the new currency. That's why everyone's afraid of the veterans—

not just because they're drug users, but because they know what's really going on."

"You're not part of any vast Afghan network, though," Arkady said. "You'd be dealing in Siberian goods, *anasha*. What's the rate of exchange as the nets go back and forth?"

Karp's smile flashed gold in the dark. "A couple of bricks from us for a spoonful from them. It seems unfair, but you know what a gram of cocaine brings at an oil rig in Siberia? Five hundred rubles. You figured out the nets; that's clever of you."

"What I don't understand is how you got *anasha* past the Border Guard and onto the *Polar Star.*"

The trawlmaster became both flattered and confiding, as if it were a shame that the two of them couldn't pull up chairs and split a bottle. At the same time, Arkady was aware that Karp was only playing a role, enjoying a situation over which he had complete control.

"You'll appreciate this," Karp said. "What can a trawlmaster ask for in the way of supplies? Net, needles, shackles, ropes. The yard always gives you the worst, you can depend on that. What's the cheapest rope?"

"Hemp." Manchurian hemp was grown legally for rope and packing; *anasha* was merely the potent, pollinating version of the same bush. "You packed *anasha* in the rope, hemp in hemp." Arkady was forced to admire it.

"And we end up trading shit for gold. Two kilos are a million rubles."

"But now you'll have to sign up for another six months to bring back a second load."

"It's a setback." Karp looked thoughtfully up the ramp. "Not like the one you're going to have, but still a setback. You say you came here in the rain in the middle of the night just to see where Zina went in? I don't believe it."

"Do you believe in dreams?"

"No."

"Neither do I."

"You know why I killed that son of a bitch in Moscow?" Karp asked suddenly.

"In the train yard with the prostitute?"

"The one you nailed me on, right."

"So it wasn't an accident; you meant to do it?"

"Long gone, fifteen years ago, you can't charge me a second time."

"So why did you kill him?"

"You know who the whore was? It was my mother."

"She didn't say. She had a different name."

"Yeah, well, that son of a bitch knew it, and he said he was going to tell everyone. It wasn't like I was crazy."

"You should have said so then."

"It would have made her sentence worse."

Arkady remembered a coarsely painted woman with hair dyed Chinese red. At that time prostitution did not officially exist, so she was sentenced for conspiracy to rob.

"What happened to her?"

"She died in corrective labor. In her camp they made padded jackets for Siberia, so maybe you or I wore one. They had a quota like anyone else. She died happy, though. There were a lot of women there with babies, a kindergarten with its own barbed wire, and they let her clean up there. She wrote and said she'd gotten better being around kids. Except she died of pneumonia, which she probably picked up from some runny-nosed brat. It's funny what can kill you."

He shook a knife from his sleeve.

Arkady turned at the sound of steps. Against the faint glow from the trawl deck he could make out someone in a hard hat descending the ramp, holding on to the rope that led to Karp.

"It's Pavel," Karp said. "He took his time getting here. So you really did come alone."

Arkady started back up the rope, pulling himself hand over hand. Karp was faster. Though the lifeline was tied around his own waist the trawlmaster didn't seem to need it and strode easily up the icy slope.

Ahead, the figure from the trawl deck stopped. Arkady would have to go wide to get by, and he knew that as soon as he left the rope he would slide down the ramp to the water. His boots slipped. How did Karp move up the ramp so quickly, like a devil flying up steps?

"This was worth waiting for," Karp said. He shook the rope so that Arkady slipped again, and then he had him by his jacket.

"Arkady?" Natasha called. "Is that you?"

"Yes."

The shape looming on the ramp above wasn't Pavel. Now that they were closer he saw that what had looked like a man's helmet was a scarf over her hair.

"Who are you with?" she demanded.

"Korobetz," Arkady said. "You know Korobetz."

Arkady could almost hear the calculations in the trawlmaster's mind. Would it be possible to kill him *and* Natasha before she reached the trawl deck and called out?

"We're old friends." Karp still held on to Arkady. "We go back a long way. Give us a hand."

"Get on deck," Arkady told her. "I'll follow."

"You two?" Natasha asked suspiciously. "Friends?"

"Go," Arkady ordered. He stayed where he was so that Karp couldn't get past.

"What's the matter, Arkady?" She stood her ground.

"Wait," Karp told her.

"Wait there," Pavel added as he came down the ramp above Natasha. An ax dangled from his free hand.

Arkady kicked Karp's leg. The trawlmaster landed on his stomach and slid down the ramp the length of his lifeline. Arkady hoped he would go into the water, but Karp stopped just above the spine of the wake. At once he was back on his feet and scaling the ramp, but by then Arkady had reached the hook where the chain holding up the safety gate was fastened. He released the chain. With a rush of air, the gate swung down and with a metallic clap slammed shut in Karp's face, trapping him on the lower end of the ramp.

Arkady got ahead of Natasha. Behind him, he heard Karp shaking the gate as if its steel mesh could come apart in his hands. Then the gate was still. "Renko"—the trawlmaster's voice came up the ramp.

Pavel hesitated as Arkady approached. His eyes were round hollows, more afraid of Karp than of Arkady. "You're fucking up everything. He said you would."

Karp's laugh filled the ramp. "Where are you going to run?"

"Piss off." Natasha said the magic words and Pavel backed away.

"We make a good team," Natasha said.

27 She was still exhilarated by their escape from the ramp, her eyes bright, a long strand of hair hanging loose. Arkady led her into the cafeteria, which they found turned into a dance floor.

There had been no announcement over the loudspeakers. Third Mate Slava Bukovsky, the officer in charge of entertainment, had for purposes of morale spontaneously gathered his band and sent word belowdecks that music would be offered to the crew. As no nets were being taken and the night was foul, the entire ship's company had been holing up, bored and stifling, in their cabins. Now they holed up happily and communally in the cafeteria. This time there were no Americans, not even reps, and for some reason no rock. The ball of mirrors spun, its reflections scattering like snow over dancers who moved in dreamy slowness. Onstage, Slava squeezed from his saxophone a sweet, dirgelike blues.

Arkady and Natasha crowded onto a back bench with Dynka and

Madame Malzeva. "I wish my Ahmed were here now." The Uzbek girl clasped her hands together.

"I've heard musicians in the Black Sea Fleet." Malzeva wrapped a babushka around her shoulders for dignity's sake, but unbent enough to add, "Actually, he's not so bad."

Natasha whispered in Arkady's ear, "We should go to the captain and tell him what happened."

"What would we say? All you saw was me and Karp. A trawlmaster has any number of reasons to be on the ramp. I don't."

"There was Pavel with an ax."

"They've been chopping ice all day. Maybe he's a Hero Worker."

"You were attacked."

"I dropped the gate on Karp, not the other way around, and all you heard him say was that we were friends. The man's a saint."

The next song was "Dark Eyes," a syrupy tale of gypsy love. The girl on the synthesizer plunked out a sound something like a guitar's while Slava produced lush, brassy melody. It was shameless and irresistible. The floor was a slowly surging tide of dancers.

"You and Karp are like a mouse and a snake," Natasha said. "You can't share the same hole."

"Not for much longer."

"Why were you on the ramp?"

"Would you like to dance?" Arkady asked.

A metamorphosis came over Natasha. Light glowed not only in her eyes but from her face. Like a woman who has arrived in sable, she slowly removed her fishing jacket and scarf, gave them to Dynka and then pulled the comb from her hair so that it cascaded softly down.

"Ready?" Arkady asked.

"Absolutely." Her voice had softened, too.

They made an unlikely pair, he had to admit: the Party's model member and a troublemaker from the slime line. As he led her between tables to the floor she met astonished glances with a gaze at once imperious and serene.

Soviet dancers don't expect much room to dance in; there's always an attendant amount of bumping, like ballbearings in a bottle. It's a good-humored aspect of the dance, especially one in the middle of the ice sheet with an Arctic wind frosting the portholes. For all her size and strength, Natasha seemed to float in Arkady's arms, her hot cheek tentatively touching his.

"I apologize for my boots," she said.

Arkady said, "No, *I* apologize for *my* boots."

"You like romantic songs?"

"I am helpless before romantic songs."

"So am I." She sighed. "I know you like poetry."

"How do you know that?"

"I found your book."

"You did?"

"When you were sick. It was under your mattress. You're not the only one who knows where to look."

"Is that so?" He pulled back for a moment. There was a frightening lack of embarrassment in her eyes. "It wasn't even a book of poetry," Arkady said. "Just some essays and letters from Mandelstam." He didn't add that it was a gift from Susan.

"Well, the essays were too intellectual," Natasha admitted, "but I liked the letters to his wife."

"To Nadezhda?"

"Yes, but he had so many other names for her. Nadik, Nadya, Nadka, Nadenka, Nadyusha, Nanusha, Nadyushok, Nanochka, Nadenysh, Niakushka. Ten special names in all. That's a poet." She laid her cheek a little more firmly on his.

Slava and his sax leaned into "Dark Eyes," extracting amber from sap. Dancers revolved slowly under the revolving ball. There was a cavelike quality to the low ceiling and flickering lights that eased the Russian soul.

"I have always admired your work on the factory line," Natasha confided.

"I've always admired yours."

"The way you handle the fish," she said. "Especially the difficult ones like hake."

"You cut the spines off so . . . well." He wasn't good at this, Arkady thought.

She cleared her throat. "That trouble you had in Moscow? I think it's possible the Party made a mistake."

A mistake? For Natasha that was like saying black might be white, or an admission that there might be gray.

"Oddly enough," he said, "this time it didn't."

"Anyone can be rehabilitated."

"Generally after they're dead. Don't worry; there's life outside the Party. More than inside."

Natasha fell contemplative. Her train of thought seemed much like the Baikal–Amur Mainline, with whole sections unfinished and tunnels going off in mysterious directions. Poetry, fish, the Party. He wondered what she would come up with next.

"I know there's someone else," Natasha said. "Another woman."

"Yes."

Was that a sniff he heard? He hoped not.

"There had to be," she finally said. "There's only one thing I ask."

"What's that?"

"That it's not Susan."

"No, it's not Soo-san."

"And it wasn't Zina?"

"No."

"Someone not on board?"

"Not on board and far away."

"Very far away?"

"Oh, very," he assured her.

"That's good enough." She rested her head on his shoulder.

Well, Arkady thought, Ridley was right. This was civilized, maybe the acme of civilization, these fishermen and fisherwomen waltzing in boots on the Bering Sea. Dr. Vainu clung to Olimpiada like a man rolling a boulder. Keeping a straight-armed, semi-Islamic distance, Dynka danced with one of the engineers. Some men were on the floor with men, some women with women, just to keep in practice. A few had taken the time to pull on fresh jerseys, but most of them had come as they were, in the spirit of a rare impromptu event. Arkady also enjoyed the dance because now he had some idea of Zina's last hours on earth. There was a nice aptness to ending up with Natasha here, as if Zina herself might come dancing by.

"He's here." Natasha stiffened.

Karp was moving slowly along the benches at the rear of the cafeteria, perfectly at ease, simply sorting out figures in the dark. Arkady steered Natasha toward the stage. "Kolya would like to dance with you," he said.

"He would?"

"If you see him, you should give him a chance. He's a bright man, a scientist, a botanist who needs to come down to earth."

"I'd rather help you," Natasha said.

"Then, half a minute after I'm gone, turn out the stage lights for just a few seconds."

"This is still all about Zina, isn't it?" Natasha's voice sank. "Why are you so involved?"

Arkady was startled into an answer. "I hate suicide."

There was something newly liberated about Slava, as if the saxophone were a divining rod that had located his soul. While the third mate wailed, Arkady and Natasha reached the galley door.

"She didn't kill herself?" Natasha asked.

"No."

"Karp killed her?"

"Now, that's the strange part. I don't think he did."

THE GALLEY WAS a narrow gamut of steel sinks, stacked trays as dented as war shields, towers of white soup bowls, industrial ranges under hanging pans of washtub size. The realm of Olimpiada Bovina. Cabbage bathed in simmering water, either being prepared for breakfast or being reduced to glue. A paddle stood upright in a mixing bowl of hardening batter. Arkady was aware he was following the same path Zina had taken during the previous dance seven nights before. According to Slava, she had removed a plastic bag from a pot. What was in the bag? Why plastic? Then the next witnesses placed her on deck.

Arkady opened the door to the corridor just enough to see Pavel anxiously sucking on a cigarette and watching for anyone leaving the dance. A moment later "Dark Eyes" ended amid shouts of "Lights!" and "Off my foot, you bloody bastard!" At once Pavel stuck his head inside the cafeteria while Arkady slipped out of the galley and down the corridor.

Who else but Kolya Mer would be at the rail taking in all the pleasures of rain turning to a wet, stinging snow that angled under a lowering fog? He grabbed Arkady as he ran past.

"I wanted to tell you about the flowers."

"Flowers?"

"Where I picked them." Bare fingers peeked out of Kolya's cut gloves.

"The irises?"

"I told Natasha I got them along the road outside the store in Dutch Harbor. Actually, irises grow higher up. I saw you check in my notebook, so you know I found them on the hill. I saw you going up after the American." Kolya took a deep breath for courage. "Volovoi asked."

"Volovoi ran into you on the hill?"

"He was looking for you. He even said he was going to take my samples away unless I told him. I didn't, though."

"I didn't think you did. Was he alone?"

Say no, Arkady thought. Say that First Mate Volovoi was with Karp Korobetz and we'll go together to Marchuk right now.

"I couldn't tell in the fog," Kolya said.

Karp would be coming on deck any second, Arkady thought, unless he was already on his way belowdecks to block him from the forward part of the ship.

Kolya was staring straight up. "Like tonight. The snow will stop and then it will really get thick. I miss the sextant."

"It's not very useful without stars," Arkady said. "Go inside. Get warm. Dance."

ONLY BECAUSE HE was away from the dance, Arkady heard the change in pitch. The reverberation of the screws was deeper, which meant the *Polar Star* was slowing down. But the stream of glittering flakes created the illusion that the factory ship was rushing forward like a sleigh. Underfoot, he felt the tremor of the engines and the cracking of ice under the plate of the prow. Overhead, snow swayed on the booms and gantries, coating the antennas, directional rings and radar bars so that they shone in a lamplight intensified by the plane of fog directly above. If the senses were anything to go by, the *Polar Star* was flying between two seas, one above and one below.

The sound of boots scurried across the deck behind him. Ahead, someone else descended the stairs from the bow. Arkady slipped through the fishing net that surrounded the volleyball court. Snow on the mesh had turned it into a gauzy tent of ice that trembled in the wind. The deck lamp was a blur. Through this screen he watched the two figures converge and talk. He should have picked up a knife in the kitchen. The volleyball apparatus had been taken down. He couldn't defend himself with a pole; there wasn't even a ball.

First one figure and then the other entered the court after Arkady. He expected them to spread out, but they stayed together as they crept forward. The bottom of the net was tied to cleats, tied and frozen; no exit there. Maybe he could climb the net like a monkey? Not likely. The deck was icy. If he knocked one down, perhaps both would fall.

"Renko? Is it you?"

The other silhouette lit a match. In a darting flame Arkady could see two faces with gnomish brows and anxious smiles with gold teeth. Skiba and Slezko, Volovoi's two slugs.

"What do you want?" Arkady asked.

"We're on your side," Slezko said.

"They're going to get you tonight," Skiba said. "They don't want you to see morning."

Arkady asked, "Who is 'they'?"

"You know," Slezko said in time-honored Soviet fashion. Why say more?

"We still know how to do our jobs," said Skiba. "There just hasn't been anyone to report to."

The match went out. In the wind the net billowed like sails of ice.

"There's no discipline, no vigilance, no line of communication anymore," Slezko said. "To speak frankly, we're at a loss."

Skiba said, "You must have done something that set them off because they're searching the entire ship for you. They'll cut your throat in your cabin if they have to. Or on deck."

"Why are you telling me?" Arkady asked.

"Reporting, not telling," Slezko said. "We're just doing our duty."

"Reporting to *me?*"

Skiba said, "We've thought about this a lot. We have to report to someone, and you're the only one with the experience to take his place."

"Whose place?"

"Volovoi's, who else?" Slezko said.

Skiba said, "We think that you might come from the appropriate organ anyway, the way you act lately."

"What organ would that be?"

Slezko said, "You know."

I know, Arkady thought. The KGB. It was insane. Skiba and Slezko had been happy to inform on him as an enemy of the people while Volovoi was alive. Once he was dead, however, they were like guard dogs thrown into confusion. Allegiance wasn't what they craved so much as a new fist on the leash. Well, a farmer sowed corn, a shoemaker made shoes, informers needed a new Volovoi. They had simply changed Arkady from victim to master.

"Thank you," Arkady said. "I'll keep your advice in mind."

"I don't understand why you don't just hold them in custody," Skiba said. "They're only workers."

Slezko said, "You won't be safe until you do."

"My advice," Arkady said, "is to watch out for your own necks."

In the dark Skiba mournfully agreed. "In times like these nothing is safe."

ON THE BRIDGE the oncoming snow was lit by bow and wheelhouse lamps so that the eye could follow flakes individually, one or two out of the millions flowing out of the dark and over and around a windshield that had been hosed down with steam and wore its own frozen sheen. Wipers rhythmically brushed snow aside, but ice was already encroaching again from the corners. What was there to see anyway, Arkady thought, except fog and ice on a line that extended over the Pole to the Atlantic?

Inside, the overhead lamp was dim. The radar and echo sounder scopes cast green halos. The gyrocompass floated in a ball of light. Marchuk was at the wheel; Hess stood at the windshield. Neither man seemed surprised to see Arkady on the bridge.

"Comrade Jonah," the captain said softly.

There was no helmsman and no one was in the navigation room. The engine telegraph was set between "Dead Slow" and "Dead Stop."

"Why are we slowing?" Arkady asked.

The captain had a pained smile. As he tapped out a cigarette he looked like a man contemplating life from the last step of a guillotine. Hess, caught in the moving shadow of a wiper, looked as if he were only one step behind.

"I should have left you where you were," Marchuk told Arkady. "You'd disappeared on the slime line, in the belly of the whale. We must have been insane to pluck you out."

"Are we stopping?" Arkady asked.

"We have a slight problem," Hess conceded. "There *are* problems besides you."

The light from outside was pale and cold, but the fleet electrical engineer appeared to Arkady to be especially white, as if all the sun lamps on earth were wasted on him.

"Your cable?" Arkady suggested.

"I told you," Hess reminded Marchuk. "He found my station today."

"Well, your station is a pearl in an oyster, so a man of Renko's abilities was bound to find it. One more reason why I should have left him where he was." To Arkady the captain said, "I told him the bottom we were going over was too grabby and too shallow, but he put the cable out anyway."

"A hydrophone cable is designed not to snag," Hess said. "It's deployed from submarines all the time."

"And now something's tangled in the cable," Marchuk said. "Maybe part of a crab pot, maybe a walrus head. Tusks dragging on the ocean floor. We can't reel the cable in and the tension on it is too great for us to go any faster."

"Whatever it is will come loose eventually," said Hess.

"In the meantime," Marchuk said, "we must proceed ahead delicately even while we're making way through ice and a Force Seven wind. The captains in the navy must be magicians." When he inhaled, his eyes reflected the ember. "Excuse me, I forgot: in the navy the cables are deployed from submarines, not from factory ships in the ice."

The *Polar Star* trembled and heaved a little in the swell hidden below the sheet. Arkady was no engineer, but he knew that in order to break ice a ship, no matter how big, needed a certain amount of momentum. Too slow at too low a gear and sooner or later the diesels would burn out. "How good a captain is Morgan?" he asked.

Marchuk said, "We'll find out. A boat like the *Eagle* should be in view of a coconut palm and looking for shrimp, nowhere near ice. Now the waves are picking up in the fairway, and his bow and deck aren't high enough. He shouldn't head into the wind, but he has to stay behind us or get iced in. He's already iced up and getting top-heavy."

Something occurred to Arkady. The quiet. A bridge always had one radio tuned to the distress frequency. Marchuk followed Arkady's eyes to the single side band. The captain left the wheel to turn up the sound, like pins dropping, of heavy static.

"Morgan hasn't sent an emergency call yet," said Hess.

"He hasn't sent any call," Marchuk said.

Arkady asked, "Why don't you raise him?" Off Sakhalin, boats always talked to each other through heavy weather.

"He doesn't respond," Marchuk said. "One of his antennas might be down."

Hess said, "Morgan can tell by our speed that something is wrong, and he probably knows that the cable is played out. A piece of the cable is what he's after. We're the ones in trouble, not him. This weather is perfect for him."

On the radar screen the fairway carved by the *Polar Star* was a narrow lane of green dots, sea returning the radar's signal. In the middle of the lane, about five hundred meters back, was the blip that was the *Eagle;* the rest of the screen was a blank. Arkady punched in a 50-k scale. Still there was nothing but the *Eagle.* Boats were supposed to be coming from Seattle, but the weather would be delaying them.

"Morgan has radar, too," Hess said. "And a directional echo sounder. If something is caught on the cable he'll detect it. This is probably the opportunity he's been waiting for."

Marchuk said, "If he's lost a radio mast, then he's lost his radar, too."

The autopilot turned the wheel a notch, minding its job.

"Captain," Hess said, "I can understand your sympathy for another fisherman. Would that Morgan was, but he's not. We are his fish. He will be silent and he will stay close to see if we make a mistake, such as picking up speed. Whatever is caught on the cable could lift it to the surface right beside the *Eagle.*"

"What if the cable breaks?" Arkady asked.

"It won't break if we stay at this speed," said Hess.

"What if it does?" Marchuk asked.

"It won't," Hess said.

What was Hess's musical instrument? The cello. The fleet electrical engineer reminded Arkady of a cellist trying to play as his strings popped one by one.

Hess repeated, "It won't, but even if it did break, the cable has negative buoyancy; it would sink. The only problem would be returning to Vladivostok and the Pacific Fleet after losing a hydrophone cable. Our voyage has been disastrous enough, Captain. We don't need any more disgraces."

"Why doesn't Morgan answer our calls?" Marchuk demanded.

"I've told you why. Except for the radio, the *Eagle* is proceeding normally. Everything else is in your imagination." Hess lost patience. "I'm going below; perhaps I can wind in the cable a little." He paused in front of Arkady. "Explain to the captain that Zina Patiashvili didn't go to the stern rail every time the *Eagle* was close in order to throw kisses. It turns out that she got plenty of them from my own radioman. If Zina were here now, I'd kill her myself."

The fleet electrical engineer left by the flying bridge. Before the door slammed shut, snow entered, spun in the dark, then died.

"It *is* humorous," Marchuk said. "After all that time in dry dock putting in the cable and it's the only thing that breaks down."

The captain leaned against the counter. He laid his hand affectionately on a compass repeater, opened its hood, closed it.

"I keep thinking things will change, Renko, that life can be honest and direct, that there's good and dignity in anyone who's willing to work hard. Not that people are perfect, not that I'm perfect. But good. Am I an idiot? Tell me, when we reach Vladivostok will you tell them about me and Zina?"

"No. But they'll take pictures of the officers and crew to the restaurant where she worked and the people there will recognize you."

"So I'm dead either way."

No, *I'm* dead either way, Arkady thought. Karp and his deck team will hunt until they find me. Marchuk was caught in the more significant drama of a trailing cable. How could he explain why Karp wanted to attack him if there was no evidence left of smuggling? At best he'd sound like a madman; more likely, he'd hang himself for Volovoi and the Aleut.

"You know how this ship was delivered?" Marchuk asked. "You know the condition in which any ship is delivered from the boatyard?"

"Like new?"

"Better than new. The *Polar Star* was built in a Polish yard. When it was handed over, it was handed over complete, with everything: tableware, linens, curtains, lights, everything, so you could go to sea right away. But they never go to sea right away. The KGB comes on board. People from the Ministry come on board. They take the new tableware and replace it with old, take the linens and curtains and replace bright lights with bulbs you could go blind by. Exactly as if they were robbing a house. Rip out the good plumbing and replace it with lead. Even mattresses and doorknobs. Replace good with shit. Then they give it to Soviet fishermen and say, 'Comrades, go to sea!' This was a pretty ship, a good ship."

Marchuk bowed his head, dropped the butt of his cigarette on the deck and stepped on it. "So, Renko, now you know why the ship is moving so slowly. Was there anything else?"

"No."

The captain stared at the bright, blinded windshield. "Too bad about us and the *Eagle,*" he said. "The joint venture is a good thing. The other way leads back to the cave, doesn't it?"

28 Arkady went through the bridge-house corridor without knowing where he was heading. He couldn't simply go to his cabin and wait. The dance wouldn't be safe. This was the sort of prison situation that an urka like Karp excelled at. The lights would go out, and when they came on again he'd be gone, down the ramp in a weighted sack. Or he'd be found in an empty bunker, paint can by his side, an obvious victim of sniffing fumes. Moral lessons would be drawn.

"We never finished our game," Susan said.

Arkady took a step back to her open door. He'd passed it without noticing because her cabin was dark.

"Don't be afraid," she said. She turned on the overhead lights long enough for him to see disconnected wires hanging from the radio and the base of the desk lamp. She sat on the lower bunk, her hair damp and disheveled as if she had just stepped out of a shower. Her feet were bare and she was dressed in jeans and a loose denim shirt. Her brown eyes seemed to have gone black. In her hand was a glass filled to the brim. The cabin smelled of scotch. She turned the light off with the bunk switch. "Close the door," she said.

"I thought you never closed the door when Soviet men came to call."

"There's always a first time. Soviet ships never have unscheduled dances, but I hear you're having one right now. That's where all my boys have gone, so it's a night of firsts."

Arkady closed the door and groped to sit where he'd seen a chair by the bunk. She turned on her bunk lamp, a twenty-watt bulb not much brighter than a waning candle.

"For example, I said to myself that I would fuck the first man who walked by my door. Then, Renko, you walked by and I changed my mind. The *Eagle*'s in trouble, isn't it?"

"I have it on good authority that the snow will stop."

"They lost radio contact an hour ago."

"We still have them on radar. They're not far behind us."

"So?"

"So their radio antenna is probably iced up. You know that happens up here."

Susan put a glass in his hand and poured from a bottle so that the scotch swelled over the brim. "Remember," she said. "First one to spill gets hit."

Arkady frowned. "The Norwegian game again?"

"Yes. They don't call them roundheads for nothing."

"Is there an American version?"

"You get shot," Susan said.

"Ah, a short version. I have a different idea. Why not the first one to spill tells the truth?"

"That's the Soviet version?"

"I wish I could say so."

"No," Susan said, "you can have anything but the truth."

"In that case," Arkady said and sipped, "I'll cheat."

Susan matched him with a swallow. She was well ahead of him, though she didn't seem drunk. The bunk light provided more corona than illumination. Her eyes were shadowed but not softened.

"You haven't been writing any suicide notes, have you?" she asked.

Arkady set his drink on the floor so he could get out a cigarette.

"Light one for me," she said.

"It's an art in itself, suicide notes." Arkady lit two Belomors off a match and put one in her hand. Her fingers were smooth, not rough and scarred from cleaning cold fish.

"You speak as an expert?"

"A student. Suicide notes are a branch of literature too often ignored. There's the pensive suicide note, the bitter one, the guilt-ridden one, rarely the comic note because there's always some sense of formality. Usually the writer signs his or her name, or else signs off in some fashion: 'I love you,' 'It's better this way,' 'Consider me a good Communist.' "

"Zina didn't."

"And the note is generally left where it will be found at the same time as the body. Or found when someone is discovered missing."

"Zina didn't do that, either."

"And always, because this is the writer's last testament, she doesn't mind using a whole piece of paper. Not a scrap, not half a page from a notebook—not for the last letter of her life. Which reminds me, how is your writing going?" He looked at Susan's typewriter and books.

"I'm blocked. I thought a ship would be the perfect place to write, but . . ." She stared at the bulkhead as if peering at some fading memory. "Too many people, too little space. No, that's not fair. Soviet writers write in communal apartments all the time, don't they? I have this cabin to myself. But it's like finally having a chance to listen to your very own seashell and there's no sound at all."

"On the *Polar Star* I think it would be hard to hear a seashell."

"True. You know, you're strange, Renko, you're very strange. Remember that poem, the one—"

" 'Tell me how men kiss you,/Tell me how you kiss'?"

"That's the one. Remember the last line?" she asked, and recited, " 'Oh I see, his game is that he knows/Intimately, ardently,/ There's nothing from me he wants,/So I have nothing to refuse.' That's you. Of all the men on this ship, you're the only one who wants nothing at all."

"That's not true," Arkady said. He wanted to stay alive, he thought. He wanted to get through the night.

"What do you want?" she asked.

"I want to know what happened to Zina."

"What do you want from me?"

"You were the last person to see Zina before she disappeared. I'd like to know what she said."

"See what I mean?" She laughed softly, more at herself. "Okay. What she said? Honestly?"

"Try it."

Susan took a more judicious sip. "I don't know. This game gets dangerous."

"I'll tell you what I think she told you," Arkady said. "I think she said she knew what the *Polar Star* was towing when we're not taking nets, and that she could give you information about the station where the cable was controlled."

She shrugged. "What cable? What on earth are you talking about?"

"That's why Morgan is where he is and that's why you're here."

"You sound like Volovoi."

"It's not an easy game," Arkady said. The scotch was good; it made even a *papirosa* taste as sweet as candy.

"Maybe you're a spy," Susan said.

"No, I don't have the world view. I'm more comfortable in a smaller, more human scale. And I'd say you're a bit of an amateur, not a professional. But you got on the ship, and if Morgan says you stay on it, you stay."

"Well, I do have a world view. I don't think Zina would have been so desperate to leave an American boat."

"She—"

He stopped and turned his ear. There wasn't so much the sound of boots in the corridor as of boots suddenly standing outside the door. Along the corridor were six cabins, with stairs at each end up to the bridge and down to the main deck. Other boots ran down the stairs and came to a halt.

The door opened in the next cabin, then shut. A door opened across the hall. There was a knock at Susan's door. "Soo-san?" Karp called.

She watched Arkady kill his cigarette. Was there panic in his eyes? he wondered. There was fascination in hers.

The second knock was harder. "Are you alone?" Karp asked through the door.

"Go away," she said, her eyes still fixed on Arkady.

The doorknob strained, resisting pressure. At least it was a metal door, Arkady thought. In Soviet housing projects the doors and frames were so easy to kick in that any locks were decorative. Susan stood, gathered a tape and cassette player from the upper bunk and turned on James Taylor very low.

"Soo-san?" Karp called again.

She answered, "Go away now or I'll tell the captain."

"Open up," Karp ordered. He hit the door with probably no more than his shoulder, and the latch, nearly persuaded, almost popped.

"Wait," she said and turned off the bunk light.

While Arkady moved himself and his chair from the line of sight, Susan took her drink across the cabin and edged open the door. The mirror over her sink was ajar, and in it Arkady found he had positioned himself directly facing Karp's reflection. A head taller than Susan, the trawlmaster gazed over her into her cabin. In the hall's dim light the rest of the deck team huddled like a pack behind a lead wolf. The room was black—black enough, Arkady hoped, so that they wouldn't see him.

"I thought I heard voices," Karp explained. "We wanted to be sure there was nothing wrong."

Susan said, "There'll be something wrong if I go to the captain and tell him his crewmen are breaking into my cabin."

"I apologize." Karp seemed to be looking right at Arkady while he talked. "It was for your own good. A mistake. Please excuse us."

"You're excused."

"Pleasant." Karp kept his foot in the door and listened to the faint music, a man singing to a guitar. Finally he looked down at Susan and his smile of appreciation turned to an expression of concern. "Soo-san, I am just a seaman, but I have to warn you."

"What about?"

"It's bad to drink alone."

When Susan shut the door Arkady stayed still. The boots outside marched away, too much in unison. He listened to her cross the cabin and turn up the volume of her player, though the words were oddly soft and meaningless. He heard her set her glass down; it sounded empty. After six months in a small space, she knew her way around it even in the dark. She crossed the cabin again and he felt her fingers touch where sweat had broken out on his temple. "Are they after you?" she asked.

He put his hand lightly on her mouth. Someone, he was sure, still stood outside. She took his wrist and slipped his hand inside her shirt.

Her breast was small. He took his hand out to unbutton the rest of her shirt. As she pulled his head close he felt the rest of her body soften and let go. He kissed her face and lifted her toward him. If it was possible to step back to that moment in Dutch Harbor when he'd suddenly left, they were there now.

She seemed weightless. The rest of the world became soundless, as if the tape were playing in another room and the listener in the corridor were on another ship in another sea. Shirt and pants collected silently at her feet. Was this what women felt like? The damp hair at the nape of the neck? Teeth biting and lips yielding at the same time? How long had it been?

His jacket and clothes fell, sloughed off like an old skin. Perhaps this was what being alive was like: the heart hammering within the chest, a second heart answering outside, being doubly alive. His body was like another man who had been entombed and, now let free, was in control. He himself was swept along. She clung to him, climbed him, wrapped herself around him. They tottered dizzily against the bulkhead and then he was in her.

At what point does antagonism twist, turn and become desire? Is heat so interchangeable, or only masked? Why do suspicions already bear their answers? How did he know she would taste like this?

"I knew I was in trouble," she whispered, "when I heard about Volovoi and Mike and my first thought was, How is Arkady?"

She curled against him as if dying even while, inside, she held him tighter. He held her and helped her move. Standing, they were like two people walking a tightrope in the dark, so high up that they preferred the dark.

"Susan—"

"Another first," she said into his ear. "My name."

They slowly sank to their knees and then to her back on the deck. He felt her wide brown eyes watching. Cat's eyes, night eyes. Her legs spread like wings.

As he had borne her standing, she carried him now, both on top and deeper within, to the unseen torch in the dark, as if the cold metal of the deck were warm water.

"I LIKE THE name," he whispered. "Susan. Soo-san. Was it Susannah and the elders?"

"A virgin, I think. You know the Bible?"

"I know a good story with elements of voyeurism, conspiracy"— he stopped to light his cigarette from hers—"seduction and revenge."

They lay on her bunk against her pillow and another one made of her blankets. Despite the cool, he wasn't cold. Her cassette player now stood on the floor, aimed at the door. Every time the tape ended, she turned it over and started it again.

"You're a strange detective," she said. "You like names?"

"There's Ridley. A riddler, someone full of riddles. Morgan? Wasn't there a pirate named Morgan?"

"Karp?"

"A fish, a big fish."

"And Renko? What does that mean?"

"Son of. Fedorenko would be son of Fedor. I'm just son of . . . something."

"Too vague." She ran a finger around the line of his lips. "A stranger detective by the minute. But then I make a strange virgin. The two of us are a perfect pair."

At least for one night, Arkady thought. The door existed as a thin line of light in the dark. If Karp was still waiting outside, his team was probably up on deck. They could try to look in through the porthole, but all they'd see was a drawn curtain.

Arkady picked up the glass. "We didn't finish the game."

"Being honest? Look at me, isn't this honest enough? I'll be more honest. My door was open just on the chance you'd go by. I didn't know what I'd say. You make me mad." In a softer voice she said, "You *made* me mad. Then I admitted to myself that this ritual of animosity between us was because you were the last person I wanted to be attracted to."

"Maybe we make a perfect pair of moths."

But it was more than that, he knew. He'd been coming back to life, and when he held her he found himself at last fully alive, as if her heat had melted some final frozen lock inside him. Though they were trapped in a small steel cabin in the middle of the ice, he was alive, even if just for a night. Or was that a moth's rationale?

"He recruited me in Athens," Susan said.

"Morgan?"

"George, yes. I was doing a graduate course in Greek, which was the passion of my life—or at least at the time I thought it was. He was the captain of a yacht that belonged to some rich Saudi. He'd send telegrams to George to meet him here or there. The Saudi never showed up, but George had to move the boat from Cyprus to Tripoli and then back to Greece. He recruited me when I finally realized there was no Saudi.

"Slavic studies were my next great passion. George said I had a talent for languages. He doesn't himself, though his Arabic is passable. He paid my way through school in Germany. I'd see him at Christmas and for a week in the summer. When I got out of school, though, he said he'd gone private. No more government hassle, he said.

"He had a small shipping company in Rhodes that specialized in beating embargoes. We relabeled canned goods from South Africa, oranges from Israel, software from Taiwan. We always had buyers from Angola, Cuba, the U.S.S.R. George said that Communists trust you as long as you're making a profit, and that they'll trust you even more if you give them a kickback.

"It made sense. He didn't have to follow directives anymore. No oversight committee, no paperwork, just lunch in Geneva every two weeks with someone from Langley. George had to visit the bank anyway, so it was convenient.

"George is smart. He was the first one to notice the fishing venture and the possibilities for the Soviets here, because he was sure you were doing the same thing he was. He folded the company in a week and moved to Seattle. There were plenty of boats available. I think he deliberately got a bad one so he wouldn't make too much of a splash. He certainly could have gotten a better crew.

"So I've known George four years and been recruited for three. I was in Germany for one, worked on Rhodes for one, have been on Soviet ships for one. In all those years, he and I have actually been together for a total of six months. Two days together in the last ten months. It's too hard to stay in love with someone that way. I end up waiting for someone like you. Is that honest enough?"

WERE SHIPS LIKE women or were women like ships? Something to cling to in a dream?

Outside in the hall, Arkady heard American voices, weary from the hour and the dance, staggering back to their separate quarters. He didn't have a watch.

He ran his hand softly down from the middle of her forehead as if he were tracing her profile. At one time he had thought of her looks as thin and triangular, but now it seemed the right frame for such a mobile mouth and wide-apart eyes, the only face for such childishly cut hair. As his fingers grazed down across her stomach she turned toward him, a warm, enfolding barque with a golden sail.

"ZINA MENTIONED SEEING something in the water," Arkady said.

"She also mentioned a navy officer she saw on board, the radio-man." Susan lay with her head resting on Arkady's chest. They shared a Winston, one of hers.

"You thought she was a provocateur?"

"At first. She did tell Volovoi about smoking grass with Lantz. It was just enough to keep him titillated."

"Just enough to give her the run of the ship," Arkady said. He passed the cigarette back to her and rested his hand where the corner of her jaw met her neck.

"Zina was too wild to be fake. Too bright," Susan said. "Men never realized that."

"She manipulated them?"

"Volovoi, Marchuk, Slava. I don't know how many others. Maybe everyone but you."

"Did she talk about Vladivostok, about her life there?"

"Just about waiting tables and fending off sailors."

"So why did she come on the *Polar Star*?" Arkady asked. "It was only more of the same."

"I wondered, too. That was her secret."

"Did she talk about a man in Vladivostok?"

"Marchuk and the radioman."

"Guns?" he asked.

"No."

"Drugs?"

"No."

"So what do you think Zina was doing every time she joined you at the stern rail?"

Susan laughed. "You never get tired of that question, do you?"

"No." He felt the pulse in her neck begin to race. "I never get tired of good questions. Was it fish? Why was she interested in fish only from the *Eagle*?"

"Men, not fish," Susan said. "Mike was on the *Eagle.*"

Arkady pictured Zina standing at the stern rail, waving to the American catcher boat. Did it matter who waved back? "Morgan was on the *Eagle,*" he said.

"All Morgan needed from Zina was confirmation that there was something like the cable. She couldn't give him any real details. He had no other use for her."

"What did she want from him?" Arkady asked.

"Too much."

"Is that what you told her the night of the dance? Was that what you said to her just before she disappeared?"

"I tried to explain that in George's terms she wasn't a valuable asset."

"Why not?" When Susan didn't answer, he asked, "What did you mean when you said she wouldn't have wanted to leave an American boat?"

"She wanted to defect."

· · ·

HE RESTED HIS head on her shoulder. This was the most quiet, he thought, like a pillow on the moon.

"Do you want to get off the *Polar Star?*" she asked.

"Yes."

He heard her hold her breath before she said, "I can help."

He held a cigarette in one hand and a match in the other, but he didn't light it. He concentrated on the soft tremor of her breast against his cheek. "How?"

"You need protection. I can ask Marchuk to make you a translator. You're wasted on the slime line. That way we can spend more time together."

"But how can you help me get off the *Polar Star?*"

"We can work on it."

"What would I have to do?"

"Nothing. Who is Hess?"

Now he struck the match, a yellow flare in the hand, and let the first sulfurous haze burn off. "Should we stop smoking?"

"No."

He inhaled. Raw tobacco fumes, Soviet again. "He's our Morgan, another fisherman."

"You saw the cable, didn't you?"

"A cover over it. There wasn't much to see."

"But you were there."

Before he blew the flame out he reached down to the floor for the glass. It was half full, the last of the scotch. "Should we stop drinking?"

"No. Go back and take another look."

"Hess won't let me in again." He killed the flame and drank half of what was left.

"You can get in. You seem to be able to go wherever you want to on this ship."

He passed the glass. "Until Karp catches me."

"Until then, yes." She swallowed what was left and turned her head away. "Then we can get you off or out."

He rose on an elbow as if he could see her. Her hair was still damp to his touch. He turned her chin toward him. "Off or out? What does that mean?"

"Just what I said."

THE BOTTLE WAS empty and the Winstons had all gone up in a floating blanket of smoke. As if he and Susan had gone up in smoke.

"I want you in, not out," she said.

The bunk lamp was more glow than light, but he could see her eyes looking up, and himself in her eyes. Inside of her and out.

"DID HESS MENTION length?" Susan asked. "Number of hydrophones? Range? He has computers and software. It would be good if you could bring me a disk, even better if you can get a hydrophone."

Arkady lit a Belomor. "Don't you find it boring?" he asked. "Doesn't spying ever seem like an endless game of cards?"

"George checked your bona fides while we were in Dutch Harbor. He has a secure line there. He wanted to know if you were for real." She took the cigarette. "The FBI says you can't be trusted."

"The KGB says so too. At least they agree on something."

"Don't you have a good reason for wanting to get out?" Her eyes were wide, trying to see into him by the sparks of the *papirosa*, the bonfire of Russian conspirators.

"At Dutch Harbor you suggested that Morgan and I might have murdered Zina together. You're attracted to murderers?" Arkady asked.

"No."

"Then why did you say it? That's the man you want me to trust?"

"It wasn't George's fault."

"Whose, then?" When she didn't answer, he said, "You and Zina were on the stern deck. The dance was still going on. It was dark, the *Eagle* tied up alongside. At the rail you told her she was asking for too much. What did she say to you?"

"She said I couldn't stop her."

"Someone stopped her. Did she show you a plastic bag?"

"A bag?"

"With a towel and clothes inside. She borrowed a bathing cap from one of her cabin mates. She never returned it."

"No. Besides, you're different, Arkady. You're a known quantity, and if you can get something from Hess for me, we really can help you. There's nothing for you at home, is there? Why would you want to go back?"

"Can you really help me? Can you really make us disappear from here and find ourselves walking on a street, sitting in a café, lying in bed on the other side of the world?"

"You have to hope."

"If you want to help, tell me what Zina was doing at the rail all those other times. Before she knew anything about Morgan or a radioman or a cable, why was she at the rail?"

She turned the lamp switch off. "Funny, this whole night has been like holding hands over a flame."

"Tell me."

Susan fell silent in the dark for a minute, and then said, "I didn't know. Not for sure. At first I thought she was simply being friendly, or was sent by Volovoi. Sometimes you become aware of something wrong going on around you, but you can't tell quite what it is. After we became friends, I stopped noticing because I liked having her there. It wasn't until you came around that I started asking questions again, and not until Dutch Harbor that I knew for sure, when I was told that I had to come back to the *Polar Star* and help keep things quiet. We had to keep the team together and cope with problems as they came up. Adjust and resolve. That's the problem with working in the private sector. There's no backup and nobody pulls you out. Instead, you compromise and the hands you hire for dirty work are that much dirtier. George is a control freak who's lost control. He'll clean it up. He's indestructible, not like us. He caught on before I did what Zina was doing at the rail, and if he says he'll deal with his side, he will. He didn't kill her, I can promise you that."

"Why did you ever think I killed her?"

"Because you were so unlikely. An investigator from the factory? And because that night she said she was coming back."

"Coming back?" Arkady thought of the girl swimming out into Vladivostok bay, borrowing a shower cap, taping up a bag. Again and again, it made no sense. There were two Zinas: the Zina who mooned over Mike and listened to the Rolling Stones, and the Zina with her secret tapes. If Zina had been defecting to the *Eagle,* she would have taken the tapes and left one false suicide note, not pages of practice notes. And she knew better than to stage a suicide when any American boat was close by. "From where?"

When Susan spoke again she sounded exhausted. "George said he needed more than fishermen, and that's what he got. He just needs some time to get the crew under control. He didn't know about Zina. He couldn't do anything about Mike and Volovoi; he was only surprised he didn't find you there too."

Arkady thought of Karp. "Tell Marchuk."

"I can't say any of this to anyone else. I'll deny every word and you know it."

"Yes," Arkady had to admit.

"It was just a game," she said. "A 'What if' game."

"Like, 'What if morning doesn't come'?" he asked.

Her hand sought his. "Now you answer a question: if you could run right now, disappear from the *Polar Star* and go to America, would you do it?"

Arkady listened to his answer, interested if it was simply a game. "No."

ON THE NARROW space of her bunk their sleeping bodies folded together as the *Polar Star* slowly rose on the angle of its plated bow and fell, crushing the ice ahead. The sound was subdued, not much more than a wind cooling the skin, or distant thunder moving farther away.

ARKADY PULLED THE curtain from a porthole of luminous gray. Not the glitter of snow, but denser and softer. The gun-slit dawn of a new day in the Bering Sea. "We've stopped," he said.

The grating of steel on ice was gone, though through his feet he felt the engines running. He flicked the bunk lamp on and off; there didn't seem to be an electrical problem. The ship seemed poised in a vacuum, not silent itself but still and surrounded by silence.

"What about the *Eagle*?" Susan asked.

"If we're not going anywhere, they're not going anywhere." He picked his pants and shirt off the deck.

"It's follow the leader, and finally you people are the leader?" Susan sat up.

"That's right."

"So much for joint ventures. The *Eagle* isn't built for ice, and Marchuk knows it."

Arkady buttoned his shirt. "Go to the radio shack," he said. "Try to raise Dutch Harbor or try the emergency channel."

"And where are you going?"

Arkady pulled on socks. "Into hiding. The *Polar Star* is a big ship."

"How long can you do that?"

"I'll think of it as a form of socialist competition."

He stepped into his boots and took his jacket from a chair. The haze covered her like dust. She was motionless, all but her eyes, which followed Arkady to the door.

"You're not hiding," she decided. "Where are you going?"

He dropped his hand from the knob. "I think I know where Zina died."

"This whole night was just about Zina?"

"No." Arkady turned to face her.

"Why do you look so happy?"

He was almost ashamed. "Because I'm alive. We're both alive. I guess we're not moths."

"Okay." Susan leaned forward. "I'll tell you what I told Zina. I said, 'Don't go.' "

But he was gone.

29 The *Polar Star* lay at the bottom of a white well. Fog bounded the factory ship on every side, and the sunlight reflected by the ice sheet and trapped by arms of fog produced an illumination that was both indistinct and overwhelming.

The ship itself glowed; ice had formed on every surface. The deck was a milky skating rink. The net around the volleyball court glittered like a house that had been built crystal upon crystal; the antennas overhead hung heavy as glass. Ice lay on the portholes in opaque extra lenses, and glazed the wood stacked on the superstructure. The ship looked as if it had surfaced like a fish from the Arctic Sea.

"IT'S THE CABLE that could not snag which is, of course, thoroughly fouled on the sea floor," Marchuk said. He had taken Arkady to a corner of the bridge away from the helmsman. The captain hadn't slept during the night. His beard was overgrown, and when he removed his dark glasses his eyes looked scoured. "We have to sit at dead stop while Hess is below, winding and unwinding the cable, trying to pull out his dick."

"What about the *Eagle*?" Arkady asked the question Susan had asked him.

Wipers were doing an effective job of smearing ice in arcs across the windshield. On the other hand, the ship was going nowhere, and there was nothing to see except blinding fog. At a squint, Arkady estimated visibility at a hundred meters.

"Be thankful you're on the right boat, Renko."

"There's been no call?"

"Their radio is dead," Marchuk said.

"Three different kinds of radio and backups, and they're all dead?"

"Maybe their mast is down. We know they iced up and that there was a lot of rolling. It's possible."

"Send someone back."

Marchuk felt his pockets for a pack, then leaned against the windshield counter and coughed, which was almost the same as having a cigarette. He cleared his throat. "You know what I'm going to do when we get back? Take a rest cure. No drinking, no smoking. Go someplace near Sochi where they clean you out, steam you in sulfur and pack you in hot mud. I want to stay in that mud for at least six months until I stink like a Chinese egg; that's how you know you're cured. I'll come out pink as a babe. Then they can shoot me." He glanced at the helmsman and then through the door to the navigation room, where the second mate was soberly working charts. The *Polar Star* was locked in ice but it had not stopped moving because, slowly and inexorably, the ice sheet itself moved. "When you get this far north, curious things happen to equipment. There are illusions not just to our eyes. A radio signal goes up and bounces right back. The magnetism is so strong that radio-direction signals are absorbed. You don't have to go to outer space to find a black hole—it's right here."

"Send someone back," Arkady said again.

"I'm not allowed to as long as the cable is not properly reeled in. If it's caught on something buoyant it could be right under the ice; perhaps it could even be seen."

"Who is the captain of this ship, you or Hess?"

"Renko." Marchuk flushed, started to bring his hands out of his pockets and stuffed them back in. "Who is a second-class seaman who should be grateful he isn't chained to his bunk?"

Arkady stepped over to the radar. Though the *Eagle* was still two kilometers behind the *Polar Star*, the green dot on the scope was a blur.

"They're not sinking," Marchuk said. "They've just iced up, and ice doesn't give you an echo the way clean metal does. Hess says they're in good shape; their radios are in working order and they have a fix on his cable. You heard him say that we're the ones in trouble, not them."

"And if they disappear from the screen completely, Hess will tell you the *Eagle* has turned into a submarine. Susan will be on the bridge in a second. How are you going to handle her and the rest of the Americans on board?"

"I'll give them a complete and frank analysis in the wardroom," Marchuk said dryly. "The main thing is to keep them away from the stern until the cable is hauled in."

Both factory ship and trawler were frozen into the sheet, bows to the southeast, aimed at the trawlers coming up from Seattle, though neither of the incoming craft showed on the screen no matter what range Arkady punched into the radar scan. He reset the scope at five kilometers to take the *Eagle*'s bearing at 300 degrees.

Marchuk said, "If after another hour Comrade Hess has still not pulled in his cable, I will personally cut it and break out of the ice. That will take time because water this cold is dense and the cable will sink slowly. Then I can go back and rescue the *Eagle.* I promise you, I am not going to let other fishermen die. I'm like you; I want them out on open water."

"No," Arkady said, "I like them right where they are."

Marchuk turned his back to the thump of the wipers. Below him the bow lifted its deck, rust and green paint wearing its ghostly sheen of ice. Beyond the gunwale there was only white: no water, no sky, no distinction of horizon.

"I can't permit anyone to leave the ship," Marchuk said. "First, I am not allowed. Second, it would be useless. You've walked on frozen lakes?"

"Yes."

"This is not the same. This is not Lake Baikal. Ice from salt water is only half as strong as from fresh water, more like quicksand than cement. Take a look. In fog like this you can't see where you're going. In a hundred steps you'd lose your way. If a crazy man did go out on the ice, he should say good-bye to everyone first. No, not allowed."

"Have you ever walked on the ice here?" Arkady asked.

Marchuk, the silhouette, bowed to memory. "Yes."

"What was it like?"

"It was"—the captain spread his hands—"beautiful."

. . .

FROM AN EMERGENCY locker Arkady took a pair of life vests and a flare gun. The vests were made of orange cotton over plastic briquettes, with pockets for missing emergency whistles, and straps that tied at the waist over his sweater. The gun was an ancient Nagant revolver, the cylinder and barrel replaced by the squat tube of a flare.

The trawl deck seemed clear. Crossing it, he noticed, too late, someone watching from the high vantage point of the crane cabin. Pavel was a shadow within the glass of the cabin, except where his face peered through a triangular crack. He didn't react, though. Not until Arkady was inside the aft house did he realize that with his hood up and the added bulk of the vests under his jacket he had, at least from a distance, disguised himself.

"Arkady, is that you?" Gury loitered in the corridor by the kitchen, passing a hot pilmeni from hand to hand. Pasta flour covered the shoulders of his leather jacket like heavy dandruff.

Arkady was startled, but realized that it was the sheer normalcy of Gury and the cabbage vapors of the mess that had surprised him. With no fishing to occupy them, people could stay below, play dominoes or chess, watch films, catch naps. The ship might be stopped for some unexplained reason, but reasons were rarely explained. They could feel the engines idling below; in the meantime, life went on.

"You've got to see this. The usual turd-shaped, meat-stuffed ravioli, but . . ." Gury bit, choked down half the pilmeni and displayed the remaining half.

"So?" Arkady asked.

Gury grinned and held the pilmeni even closer to Arkady's eyes, as if displaying a diamond ring. "No meat. I don't mean the usual 'no meat,' with gristle or bone. I mean not within light-years' distance of any mammalian life form. I mean fish meal and gravy."

"I need your watch."

Gury was nonplussed. "You want to know what time it is?"

"No." Arkady unbuckled the new safari watch on Gury's wrist. "I just want to borrow your watch."

" 'Borrow'? You know, of all the words in the Russian language, including 'fuck' and 'kill,' 'borrow' is probably the lowest. 'Lease,' 'rent,' 'time-share'—these are the words we must learn."

"I'm stealing your watch." The compass built into the band was even notched to indicate degrees.

"You're an honest man."

"You're going to report Olimpiada for adulterating our food?"

It took Gury a moment to get back on track. "No, no. I was thinking when we get back to Vladivostok of maybe opening an enterprise, a restaurant. Olimpiada's a genius. With a partner like her I could make a fortune."

"Good luck." Arkady strapped on the watch.

"Thank you." Gury pulled a face. "What do you mean, 'Good luck'?" He became more concerned as Arkady moved toward the trawl deck. "Where are you going dressed like that? Will I get my watch back?"

Arkady took the walkway to the stern deck, consciously assuming the deliberate gait of a heavier man. He didn't glance back at the boat deck in case one of Karp's team was watching. The red ensign at the stern rail hung stiff with ice. Few footsteps had marred the shiny patina of the deck. At the well over the stern ramp stood a pair of long-suffering crewmen with the red armbands of public-order volunteers: Skiba and Slezko in sunglasses and rabbit-fur hats. When Arkady neared, they recognized him. As they started to block his way he waved them aside. It was a gesture he had seen enough in Moscow, a brusque gesture more with the hand than the arm, but sufficient to prompt the trained response, to chase pedestrians away from speeding motorcades, send dogs racing around a perimeter, dismiss orderlies or disperse prisoners.

Slezko said, "The captain ordered that—"

"No one is allowed—" said Skiba.

Arkady took Skiba's glasses.

"Wait," Slezko said. He handed Arkady his Marlboros.

"Comrades." Arkady saluted them. "Consider me a bad Communist."

He went down the well. At the landing, the platform where the trawlmasters usually watched nets rise from the sea, the rope was frozen to the rail and he had to kick it free. He climbed over the rail and wrapped the rope around his sleeve. Going down the rope was not much different from sliding down an icicle. He landed on his heels, which at once went out from under him; letting go, he slid the rest of the way down the ramp and onto the ice.

High overhead, Skiba and Slezko crowded to the stern rail like a pair of stoats peeking over a cliff. On his feet again, Arkady took a bearing from the compass built into the band of Gury's watch. The ice was solid as stone. He started to walk.

He should have worn double underclothes, socks and felt boots. At least he had good gloves, a wool cap inside his hood and the two life preservers, which provided a surprising amount of insulation. The more he walked, the warmer he got.

And the less he cared. The glasses didn't so much shade the brilliant fog as define it so that he could appreciate the veils of white vapor shifting around him. He'd once had a similar sensation looking through the window of a plane flying through clouds. The ice was solid, white the way sea ice is when the brine freezes out.

Bright as a mirror, though he couldn't see his image, only an aerated haze frozen within the ice. When he looked back, the ship was fading into the fog. And out of context, Arkady thought. The *Polar Star* was no longer a ship in water so much as a gray wedge dropped from the sky.

Two kilometers at a brisk pace. Twenty minutes, maybe half an hour. How many people got to walk upon the sea?

He wondered whether Zina had looked up from the waves at the looming gray flank of the ship. It was much easier for him; the water was flat, frozen, so much alabaster pavement. When he glanced back again, the *Polar Star* had disappeared.

He was still on a bearing of 300 degrees, though the compass needle swung from side to side. This close to the magnetic pole the vertical pull was so strong that the needle's tip seemed to be jerked left and right by strings. There was nothing else to get a fix on—no feature on the horizon, no horizon at all, no seam between ice and fog. Every direction was the same, including up and down. Total whiteout.

First he wanted to check the wardrobes in the *Eagle*'s cabins, then storage lockers and engine room. Zina had been stowed somewhere.

Marchuk was right about illusions. Ahead Arkady saw an old-fashioned black vinyl 78 record spinning by itself and without a sound in the middle of the ice. It was as if his mind had decided to fill in the white void with the first object it could grab from his memory. He checked the compass. Perhaps he had been going in a circle. That happened in fog. Some scientists said travelers wandered because one leg was stronger than the other; others even cited the Coriolis effect of the rotation of the earth, assuming that men had no more control over their direction than wind or water.

The record spun faster as he approached, then wobbled out of control; with his last steps, it trembled and dissolved into a rough circle of tar-black water edged by broken ice soaked red with blood.

Polar bears sometimes crashed through a seal's breathing hole just as the seal was coming up for air. The bears hunted two hundred or three hundred kilometers out on the sea ice. The sound of an icebreaker usually chased them away, but the *Polar Star* was at dead stop. Arkady hadn't heard the attack, so it couldn't have just happened. On the other hand, no blood or tracks led away from the hole. The bear had taken its kill straight down into the water and either hadn't come back up yet or else had headed underwater for another hole. The ice looked as if it had exploded. From the amount of blood ringing the hole, perhaps the seal had exploded too. Only a piece or two of ice bobbed in the water, evidence of the currents still moving under the sheet.

Now, that would be an unexpected conclusion to an investigation, Arkady thought: being eaten by a bear. A first? Not in Russia. How surprised that seal must have been. He knew the feeling. He took another reading from the compass and set off again.

Ahead he heard the sharp sound of a crack. At first he thought it might be the bear erupting through the ice; then it occurred to him that perhaps the ice sheet was splitting. On open water, pulled by tides and currents, the sheet shifted, broke and realigned. He didn't feel in any particular danger. Water carried sound faster and farther than dry air. Fog didn't muffle sound; it amplified it. If there was a fissure, it was probably far in the distance.

He wished the needle of the compass would stop jumping. How many minutes had he been walking? Twenty by the watch. How was Japanese quality control? There was no sign of the *Eagle,* but looking back he could see, on the outer ring of visibility, something following him, a figure so gauzy it seemed an apparition.

A gray streak of ice started to sag under his feet. He moved laterally to whiter ice and picked up the bearing again. Ice tended to break on a southwest-northeast axis, the wrong way for his path. It kept him alert. The object behind him moved at a steady lope, like a bear, but it was upright and black.

By now Arkady knew he was lost. Either he had gone off at an angle, or else he had underestimated the distance to the *Eagle*. As the fog stirred it flowed from left to right. For the first time he noticed the sideways movement of what he'd thought was a stationary bank, which might have been leading him astray the entire time. The cloud also flowed forward, enveloping him. Behind him, within a hundred meters now, his pursuer had developed legs, arms, head and beard. Marchuk. Skiba and Slezko would have run directly from the stern to the captain, and it was perfectly characteristic of a Siberian like Marchuk to follow by himself. In a matter of steps Arkady was into the fog and Marchuk faded away.

The captain hadn't called out. What Arkady wanted now was to reach the *Eagle* before Marchuk caught up and ordered him back to the *Polar Star*. They could go on board the trawler together, as long as Arkady got to look around. Actually, it would be safer with Marchuk along, since Ridley and Coletti were working with Karp. Morgan probably was not, though no captain could be entirely unaware of what happened on his own boat.

Although he was walking blindly in the fog, in his mind's eye Arkady saw his footprints leading straighter than an arrow across the ice to the *Eagle*. It had a rightness, a sense of the magnetic—unless, of course, he'd already missed the trawler and was heading for the Arctic Circle.

The cracking sound came again, more distinctly this time. Not ice splitting: ice being hammered, impact followed by an echo like splintering glass. Arkady found himself turning his head in a searching motion as if he could trace the source of the noise. Sound could mislead in fog by seeming too close, and he resisted the temptation to run because it would be easy to veer in the wrong direction. By now the fog itself rushed over him like surf trying to bear him away. Imagine, he thought, how much courage it took to swim even a few meters in water almost this cold. He had seen men fall off a trawler and almost instantly go into shock before they were rescued.

Suddenly the hammering was loud. The *Eagle* emerged no more than ten meters away, thrust up and tilted by ice. Yet the fog whipping over it made it appear as if it were speeding through heavy seas.

Breaking the way, the *Polar Star* had iced up from clean snow. On the fairway, the *Eagle* had iced up from salt spray, which froze in a gray ice that had accreted grotesquely like stalactites, then glazed as the temperature dropped. Ice seemed to cascade down the wheelhouse stairs and flood from the scuppers. Icicles hanging off the gunwales were rooted in the ice sheet. Coletti was outside the wheelhouse using a blowtorch to melt ice into sockets around the windows; the flame of the torch lit his sallow face. The light inside the bridge was as dim as a candle, but Arkady could see a figure sitting in the captain's chair. Ridley was hammering ice off the rungs of the radio mast. At the top of the mast the dipoles had disappeared and the whip antennas were bent at 90 degrees. Ice hung from them like torn rigging; the best Morgan would hear from them was static. The fog shifted, obscuring the *Eagle* again. They hadn't seen him. He began circling toward the stern.

How far ahead of Marchuk was he? Ten steps? Twenty? Sound would draw the captain, too. Arkady almost stepped onto the stern ramp before he saw it. A net was reeled onto the gantry overhead, strips of black and orange plastic turned into a dull shroud of ice. Fog was driving so hard over the boat that it left a ghostly wake, a dark tunnel at the end of which Marchuk was already visible. No matter, the captain couldn't send him back now. It was all working out.

As the trailing figure separated more clearly from fog, Arkady saw that its beard was actually a sweater drawn up over the man's mouth. Karp pulled the sweater down as he neared. Better prepared than Arkady, he had dark glasses and Siberian felt boots. In one hand he held an ax.

For a moment Arkady considered his options. A dash right to the North Pole? The long run left to Hawaii?

The *Eagle*'s ramp was low but slick and he pulled himself up on his stomach. On deck, fish and crabs were cemented in ice. Icicles fringed the shelter deck. Riding the fog high on the radio mast, Ridley had reached the radar bar, which was frozen solid in a white cowl. The fisherman's long hair and beard were frosted from his breath. With the care of a jeweler, he started to tap the bar free. Arkady estimated the distance from ramp to wheelhouse at fifteen meters, but the most exposed were the first five meters to the shelter deck that ran along the side.

Karp was closing in. Carrying the ax like a spare wing, he seemed to glide across the ice.

30 Arkady ran the few steps to the shadow of the shelter deck. He could no longer see the bridge, but the bridge could no longer see him. Behind, Karp came up the ramp with the sure foot of a deckhand.

Arkady slipped into the wheelhouse through a wet room that opened into the galley of the *Eagle.* He removed his glasses to see in the dim light that filtered through two portholes crusted with ice; it was like visiting the murk of an underwater ship. A banquette curved around a table with antiskid mats. Pots leaned on the sea rails of the stove top. Forward were two cabin doors and stairs up to the bridge and down to the engine room.

The port-side cabin had two bunks, though only the lower one looked used. Immediately, Arkady saw that there was no Soviet-style wardrobe where a body could have been stowed. On the bulkhead was an empty rifle rack. He felt under the mattress for a handgun, a knife, anything. Under the soiled pillow was a magazine with nudes. Under the bunk was a drawer with dirty clothes, more magazines of nudes, of firearms and of survival tactics; a sock with a roll of $100 bills; a well-carved whetstone; a carton of cigarettes; an empty box of shotgun shells.

"Coletti's," Karp said as he came in. He looked like a woodsman who had set off into the taiga for a vigorous morning of felling trees. No jacket or life vest, just an extra sweater, heavy gloves, boots, cap and dark glasses resting against his brow. Not even out of breath.

"You make it so easy," Karp said. "Getting rid of you on the ship was a little difficult. Out here you just disappear, and no one will know I was ever gone."

The ax was probably from the wide selection of firefighting equipment on the boat deck of the *Polar Star,* and Arkady suspected that Karp had brought it for a practical reason—to break through the ice and dispose of a body. As usual, the trawlmaster's plan had the virtue of simplicity. From outside came sounds of the ongoing war on ice, more the hammer blows of a foundry than of a boat. The Americans still didn't know anyone else was on board.

"Why did you come?" Karp asked.

"I was looking for signs of Zina."

There was a flare gun in Arkady's jacket pocket; that would be a dazzling sight in a small cabin. As Arkady moved his hand, Karp flicked it aside with the ax.

"Another investigation?"

"No, just me. No one else knows. No one besides me even cares." His wrist where the ax had hit it was numb. This is what it would be like to be cornered by a wolf, he thought.

Karp said, "Whenever someone is dead, you usually accuse me."

"You were surprised when she came up in the net. You could have poured her with the fish into a bunker and dumped her later. Instead you cut her out. You didn't know. Last night on the ramp you still didn't know."

Casually the ax nudged Arkady's hand from the pocket again. It wasn't fair to die feeling quite so helpless, yet panic was shutting the brain down.

"You're stalling," Karp said.

Arkady had been too scared to stall. "Don't you want to know who killed her?" he asked. *Now* he was stalling.

"Why should I?"

"You brought her," Arkady said. "I must have been smarter back in Moscow. For a long time I couldn't even understand how Zina got herself assigned to the *Polar Star.* It was Slava, of course. But who pointed him out to Zina when he was sailing on the bay? Who'd shipped with Slava before?"

"A whole crew."

"But only three coming on the *Polar Star:* Marchuk, Pavel and you. You saw him from the dock."

"Daddy's boy on his toy boat. His father was the only way he'd get on a real ship."

"With Slava she acted the innocent. That's why she never took him to your apartment."

Karp peeled off his sunglasses. "You knew that was me?"

"Someone with money, rifles, the nerve to run drugs." Arkady spoke quickly; it was wonderful what adrenaline could do for the ability to add two and two. "The only man on the *Polar Star* who fits that description is you. Since she was making money at the Golden Horn, she would have come only for something better than rubles. You kept away from each other on board, but not as much as you claimed. You said you never saw her except in the mess, but every time the *Eagle* brought in a net you saw her on the stern deck. Before she knew any men from any boat, she was at the rail waiting for the *Eagle.* She was yours."

"That's right," Karp said proudly. "You're not so dumb."

Arkady imagined the Americans overhead, surrounded by the abrasive static of the radio, the anvil-hammering on ice. He and Karp were conversing as quietly as conspirators; no one knew they were on board.

"Volovoi's fear," Arkady said. "The theme of his life was smuggling. He had to inspect every package, even one thrown from one Soviet boat to another. The watchword is what?"

"Vigilance." Karp smiled in spite of himself. He lifted the ax and shouldered it. "Keep your hands where I can see them."

"The one thing he couldn't stop was the net going back and forth. How did you know when a package was coming?"

"Simple," Karp said. "Ridley waved if they were delivering something besides fish and Coletti waved if they weren't. I looked to see where Zina stood at the rail, starboard side or port. Then I told the men on the ramp the net looked heavy or it didn't."

"If it was, they found a waterproof package on the headrope of the bag?"

"You'd be good at this. Pavel would cut it off and slip it in his life vest. Then Zina signaled if we were sending a package back. Renko, what's the point? You're not getting away alive."

"When you don't worry about that, you can learn a lot."

"Yeah." Karp saw merit in the concept.

"And I'm interested in Zina," Arkady added.

"Men were always interested in Zina. She was like a queen." Karp's gaze wandered up toward the percussive chorus of hammers on deck, then dropped back; Arkady had never felt eyes so attentive.

"Could you have caught up with me on the ice?" Arkady asked.

"If I'd wanted to."

"You could have killed me a minute ago, ten minutes ago?"

"Whenever."

"Then you want to know what happened to Zina, too."

"I just want to know what you meant on the ramp last night about Zina being thrown into the water."

"Simple curiosity?"

Karp had the metallic stillness of a statue. After a long pause he said, "Go on, Comrade Investigator. Zina was at the dance. . . ."

"Zina went and flirted with Mike, but she didn't say good-bye to him when he transferred back to the *Eagle* because she'd gone to the stern deck forty-five minutes before. She was seen there by Marchuk, Lidia, Susan. Thirty minutes before Mike transferred, Zina wasn't seen on the *Polar Star* again. By the time he transferred, she was dead." From his jacket Arkady slowly took out a piece of paper that he unfolded for Karp. It was a copy of the physical examination. "She was killed by a blow to the back of the head. She was stabbed so she wouldn't float. She was stowed somewhere on this boat, bent and crammed in some small space that left these regular marks on her side. That's what I came to find—that space. A wardrobe, a closet, a hold, a bin."

"A piece of paper." Karp shoved it back.

"That space is here or it isn't. I have to look in the other cabin," Arkady said, but he didn't dare move.

Karp rolled the ax handle thoughtfully. The single-edged head turned reflectively, like a coin. He pushed the door open. "We'll look together."

Passing through the galley, Arkady heard hammers taking full swings, as if the Americans were trying to carve their way home. He felt the ax cocked at his back and sweat rolling down his spine.

Karp prodded him into the starboard cabin. A real blanket covered this bunk. A railed shelf displayed books on philosophy, electronics and diesel mechanics. On the bulkhead hung a holster and a picture of a man sticking out his tongue. The man in the picture was Einstein.

"Ridley," Arkady said in answer to himself.

"She disappeared from the *Polar Star* . . . then what?" Karp demanded.

"Remember, you pointed out Slava to her when he was sailing." Arkady spoke faster. Ridley's bunk drawer held clean clothes neatly folded; leather wristbands and silver ear studs; photos of himself skiing with two women, touching wineglasses with a third; books of Hindu prayer; playing cards; an electronic game of chess; a lapel pin of Minnie Mouse. Arkady turned the cards face up, flipped through them and spread them on the bed.

"I wanted her on the ship, and Bukovsky had the connection. So?"

"She liked to visit men on their boats, and it must have seemed easy for a swimmer as strong as she was to take a few strokes to the *Eagle* when it was tied up to the *Polar Star.* She simply stepped off the stern ramp of the ship, Madame Maltseva's shower cap on her head, her shoes and a change of clothes in a black plastic bag tied to one wrist. From the rail she was probably invisible."

"Why would she do that?"

"That was her method. She moved from man to man and boat to boat."

"No, that doesn't answer my question," Karp said. "She wouldn't have taken the chance just to visit. So, Comrade Investigator, why would she do it?"

"I asked myself the same question."

"And?"

"I don't know."

Karp used the ax like a long hand to push Arkady to the wall. "See, where you went wrong, Renko, is saying that Zina would ever leave me."

"She slept with other men."

"To use them; that didn't mean anything. But the Americans were partners; that's different."

"She was here."

"Now that I look around, I don't see any space like you said she was put in. Not a sign of her." Karp glanced at the open drawer. "If you were hoping to find a gun, forget it. On this boat everyone carries his gun all the time."

"We have to look around more," Arkady said. He remembered fighting the trawlmaster in the bunker; the last place he wanted to dodge an ax was in the confines of a trawler cabin.

Karp's attention fell on the playing cards spread across the bunk. Still holding the ax high, he scanned the cards back and forth. "Don't move," he warned. He set the ax down to pick up the cards and painstakingly thumb through them. When he was done, he squeezed them back into a pack, which he replaced in the drawer. His small eyes receded into a stricken white face of love. For a moment Arkady thought Karp would actually drop to the floor. Instead, he picked up his ax and said, "We'll start in the engine room."

As they opened the door to the galley another furious assault on ice began overhead. The trawlmaster only glanced upward as if at the sound of heavy rain.

THE *EAGLE*'S TWO diesel engines throbbed on their steel beds, a six-cylinder main and a four-cylinder auxiliary. This was Ridley's domain, the warm inner boat beneath the deck where it took maneuvering to walk safely around layshafts and pulleys, generators and hydraulic pumps, wheel valves and convoluted piping. Low pipes, belt guards and every other dangerous possibility were painted red. The path between the engines was crosshatched plating.

While Karp prowled Arkady went into the forward space, a repair room with tools, hanging belts, a table with a threader and vise, a rack with saws and drills. There was also what appeared to be the door of a refrigeration unit, though since the *Eagle* delivered its catch to the *Polar Star*, why would it need refrigeration? When he opened the door he had to laugh. Stacked to waist level were mahogany-brown, resinous one-kilo bricks of Manchurian hemp, *anasha*. Well, it was the way the major companies worked. Because the ruble wasn't hard currency, international business was always done by barter. Soviet gas, Soviet oil, why not Soviet *anasha*?

In the narrow bow end of the refrigerator were crammed a table and chair, headphones and oscilloscope, amplifier and equalizer, mainframe, dual console and a file of floppy disks. It was much the same as Hess's station except that the hardware was shinier and more compact, with names like EDO and Raytheon. Sure enough, below the table was a fiberglass dome. He picked a disk from the file; the label read, "Bering Menu. File: SSBN–Los Angeles. USS Sawtooth, USS Patrick Henry, USS Manwaring, USS Ojai, USS Roger Owen." He flipped through the other disks; their labels read "SSBN–Ohio," "SSGN," "SSN." On the table was a clipboard with a paper divided into columns that listed "Date," "Boat," "Position," "Transmission Time," "Duration." The last transmission had been of the *Roger Owen* two days before. Arkady opened the desk drawer. Inside was an assortment of manuals and schematics. He flipped through the pages. "Acoustic simulator . . ." "Polyethylene-covered tow cable with acoustic section and vibration isolation module . . ." "Winch drum traverses axially . . ." There was a book titled in red letters: "You Cannot Take This Book from This Office." The subtitle was "Reserve, Decommissioned, Dismantled Status—1/1/83." Under "submarines" he found that the USS *Roger Owen* had been dismantled a year ago, and that the USS *Manwaring* and the USS *Ojai* had been removed from service.

The outline of a wonderful joke was taking shape. The electronics were similar to Hess's, with one difference: at the end of Morgan's cable wasn't a hydrophone for listening; instead, there was a waterproof acoustic transmitter trailing sounds like a lure. The disks were recordings, and all the submarines on them had been decommissioned or dismantled. Morgan and Hess were circling the Bering Sea, one spy sending false signals for another spy to collect in triumph. Hess must think that American subs were swarming like schools of fish. Arkady replaced the book, but pocketed the disks. From the engine room Karp paid no attention, as if nothing Arkady did at this point could matter.

Together they returned to the wet room's intermediate damp and pegs of slickers and boots, then went back outside. Under the cover of the shelter deck lay rolls of mesh laced with ice, net bags of buoys, a welder's table with a vise, storage lockers and oil drums of shovels and grappling hooks. The hammering overhead was intermittent, but there was no stopping Karp now. The *Eagle* had fishholds it had never used since it began transferring nets to factory ships. With his ax, the trawlmaster chipped away the ice covering the holds. As it split it flew up in prismlike flashes. He had to use a grappling hook to lift the hatch. After all his effort, the hold was empty.

Arkady hastily concentrated on the storage lockers under the shelter deck. From the first one he emptied loose rope and blocks; from the second, rubbery legs of coveralls, gloves, torn slickers, tarp. At some previous point the box must have held wire rope, because the bottom had a mixed residue of lubricant and rust. A coffin. He could see clearly the marks where Zina's knees and forearms had rested. On one wall was a row of six nuts, about five centimeters apart, that had bruised her side.

"Come and look," Arkady whispered.

Karp leaned in and came up with a tuft of hair, blond with dark roots. As Arkady reached for it, he felt something brush his neck.

"What are you doing here?" Ridley pressed the gun's cold muzzle more firmly against Arkady's head as Coletti came through the wet-room door with a double-barreled shotgun.

"This is an unofficial visit?" Morgan stood halfway down the wheelhouse ladder.

Ridley and Coletti looked inflated by the parkas under their slickers. Their left hands were huge with heavy gloves, their right hands bare to fit in trigger guards. Their mouths were raw and frosted by their breath, proper faces for a boat draped in white. In contrast, with his down vest and cap, Morgan looked as if he'd stepped out of a different climate. Except for his eyes; they had facets as crystalline as ice. Slung over one shoulder was a stubby automatic weapon, a military piece, its ammunition clip longer than its barrel.

"Looking for vodka?" Morgan asked. "You won't find it there."

"The *Polar Star* sent us," Arkady said. "Captain Marchuk would probably appreciate a call that we made it."

Morgan pointed to the mast. For all Ridley's labor, the radar bar was still locked in place, the antennas still bent and sheathed in ice. "Our radios are down. Besides, you two don't look like an official rescue party."

"Here we are, freezing our asses off to de-ice this tub and we hear this banging on the deck and come around to find you two going through gear like a pair of bag ladies. You understand 'bag ladies'?" Ridley twisted the barrel into the back of Arkady's head.

"I think so."

"I have the feeling," Morgan said, "that no one on the *Polar Star* knows you're gone. And if they do, there's no way they can know you and the trawlmaster made it here. What were you looking for?"

"Zina," Arkady said.

"Again?" the captain asked.

"This time we found her, or the only evidence that's left of her here."

"Like what?"

"Some hair. I took a sample from the muck at the bottom of this box, and I think I can match that with the marks on her pants. I'd prefer to have the whole storage box, of course."

"Of course," Morgan said. "Well, we'll have the box clean before you get back to the *Polar Star,* and as for the hair, you could have gotten that anywhere."

All Arkady could see of Ridley's weapon was the cylinder of a large revolver, a cowboy gun. The approach to the back of the skull was the same style used on Mike and Zina, but whoever killed them had been a knife artist. There was no help from Karp; the trawlmaster stood immobilized, his eyes desperately chasing a foreign conversation, the grappling hook hanging limply from his hand.

"Consider the situation," Ridley said to Morgan. "We have a lot to lose and you have a lot to lose."

"You mean the *anasha,*" Arkady asked.

Ridley paused, then told Coletti, "They've been below."

"This is where I draw the line," Morgan told Ridley. "I'm not going to let you kill someone in front of me."

"Captain, my captain," Ridley said, commanding the stage as usual. "We're trapped in the fucking ice. If Renko goes back and reports what he's seen, the next thing you know we've got fifty more Soviets traipsing over for an interested look. This is a case of national security, right?"

"You just want to protect your drugs," Morgan said.

"I could get personal, too," Ridley answered. "At Dutch Harbor,

Renko was balling your woman. He took her right away from you. He's probably been balling her on the big ship ever since."

Morgan looked at Arkady. The moment of denial came and went.

"How about that?" Ridley said. "Bingo! Cap, you going to let him go back now?"

"That's the difference between you and me," Morgan said. "I'm a professional and you're a greedy little bastard."

"We have a right to our stake, too."

Arkady asked, "Why didn't you unload the *anasha* at Dutch Harbor?"

"Mike was crazy about Zina," Ridley said. "He ratted to the captain. Then when he was dead, with all those Aleuts watching we just wanted to get out of port. We'll off-load on the mainland later." Ridley turned to Morgan. "Right, Captain? We all have different interests, some rational and some purely patriotic. The question is," he went on, switching to Russian to ask Karp, "what team are you on? Are you Renko's partner or are you our partner?"

"You speak Russian," Arkady said.

"Better than Esperanto," Ridley said.

"I followed Renko to get rid of him," Karp said.

"Do it," Ridley said.

"Let Renko go, alone," Morgan ordered.

Ridley sighed and asked Coletti, "Who needs this shit from Captain Bligh?"

Arkady was amazed at Morgan's reaction time. Coletti turned, aimed and fired, and only punched in a window by the stairs Morgan jumped from. But while Morgan was in midair, Coletti fired the second barrel. The vest exploded. The captain landed on the deck covered in feathers and blood.

"Like a fucking duck." Coletti broke the shotgun and reloaded a single shell.

Morgan squirmed against the winch, trying to rise and reach his own weapon, which lay under him. His right shoulder and ear were red pulp. His jaw was pocked red.

"Your turn," Ridley told Karp. "You wanted Renko? Take him."

"Who killed Zina?" Karp asked.

Coletti stood over Morgan, the shotgun at the captain's head, but he paused at the sound of Karp's voice.

"Renko told us she drowned," Ridley said.

"We know Zina was here," Arkady said. "At the dance you pretended to be drunk. You came back early to the *Eagle* and you waited for her to swim over."

"No," Ridley said. "I was sick, I told you before."

"She followed you," Arkady said. "We found marks, her hair; there's no doubt she was here."

"Okay, I came back and suddenly she was on board." Although Ridley was behind him, Arkady could feel the gun waver. "Look, Karp, the entire enterprise depended on everyone acting normal and staying in place: Americans here, Soviets there, a joint venture."

"Zina was very attractive," Arkady said.

"Who killed her?" Karp repeated.

Coletti's shotgun rose from Morgan.

"No one," Ridley said. "Zina sprang this crazy plan. She had this bag and she wanted to take back one of our survival suits so she could wear it the next time she went overboard. Insane. She'd jump when we were far away, then we'd pick her up miles away from the *Polar Star.* She said that as long as they weren't missing any survival gear they'd give her up for dead."

"I'm sure you have excellent survival suits." Arkady admired Zina's plan. That was what she'd come for, of course. "It could have worked."

"Karp, I blame myself," Ridley said. "I told her she was your girl and she'd have to go back to the *Polar Star* the way she came. I guess she didn't make it."

"You're missing a card," Karp said.

Ridley paused. "Missing a card?"

"The queen of hearts," Karp said. "She collected them from lovers."

Coletti was exasperated. "What the fuck is Karp talking about?"

"I don't know, but I think we've got another bad partner," Ridley said. "Cover the ape." He took the gun from Arkady's head. "Have to save shots." From inside his slicker he took an ice pick. As Arkady tried to turn, Ridley drove the pick into his chest.

The force of the blow dropped Arkady to the deck. He sat against the storage box and groped inside his jacket.

Ridley turned to Karp. "She seduced me. Who was going to resist Zina after four months at sea? But blackmailing me to help her defect?" He raised his gun. "You people live in a different world. A fucking different world."

Arkady fired the flare gun. He'd aimed at Ridley's back, but the flare caromed off the engineer's cap, leaving it ablaze like a match-head.

Ridley whipped off the burning cap. As he swung around to Arkady a black spider flew over the engineer's shoulder and stretched across his face. It was the three-legged grappling hook that the trawlmaster had been holding. While one prong sank through a cheek, another probed his ear. Karp wrapped the line around Ridley's neck, shutting off the air to his scream. Coletti looked for an angle of fire, but Karp and the engineer were too close together. Karp wrapped the line around Ridley like a man binding barrel staves. Ridley fired his cowboy gun wide twice, and the third time the hammer came down on an empty breech. His eyes twisted back as he dropped the gun.

"Jesus Christ," Coletti said.

Arkady freed the pick. The tip was red, but the rest of the shaft had been buried in the two life vests he wore.

"You only have one shell left." Morgan nodded at Coletti's shotgun. The captain had finally rolled off his own weapon. He pointed it at his deckhand.

Ridley struggled as Karp yanked him backward along the gunwale, snapping icicles like chimes. Sometimes a boat brought up halibut, a fish that was as big as a man and could thrash like a man and had to be killed as quickly as possible with a spike through the brain. With his arms tied tight, Ridley looked a little like a landed fish, though Karp was taking his time finishing him.

Arkady got to his feet. "Where are her jacket and bag?"

"We dumped them at sea long ago," Coletti said. "No one will ever find them. I mean, what were the odds she was going to come up in a fucking net?"

"Ridley killed Zina. Mike, too?" Arkady asked.

"Not me. I was in the bar. I have witnesses," Coletti said. "What does it matter?"

"I just like to be absolutely certain."

Karp threw the loose end of the line four meters high over the stern gantry, caught the line on the way down and started hauling Ridley up hand over hand. The engineer was good-sized, but the rope slipped friction-free over the icy transom. He'd stopped kicking.

"How are you?" Arkady asked Morgan.

"Nothing broken. I have morphine and penicillin." Morgan spat beads onto the deck. "Steel shot. Not as bad as lead."

"Really?" Arkady recalled that Susan had called Morgan invulnerable; perhaps not impenetrable, he thought, but fairly invulnerable. "Even a superman can't run a boat with one arm."

"The captain and I can work something out." Coletti's face

showed the strain of a man making fresh calculations. "I'll tell you this, I've got a better chance than you. How far do you think Karp will let you get?"

Karp secured the rope around the hydraulic levers on the gantry post so that Ridley swayed clear of the deck. His head seemed to be unscrewing from his shoulders, east to west.

"This is an American boat in American waters," Morgan said. "You don't have proof of anything, not really."

As Karp took a step from the gantry, Coletti raised the shotgun. "I still have one shell," he told Arkady. "Get that psycho out of here."

Karp eyed Coletti speculatively, gauging the distance across the deck and his chances against the spreading pattern of a shotgun, but the fire in him was gone.

Arkady joined Karp. "Now you know."

"Renko," Morgan called.

"Morgan," he called in return.

"Go back," Morgan said. "I'll get the radios up and tell Marchuk everything is under control."

Respectfully Arkady gazed around the frozen ship, the shattered window, Ridley's smoldering cap on the deck, his body dangling from the crosspiece of the gantry.

"Good," Arkady said. "Then you can tell Captain Marchuk he has *two* fishermen coming back."

31 Arkady fished out Slezko's cigarettes, which he shared with Karp. The walk had the aspect of a stroll.

"You know the song 'Ginger Moll'?" Karp asked.

"Yes."

" 'Why've you gone and plucked your eyebrows, bitch? And why've you put your blue beret on, you whore?' " Karp's voice rose to a husky tenor as he sang. "That was Zina and me. She treated me like dirt. 'You know for a fact that I'm crazy about you, I'd be glad to spend all my time thieving for you, but lately you've been stepping out a bit too much.' "

"I heard you on her tape."

"She liked my songs. That's how we met. I had a table of friends at the Golden Horn. We were singing and having a good time, and I could see her watching and listening from across the restaurant. I said to myself, 'That's for me!' She moved in a week later. She slept around, but men meant nothing to her, so how could I be jealous? She operated outside the rules. If Zina had a weakness, it was all her ideas about the West, as if it was paradise. That was her only flaw."

"I found a jacket with a hemful of jewels."

"She liked jewels," Karp granted. "But I watched her take over the *Polar Star*. I couldn't get her on board with any amount of money. Then we found Slava, and she took care of Marchuk. When we left port she worked her way through the ship. If she'd wanted you, she'd have had you."

"In a way she did." Arkady thought of the tapes.

By the compass, they were on a line to the *Polar Star*. A curiosity of the fog was that they seemed to be making no progress. With every step they were surrounded by the same periphery of fog, as if they were continually stepping in place.

The ache in Arkady's chest seeped through the rest of his body. Hail to tobacco, the poor man's sedative. Morgan might radio Marchuk that two men were returning, but who could prove one hadn't lost his way, met a bear, walked onto soft ice and slipped from the glittering face of the earth?

"You met Ridley when he spent those two weeks on the ship?" Arkady asked.

"The second week he said to me, 'Religion is the opium of the masses.' He said it in Russian. Then he said, 'Cocaine is the business of the masses.' I knew right then. When I got back to Vladivostok, I told Zina about this fantastic connection, and that it was too bad she couldn't get on board. But she found a way. What is fate? Birds fly from a nest in Africa to a branch in Moscow. Every winter the same nest, every summer the same tree. Is it magnetic? Can they tell by the angle of the sun? Every eel in the world is born in the Sargasso Sea, then each one heads to his predestined stream, sometimes swimming for years. When Zina was born in Georgia, what led her to Siberia, then to the sea?"

"The same things that led you to me," Arkady said.

"What's that?"

"Murder, money, greed."

"More than that," Karp insisted. "Someplace to breathe. Right now this is the freest you or I will ever be. Morgan isn't going to report what happened to Ridley; he was ready to kill him too. I sank what I was smuggling. So far I haven't done anything wrong at all."

"What about Volovoi? When Vladivostok takes a look at his slit throat, there'll be questions asked."

"Fuck! I can't go straight even if I wanted to."

"It's tough."

Karp coaxed a drag from his butt. "Rules," he said. "It's like the blue line you see on the wall at school. Blue line on a shitty plaster wall. In every room, every hall, every school. It starts at shoulder level, and as you get bigger the line sinks to your belt, but it's always there. I mean, it seems to stretch right across the country. In reform camp, same line. Militia office, same line. You know where it stops? I think it stops at about Irkutsk."

"Norilsk for me."

"East of there, no more line. Maybe they ran out of paint, maybe you can't paint Siberia. You know, what I feel worst about is Ridley sleeping with Zina. She always took a playing card, a queen of hearts, like a trophy. Did you see the cards on Ridley's bunk? I looked through the whole deck. No queen of hearts. That's how I knew she'd been on the *Eagle.*"

Arkady pulled up his jacket sleeve and gave Karp a card with a stylized queen in a robe of hearts. "I palmed it before I spread the deck," Arkady said.

"You prick!"

"It took you forever to notice."

"Brass bastard." Karp stopped to stare at the card in disbelief. "You're the one man I thought was honest."

"No," Arkady said. "Not when I'm trapped by a man with an ax. Anyway, it worked; we did learn who killed her."

"Fucking devious all the same." Karp threw the card away.

They started walking again. "Remember the director at the slaughterhouse?" Karp asked. "His girls raised a reindeer like a pet, and one day it wandered into the wrong pen and they went running through the slaughterhouse looking for it. It was funny. Who can tell one dead reindeer from another? One of the girls left after that. She was the one I liked."

Ahead, sooner than Arkady had expected and clearer with every step, was the breathing hole. On an otherwise featureless surface it was a black pool within a ring of red ice, a startling break in the mist.

Automatically Karp began to slow down and look around. "We should have gotten drunk together sometime, just the two of us." He snapped his butt into the water.

Arkady tossed his in, too. Pollution of the Bering Sea, he thought: one more crime. "Morgan radioed the *Polar Star* to expect two of us," he reminded Karp.

"If he ever got his radio going. Anyway, it's dangerous out here. A call doesn't mean anything."

The hole was more circular than Arkady remembered. It was only two meters across, but it gave definition to the fog. A Pole of Inaccessibility reached. Some of the ice was soaked through with blood, some pinkly tinged. The black water lapped against it with rhythmic slaps. There was a pulse in there, Arkady suspected, that a man watching long enough might detect.

"Life is shit," Karp said. With a sideways kick, he knocked Arkady's feet from under him, straddled his back and started to twist his head. Arkady rolled and swung his elbow against Karp's jaw, turning the trawlmaster over.

"It feels like I've been trying to kill you forever," Karp said.

"Then quit."

"I can't now," Karp said. "Anyway, I've seen guys get stuck before. I think you're hurt worse than you know." He hit Arkady in the chest, directly on the wound, and it felt as if a lung had collapsed. Arkady couldn't move. Karp punched him again, and all the air seemed to leave his body.

The trawlmaster rolled him over, sat on him and pressed Arkady's shoulders back over the edge of the ice. "Sorry," he said and pushed Arkady's head under. Air bubbles exploded from his mouth. He saw silvery air in his lashes and hair. The water was incredibly cold, like molten ice, stinging salty but clear, not black, magnifying Karp as he leaned forward, pushing Arkady down. He actually did look sorrowful, like a man performing an unpleasant but necessary christening. Arkady's hand came out of the water, took Karp's sweater and pulled him down.

As Karp reared back Arkady came out of the water, holding in his other hand the ice pick Ridley had used on him, and pressed its stained tip against Karp's neck, twisting the jaw back from the bulging vein. Karp's eyes rolled as he tried to watch the shaft. Why not stab him? Arkady thought. Put his whole weight behind the steel, prick the vein and press straight through to the backbone? Eye to eye, what better time?

Karp rolled to the side. He was uninjured except for a scratch, yet all his strength seemed to have left him, as if the gravity of a lifetime had suddenly fallen on his chest. "Enough," he said.

•••

"YOU'RE STILL GOING to freeze. It won't take long," Karp said. He sat by the water, legs crossed, relaxing with a cigarette like a Siberian at ease. "Your jacket's soaked. You're going to be a walking block of ice."

"Then come on," Arkady said. It was already hard to choose between the dull pain of the wound and the shakes of the cold.

"I was just thinking." Karp didn't stir. "What do you think life would have been like for Zina if she'd made it? That's the sort of thing you can spend the rest of your life dreaming about. Ever know anyone who went over?"

"Yes, but I don't know how she's doing."

"At least you can wonder." Karp blew a trail of smoke the same color as the fog; he seemed surrounded by a puffy world of smoke. "I've been thinking. Pavel's already shitting like a rabbit. You're right, once we get to Vladivostok they're not going to let up until somebody talks—Pavel or one of the others. It doesn't matter whether you get back or not; I'm finished."

"Admit to the smuggling," Arkady said. "Testify and they'll give you only fifteen years for Volovoi, and you might get out after ten."

"With my record?"

"You've been a leading trawlmaster."

"Like you've been a worker on the leading slime line? The winners of socialist competition, you and me! No, it will be aggravated murder. I don't want to to lose my teeth in a camp. I don't want to be buried in a camp. Ever see those little plots right outside the wire? A few daisies for those miserable souls who never left. That's not for me."

Ice had formed on Arkady's hair and brows. His jacket was glazed with ice, and when he moved, his sleeves cracked like glass. "Alaska is a little out of reach. Let's go; we'll argue on the way to the ship. It will keep us warm."

"Here." Karp got to his feet and pulled off his sweater. "You need something dry."

"What about you?"

Karp pulled off Arkady's jacket and helped him on with the sweater. The trawlmaster wore another one underneath.

"Thanks," Arkady said. Along with the life vests, the sweater might provide enough insulation. "If we walk fast enough, we may both make it."

Karp brushed ice from Arkady's hair. "Someone who's been in Siberia as long as you have should know you lose most of your heat from your head. Your ears are going to be frostbit in another minute. It's a trade." He placed his cap on Arkady's head, pulling it tight over his ears.

"What do you get?" Arkady asked.

"The cigarettes." Karp fished them out of the jacket before handing it back. "I worry about you sometimes. There's got to be a dry one here."

He broke off an unsoaked half and lit it from the fag he was about to toss. Though Arkady felt as if his blood were congealing in ice, Karp didn't seem cold. "Joy." He exhaled. "That was one of the signs at the camp. 'Rejoice in Work!' and 'Work Makes You Free!' We made cameras, actually—New Generation. Look for them."

"Are you coming?"

"Our last day in Valdivostok, Zina and I went on a picnic outside town, on the cliffs overlooking the water. There's that lighthouse there at the cape, looks like a gray castle going to sea, with a red-and-white candle stuck on top. Renko, it's fantastic. Waves crash at the foot of the cliffs. Seals stick their heads out of the water. On top of the cliffs, pines are bent by the wind. I wish I'd had a camera then."

Holding the cigarette in his lips, Karp peeled off his other sweater.

He still seemed clothed because of the urka tattoos that covered his torso and arms to his neck and wrists.

"You're not coming?" Arkady asked.

"Or you can go into the woods. It's not the taiga; it's not what people expect. It's a mixed forest—fir and maple on the hills, slow rivers with water lilies. You want to sleep in the woods so you can hear a tiger. You'll never see one, and anyway, they're protected. But to hear a tiger at night, that's something you never forget."

Karp stepped naked from his pants and boots. He pinched the butt of his cigarette in his mouth; he was smoking an ember. As his skin pinkened from the cold his tattooed decorations stood out.

"Don't do this," Arkady said.

"The main thing is, nobody can say I ever hurt Zina. Not once. If you love someone, you don't hurt them and you don't run away. She wouldn't have stayed away."

The tattoos were freshened by the air. Oriental dragons climbed Karp's arm, green claws splayed from his feet, ink-blue women wrapped around the columns of his thighs, and with each steamy breath the vulture picked at his heart. More vivid were the whitening scars, dead stripes on his chest, where the accusations had been burned away. Across his narrow brow spread a livid band. The rest of his skin was reddening, the muscles trembling and jumping in reaction to the cold, animating each tattoo. Arkady remembered what agony it had been for him, even when dressed, in the fishhold. Each second it visibly took more effort and concentration for Karp to get out a word, even to think.

"Come back with me," Arkady said.

"To what? For what? You win." By now Karp shook so hard that he could barely stay upright, but he took a final, burning drag before dropping a butt that was no more than a spark into the water. He spread his arms triumphantly. " 'I smile at the enemy with my wolfish grin, baring my teeth's rotten stumps. We're not wolves anymore.' " He grinned at Arkady, took a deep breath and dived in.

Arkady could see Karp swimming straight down in powerful strokes as glutinous air bubbles trailed behind. The tattoos looked appropriate, more like scales than skin in the twilight water beneath the ice. About four meters down, he seemed temporarily stalled, until he released a chestful of air and descended to the next, darker layer of water. There a current caught him and he began to drift.

The soles of Karp's feet were not tattooed. After the rest of him disappeared, Arkady saw his feet still swimming, two pale fish in black water.

32 Arkady looked down at the patrol boat's broad radar rig, gray turtleshell guns, torpedo tubes. All night, it seemed, sailors from naval intelligence had clambered on and off the *Polar Star* removing sealed boxes of equipment. Now, before dawn, the time had come for Anton Hess to make his exit; like an actor between costume changes the fleet electrical engineer still wore a fishing jacket over pants with a military crease.

"It's good of you to come to see me off. I always believed that you would prove yourself useful with the right goad, the right prize. So here we are."

"In the dark," Arkady said.

"In the clear." Hess gathered Arkady from the rail. "You don't know how toothsome a bone a failure of naval intelligence can be to the KGB. This will not go unappreciated." He ended his sigh with a laugh. "Did you see Morgan's face when we freed the *Eagle* from the ice? Of course he was in some pain. Worse, he knew what you had brought back to us."

As soon as it was independently free of the ice sheet the *Eagle* had limped toward the Alaska mainland, while the *Polar Star* had canceled the rest of its fishing. The ship had dropped Susan Hightower, the other reps and Lantz off on a pilot boat outside Dutch Harbor.

"The only thing I didn't understand was Susan, when she left," Hess said. "Why was she so amused?"

"We shared a joke. I told her how valuable her help had been." After all, she had told him what to steal, even if he had used her advice on a different boat.

Nikolai was waiting inside the transport cage with a marine. The soldier, moon-faced between black fatigues and a beret, carried an assault rifle. The young radioman did not appear happy; on the other hand, he was not in irons. For a moment Hess seemed reluctant to leave, like any man reflecting at the end of a long and successful trip.

"Renko, you understand that your name can't come up in connection with the disks. We don't want to taint them. I wish I could share the credit."

"Credit for the sounds of submarines that were dismantled years ago? You were listening to submarines that don't exist," Arkady said.

"That doesn't matter. Morgan was compromised, and this time we have the trophy."

"Disks of nothing."

"Very well, ghosts and phantoms hissing in the dark. Careers have been made on less." Hess boarded the cage and hooked the chain across the gate. "Let me tell you something, Renko. It's round after round and it never stops. I'll be back."

"That's another reason Susan was smiling," Arkady said. "She won't be."

Hess's good humor could not be defeated. "Nevertheless." He put out his hand and shook Arkady's. "We shouldn't argue. You served well. You rose early to say good-bye."

"Not really."

"Nevertheless," Hess insisted.

"Good luck." Arkady shook Nikolai's hand.

WITH THE PATROL boat gone, the *Polar Star* picked up speed again. Coastal trawlers increased by the hour on the night horizon. A kilometer away, they made a dazzling string of fishing lamps, each boat its own constellation, a different scene from the leave-taking at Dutch Harbor; there it had been a wet afternoon, with the kind of damp that was a second skin and the Americans huddled inside the bridge for the ride to the dock—all but Susan, who stood on deck, not waving, but never taking her eyes off the ship she was leaving.

A curious life, Arkady thought; he always cared most for whatever he was losing. He'd felt her gaze across the widening water as strongly as when they'd been in bed. Some flaw in him led to futile connections.

"Comrade Jonah." Marchuk joined Arkady.

"Captain." Arkady stirred from his reverie. "I always like night fishing."

"It will be day in a minute." Marchuk leaned on the rail. The captain tried for a casual attitude, though for the first time on the voyage he wore dress blues, four gold stripes on the cuffs, gold braid on his cap, bright smudges in the dim light of the deck. "Your cut is better?"

"It proved to be within Vainu's level of competence," Arkady said, though he wasn't taking any deep breaths. "Too bad about your quota."

"We revised the quota." Marchuk shrugged. "That's the beauty of a quota. But it was good fishing. We should have just fished."

With the start of dawn, the trawler lamps began to fade into traceries of ordinary gantries and booms against a background of retreating shadow. Chains rang across the surface of the water as the fleet dipped its nets. In the twilight, claques of gulls shifted from boat to boat. On the *Polar Star,* more crew came up on deck all the time. Arkady could see them by their cigarettes up on the boat deck and along the rail.

"You weren't the Jonah," Marchuk added. "You know, on the radio they're starting to refer to you as *Investigator* Renko, whatever that suggests."

Below, a line of angular shadows flew by, their bills tucked, skimming the trough behind the bow wave, pelicans at work.

"It could mean anything," Arkady said.

"True."

The trawlers shimmered in a gray haze, not fog but the normal exhalation of the sea. This was the in-between moment when the eye had to complete each ship, connect a bow here or a stack there, paint them, people them, give them life. Arkady looked up at the boat deck, where Natasha had turned her face toward the breaking sun, her eyes shining, her black hair momentarily edged with gold. Beside her Kolya checked his watch, and Dynka rose on tiptoes as she looked east. Along the rail he saw Izrail in a sweater so clean of fish scales that he looked like a burly lamb; Lidia, her face wet with tears; Gury unfolding his dark glasses.

Arkady hadn't risen to see Hess off; what he'd waited all night for was only now emerging.

Gulls burst over the *Polar Star* as if blown by light that rolled like a wind over the factory ship. Clouds lit. The windows of the trawlers flashed, and at last, out of the dark rose the low green shore of home.

About the Author

MARTIN CRUZ SMITH lives with his wife and three children in northern California. This year he will go to Russia, which he has not been able to visit since *Gorky Park* appeared, to attend the long-delayed publication of that novel in Moscow.